P9-DNM-948

A man with no name
may you claim,
heart, body and soul

"Touching you is like bathing in a magical fire," Amber said. "But I must confess something to you."

"Why?" asked Duncan. "Do I look like a priest?"

Amber laughed. "Nay. You look like what you are, a warrior both fierce and sensual."

"Then why confess to me?"

"Because I smoothed healing oil over your body long after the danger of fever was past."

Duncan's breath caught. "Why?"

"For the forbidden pleasure of touching you."

Avon Books are available at special quantity discounts for bulk
purchases for sales promotions, premiums, fund raising or edu-
cational use. Special books, or book excerpts, can also be created
to fit specific needs.

For details write or telephone the office of the Director of Special
Markets, Avon Books, Dept. FP, 1350 Avenue of the Americas,
New York, New York 10019, 1-800-238-0658.

Elizabeth Lowell

Lowell

FORBIDDEN

AVON BOOKS ◆ NEW YORK

FORBIDDEN is an original publication of Avon Books. This work has never before appeared in book form. This work is a novel. Any similarity to actual persons or events is purely coincidental.

AVON BOOKS
A division of
The Hearst Corporation
1350 Avenue of the Americas
New York, New York 10019

Copyright © 1993 by Two of a Kind, Inc.
Published by arrangement with Two of a Kind, Inc.
Library of Congress Catalog Card Number: 93-90321
ISBN: 0-380-76954-9

First Avon Books Printing: October 1993
First Avon Books Special Printing: July 1993

AVON TRADEMARK REG. U.S. PAT. OFF. AND IN OTHER COUNTRIES, MARCA REGISTRADA, HECHO EN CANADA

Printed in Canada

UNV 10 9 8 7 6 5

For
Marjorie Braman
whose sense of humor has enlivened
many a tedious editorial task.

CHAPTER ONE

1

HE *will come to you in shades of darkness.*

The words of the dire prophecy rang in Amber's mind as she looked at the naked, powerful man whom Sir Erik had dumped senseless at her feet.

Candle flames bent and whipped as though alive, called by the cold autumn wind pouring through the cottage's open door. Light and darkness licked over the stranger's body, underlining the strength of his back and shoulders. Sleet shone in the near-black of his hair. Icy rain gleamed on his skin.

Amber felt the man's chill as though it were her own. Silently she looked up at Erik. Her wide golden eyes asked questions for which she had no words.

It was just as well, for Erik had no answers. All he had was the slack body of a stranger found in a sacred place.

"Do you know him?" Erik asked curtly.

"Nay."

"I think you are wrong. He wears your sign."

With that, Erik turned the man over. Candlelight and water streamed across the muscular torso, but it wasn't the stranger's naked male strength that drew a gasp from Amber.

A piece of amber shone against the intense darkness of the hair on his chest.

1

Careful not to touch the stranger, Amber knelt at his side and held the candle so that she could study the talisman. Elegant runes had been incised on the gem. The runes commended the wearer to the protection of Druids.

"Turn the pendant over," she said in a low voice.

Deftly, Erik flipped the amber talisman. On the other side, Latin words in the shape of a cross proclaimed the glory of God and asked His protection for the wearer. It was a common Christian prayer carried by knights who had gone off to battle the Saracen for possession of the Holy Land.

Amber let out a long sigh, relieved that the stranger was not some black sorcerer dropped into the Disputed Lands for the sake of mischief. For the first time she looked at the stranger as a man rather than as an object brought to her so that she might discover truth or treachery.

Wherever Amber looked, the overwhelming reality of the stranger's strength looked back at her. The only hints of delicacy in the man were his dense, faintly curling eyelashes and the clean, curving line of his lips.

The stranger was handsome in the way a warrior is handsome, the beauty of a storm rather than the beauty of a flower. Recent bruises, cuts, and scrapes mingled with the scars of other, older battles. The marks served to enhance rather than to diminish his aura of male power.

Though he had no possessions beyond the talisman, not even clothes, Amber had no doubt that the stranger was someone to be reckoned with.

"Where did you find him?" she asked.

"The Stone Ring."

Amber's head snapped up.

"What?" she demanded, hardly able to believe.

"You heard me."

Amber waited expectantly.

Erik simply watched her with unflinching wolf's eyes.

"Don't make me pluck words from you like feathers from a chicken," Amber said in exasperation. "Speak!"

The hard lines of Erik's face flowed into an amused smile. He stepped over the senseless stranger and shut the cottage door, putting an end to the frisking of the cold autumn wind through the room.

"Do you have some mulled wine for an old friend?" Erik asked mildly. "And a blanket for whomever this might be. 'Tis too cold to be lolling there uncovered, friend or foe."

"Aye, *lord*. Your slightest wish is my greatest command."

The dryness of Amber's voice was as unmistakable as the affection that lay beneath. Sir Erik was the son and heir of a great Scots thane, but Amber had always felt a curious ease with him despite her own lack of high birth and the fact that she had no more kin than the wild autumn wind.

Erik shrugged out of his costly mantle. He covered the stranger with a swirl of thick, warm wool that was the indigo of twilight. There was very little of the mantle left over.

"He is a big one," Erik said absently.

"Even bigger than you," Amber said from the other side of the cottage. "The knight who felled this man must have been a mighty warrior."

Erik watched through narrowed eyes as Amber hurried toward him, her arms overflowing with the thick fur cover that normally warmed her bed.

"If the evidence of the tracks is to be believed, he was felled by a bolt from the sky," Erik said distinctly.

The swirling length of Amber's nightclothes wrapped about her ankles, tripping her. She stumbled and would have fallen on the stranger if Erik hadn't caught her. He set Amber aright and released her in the same swift motion.

"Forgive me," he said quickly.

Though Erik had touched her for only the briefest moment, she couldn't conceal the unease it had caused.

"There is nothing to forgive," Amber said. "Better your flesh than the stranger's."

Despite her reassuring words, Erik watched Amber closely, wanting to be certain that whatever difficulty his touch had caused her was truly fleeting.

"I can't say why your touch doesn't pain me," Amber added wryly. "God knows that your heart is no more pure than it must be."

The smile that edged Erik's mouth was as brief as Amber's discomfort had been.

"For you, Amber the Untouched," he said, "my heart is as pure as unfallen snow."

She laughed softly. "Perhaps it is the legacy of our childhood sharing Cassandra's lessons."

"Yes. Perhaps."

Erik smiled almost sadly. Then he bent and wrapped the unmoving stranger in the fur cover.

Amber hastily pulled a mantle around her own shoulders and stirred up the fire in the center of the room. Soon the friendly leap of flames warmed the room and ran like sunlight through Amber's long golden braids. She suspended a pot from the trivet over the fire.

"What of the man's companions?" she asked.

"They scattered to the winds, and so did their horses." Erik smiled rather savagely. "The ancient Stone Ring must not have cared for Normans."

"When did this happen?"

"I don't know. Though the tracks were deeply cut, they were all but washed away by the rain. The lightning-struck oak was little more than a blackened stump and sullen embers."

"Bring him closer to the fire," Amber said. "He must be sore chilled."

Erik moved the stranger with an ease that belied the man's size. The dance of flames brought out the gold in Erik's hair and beard.

The stranger's hair remained a rich shade of darkness. He was clean-shaven but for a mustache that was also dark.

"Does he breathe?" she asked.

"Aye."

"His heart—"

"Beats as strongly as a war stallion's," Erik interrupted.

Amber sighed with a relief that was too intense to be feeling for a stranger.

Yet she felt it just the same.

"Is one of your squires fetching Cassandra?" Amber asked.

"No."

"Why not?" she asked, startled. "Cassandra has greater skill at healing than I."

"And far less skill at scrying."

Amber took a deep, hidden breath. She had been afraid of this since the instant Erik had dumped the naked stranger at her feet. Slowly she reached inside her mantle and nightgown.

Though she had many necklaces and bracelets, pins and hair decorations of precious amber, there was only one piece of jewelry she wore at all times, even in bed. The necklace's chain was of gold wire finely twisted. A pendant of transparent amber half the size of her palm hung from a golden loop inscribed with tiny runes.

Ancient, priceless, mysterious, the pendant had been given to Amber at her birth. Within the precious gem, captured sunlight pooled and flashed, brooded and laughed and burned, defined by the fragments of darkness that were also caught inside the golden pool.

Murmuring ancient words, Amber held the pendant between her cupped palms. The heat of her body went into the fey stone as her breath bathed it. When the substance was infused with her living warmth, a haze formed.

Quickly Amber bent to the fire, holding the pendant just beyond the reach of flames. As the haze began to clear, the stone shimmered with light and shadow shapes constantly changing.

"What do you see?" Erik asked.

"Nothing."

He made an impatient sound and looked at the stranger, who still lay slack, seemingly unhurt save for his unnatural sleep.

"Surely you see something," Erik muttered. "Even I can see into amber when I—"

"Light," Amber interrupted. "A circle. Ancient. The graceful line of a rowan tree. Shades of darkness. At the foot of the rowan. Something . . ."

Her voice faded. She looked up and found Erik watching her with eyes that were like amber seen at night, darkly golden, unreadable.

"The Stone Ring and the sacred rowan," he said flatly.

Amber shrugged.

Body poised as though for battle, Erik waited.

"There are many sacred circles," she said finally, "many rowans growing, many shades of darkness."

"You saw him as I found him."

"Nay! The rowan is *inside* the Stone Ring."

"So was he."

Erik's calm statement sent chills racing through Amber. Speechless, she glanced from him to the stranger who lay wrapped in rich cloth and fur.

And a thousand shades of darkness.

"Inside?" she whispered, crossing herself quickly. "Dear God, who is he?"

"One of the Learned, certainly. No other man could pass between the stones."

Amber looked at the stranger as though seeking his identity written in runes on his face. She saw only what she already knew—his face was strongly made, very male.

It appealed to her as nothing ever had but amber itself.

She wanted to breathe his breath, to learn his unique scent, to absorb his warmth. She wanted to know his textures, to savor his maleness.

She wanted to touch him.

The realization shocked Amber. She, the Untouched, wanted to risk agony by touching a stranger.

"Was the rowan blooming?" Erik asked.

Amber started and looked at him warily.

"It hasn't bloomed in a thousand years," she said. "Why would it offer this stranger a lifetime of blessings?"

Erik said only, "What else did you see in the pendant?"

"Nothing."

"Talk about plucking feathers," he muttered. "All right, then. What did you *sense*?"

"I felt . . ."

Erik waited.

And waited.

"God's teeth! Speak to me," he demanded.

"I have no words. Simply a feeling, as though . . ."

"As though?" he prodded.

" . . . I am balanced on a cliff's edge and have only to spread my wings to fly."

Erik smiled with a combination of memory and anticipation.

"A fine feeling, is it not?" he asked softly.

"Only for those who have wings," Amber retorted. "I have none. I have only a long fall and a harsh landing."

Erik's laughter filled the small cottage.

"Ah, little one," he said finally, "if it wouldn't

hurt you, I would hug and pat you like a child."

Amber smiled. "You are a dear friend. Come. Take this man to my bed until Cassandra can care for him."

An odd look was Erik's only answer.

"I would hate to lose to simple cold a man who can walk between the sacred stones," she explained.

"Perhaps. But on the whole, I think it would be easier for me to order his death if he weren't a guest in your cottage. And your bed."

Shocked, Amber stared at Erik.

The smile he gave her was as cold as the wind prowling beyond the cottage.

"Why would you condemn a stranger found in the sacred grove?" she asked.

"I suspect that he is one of Duncan of Maxwell's knights come to spy out the land."

"Then the rumor is true? A Norman granted his Saxon enemy the right to rule Stone Ring Keep?"

"Aye," Erik said bitterly. "But Duncan is no longer Dominic's enemy. The Scots Hammer swore fealty to Dominic at the point of a sword."

Amber looked away from Erik. She didn't have to touch him to gauge the extent of his leashed rage. Duncan of Maxwell, the Scots Hammer, was both bastard and landless. Nothing could change his bastardy, but Duncan had been given control of Stone Ring Keep and its surrounding land by Dominic le Sabre.

Yet Stone Ring Keep was part of Erik's estates.

Erik had fought outlaws, bastards, and ambitious cousins for the right to rule Lord Robert's various estates in the Disputed Lands. There was little doubt that he would have to fight again. It was the nature of the Disputed Lands to belong only to the strong.

"What clothes did you find with the stranger?" Amber asked.

"I found him as you saw him. Naked."

"Then he isn't a knight."

"Not all knights returned from the Saracen with caskets of gold and gems."

"Even the poorest knight has armor, arms, a horse, clothing," she protested. "Something."

"He has something."

"What?"

"The pendant. Do you recognize it?"

Amber shook her head, making her hair burn as though it were the sun itself.

"Have you ever seen or heard of its like?" he persisted.

"Nay."

Erik let out an explosive sigh that was also a curse.

"Perhaps Cassandra?" Amber offered.

"Doubtful."

The room seemed cold despite the cheerful fire, for Amber felt the jaws of a trap both delicate and insatiable closing around her.

Erik had come to her as he had many times before, seeking the truth about a man who could not or would not speak the truth for himself. In the past, Amber had learned what she could in whatever way she could.

Even touching.

The pain of touching was a small repayment to the son of the great lord who had been so generous to her. Touching hadn't frightened Amber before.

Yet she was frightened now.

The prophecy that had attended her birth quivered in the room like a bowstring just released . . . and Amber feared the death that would be launched on the invisible, deadly arrow.

But at the same time, a need to touch the stranger was growing inside her, pressing at her, barely leaving her room to breathe. She needed to know him as she had never needed to know anything, even her own true name, her own lost parents, her own hidden heritage.

The ravenous need frightened Amber most of all. The stranger called to her in his silence, sung to her in a voice unheard, compelled her in a way she could not deny.

"Cassandra knows more than both of us together," Amber said tightly. "We must wait for her."

"At your birth, Cassandra named you Amber. Do you think it was a whim?"

"No," she whispered.

"You were born to things amber in a way that Cassandra recognized but could not hope to equal."

Amber looked away from Erik's intent eyes.

"Do you deny that this stranger wears your sign?" Erik demanded.

Amber said nothing.

"God's blood," Erik muttered, "why are you being so difficult?"

"God's blood, why are you being so dense!"

Shocked by Amber's unaccustomed anger, he simply stared at her.

"Do you know this man's name?" she demanded.

"If I knew that, I wouldn't have to—"

"Have you forgotten Cassandra's prophecy?" Amber interrupted.

"Which one?" he retorted. "Cassandra sheds bits of prophecy like an oak sheds leaves hard kissed by frost."

"Spoken like a man who has never seen beyond his own hands."

"The sword master praised the length of my reach," Erik countered, smiling thinly.

Amber made a frustrated sound. "Arguing with you is like wrestling shadows."

"Cassandra used to mention *that* even more often than she mentioned casting pearls before swine. Her wisdom, my swine, of course."

For once Amber wasn't swayed by Erik's quick wit and wry tongue.

"Hear me," she said urgently. "Listen to what Cassandra saw for me at my birth."

"I've heard what—"

But Amber was already speaking, words tumbling out, retelling the prophecy that had been born with her, casting a shadow across her life.

" 'A man with no name may you claim, heart and body and soul. Then rich life might grow, but death will surely flow.

" 'In shades of darkness he will come to you. If you touch him, you will know life that might or death that will.

" 'Be therefore as sunlight, hidden in amber, untouched by man, not touching.

" 'Forbidden.' "

Erik glanced broodingly at the stranger and then at the girl who was indeed like sunlight captured within amber, colors of golden brightness defined by a single dark truth: simple touch could cause her great pain.

Yet he was going to ask her to touch the stranger. He had no choice.

"I'm sorry," Erik said, "but if spies of Dominic le Sabre or the Scots Hammer are abroad in Stone Ring Keep's land, I must know it."

Slowly Amber nodded.

"But most of all, I must know where the Scots Hammer himself is," Erik continued. "The sooner Duncan of Maxwell is dead, the safer Lord Robert's holdings in the Disputed Lands will be."

Again Amber nodded, yet she made no move to touch the man who lay senseless at her feet.

"No man gets to this stranger's age without having a name of some sort," Erik said reasonably. "Even slaves, serfs, and villeins have names. 'Tis foolish to fear Cassandra's prophecy."

The pendant on Amber's palm burned like trapped flames. She stared at it, yet saw only what she had seen before. Sacred ring. Sacred rowan.

Shades of darkness.

"So be it," Amber whispered.

Clenching her teeth against the pain to come, she sank to her knees by the fire and laid her palm against the stranger's cheek.

The pleasure was so sharp Amber cried out and snatched her hand back. Then, realizing what she had done, she slowly reached for the stranger again.

Involuntarily, Erik moved as though to protect Amber from more pain. Then he controlled himself and stood watching, his mouth flattened into a thin line beneath his short, tawny beard. He disliked causing Amber any discomfort, but he disliked the thought of killing a stranger needlessly even more.

The second time Amber's hand touched the stranger, she didn't flinch. With a soft sound she settled more closely to him. Closing her eyes, shutting out the rest of the world, she savored the purest pleasure she had ever known.

It was like being suspended in a pool of sweet fire, caressed by warmth, knowing the heart of light.

And beyond the golden warmth of the pool, knowledge lay in shades of darkness.

Waiting.

Amber gave a low cry. She could think of few men who would have such a certainty of their own prowess in battle. Dominic le Sabre and Duncan of Maxwell were two. A third was Erik.

A great warrior lies beneath my hand, light and darkness, pleasure and pain, soul mate and deadly foe in one.

"Amber."

Slowly she opened her eyes. The look on Erik's face told her that he had called to her more than once. Intent, tawny eyes watched her. His concern for her was tangible, and warming. She forced a smile despite the turmoil seething beneath her calm surface.

She owed Erik so much. His father had given her clothes, the cottage, men to work the land, and land for men to work. Erik trusted her as though she were a clansman rather than a waif with neither parent nor sibling to call her own.

And she knew she was going to betray Erik's trust for a stranger who might well prove to be Erik's foe.

Having touched the stranger, Amber could not deliver him to death at Erik's hands. Not until she was certain that the man was whom she feared.

Perhaps not even then.

He could simply be a stranger, known to no one.

The thought was as seductive as a hearth fire on a winter day.

Aye! A stranger. Other knights have come to the Disputed Lands. I have heard their tales of being tested in the Saracen crucible. They were confident of their own might.

This man could be such a warrior.

He must be.

"Amber?"

"Leave him here," she said huskily. "He belongs to me."

The temptation to continue touching the stranger was very great. Reluctantly she withdrew her hand. The emptiness she felt at the loss of touch dismayed her. Until that instant she wouldn't have described herself as lonely.

Erik let out a long, relieved sigh as he realized that touching the stranger had unsettled Amber, but hadn't caused her true pain.

"God must be listening to my prayers," Erik said.

Amber made a questioning sound.

"I need skilled warriors," Erik said. "The Scots Hammer is only the first problem I must face."

"What else?" Amber asked, concerned.

"Norsemen have been seen just north of Winterlance. And my dear cousins grow restless once again."

"Send them to fight the Norsemen."

"More likely, they would ally themselves and attack my father's estates," Erik said, smiling thinly.

Amber forced herself not to look at the stranger. Having a warrior such as Dominic le Sabre or the Scots Hammer fighting with Erik rather than against him could easily make the difference between peace and prolonged war for the Disputed Lands.

Yet she could as well wish to pour sunlight from hand to hand like water as wish the great Norman lord or his Scots vassal to ally with Lord Robert of the North.

"What is my new warrior's name?" Erik asked.

"I'll ask him when he wakens," Amber said.

"Why did he come to the Disputed Lands?"

"That will be the second thing I ask him."

"Where was he going?" Erik asked.

"That will be the third."

Erik grunted. "You didn't learn much when you touched him, did you?"

"No."

"The stranger's sleep isn't natural."

Amber nodded.

"Is he spellbound?" Erik pressed.

"No."

Erik's eyebrows rose at the quickness of her response.

"You sound quite certain," he said.

"I am."

"Why?"

Frowning, Amber probed her memory. The certainties that had flowed from the stranger into her were unlike any she had ever discovered by touch in the past. His basic nature—fierce, proud, generous, passionate, determined, bold—had been frighteningly easy to discover.

Yet there were no shifting, chaotic images of the hours or days or weeks or years before he came to the Stone Ring and the sacred rowan. There was no bright sense of purpose stitching like lightning through darkness. There were no faces beloved or hated.

It was as though the stranger had no memories.

Without realizing it, Amber reached out to the man again. She willed herself to ignore the pleasure as she once had taught herself to ignore pain. Peeling away petal after petal of beguiling sensation, she searched for the stranger's memories.

There were none. There were only faint, fading glimmers of light that retreated even as she pursued.

The man was as though newly born.

"I don't sense anything corrupt gnawing away inside him," she said finally. "It is like touching a babe."

Erik snorted. "A babe? God blind me, but he is the biggest babe I've ever seen!"

Amber withdrew her hand.

"What else can you tell me?" Erik asked.

She laced her fingers together so tightly that they ached. She didn't want to share her fears with Erik, yet his questions were circling closer and closer to the core of her unease, a fear she acknowledged each time she denied it.

Great warrior, deadly enemy, and soul mate in one.

Nay! I don't know who he is!

I know only that he is a man with no name who is supremely confident of his own fighting skills.

"Normally you ask the question, the person I'm touching answers, and my touch tells me if the truth was spoken," Amber said slowly. "This time was . . . different."

Erik looked from the senseless stranger to Amber, who seemed almost a stranger herself at the moment.

"Are you well?" he asked softly.

She jumped. "Aye."

"You seem dazed."

A smile was difficult to manage, but Amber did.

" 'Tis the touching," she said.

"I'm sorry."

"Don't be. God sends us nothing that we can't endure."

"Or die trying," Erik said dryly.

Amber's smile slipped as the words of the prophecy rang once again in her mind.

Death will surely flow.

2

THE smell of timeless evergreens permeated Amber's cottage. Candles flickered in holders above the bed. They cast a shivering golden light over the man with no name. A man who lay captive in a sleep that had no dreams.

Amber was certain he wasn't dreaming, for she had spent the past two days rubbing precious oils and warmth into his body. During that time she had sensed nothing new. Nor had the pleasure that came with touching him changed. It was as keen now as it had been the first time.

As Amber worked, she spoke to the stranger, trying to reach him with words as well as with the warmth of her touch and the pungent, healing power of evergreen and amber.

"My dark warrior," Amber murmured as she had many times before. "How did you come to the Stone Ring?"

Her hands massaged first one powerful arm, then the other, shaping muscles that were firm even in relaxation. The dark hair on his forearms gleamed with oil and candlelight. The sight of the strong cords binding him to the bed frame made her frown. She touched one of the cords and sighed, but didn't remove it.

Erik had said the stranger was to be bound or else one of Erik's squires would be with Amber at all times. She had chosen the bonds, for she wanted no one else around if the man woke up and was discovered to be the enemy she feared.

Amber didn't know what she would do if that happened. It was a thing she refused to think about, for there was no solution to the dilemma it would cause.

Enemy and soul mate in one.

"Were you afoot?" Amber asked. "Were you alone?"

There was no answer but the rhythmic rise and fall of the stranger's broad chest.

"Are your eyes the gray of ice and winter, the gray of Dominic le Sabre's? Or are your eyes darker, as the Scots Hammer's are reputed to be?

"Or are you a third warrior, unknown, come back from the Saracen full of certainty of your own ability?"

There was no change in the stranger's deep, even breathing.

"I pray you are unknown," Amber whispered.

With a sigh, she resumed stroking the patterns of hair across the man's chest. The masculine hair both intrigued and pleased her. She liked smoothing the crisp mat, feeling its resilience and tickling caress over her palms.

"Did you take off your clothes so that you could enter the sacred circle and sleep safely at the rowan's feet?"

The man made a murmurous sound.

"Yes," Amber said eagerly. "Oh, yes, my warrior. Come to the golden light. Leave all the shades of darkness behind."

Though the man made no response, Amber was elated. Slowly, slowly, he was emerging from his unnatural sleep. She sensed his pleasure in being stroked and petted as clearly as if he could speak.

Yet still no memories came from him to her, no images, no names, no faces.

"Where are you hiding, my dark warrior?" she asked. "And why?"

Amber smoothed thick, slightly wavy hair back from the stranger's forehead.

"Whatever you fear, you must awaken soon. Else you will be lost forever in a darkness that won't end short of death."

The stranger made no sound. It was as though she had imagined the brief stirring.

Straightening wearily, Amber looked at the incense bowl that was set like a candle holder into the wall. The teardrop-shaped bit of gemstone was almost consumed. She added another precious fragment from her store of medicinal amber. A tendril of thin, fragrant smoke curled upward.

The stranger's body twitched but he didn't awaken. Amber was beginning to fear he wouldn't. Too often that was what happened to people who were struck by stone or broadsword or horse's hoof. They fell into dreamless sleep. Nor did they awaken. Ever.

That can't happen to this man. He is mine!

The intensity of Amber's feelings startled her. Uneasily, she began pacing the cottage. After a time she realized that dawn was sending tiny lances of light between the cottage's shutters. Beyond the walls, cocks crowed their triumph into the dying night.

Amber peeked through a crack where the shutters didn't quite meet. The autumn storm that had been the stranger's undoing had passed over the land. In its wake lay a world newly made, glittering with dew and possibilities.

Normally Amber would have been up and about in the garden, checking on the herbs she grew for Cassandra and herself. Or she would walk to the fens to see if flights of plump geese had arrived, bringing with them the certainty of the coming winter.

But there was nothing normal about today. There had been nothing normal since the instant Amber had touched a man with no name and discovered that she had been born to be this one man's mate.

She went to the bed and rested her fingers lightly on his cheek. He was still in the coils of unnatural sleep.

"But not so deeply, I think. Something is changing."

The cocks outside no longer crowed, telling Amber that the sun was lifting to its accustomed rounds.

"If you do awaken, I'll scare you back to sleep with my appearance," she said. "I must look as bedraggled as a winter garden."

Amber refreshed herself with a basin of warm water and evergreen-scented soap. She put on a clean linen shift, tugged bright red stockings into place, and pulled a dress of thick, soft wool over her head.

The dress was another gift of Lord Robert, through his son, Erik, in thanks for the fine, dried herbs Amber supplied to Robert's household. The gold embroidery around the front neck opening made a rich contrast to the indigo color of the wool itself. The dress was lined with yellow linen, which showed inside the long, trailing sleeves and at the hem of the dress.

When she was finished dressing, the soft cloth clung to the curving lines of her breasts and waist and hips. She caught the wide hem of the sleeves and bound them with ribbons around her wrists where the cloth would be out of her way.

With flying fingers she wrapped a triple strand of gold-painted leather around her hips and tied the belt in front. At the end of each of the six leather strands, opaque rings of amber glowed in shades of gold. A sheath of gilded leather hung securely from her waist. Within the sheath lay a silver dagger whose hilt held a single eye of blood-red amber.

Grabbing a comb made of rowan wood set with orange amber, she hurried over to the stranger's bed. A brief touch told her that he was still swimming like a trout beneath the surface of unnatural sleep. And like a trout, he was struggling to rise toward the gleaming lure of the sun.

Amber shook him lightly. There was no response other than a muttering that had no meaning. She stood next to the bed and combed tangles from her long golden hair while she watched him anxiously.

"You are closer to the sunlight with each heart-beat," she said hopefully. "Please awaken and tell me your name."

His head turned restlessly and a hand twitched. Amber touched him but discovered nothing new.

Amber felt as restless as the stranger's sleep. Pacing, combing her hair, pacing again, she finally cracked the shutters just beyond the bed and looked out. No one was coming up the path from Stone Ring Keep to her secluded cottage.

She pushed the shutters a bit apart and began braiding her hair, ignoring the bracing rush of air into the room. Her fingers were clumsy with impatience and anxiety. The comb slipped and fell onto the rush-covered floor next to the bed. She slammed the shutter closed.

"What a bother my hair is," Amber muttered.

As she bent down to retrieve the comb, her hair fell across the stranger's bound right hand. Long, powerful fingers clenched in her hair, holding her captive.

Amber froze, then stared into piercing hazel eyes that were only a few inches from her own.

Not gray. Thank God, not the gray of Dominic le Sabre's! I haven't lost my heart to a man who is already wed.

"Who are you?" demanded a deep male voice.

"You have your wits! You have slept for two days and I feared—"

"Two?" he interrupted.

"Don't you remember?" Amber asked softly, stroking the hand whose fingers were wrapped in her hair. "There was a storm."

She waited hopefully.

"I remember nothing," he said.

Amber didn't doubt it. All that came to her from touching the stranger was the depth of his confusion.

"I—remember—nothing!" the stranger said violently. "By God's holy blood, what has happened to me?"

There was fear as well as confusion in his voice. He tried to get up, only to realize that he was bound hand and foot. He could move his fingers and his head, but no more. He was so surprised that he released his grip on Amber's hair and began straining at the cords binding his right arm.

His sword arm.

"'Tis all right," Amber said, reaching for his hand.

"I'm bound! Am I a prisoner?"

"Nay, it's just—"

"What in the name of Jesus and Mary is going on!"

She touched the stranger's clenched hand. She sensed fury at being bound, turmoil at lack of memory, fear at his own helplessness; but nowhere did she sense any desire to hurt her.

"I wish you no harm," Amber said soothingly. "You've been ill and out of your senses."

She might as well have been talking to the wind. The man's muscles bunched as he fought against his bonds. The wooden supports of the bed creaked and cords bit into his flesh, but none of the bonds gave way.

A feral snarl rippled from his throat. His body bucked and covers flew off as he struggled to free himself. Cords cut into flesh until blood flowed. He kept fighting.

"Nay," Amber said urgently. "Stop!"

She threw herself across the stranger's body and hung on to him as though he were an unruly horse, trying to hold him still so that he wouldn't hurt himself any more.

The shock of being surrounded by a soft, fragrant woman and a wild fall of golden hair was so startling that the man stopped struggling for an instant.

It was all Amber needed. She brushed a kiss across his naked chest, further shocking him into stillness. Then she touched his lips with her fingers as though to stop his cries.

"Lie still, my dark warrior. I will free you."

A shudder went through him. He counted each heartbeat in the savage agony hammering inside his head. Slowly, with a visible act of will, he forced himself not to fight against his bonds.

The feel of Amber's hands on his bare skin sent another shudder through him, as did the silky fall of her hair across his groin. His heart raced with more than the brief fight to free himself.

Then he saw the ancient silver dagger she had taken from her belt.

"Nay!" he said hoarsely.

Abruptly he realized that the dagger was to be used on the knots rather than on him. With a groan, he stopped struggling. When the force of his blood slowed, the pain in his head subsided.

Amber looked up from her work and smiled encouragingly.

"I'm sorry you were bound," she said. "You were . . . not yourself."

Whomever that might be.

"No one knew how it would go with you when you awoke," she added.

The man let out a long breath as his right hand was freed. The other bonds gave way quickly to the flashing dagger. Before the sweat of his brief battle had dried on his body, he was free.

"I'm sorry," Amber said again. "Erik insisted that you be tied for my safety. But I know you won't hurt me."

A shake of the stranger's head was his only answer. For the space of several breaths he lay and watched Amber, trying to understand what had happened to him.

All he knew for certain was that the less he moved, the less his head hurt.

"Ill?" he asked after a few moments. "I've been ill?"

Amber nodded.

"What kind of illness is it that leaves a man with no memory, nothing—not even his own name!"

A chill lanced through Amber. She sheathed the dagger with trembling hands.

This can't be what Cassandra prophesied.

I haven't been reckless. I haven't been foolish.

He can't be a man with no name.

But he was.

"You don't remember your name?" she asked in an aching voice.

"Nay, nor anything but . . ."

"Yes?" Amber asked eagerly.

"Darkness. A thousand shades of black."

"Is that all?"

Thick lashes flickered for a moment as the stranger rubbed his raw wrists and looked at the ceiling, searching for something only he could see.

"A golden light," he said slowly, "a sweet voice calling to me, luring me from that fell night, breathing the scent of larch and pine over me."

Hazel eyes flecked with gray and green and blue focused intently on Amber. His hand moved so swiftly that she was captive before she knew what had happened. His fingers slid into her hair all the way to her scalp. He held her gently this time, but so securely there was no chance to get away.

Nor did Amber want to. A curious pleasure was coursing through her. She had touched the stranger many times, but never had she been touched *by* him. The difference was quite thrilling, despite her clear understanding that his emotions were a seething, unpredictable storm that might slip his control at any moment.

Slowly the man drew Amber down onto the bed next to him. He buried his face in her hair and inhaled deeply, drinking her scent. Amber brushed her lips across his cheek and chest as had become her custom through the long hours that she had tended him.

"It was you," he said huskily.

"Yes."

"Do I know you?"

"You know only what is in your own mind," she said. "Do you know me?" she countered.

"I think I have never seen a girl more beautiful. Not even . . ."

The man's deep voice faded and he frowned heavily.

"What is it?" Amber asked.

"I can't remember her name."

"Whose?"

"The one who was the most beautiful girl I had ever seen. Until you."

As the stranger spoke, Amber deliberately flattened both palms against the naked skin of his shoulders. A vague image came to her of a girl with hair as red as flame and far-seeing eyes of jeweled green.

The image faded, leaving him without a name to put to the delicate face. He shook his head and cursed roughly in frustration.

"Give yourself time to heal," Amber said. "Your memory will return."

Big hands clamped around her shoulders and strong fingers dug urgently into her flesh.

"There is no time! I must—I must—God's teeth, I can't remember!"

Tears came to Amber's eyes as the stranger's anguish swept through her. He was a man whose honor was his greatest possession. He had given vows that must be kept.

But he could not remember who had accepted those vows.

Nor could he remember what the vows had been.

A cry was dragged from Amber's throat, for the man's pain and fear and rage were also hers while she touched him.

Instantly the pressure on her shoulders was relieved. Battle-hardened hands began caressing rather than digging into soft flesh.

"Forgive me," he said hoarsely. "I didn't mean to hurt you."

Surprisingly gentle fingers brushed over Amber's eyelashes, taking her tears. Startled, she opened her eyes.

The man's face was very close to hers. Despite his own agitation, he was concerned for her. It was as clear to her as the dark, thick lashes that framed his hazel eyes.

"You d-didn't hurt me," Amber said. "Not in the way you mean."

"You're crying."

" 'Tis your anguish. I sense it so very clearly."

Dark eyebrows rose. The backs of the man's fingers brushed very lightly over Amber's cheek. Hot tears burned against his skin.

"Don't cry, gentle fairy."

Amber smiled despite her tears. "I'm not a fairy."

"I don't believe you. Only a creature of magic could have pulled me from that savage darkness."

"I'm a student of Cassandra the Wise."

"Ah, that explains it," he said. "You're a witch."

"Not at all! I'm simply one of the Learned."

"I meant no insult. I have a fondness for witches who can heal."

"You do?" Amber asked, startled. "Have you known many?"

"One." The man frowned. "Or is it two?"

His control threatened to break at the new evidence that he had none of the memories other people take for granted.

"Try not to fight so," Amber said. "It only makes things worse. Can't you feel that?"

" 'Tis hard not to fight," he said through his teeth. "Fighting is what I do best!"

"How do you know?"

The man went still.

"I don't know," he said finally. "But I know it's true just the same."

"It's also true that a man who fights himself can't win."

Silently the stranger absorbed that unhappy truth.

"If you are meant to remember," Amber said, "you will."

"And if I'm not?" he asked starkly. "Will I go through the rest of my life a man with no name?"

His words were too close to the bleak prophecy that had haunted Amber's life.

"Nay!" she cried. "I will give you a name. I will call you—*Duncan*."

The echoes of the name beat at Amber, horrifying her. She hadn't meant to say that name. She truly hadn't.

He can't be Duncan of Maxwell. I refuse to believe it. Better that he remain forever a man with no name!

But it was too late. She had given him a name. Duncan.

Breath held, her hands clenched around one of

his, Amber waited for Duncan's response.

There was a distant sense of straining, of shifting, of focusing, of . . .

Then it was gone, fading like an echo heard for the third time.

"Duncan?" he asked. "Is that my name?"

"I don't know," Amber said unhappily. "But the name suits you. It means 'dark warrior.' "

His eyes narrowed.

"Your body bears the marks of battle," Amber said, touching the scars on his chest, "and your hair is a most pleasing shade of darkness."

The light caress of her fingers lured and beguiled Duncan, encouraging him to accept his strange awakening into a world both familiar and forever changed.

And whether it was strange or familiar, Duncan was too spent to fight anymore. The long climb up from darkness had sapped even his great strength.

"Promise you won't bind me if I sleep again," he said huskily.

"I promise."

Duncan looked at the intent, intense maid who was watching him with such concern. Questions crowded his thoughts, too many questions to sort out.

Too many which had no answer.

He might not remember the details of his life before he had awakened, but he hadn't forgotten everything. At some time in the past he had learned that a frontal attack wasn't always the best way to take a fortified position.

And in any case, at the moment he hadn't the strength to attack a butterfly. Every time he gathered himself to fight, the pain in his head all but blinded him.

"Rest for a bit," Amber said encouragingly. "I'll make some tea to ease the pain in your head."

"How did you know?"

Amber reached for the fallen covers without answering. Her unbound hair fell over Duncan and was drawn beneath the covers as she pulled them up. With an impatient sound, she swept the long mass back over her shoulders, only to have a handful escape once more.

"You hair is like amber," Duncan said, stroking a soft lock. "Smooth and precious."

"That is my name."

"Precious?" he asked, smiling slowly.

Amber's breath caught. Duncan had a smile to melt sleet and call meadowlarks from a midnight sky.

"No," she said with a soft laugh, shaking her head. "My name is Amber."

"Amber . . ."

Duncan looked from her long hair to her luminous golden eyes.

"Yes," he said. "Precious Amber."

Duncan released the silky strand of hair, stroked her wrist, and let his hand settle onto the thick fur cover.

The lack of Duncan's touch was like having a fire go out. Amber had to swallow a sound of protest.

"So I am Duncan and you are Amber," he said after a few moments. "For now . . ."

"Yes," she whispered.

Desperately Amber wished that she had called Duncan by any other name.

Yet at the same time she knew she couldn't have withheld what she feared could be his true name. She, called simply Amber, knew only too well the hole in the center of life that came from having no name, no real heritage.

Perhaps it is simply my fears playing upon me, drawing shadow monsters upon an empty wall.

Do I fear that he is Duncan of Maxwell simply because I want so much for him to be someone else?

Anyone else.

"Where am I?" Duncan asked.

"In my cottage."

He glanced around, seeing beyond Amber to the large room. There was a central fire burning cheerfully as smoke was drawn to the hole at the peak of the thatched roof. Something savory cooked in the small cauldron suspended from a trivet over the fire. The walls had been limed to whiteness and the floor was covered with clean rushes. Shuttered windows were set in three walls. In the fourth was a door.

Thoughtfully Duncan fingered the bedding. Linen and soft wool and luxurious fur, rich curtains of cloth pulled aside for the day. Nearby was a table with a chair, an oil lamp, and, astonishingly, a handful of what appeared to be ancient manuscripts.

Duncan looked back to the girl who had attended his illness, a girl who was familiar and unknown at once.

Amber's clothes were like the bedding, wonderfully rich, soft, warm, and colorful. At her wrists and neck, amber gems gleamed in costly shades of warm yellow and gold.

"You live far better than most cottagers," Duncan said.

"I have been fortunate. Erik, heir to Lord Robert of the North, watches over me."

Amber's affection for Erik was clear in her voice and in her smile. Duncan's expression darkened, making him look every bit the formidable warrior he was.

For an instant, Amber wondered if she hadn't been a bit too hasty in untying him.

"Are you his leman?" Duncan asked.

At first Amber didn't understand the blunt question. When she did, she flushed.

"Nay! Lord Robert is a—"

"Not Robert," Duncan interrupted curtly. "Erik,

the mere mention of whose name makes you smile."

Amber smiled widely.

"Erik's leman?" she repeated. "He would laugh fit to choke at the thought. We've known one another since we were no bigger than goslings."

"Does he give costly gifts to all his childhood friends?" Duncan asked coolly.

"We were both students of Cassandra the Wise."

"So?"

"So Erik's family befriended me."

"At some expense to themselves," Duncan said pointedly.

"Their gifts, though generous indeed, do not strain Lord Robert's wealth," Amber said in a dry tone.

As Duncan opened his mouth to question Amber further, he realized that he was reacting with far too much jealousy over a maid he had just met.

Or had he?

He was quite naked in her bed. Her hands weren't hesitant to touch him. She had neither blushed nor turned away when the bed covers went sliding in disarray, revealing his nakedness. Nor had she been in any great haste to cover him again.

But how did one delicately ask a maid if she was his betrothed, his wife, or his leman?

Or, God forbid, his *sister*?

Duncan grimaced. The thought that he and Amber might be close in blood appalled him.

"Duncan? Are you in pain?"

"No."

"Are you certain?"

He made a harsh sound. "Tell me . . ."

His voice and his courage faded. The sensual heat in his blood did not.

"Yes?" Amber said encouragingly.

"Are we related by blood?"

"Nay," she said instantly.

"Thank God."

Amber looked startled.

"Is Cassandra one of those whom you call Learned?" Duncan asked, changing the subject before Amber could pursue it.

"Yes."

"Is that a tribe or a clan or a priesthood?"

At first Amber wondered if Duncan were toying with her. Any man who was found inside the Stone Ring asleep at the foot of the sacred rowan was certainly one of the Learned!

The thought was like a balm. She had heard many things about Duncan of Maxwell, the Scots Hammer, but never had it been so much as hinted that he was one of the Learned.

Whatever or whomever the stranger she had named Duncan had once been, he was now a different man, riven from past Learning by a bolt of lightning.

Frowning, Amber tried to find the words to describe her relationship with Cassandra and Erik and the few other Learned whom she had met. She didn't want Duncan to look at her with superstition or fear, as some of the simple folk did.

"Many Learned are related by blood, but not all," Amber said slowly. "It is a kind of discipline, like a school, but all those who attempt to learn aren't equally apt."

"Like hounds or horses or knights?" Duncan asked after a time.

She looked puzzled.

"Some are always better than others at what they do," he said simply. "A few, a very few, are far better than any."

"Yes," Amber said, relieved that Duncan understood. "Those who can't be taught say that those who can learn are cursed or blessed. Usually cursed."

Duncan smiled wryly.

"But we aren't," she said. "We are simply what God made us to be. Different."

"Aye. I have met a few people like that. Different."

Absently, Duncan flexed his right hand as though to grasp a sword. It was a movement made without forethought, as much a part of him as breathing. He didn't even notice the act.

Amber did.

She remembered what she had heard about the Scots Hammer, a warrior who had been defeated in battle only once, and that by the hated Norman usurper, Dominic le Sabre. In exchange for his own life, Duncan had sworn fealty to the enemy.

It was rumored that Dominic had defeated Duncan with the help of his Glendruid witchwife.

Amber remembered the face she had glimpsed through Duncan's thick veil of forgetfulness—hair of flame and eyes of an unusually intense green.

Glendruid green.

Dear God, could he be Dominic le Sabre, Erik's sworn enemy?

Staring at Duncan's eyes, Amber tried to see them as gray, but honestly could not. Green, perhaps. Or blue. Or brown. But not gray.

Amber let out a long sigh and prayed she wasn't deluding herself.

"Where did you meet these unusual men?" she asked. "Or were they women?"

Duncan opened his mouth, but no words came. He grimaced at the fresh evidence of his lack of memory.

"I don't know," he said flatly. "But I know that I have met them."

Amber went to Duncan and put her fingers over his restless sword hand.

"Their names?" Amber asked in a soft voice.

Silence answered her, followed by a curse.

She sensed Duncan's raw frustration and growing anger, but no faces, no names, nothing to call forth memories.

"Were they friend or foe?" she asked quietly.

"Both," he said hoarsely. "But not . . . not quite."

Duncan's hand clenched into a heavy fist. Gently Amber tried to soothe the fingers into relaxation. He jerked his hand away and pounded on his thigh.

"God's blood!" he snarled. "What kind of dishonorable cur can't remember friend or foe or sacred vows?"

Pain twisted through Amber, pain that was both Duncan's and, eerily, her own.

"Have you made any such vows?" she asked in a low voice.

"I—don't—know!"

The words were almost a shout.

"Gently, my warrior," Amber said.

While she spoke, she stroked Duncan's hair and face as she had through the long hours when he had been lost in an odd kind of sleep.

At the first touch, Duncan flinched. When he looked into Amber's troubled golden eyes, he groaned and unclenched his hands, allowing her gentle caresses to soothe him.

"Sleep, Duncan. I can feel your exhaustion."

"No," he said grimly.

"You must let yourself heal."

"I don't want to go into that fell darkness again."

"You won't."

"And if I do?"

"I'll call you forth again."

"Why?" he asked. "Who am I to you?"

Amber hesitated at the blunt question, then smiled an odd, bittersweet smile as Cassandra's prophecy echoed like distant thunder.

He will come to you in shades of darkness.

And he had.

She had touched a man with no name and he had claimed her heart.

Amber didn't know if she could bend events so that life as well as death flowed from her reckless action. She knew only one thing, and she knew it with a certainty greater than that of the sun's burning progress across the sky.

"Come heaven, come hell," Amber said in a low voice, "I will protect you with my life. We are . . . joined."

Duncan's eyes narrowed as he realized that Amber had just given him a vow that to her was every bit as binding as any that lords might make among themselves. The fierceness with which she was prepared to defend him against the darkness that had claimed his memory both reassured Duncan and made him smile.

She was so fragile-looking, a handful of sunlight and softness, a fragrant breeze, a sweet warmth.

"Are you another ruthless Boadicea, to lead men into battle?" Duncan teased gently.

With a small smile, Amber shook her head. "I've never held a broadsword. They look like great, clumsy things to me."

"Fairies weren't meant to wield swords. They have other weapons."

"But I am not a fairy."

"So you say."

Smiling, Duncan traced the long fall of Amber's unbound hair.

"Odd to think that you are mine and I am yours . . ." he murmured.

Amber didn't correct Duncan's misunderstanding, for there was a curious difference in his touch now. It sent tendrils of sweet, secret fire through her.

"Only if you wish it," she whispered.

"I can't believe I would forget such a fey, beautiful creature as you."

"That's because I'm not beautiful," she retorted.

"To me you are as beautiful as dawn after a long winter's night."

The genuine belief in Duncan's voice and eyes was reinforced by his touch. He was not paying her courtly compliments. He had spoken what was to him the simple truth.

Amber shivered as Duncan's thumb outlined the curve of her parted lips. He felt her response and smiled despite the headache that had returned with the renewed beating of his blood. The smile was nakedly male, frankly triumphant, as though he had been given an answer to a question he hadn't wanted to put into words.

Duncan's other hand slid deeply into Amber's hair, both caressing and chaining her. Strange sensations coursed from his touch. Before she could put a name to them, she found herself stretched across his chest, her lips against his, and his tongue within her mouth.

Surprise overcame the other feelings racing wildly through Amber. Instinctively she struggled against Duncan's heavy embrace.

At first his arms tightened. Then slowly, reluctantly, he loosened his grip on her just enough so that he could speak.

"You said you were mine."

"I said we were *joined*."

"Aye, lass. That's what I had in mind. Joining."

"I meant—that is—"

"Yes?"

Before Amber could answer, the excited yaps and howls of a pack of hunting dogs burst into the clearing that surrounded her cottage. She knew without looking that Erik had come to check on the stranger who had been left in her care.

Erik would be furious that Amber had disobeyed him and untied the man who had no name.

3

Duncan sat up in a rush, then groaned at the hammer blow of pain behind his eyes.

"Lie back," Amber said quickly. " 'Tis only Erik."

Duncan's eyes narrowed, but he did as she asked, giving way to the firm pressure of her hands on his shoulders.

An outraged squawking and screeching from the yard announced that Erik's hounds had discovered the chickens. As Amber opened the front door, the hound master blew on his horn, calling the dogs back to order.

The youngest hound in the pack didn't come to the command. The half-grown dog had just discovered an old goose. Certain of an easy rout, the hound romped forward with delighted barks. The gander arched its long neck, lowered its head, spread its wings, and hissed menacingly.

The hound kept coming.

"Erik," Amber said, "call him off!"

"It will do him good."

"But—"

The rangy, rough-coated dog attacked. The gander's right wing came down in a blur of motion. The hound was knocked off its feet. Crying in surprise and pain, the dog scrambled upright and raced back to the pack, tail tucked low.

Erik laughed so hard it upset the peregrine riding on a perch on the pommel of his saddle. Silver bells on the trailing ends of the jesses jangled harshly, telling of the bird's disturbance. The falcon flared its narrow, elegant wings and gave a sharp, piercing cry.

Erik's answering whistle was as high and wild as the falcon's. The bird cocked her head and whistled again. This cry was different, as was Erik's whistled response.

The falcon folded its wings and was quiet once more.

Swift glances passed among the squires and knights who were hunting with Erik. His uncanny way with wild beasts was a matter of much speculation among the people. Though none called Erik sorcerer to his face, men whispered it among themselves.

"Be easy, my beauty," Erik said softly.

He stroked the bird with his bare hand. His other hand wore a thick leather gauntlet for protection when the falcon rode his wrist.

"Robbie," Erik said to the hound master. "Take the hounds and my men off to the forest. You're disturbing Amber's peace."

Amber opened her mouth to say that wasn't true. A glance from Erik silenced her. Without a word, Amber waited until the hounds, horses, and men rode back into the forest in a flurry of noise and motion.

"How fares the stranger?" Erik asked bluntly.

"Better than your hound."

"Maybe next time Trouble will come when Robbie sounds the hunting horn."

"Doubtful. Half-grown males have much passion and little brain."

"I'd be insulted if I weren't fully grown," Erik said.

Amber widened her eyes. "Are you? Since when, my lord?"

A smile flashed and faded on Erik's handsome face. Silently he waited for Amber to speak of the fully grown male who lay within her cottage.

"He is awake," she said.

Erik's right hand settled on the hilt of the sword he always wore.

"His name?" Erik demanded.

"He doesn't remember."

"What?"

"He remembers no names from his past, not even his own."

"He is as cunning as a fox," Erik said flatly. "He knows he is in enemy hands and—"

"Nay," Amber interrupted. "He knows not whether he is Norman or Saxon, serf or thane."

"Is he bewitched?"

Amber shook her head. The sudden weight and shimmer of her hair falling around her shoulders reminded her that she hadn't yet managed to bind the locks properly. Impatiently she tossed her head and pulled the mantle's cowl over her hair, concealing it.

"There is no feel of compulsion about him," Amber said.

"What else did you sense?"

"Courage. Strength. Honor. Generosity."

Erik's eyebrows rose.

"A saint," he said dryly. "How unexpected."

Color showed along Amber's slanting cheekbones as she remembered Duncan's distinctly unsaintly desire for her.

"There was also confusion and pain and fear," she said crisply.

"Ah, he's human, then. How disappointing."

"You're a devil, Erik, son of Robert of the North!"

His smiled. "Thank you. 'Tis nice to have my true character appreciated."

Amber laughed despite trying not to.

"What else?" he asked.

Her amusement faded. "Nothing."

"What?"

"Nothing."

The falcon's wings flared in swift reflection of its master's irritation.

"Why is he in the Disputed Lands?" asked Erik in a clipped voice.

"He doesn't remember."

"Where was he going?"

"He doesn't know," she said.

"Does he owe fealty to a lord or is he a free lance?"

"He doesn't know."

"God's wounds," Erik hissed. "Is he a fool?"

"Nay! He just doesn't remember."

"Have you questioned him with your touch?"

Amber took a deep breath and nodded slightly.

"What did you sense?" Erik pressed.

"When he tries to remember, there is confusion. If he pursues, there is a blinding light, harsh pain . . ."

"Like lightning striking?"

"It could be," she said.

Erik's eyes narrowed into amber slits.

"What's wrong?" he asked after a moment. "You've never been so uncertain before."

"You've never brought me a man found sense-less within Stone Ring before," she retorted.

"Is that a complaint?"

Amber sighed. "I'm sorry. I've slept little since you brought him. It was very difficult to call him from the darkness."

"Yes. I can see that in the shadows beneath your eyes."

She smiled wanly.

"Amber? Is he friend or foe?"

The blunt question was the very one that she had feared.

"Friend," she whispered. Then honesty and affection compelled her to add, "Until he regains his memory. Then he will be whatever he was before you brought him to me. Friend or enemy or free lance bound to no lord."

"Is that the best you can do in assessing him?"

"He isn't a criminal or a beast to savage his own kind. He was gentle with me despite his fear."

Erik grunted. "But?"

"But if he regains his memory, he might not consider himself our friend. Or he might be a long-lost cousin happy to find himself at home. Only he can say."

"If he regains his memory . . ."

Silently, Erik stroked his peregrine's shining back while he considered the possibilities. A persistent sense of uneasiness threaded through his thoughts. Something was wrong. He knew it.

He just didn't know what it was.

"Will he regain his memory?" Erik asked.

"I don't know."

"Guess," he said succinctly.

A chill went through Amber. She didn't like to think of what would happen if Duncan's memory returned. If he were enemy and soul mate in one . . .

It would tear her apart.

Nor did she want to think of what it would be like for Duncan if he didn't remember. He would be restless, savage, driven mad by names never remembered, sacred vows never honored, a man forsworn.

It would tear him apart.

Amber's breath froze in her chest. She wouldn't cause such dishonor and anguish even to an enemy, much less to the man who had stolen her heart with a touch, a smile, a kiss.

"I . . ." Her voice died.

"Little one?" Erik asked, troubled by Amber's haunted golden eyes.

"I don't know," she said in a shaking voice. "So much ill could come. So little good."

Rich life might grow, but death will surely flow.

"Perhaps I had better take the stranger to Stone Ring Keep," Erik said.

"Nay."

"Why not?"

"He wears sacred amber. He is mine."

The flat certainty in Amber's voice both surprised and worried Erik.

"What if he regains his memory?" Erik asked.

"Then he will."

"You could be in danger." ·

"As God wills."

A surge of anger went through Erik. The falcon cried and his horse moved restlessly and champed at the bit. Erik curbed his mount and soothed his falcon without looking away from Amber's steady gaze.

"You make no sense," he said finally. "I'll send my squires for the stranger as soon as we're through hawking."

Amber's head came up defiantly. "As you will, *lord*."

"God's teeth, are you possessed? I'm trying only to protect you from a man with no name."

"He has a name."

"You told me he didn't remember his name."

"He doesn't," Amber retorted. "I gave him one."

"What is it?"

"Duncan."

Erik's mouth opened, then snapped shut with a distinct sound of clicking teeth.

"Explain," he demanded.

"I had to call him something. 'Dark warrior' suits him."

"Duncan," Erik said neutrally.

"Yes."

In the distance a horn blew, telling of hounds

being sent after birds, scaring them into flight for the hawks that rode on the arms of knights. The peregrine on Erik's saddle keened restlessly, recognizing the call to a hunt that had left her behind.

Overhead, a merlin's cry announced yet another hawk on the wing. Erik looked up, searching the brilliant sky with eyes that were the equal of any hunting bird's.

A small, fierce falcon shot down like a dark bolt from the blue, trailing silver jesses that flashed in the sunlight. Though the falcon's stoop ended behind a rocky rise, Erik had no doubt about the outcome.

"Cassandra will have partridge before I have mallard," he said. "Maid Marian flies with her customary lethal grace."

Amber closed her eyes and let out a soundless sigh of relief that Erik was no longer pursuing the uncomfortable subject of the stranger whom she had named Duncan.

"Cassandra will come to you at supper," Erik said. "And so will I. Be here. See that the man you call *Duncan* is here as well."

Amber found herself looking into the cold, topaz glance of the wolf that lived within her childhood friend. Her chin came up. She watched him through narrowed yellow eyes that were as cold as his own.

"Aye, lord."

Erik's smile flashed beneath his dark gold beard. "Do you still have smoked venison?"

She nodded.

"Good," he said. "I'll be hungry."

"You're always hungry."

Laughing, Erik urged the peregrine onto his wrist, set his spurs lightly to his mount, and galloped off into the forest. Sun struck golden fire from his hair and stormy gray from his mount.

Amber watched until there was nothing to see but the rocky rise. Just as she turned to go back to the cottage, the merlin rose keening on the wind, seeking other prey. Amber cocked her head, listening, but heard no sound of hoofbeats approaching. Unlike Erik, Cassandra would wait until the hunt was over to talk with Amber.

Relieved, Amber went into the cottage and shut the door quietly behind. Just as quietly, she lowered a stout piece of wood across the frame. Until she lifted that board, no one could enter short of chopping through the door.

"Duncan?" Amber asked softly.

There was no answer.

Fear sank cold talons into her. She ran to the bed and yanked aside the curtain.

Duncan lay on his side, his body relaxed, his eyes closed. Amber put her hand out and touched his forehead. Her breath came out in a rushing sigh of relief. His sleep was deep, but normal.

The contrast between the powerful line of Duncan's shoulders and the pale lace on the linen bedding made Amber smile. Gently she brushed his hair back from his forehead, savoring the warmth and smoothness of his skin.

Duncan stirred, but not to turn away. Instead, he moved toward her touch. Blindly his hand found hers, circled it, and held on. When she would have withdrawn, his grip tightened. She sensed him awakening.

"Nay," she whispered, stroking Duncan's cheek with her free hand. "Sleep, Duncan. Heal."

He slid back toward sleep, but he didn't release Amber's hand. She kicked off her shoes and sat on the edge of the bed, fighting against the exhaustion that she had held at bay through the long days and nights since Duncan had been dropped naked on her doorstep.

She couldn't sleep yet. She needed to think, to plan, to find the single thread in the tangled tapestry of Duncan's and her own fate that would lead to enriched life rather than untimely death.

So much depends on his memory. Or lack of it.

So much depends on the prophecy.

Aye. The prophecy. I must be certain that no more of its words come true. I fear my heart has been given, but not my body, not my soul.

It must stay that way. I must not touch him.

Yet even as the thought came, protest welled up from deep within Amber. Touching Duncan was the greatest pleasure she, the Untouched, had ever known.

He is forbidden to me.

Nay. Only the special touching of lovers is forbidden between us. Then my body will remain my own.

Untouched.

The prophecy will remain unfulfilled.

Weariness finally claimed Amber. Her eyelids closed and she swayed forward, asleep before her head touched the bed. As her weight stretched along Duncan's side, he woke slightly, gathered her closer along his body, and fell back into a healing sleep.

Held within the very arms that were forbidden to her, Amber enjoyed the most peaceful sleep of her life.

She didn't awaken until a wolf's harmonic howl rose into the twilight. Her first sensation was that of extraordinary peace. Her second was of a warmth like that of the sun behind her. Her third was the realization that Duncan's naked body was cradling her and his sword hand was cupped around her breast.

A curious heat shot through Amber. In its wake came a flush that made her cheeks burn. She began to ease out of Duncan's grasp. He made a sleepy, protesting sound and tightened his hand. She gasped at the sensations radiating from her breast.

Nay, this is the very kind of touching that is forbidden to us!

Dear God, why is it so sweet?

The wolf howled again, calling kindred spirits to a twilight hunt.

As quickly as Amber dared, she eased from the bed. When Duncan threatened to awaken again, she soothed him with light touches and soft words until he lay quietly once more.

Letting out a long sigh of relief, Amber hurried from the bed. She had to be alone when she talked to Erik and Cassandra. It would be much safer for Duncan that way.

Amber threw on a mantle of green wool and fastened it with a large silver pin in the shape of a crescent moon. Ancient runes ran down the crescent, giving texture and grace to the beaten silver. When she set aside the board barring the door and stepped into the twilight, the pin shimmered as though made to gather light and hold it against the coming night.

No sooner had Amber closed the door behind her than Cassandra appeared on the path from the forest. She was afoot, wearing her customary robes of scarlet embroidered at the edges with blue and green, but twilight turned the colors nearly black.

Her pale, almost colorless hair was plaited and concealed beneath a headdress of fine red cloth. The cloth was held in place by a ring of woven silver strands. The sleeves on her dress were long and deeply flared at the cuff.

Despite a lack of family that equaled Amber's, Cassandra looked every inch a highborn lady. Older than Amber, wiser, Cassandra had raised Amber as though she were her own. Yet Cassandra made no move to embrace the child she had raised. She had come to the cottage as Stone Ring Keep's wise woman rather than as Amber's friend and mentor.

Uneasiness prickled along Amber's skin.

"Where is Erik?" Amber asked, looking beyond Cassandra.

"I asked to see you alone for a time."

Amber smiled with a brightness she was far from feeling.

"Was Maid Marian's hunt successful?" she asked.

"Very. Was yours?"

"I didn't go hawking."

"I refer to your quest for information about the man Erik found asleep within the Stone Ring," Cassandra said mildly.

Saying no more, Cassandra watched Amber with penetrating gray eyes. Amber had to fight not to fidget or mumble the first words that came to her mind. At times Cassandra's silences were as unnerving as her prophecies.

"He hasn't awakened since morning," Amber said, "and then only for a few moments."

"What were his first words upon awakening?"

Frowning, Amber cast about in her memory.

"He asked me who I was," she said after a moment.

"In what language?"

"Ours."

"Accented?" Cassandra asked.

"No."

"Continue."

Amber felt as though she were being quizzed on a lesson. But she didn't know what the lesson was, didn't know the answers to the questions, and feared true answers in any case.

"He asked if he was a prisoner," Amber said.

"Did he? An odd thing for a friend to ask."

"Not at all," Amber retorted. "Erik had bound him hand and foot to my bed."

"Mmmm," was all Cassandra offered.

Amber said no more.

"You have few words," Cassandra said.

"I follow your teaching, Learned," Amber replied formally.

"Why are you so distant?"

"Why are you quizzing me like a stranger caught within the keep's walls?"

Cassandra sighed and held out her hand.

"Come," she said. "Walk with me in the hour that is neither day nor yet night."

Amber's eyes widened. Cassandra rarely offered to touch anyone, especially Amber, to whom touch was often painful and always uncomfortable.

Except for the stranger. His touch had been purest pleasure.

"Cassandra?" Amber whispered. "Why?"

"You look hunted, daughter. Touch me and know that I am not one of your pursuers."

Hesitantly, Amber brushed her fingers along the other woman's hand. As always, a sense of fierce intelligence and deep affection flowed from Cassandra.

"I want only joy for you, Amber."

The truth of Cassandra's words flowed through the touch like a bright scarlet ribbon.

A bittersweet smile curved Amber's lips as her hand dropped to her side. She doubted that Cassandra knew what a joy touching Duncan was to Amber.

And if Cassandra had known, Amber doubted that she would wish more of it for her pupil.

When the wise woman turned and walked slowly toward the moonlight pooled in the meadow just beyond the cottage, Amber followed, walking by Cassandra's side.

"Tell me about the man you have chosen to call Duncan," Cassandra said.

The words were as soft as twilight, but the command just beneath them was not soft at all.

"Whatever he was before he came to the Stone Ring," Amber said, "he knows none of it."

"And you?"

"I saw the marks of battle on his body."

"Dark warrior . . ."

"Yes," Amber whispered. "Duncan."

"Is he a brute, then?"

"No."

"How can you be so certain? A bound man can do little save try to free himself by strength or guile."

"I cut his bonds."

Cassandra's breath came out in an audible rush as she crossed herself.

"Why?" she asked in a strained voice.

"I knew he meant me no harm."

"How?" Cassandra asked, fearing the answer even as she demanded it.

"The usual way. I touched him."

Hands clasped, Cassandra stood, swaying like a willow in a slow wind.

"When he came to you," she asked in a strained voice, "was it night?"

"Yes," Amber said.

In shades of darkness he will come to you.

"Are you mad?" Cassandra asked in a horrified tone. "Have you forgotten? *Be therefore as sunlight, hidden in amber, untouched by man, not touching man. Forbidden.*"

"Erik required that I touch the stranger."

"You should have refused."

"I did, at first. Then Erik pointed out that no man gets fully grown without a name. Therefore, the prophecy holds no—"

"Don't presume to teach a falcon how to fly," Cassandra interrupted angrily. "Did the man know his own name when he awakened?"

"No, but that could change at any moment."

"By Mother Mary's sweet smile, I have raised a reckless fool!"

Amber wanted to defend herself, but could think of nothing to say. When she was away from Duncan, the recklessness of her own actions in touching him appalled her.

Yet when she was with him, no other action seemed possible.

As one, both women turned around to go back to the cottage. As one, they stopped.

Erik was standing a few feet ahead of them.

"Are you proud of your work?" Cassandra asked him acidly.

"And a good evening to you, too," Erik said. "What have I done now to earn the sharp side of a Learned woman's tongue?"

"Amber has touched a man with no name who came to her in shades of darkness. Brought, I might add, by a young thane with no more brains than a drystone wall!"

"What would you have had me do?" Erik asked. "Gut him as though he were a salmon to be salted?"

"You could have waited until I—"

"You do not rule Stone Ring Keep, madam," Erik interrupted coolly. "I do."

"Just so," Cassandra said with a thin smile.

Erik let out an explosive breath. "I respect your wisdom, Cassandra, but I am no longer yours to order about like a squire."

"Aye. And that is as it should be."

"We are in agreement on that, at least." But Erik smiled as he spoke. "Since it is impossible to undo that which has been done, what do you suggest we do?"

"Try to bend events so that life rather than death follows," Cassandra said succinctly.

Erik shrugged. "Death always follows life. 'Tis the nature of living. And dying."

" 'Tis the nature of my prophecies to be accurate."

"In any event, the prophecy's requirements haven't been met," Erik pointed out.

"He came to her in—"

"Yes, yes," Erik interrupted impatiently. "But her heart and soul and body aren't his!"

"I can't speak for her soul or body," Cassandra retorted, "but her heart is already his."

Erik shot Amber a surprised look. "Is that true?"

"I understand the prophecy's three requirements better than anyone," Amber said. "All three have not been met."

"Perhaps I should gut him like a salmon after all," Erik muttered.

"You might be gutting yourself at the same time," Amber said with a composure she didn't feel.

"How so?"

"You need to be in the north to hold Winterlance against the Norse raiders. Yet if you don't stay here, you will lose Stone Ring Keep to your cousins."

Erik looked at Cassandra.

"You need no prophetess to tell you of your cousins' ambitions," Cassandra said dryly. "They were so certain that Lady Emma would die without conceiving an heir for Robert that they had already begun fighting among themselves as to who would rule Stone Ring, Sea Home, Winterlance, and all the rest of Robert's estates."

Without a word, Erik looked to Amber.

"Duncan thinks of himself as a powerful warrior," Amber said to Erik. "He could be very useful to you."

She gave Erik a shuttered look, wondering if he was truly listening or merely humoring her. There was no way to tell short of touching him. In the moonlight his eyes had the veiled gleam of a wolf's.

"Go on," Erik said to Amber.

"Give him time to heal. If his memory doesn't return, he will vow fealty to you."

"So you think he is a Saxon or Scottish free lance looking for a powerful lord?"

"He would not be the first such knight to come to you."

" 'Tis true enough," Erik muttered.

Cassandra started to object again, but was cut off by Erik.

"You may have a fortnight's grace while I search out the stranger's past," he said to Amber. "But only if you will answer one question."

Amber waited, breath held.

"Why do you care what happens to the man you call Duncan?" Erik asked.

The calmness of his voice was at odds with the intensity of his eyes.

"When I touched Duncan . . ." Amber's voice died.

Erik waited.

She clenched her hands within her long, loose sleeves and tried to think of a way to tell Erik that she suspected he had within his grasp one of the finest warriors ever to be born of human woman.

"Duncan has no memories, as such," Amber said slowly, "yet I would vow on my soul that he is one of the greatest warriors ever to hold a sword. And that includes even you, Erik, whom men call the Undefeated almost as often as they call you the Sorcerer."

Cassandra and Erik exchanged a long look.

"With Duncan on your side, you could hold Lord Robert's land against Norsemen, Normans, and cousins combined," Amber said flatly.

"Perhaps," Erik said. "But I'm afraid that your great, dark warrior belongs to Dominic le Sabre or the Scots Hammer."

"That might be true. *But not if Duncan's memory doesn't return.*" Amber drew a deep breath. "Then he is yours."

Silence spread while Cassandra and Erik considered Amber's suggestion.

"Such a ruthless little thing," Erik said, grinning. "You would have made a fine peregrine."

And he laughed.

Cassandra did not. "Are you certain Duncan won't regain his memory?"

"No," Amber said.

"What if he does?" the other woman asked.

"He will be either friend or enemy. If he is a friend, Erik has an invaluable knight. A risk well worth taking, surely?"

"And if he is an enemy?" Erik asked.

"At least you won't have on your soul the cowardly murder of a man struck senseless by lightning."

Erik turned to Cassandra. "Madam?"

"I like it not."

"Why?"

"The prophecy," she said curtly.

"What would you have me do?" he asked.

"Take the stranger out into the Disputed Lands and leave him naked to find his own way."

"Nay!" Amber said before she could stop herself.

"Why not?" Cassandra said.

"He is mine."

The fierceness in Amber's soft voice shocked the others. Erik glanced aside at Cassandra. She was watching Amber as though she had never seen her before.

"Tell me," Cassandra said warily. "When you touched him, what was it like for you?"

"Sunrise," Amber whispered.

"What?"

"It was sunrise after a night as long as time."

Cassandra closed her eyes and crossed herself.

"I will consult my rune stones," she said.

Amber let out a sigh of relief and looked hopefully at Erik.

"I will wait a fortnight, no more," Erik said. "If your Duncan is revealed as my enemy during that time . . ."

"Yes?" she whispered.

Erik shrugged. "I will treat him just as I would any other outlaw found skulking about my keeps. I will hang him where I find him."

4

DUNCAN spun toward the soft, unexpected sound. The movement drew the folds of his new under tunic tightly across his body, outlining its muscular lines in swaths of pale linen and shadow. As he turned, his right hand went to his left side, fingers grasping for the sword that wasn't there.

When the cottage door opened to reveal only Amber, his hand relaxed.

"You make no more sound than a butterfly," Duncan said.

"It's a dreary day for butterflies. The rain is like buckets upended."

Amber shook water from her hooded mantle, shrugged it off, and hung it on a peg to dry. The other mantle, the one she had kept dry beneath her own, she kept folded over one arm. When she turned back to Duncan, he was pulling an outer tunic into place. The costly green wool was sewn with embroidered ribbons in gold and red and blue at the hem.

"You look like a thane," Amber said admiringly.

"A thane would have a sword."

She smiled despite the fear that had become her constant attendant since talking with Erik four days ago. Each day Duncan revealed his warrior heritage

55

in many ways, but never more so than when he was taken by surprise.

And each day was another drop in the pool of fear that grew uneasily in Amber. She could not bear to think of what Erik would do if Duncan proved to be the Scots Hammer rather than a bold knight looking for a worthy lord to serve.

If he is my enemy . . . I will hang him where I find him.

"Is this clothing more comfortable than the last?" Amber asked in a strained voice.

Duncan stretched his arms and flexed his shoulders, testing the width of the fabric. It was tight, but better than the first tunic Amber had brought. That one barely had taken his head through the neck opening, much less the breadth of his chest and shoulders across the back.

"It's much better," Duncan said, "though I fear it would give way in a battle."

"You're among friends," she said quickly. "There is no need to fight."

For a moment Duncan said nothing. Then he frowned as though searching for a memory that was no longer there.

"I hope you're right, lass. I just keep feeling . . ."

Heart in her throat, Amber waited.

With a throttled curse, Duncan abandoned the hunt among the shadow memories that mocked and teased him, retreating as soon as he approached.

"Something is not right," he said flatly. "I am a man out of place. I know it as surely as I know that I breathe."

"It has been only a handful of days since you awakened. Healing takes time."

"Time. Time! God's teeth, I have no time to stand around like a squire waiting for his lord to sleep off a night of folly. I must—"

Duncan's words ended as though cut off by a sword. He didn't know what he had to do.

It was worse than a fox gnawing at his vitals.

He struck his fist against his hand and turned away from Amber. Though he said nothing more, tension radiated from him like heat from a hearth fire.

When Amber approached and stood close, his nostrils flared at the evergreen freshness of her scent.

"Be at peace, Duncan."

A warm, gentle hand caressed his fist. He flinched subtly, surprised. She had been very careful not to touch him since he had stolen that single, hungry kiss from her. Just as he had been careful not to touch her again.

Duncan told himself that he was wary because he had no way of knowing whom Amber had been to him in the past or would be in the future. They might very well be lovers separated by conflicting vows.

Yet the instant Duncan felt the sweetness of Amber's brief caress, he knew the real reason he hadn't touched her again. The torrent of passion and yearning she aroused in him was like nothing he had ever felt for a woman.

The passion Duncan understood, for he was a healthy man in the presence of a girl whose very scent made him harden in a wild rush of blood. But the hungry yearning to hold and be held was as new and unexpected as his lack of memory.

The surprise that came each time Duncan confronted the depth of his response to Amber was what finally had convinced him that he had never felt such passion for a woman before. Just as the fact that he kept reaching for a sword told him that he had worn one in his unremembered past.

"Duncan," Amber whispered.

"Duncan," he repeated sardonically. "A dark warrior, am I? But there is no sword at my side,

no cold weight of metal to keep me company when
danger calls."

"Erik—"

"Aye," Duncan interrupted. "The all-powerful
Erik, who is your protector. The great thane who
decreed I would go unarmed for a fortnight, yet
still his squire lounges ever within reach of your
shout."

"Egbert the Lazy?" Amber asked. "Is he still
about?"

"Dozing in the shed. The fowl are quite put out
to share their roost."

"Turn to face me," she said, changing the subject. "Let me see to the fit."

Slowly Duncan complied.

Amber tugged at a lace here and there, tucked
in a stray fold of cloth, and handed over the beautiful indigo mantle that she had brought through
the rain from Stone Ring Keep.

"For you," she said.

Duncan looked down into the golden eyes that
watched him with such transparent eagerness to
bring him ease.

"You are very kind to a man with no name, no
past, and no future," he said broodingly.

"We have been over that many times to no avail.
Unless . . . are you remembering more?"

"Not in the way you mean. No names. No faces.
No deeds. No vows. Yet I feel . . . I *feel* that something both grand and dangerous is waiting for me,
just beyond my grasp."

Amber's slender hand settled on Duncan's fist
again. She sensed no memories looming from his
past, no condensing of the shadow memories that
swirled and faded, only to be reborn, taunting and
hinting. Everything was as it had been.

Especially the sensual hunger for her that pervaded Duncan's being as deeply as the shadows
of his lost memory.

Knowing of Duncan's need made a curious kind
of heat uncurl throughout Amber's body. It was as
though an invisible fire lived in the pit of her stomach, waiting only for the breath of Duncan's desire
to burst into flame.

Amber told herself that she must lift her hand
and not approach Duncan again, but her hand
remained where it was, touching him. Such contact was a sweet, subtle drug. The joy it gave her
should have terrified her, yet it only lured her even
more deeply.

"Life is both grand and dangerous," Amber said
in a low voice.

"Is it? I don't remember."

Duncan's barely restrained emotions lashed
through Amber, a seething mixture of frustration, anger, and impatience.

With an act of will that left Amber aching, she
forced herself not to thread her fingers deeply
into Duncan's hair and hold him until pleasure
at her caresses overcame all other emotions. Yet
she couldn't prevent herself from touching Duncan
just a little.

So little.

Just her fingertip tracing the clenched power of
his fist.

"Has it been so bad for you here, then?" Amber
whispered unhappily.

Duncan looked down at the bent head of the girl
who had done nothing to earn his anger and much
to earn his gratitude. Slowly his fist uncurled. Just
as slowly he caught Amber's right hand in his own.
Her body jerked subtly at his touch.

"Don't be afraid, golden fairy. I won't hurt you."

"I know."

The certainty in Amber's voice was reflected in
her eyes. Duncan was too pleased by her trust to
ask why she was so confident. He lifted her hand
to his lips for a kiss.

The sound of Amber's breath rushing out made

Duncan's heartbeat speed. He had meant only to kiss her hand, but her response was an irresistible lure. He turned her hand over, cradling it in his palm while his lips found the pulse point of her wrist and brushed it repeatedly.

When his lips parted and the tip of his tongue traced the fragile blue vein, her heart's blood visibly raced in response to the caress. Desire arced through Duncan like a bolt from an invisible storm.

Yet the gentleness of his caress never varied. He remembered too well Amber's retreat when he had tried a bolder kind of love play.

"Duncan," Amber whispered. "I . . ."

Her voice vanished as a sensuous shiver took her. Being touched by Duncan under any circumstances was a piercing pleasure. Knowing the full force of his passion for her while being kissed so very tenderly by him was like being wrapped in delicate, consuming fire.

Duncan lifted his head and looked down into the dazed golden eyes of the girl who was as much a mystery to him as his own past.

"You come to my lure like a falcon to its master's call," he said in a deep voice. "You burn for me and I for you. Were we lovers in the time I don't remember?"

With a small cry Amber jerked her hand free and turned her back.

"I was never your lover," she said in a strained voice.

"I find that hard to believe."

" 'Tis true just the same."

"God's teeth," Duncan hissed. "I can't believe that! We are too strongly drawn. You know something about my past that you aren't telling me."

Amber shook her head.

"I don't believe you," he repeated.

She spun back to Duncan with a speed that made her clothing flare.

"As you will," she said angrily. "Before you came to the Disputed Lands, you were a prince."

Duncan was too shocked to speak.

"You were a freeholder," Amber continued.

"What are you—"

"You were a traitor," she said ruthlessly.

Stunned, Duncan simply stared at Amber.

"You were a hero," she said. "You were a knight. You were a squire. You were a priest. You were a lord. You were—"

"Enough," Duncan interrupted in a savage voice.

"Well?" she demanded.

"Well what?"

"One of those things is the truth."

"Is it?"

Amber shrugged. "What else could you have been?"

"A serf or a sailor," he said sardonically.

"No. You haven't the calluses for it. Nor the thick head, though lately I begin to wonder."

Abruptly, Duncan laughed.

Against her will, Amber smiled. "You see? Whatever I tell you isn't the same as *knowing*. That you must do for yourself. No one can do it for you."

Duncan's laughter stopped. For the space of several breaths he said nothing.

The temptation to touch him and discover what he was feeling almost overwhelmed Amber. She fought her own hunger, her own need.

And she lost.

Her fingertips smoothed lightly over Duncan's clean-shaven cheek.

Anger.

Bafflement.

A loss so great it couldn't be described, only felt like thunder from a distant storm quivering through the air.

"Duncan," Amber whispered painfully. "My dark warrior."

He watched her with eyes that were narrowed, glittering, the eyes of an animal caught within a trap.

"Fighting yourself only wounds you more," she said. "Let yourself grow used to the life you have now."

"How can I?" Duncan asked in a rough voice. "What of the life I left behind? What if there is a lord expecting me to honor my vow? What if there is a wife? Heirs? Land?"

When Duncan spoke of lord and land, Amber sensed the dark seething of his memory. No such response came at the mention of wife or heirs.

Her relief was so acute that Amber's knees weakened. The thought of Duncan bound by sacred vow to another woman had been like a knife turning in Amber's heart. She hadn't known how great her fear had been until it was banished by the unspeakable certainty that lay beneath Duncan's elusive memory.

Pray God that his memory doesn't return. The more he remembers, the more I fear.

Enemy, not friend.

Soul mate.

In shades of darkness Duncan came to me. In shades of darkness he must remain.

Or die.

And that thought was even more unbearable than Duncan alive and bound to another woman.

THE merlin's quick, shallow wingbeats brought it swiftly toward the lure Duncan was casting with smooth, powerful sweeps of his arm.

"Well done," Amber said, clapping her hands in excitement. "You must have cast the lure many times before."

The lure jerked, then resumed its steady circling.

Instantly Amber regretted her words. For the last five days she had refused to discuss Duncan's past in any way at all. Nor had his memory returned, though it had been nine days since he had awakened.

After that first, swift look at Amber, Duncan concentrated only on the smooth circling of the lure, calling the winged predator down from the cloud-tossed sky. Without warning the small falcon stooped, hit the lure with deadly speed, and settled to the ground to feed, mantling its wings protectively over its "prey."

Quickly Amber lured the merlin with a bit of meat and piercing whistles. After a few sharp protests, the falcon surrendered and came to Amber's wrist.

"Don't sulk, little beauty," Amber murmured as she smoothed the jesses so that they hung evenly over her gauntlet. "You did very well."

"Well enough to earn a true hunt?" Duncan asked.

She smiled. "You sound as eager as a falcon."

"I am. I'm not used to being shut up in a cottage with only a wary maid and my own thoughts for company—or lack thereof," he added ironically.

Amber winced.

Duncan had shown little interest in her prescribed course of rest, food, and more rest. When the cold rains came, it wasn't difficult to keep Duncan indoors, for all that he paced like a caged wolf.

But today, when the sun poured down until mist lifted in great silver flags from the land, keeping Duncan inside hadn't been possible.

"I was afraid," she said.

"Of what? I'm not ice to melt in sunshine or rain."

"I feared enemies."

"Who?" he asked swiftly.

"The Disputed Lands are . . . disputed. Landless

knights, ambitious bastards, second and third sons, outlaws. All of them roam, seeking prey."

"Yet you went to Stone Ring Keep alone to bring clothes for me?"

Amber shrugged. "I don't fear for myself. No man will touch me."

Duncan looked skeptical.

" 'Tis true," she said. "It is known throughout the Disputed Lands that Erik will hang the man who touches me."

"I have touched you."

"Besides, you grumbled so about having to wear bed covers, like a Saracen . . ." Amber said, changing the subject.

Duncan said a few profane words in the language he had learned in the Holy Land.

"What does that mean?" she asked curiously.

"You don't want to know."

"Oh." She sighed. "In any case, I wanted to make sure you were healed from all the effects of the storm before you went out."

"All?" Duncan retorted.

"Almost all," Amber said tartly. "If I waited for your temper to mend, I would be wrapped in winding sheets and on my way to the grave."

Duncan shot her a glittering hazel glance, but had the grace to realize she was right. He had been in a foul temper since morning, when he had awakened from dreams that seethed with shadows and sensual heat.

"I'm sorry," he said. "Bad enough that my memory of the past is gone. But having the past stand in the way of my present and future is more than I can bear with a smile."

"There is a future for you here, if you want it," Amber said.

"As a freeholder or squire?"

She nodded.

"That's generous of you," Duncan said.

"Not I. Erik. He is lord of Stone Ring Keep."

Duncan frowned. He had yet to meet the young lord, but doubted that they would do well together. Amber was too fond of Erik for Duncan's ease.

As always, the depth of his possessiveness toward Amber bothered Duncan, but he was helpless to change it. Just as he was helpless to know why he felt as he did.

We must have been lovers. Or wished to be.

Duncan waited, testing his response the way a tongue tests a sore tooth. Cautiously. Relentlessly.

Nothing happened. Absolutely nothing.

He felt neither a sense of right nor of wrong, as had been the case when he noted the absence of a sword, and the certainty that he had never felt so strongly about a woman before.

"Duncan?" Amber said softly.

He blinked and came back from his thoughts.

"I don't think I would be happy as a freeholder or a squire," Duncan said slowly.

"Then what do you want?"

"Whatever I lost."

"Dark warrior . . ." she whispered. "You must let go of the past."

"That would be like dying."

Unhappily, Amber turned aside and hooded the merlin. The bird tolerated it calmly, satisfied for the moment by the recent flight and taste of blood.

"Even the most fierce falcon accepts the hood without great complaint," she said.

"It knows the hood will be removed," Duncan retorted.

Amber turned and walked toward the mews that were nestled along one side of the cottage. Squire Egbert, more boy than man, came slowly to his feet, stretched, and opened the door for her to enter. When the merlin was safely inside, Amber shut the door behind her and waved the red-haired Egbert back to his idle counting of clouds.

As soon as she and Duncan were beyond the reach of the squire's eyes, Amber turned to her companion. Delicately she put her hand on his.

"If you can't have the past," she asked in a low voice, "what do you most want?"

The answer was immediate.

"You."

A stillness came over Amber. Joy and fear warred within her, shaking her.

"But that won't be," Duncan continued evenly. "I won't take one maid without knowing what I might have vowed to another."

"I don't believe you are joined to another woman."

"Nor do I. But I was born of an adulterous union," he said distinctly. "I'll leave neither bastard son to beg his way through the world, nor bastard daughter to become a nobleman's whore."

"Duncan," Amber whispered. "How do you know?"

"What?"

"That you were born a bastard. That one of your parents committed adultery."

Duncan's mouth opened but no words came. He shook his head sharply, as though to banish a blow.

"I don't know," he groaned. "I don't know!"

But he had known. Just for an instant. Amber had sensed it as clearly as she sensed the heat of his body.

For a moment the shadows had lost some of their power. A few bright stars had glimmered through the dense night that shrouded Duncan's past.

"*Why can't I remember?*" he asked savagely.

"Let it be," Amber said softly. "You can't batter down shadows. You can only slide between them."

She sensed the tension leaving Duncan before he did. Taking her hand from his, she gave him a bittersweet smile and opened the cottage door. Before

she could cross the threshold, Duncan pulled her
back.

Startled, Amber turned to him. His hard hand
fitted beneath her chin with surprising delicacy.
She closed her eyes for a moment to savor the
sweetness pouring through her from Duncan's
touch. His concern for her was like spring sunlight, warming without burning.

And the passion just beneath his concern was a
wild torrent of fire.

"I didn't mean to make you unhappy," Duncan
said.

"I know," she whispered, opening her eyes.

Duncan stood so close that Amber could see the
shards of green and blue, gold and silver that made
up the hazel of his eyes.

"Then why do tears cling to your eyelashes?" he
asked.

"I am afraid for you, for me, for us."

"Because I can't remember?"

"No. Because you might."

His breath came in sharply. "Why? What could
be wrong with that?"

"What if you are married?"

"I think not. Surely I would feel its absence as I
do my missing sword."

"What if you owed fealty to a Norman lord?"
Amber asked desperately, trying to quench the passion in Duncan's eyes.

"What would it matter? Saxon and Norman are
at peace."

"That could change."

"The sky could fall, too."

"But what if you are Lord Robert's enemy? Or
Sir Erik's?"

"Would Erik have brought an enemy to you?"
Duncan countered.

When Amber started to speak, he talked over
her.

"What if I'm merely a knight back from the Holy Land looking for a lord to serve?"

Duncan's words went through Amber like delicate lightning, making even darkness bright, if only for a moment.

Amber's smile trembled uncertainly. "Have you fought the Saracen?"

"I . . . yes!" Duncan's smile flashed against the silky darkness of his mustache as a memory gleamed briefly. "I fought them in a place called . . . God's blood, 'tis gone again!"

"It will return."

"But I fought. I know it," he said. "Just as surely as I know I want this."

Duncan bent until his lips were all but brushing Amber's. When she would have withdrawn, his hand tightened on her chin and his arm slid around her body.

"Just a single kiss. 'Tis all I ask. One kiss for the man you brought out of darkness."

Amber stiffened, but couldn't fight against the lure of his passion and her own.

"We shouldn't," she said.

"Aye," he murmured, smiling.

" 'Tis dangerous."

" 'Tis sweet beyond belief."

Amber tried to argue, but could not. It was indeed sweet beyond belief to be held by her dark warrior.

"Open your lips for me," Duncan whispered against her mouth. "Let me taste your nectar as delicately as a bee tastes a violet."

"Duncan . . ."

"Yes. Like that."

This time Amber wasn't shocked to feel the living warmth of Duncan's tongue gliding into her mouth, but she was amazed by his restraint. She could feel the passion in him like a wild sea battering against the shores of his will.

His whole body was taut, fierce. He quivered with hunger. Yet his kiss was barely a breath of warmth, a fragile pressure that came and went like a flame.

Without knowing it, Amber made a soft, tiny sound and opened her lips wider, seeking more than Duncan had offered. Hands hardened by war shifted gently on her body, coaxing her closer and then closer still, luring her nearer the fire that was burning in his loins.

"Duncan," she whispered.

"Yes?"

"You taste of sunlight and storm at once."

His breath caught as his heartbeat quickened.

"You taste like spiced honey," Duncan said. "I want to lick up every sweet drop."

"And I want you to," Amber admitted.

His breath came out in a groan. His mouth came down over hers less gently, seeking a deeper mating. His arms molded her supple warmth to his body until she could feel every bit of his strength. His strong hands rocked her hips in a rhythm as ancient as desire and as new to her as dawn.

After a long time Duncan lifted his head and took a deep, harsh breath.

"My body knows you," he said in a gritty voice. "It responds to you as to none other."

Amber trembled and fought against the twin torrents of passion—his own, hers, their hunger combining until it was like a river in flood, and she stood on crumbling banks, ripe to fall at any moment.

"How many times have we lain in darkness together, our bodies joined and slick with desire?" he asked.

Amber started to speak, but the feel of Duncan's hand over her breast stole her thoughts.

"How many times have I undressed you, kissed your breasts, your belly, the creamy smoothness of your thighs?" he asked.

A broken sound of desire was her only answer.

"How many times have I opened your legs and sheathed myself within your eager heat?"

"Duncan," she said raggedly. "We mustn't."

"Nay, lass. Why not do again what we must have done so many times before?"

"We have—" Her breath fragmented. "Never."

"Always," Duncan countered.

"But—"

Gently he caught Amber's lower lip in his teeth, stopping her words. When his fingers slid beneath her mantle, finding and teasing nipples that hardened at his touch, her knees buckled.

"Desire is a road we've traveled many times together," Duncan said, smiling, bending to her breast. "That's why our bodies respond to each other so quickly."

"No, it's—"

Amber's voice splintered as she felt the heat and pressure of Duncan's mouth over her breast. When his teeth raked lightly, she could barely stand.

"Duncan," Amber said brokenly, "you are a fire burning me."

"It is you who burns me."

"We must stop—touching."

Duncan smiled rather darkly.

"In time," he agreed. "But first I will quench the fire within your body. And you will quench mine."

Trembling, Amber thought of being naked with Duncan, no clothing to dull the piercing joy of his touch, nothing between them but the sultry heat of their shared breath as she gave her body to her dark warrior.

A man with no name may you claim, heart and body and soul.

"Nay!" she cried suddenly. "It's too dangerous!"

Strong hands tightened, holding Amber when she would have wrenched herself away.

"Let me go," she cried.

"I can't."

"You must!"

Duncan looked down into Amber's wild, golden eyes. What he saw there so astonished him that he released her. Instantly she retreated beyond his reach.

"You're afraid," he said, hardly able to believe it.

"Yes."

"I wouldn't hurt you, precious Amber. You must know that. Don't you?"

Amber backed away from Duncan's outstretched hand.

With a savage curse, Duncan turned on his heel and stalked back out into the yard.

5

"YOUNG Egbert told me that you want to go to Sea Home with me and watch my men train for battle," Erik said.

"Yes," Amber and Duncan said as one.

The three of them stood just inside the cottage. A few steps outside, Egbert waited with outward patience in the drizzle, holding the horses Amber and Duncan were to ride. One of the spare horses stamped and snorted, irritated by a trickle of rainwater down its leg.

Erik shot a hooded glance at Duncan before he turned his attention to Amber.

"You were never keen to watch my men train before," Erik said mildly.

"Like Duncan, I tire of the four walls of my cottage," Amber said in a tight voice. "Autumn rains can be tedious."

Erik turned toward the other man. Duncan offered a smile that lacked both humor and comfort.

"The witch and I—excuse me," Duncan said sardonically, "the *Learned* female and I are weary of shadow games, unanswerable questions, and Squire Egbert's company."

The squire in question gave a heartfelt sigh. He was heartily tired of tiptoeing around a witch of uncertain temper and a warrior whose temper was very certain—and quite vile.

"Then by all means," Erik said, stepping away from the cottage door, "let's be off to Sea Home."

Amber pulled the hood of her mantle over her hair and walked across grass that shone with thick drops of water. The smoke of wood and peat fires curled through the early morning, finding space between drops of moisture that were too fine to be rain and too thick to be mist.

When Amber approached, Egbert whisked a protective cloth from the saddle of a dainty little chestnut mare. The squire made no move to help Amber into the saddle. That would have required touching her, and Egbert knew that no man touched Amber without her specific invitation.

Duncan didn't know any such thing. He threw a disbelieving look at the stripling squire, stepped forward quickly, and lifted Amber into the saddle before the other men realized what he was doing.

Erik drew his sword half out of its sheath before he saw that Amber made no protest. With narrowed eyes he watched Duncan and Amber together.

Even in the act of releasing her, Duncan let his hands caress subtly, testing the resilience of Amber's waist and hips, brushing over her thigh.

"Thank you," she said.

Amber's voice was breathless and her cheeks were flushed. The desire that Duncan had for her burned more brightly with each touch, each look, each day of enforced intimacy in the one-room cottage.

Once Duncan had gotten over his anger at Amber's fear of him as a lover, he had set about seducing her with a single-minded focus that was in itself seductive. Instead of banking the fires of mutual desire, Egbert's presence had acted to heighten the intimacy of the ordinary. Stolen caresses, a smile revealed and then hidden, strong fingers closing over a more delicate hand as a pot was lifted from the fire, all of these worked to increase passion until the very air quivered with it.

Amber had felt nothing similar in her life. It was as though she were a harp being plucked by a master's fingers. Each of Duncan's touches vibrated through her, setting off haunting harmonies in unexpected places. The racing of her heart combined with a curious melting deep inside her body. Her shortened breath was matched by the exquisite sensitivity of her skin.

Sometimes just watching Duncan was enough to make a sweet lassitude steal through Amber, turning her bones to honey. Now was one of those times. Duncan mounted the spare horse with the grace of a cat leaping onto a fence. His hand rubbed reassuringly down the length of the horse's neck.

With a deep, aching breath, Amber tried to still the clamor of her body for the one man she must not have. Yet she couldn't stop her memory of Duncan's eyes as he watched her, and his lips as he spoke the words that set her on fire.

How many times have I undressed you, kissed your breasts, your belly, the creamy smoothness of your thighs?

"Are you all right?" Erik asked.

"Yes," Amber said faintly.

"You don't sound it."

Turning, Erik gave Duncan a narrow look.

"No one touches Amber without her permission," Erik said. "Is that quite clear?"

"Why?" Duncan asked.

"She is forbidden."

Surprise showed in Duncan's expression, but he controlled it immediately.

"I don't understand," he said carefully.

"You don't have to," Erik retorted. "Just don't touch her. She doesn't wish it."

Duncan smiled slightly. "Truly?"

"Aye."

"In that case, I will do as the lady wishes."

With a darkly sensual smile, Duncan turned his horse aside and waited for Erik to lead off into the liquid gray of the morning.

Erik turned to Amber.

"Haven't you warned him about touching you?" he asked.

"There was no need."

"Why?"

"Even after Duncan awakened, his touch didn't distress me."

"Odd."

"Yes."

"Does Cassandra know?" Erik asked.

"Yes."

"What did she say?"

"She is still consulting her runes."

Erik grunted. "I've never known Cassandra to labor so long over a prophecy before."

"No."

"God's blood, no wonder Duncan is eager to be free of the cottage," Erik muttered.

Amber gave him a sideways look from golden eyes, but said nothing.

"You're as talkative as a turnip," Erik said.

She nodded.

And spoke not one word.

With an impatient oath, Erik reined his horse aside and spurred into the lead. Two knights and their squires trotted across the meadow to join the small party. The men were wearing chain-mail hauberks beneath their mantles. They also had metal helms on their heads and carried the long, teardrop-shaped shields that Saxons had adopted from their Norman conquerors. Both knights were mounted on war stallions.

Duncan looked from the fully armed knights to Erik.

"Despite the clothes Stone Ring Keep has provided, suddenly I feel as naked as when I was found," Duncan said dryly.

"Do you think you once wore armor?" Erik asked.

"I know it."

There was no doubting the certainty in Duncan's voice.

"It makes me wonder if perhaps the man who discovered me didn't take my armor to pay for his trouble," Duncan added.

"He didn't."

"You sound confident."

"I am. I was the man who found you."

Duncan's right eyebrow rose in a questioning arc.

"Amber told me only that you had brought me to her," Duncan said.

At Erik's signal, the knights turned and rode from the cottage yard. After a time, Erik reined his horse alongside Duncan's.

"Is your memory returning?" Erik asked.

"Bits and fragments, no more."

"Such as?"

Though asked politely, the question was a command. Both men knew it.

"I fought the Saracen," Duncan said, "but I don't know when or where."

Erik nodded, unsurprised.

"I feel naked without weapons or armor," Duncan said. "I have some skill at hawking."

"You ride well," Erik added.

Duncan looked surprised, then thoughtful. "Odd. I assumed everyone did."

"Knights, squires, and warriors, yes," Erik said. "Serfs, villeins, merchants, and the like, no. Some priests ride well. Most don't, unless they came of highborn families."

"I doubt I'm a priest."

"Why not? Many a fine warrior-priest has ridden against the Saracen for Church and Christ."

"But the Church desires—yea, of late it even demands!—celibacy."

Without realizing it, Duncan looked over his shoulder, where Amber rode alone.

She saw his glance and smiled.

Duncan smiled in return, watching Amber with a longing he couldn't conceal. Even in the gray drizzle, she seemed to gather light into herself, becoming a golden presence that warmed everything within reach.

He wished he were free to ride next to Amber, his leg brushing hers occasionally. He loved to see the color flood her cheeks at his touch, to hear her breath shorten, and to sense the hidden stirring of her sensuality.

"No," Duncan said, turning back to Erik, "celibacy is not for me. Now or ever."

"Don't even think of it," Erik said icily.

Duncan gave the younger man a wary look.

"Think of what, my lord?" Duncan asked.

"Seducing Amber."

"No maid is *seduced* without her permission."

"Amber is called the Untouched. She is totally innocent. She wouldn't have the least idea of what a man wanted until it was far too late."

Duncan laughed, shocking Erik.

"No untouched maiden would be so vividly, sensually aware of a man," Duncan said, amused.

Erik's shock gave way to cold fury.

"Understand this, Duncan the Nameless," Erik said distinctly. "If you seduce Amber, you will face me in single combat. And you will die."

For a moment Duncan said nothing. Then he looked at Erik with the coolly measuring glance of a man to whom battles were neither new nor feared.

"Don't force me to fight you," Duncan said, "for

I will win. Your death would grieve Amber, and I have no desire to bring her sadness."

"Then keep your hands off her."

"As the lady wills. If she is, as you say, untouched, there will be no difficulty. She won't respond to the sensual lure."

"Don't offer it," Erik said in a clipped tone.

"Why not? She is well beyond the age of marriage, yet she is neither betrothed nor under a lord's private seal." Duncan paused, then added, "Is she?"

"Betrothed? Nay."

"Is she some lord's leman?"

"I just told you, Amber is untouched!"

"Is she yours?" Duncan pressed.

"Mine? Haven't you been listening? She is—"

"Untouched," Duncan interrupted. "Aye. So you say."

Duncan frowned, wondering why Erik was so intent on believing that Amber was a virgin, when Duncan had no doubt that the opposite was the case.

"Do you fancy Amber for yourself?" Duncan asked after a moment.

"Nay."

"I find that hard to believe."

"Why?"

"Amber is . . . extraordinary. No man could look at her without wanting her."

"I can," Erik said bluntly. "I no more desire Amber carnally than I would a sister."

Duncan gave the other man a startled look.

"We were raised together," Erik explained.

"Then why do you object to my touching her? Do you have a marriage in mind for her? Does she feel a calling to the nunnery?"

Erik shook his head.

"Let me be certain I understand," Duncan said carefully. "You have no desire for Amber yourself."

"None."

"You have no marriage planned for her."

"None," Erik said.

"Yet you forbid me to touch her."

"Yes."

"It is because I have no memory of who—or what—I was before I woke up in Amber's cottage?" Duncan asked.

"It is because Amber is what she is. Forbidden."

With that, Erik spurred his horse forward, joining his knights. He didn't speak to Duncan again until they had finally reached and passed through the hamlets and stubble fields that radiated outward from Sea Home.

When the group of riders was within the first ring of palisades that defended Sea Home, Erik turned his horse and waved for Amber and Duncan to join him on a hillock overlooking the lower earthworks. From that vantage point, it was obvious that the defenses of Sea Home Manor were being reshaped into those of a true keep. Many men labored in the wet day, dragging stones on sledges, hauling logs, ramming earth between stone walls.

A second log-and-earth palisade was being raised just beyond the base of a rocky knoll that overlooked the fen and the salty sweep of the firth. On top of the knoll, the manor itself was nearly invisible behind the newly erected stone walls of what would become the keep itself. Gatehouse and turrets, parapets and inner bailey, moat and drawbridge could all be seen either in outline or in finished form.

Beyond the defensive rings, little was visible but dense mist, darkly gleaming saltwater channels, and rain-beaten grass. Though hidden by cloud, the vast presence of the ocean could be tasted in the air. The bay that Sea Home defended was wide and shallow, ringed with mud flats at low tide and salt marsh at high tide. Fresh water welled

up throughout the marsh and small streams trickled in from the green and rumpled countryside.

"How do you like it?" Erik asked Amber as she
and Duncan came alongside.

"The work has gone so fast," Amber said. "I can
barely believe it. Last time I was at Sea Home, there
was little more than a palisade to protect the manor
house."

The import of the frenzied building hadn't
escaped Duncan. Sea Home was being fortified
as quickly as men could drag log, stone, and bas-
kets of earth into place.

"After the defenses are finished, I'm going to
rebuild the house entirely of cut stone," Erik said.
"Then I will replace the outer palisades with stone
walls and put yet another log-and-earth palisade
beyond the inner and outer baileys."

"It will be quite grand," Amber said.

"Sea Home deserves no less. When I marry, this
will be my primary residence."

"Has Lord Robert chosen a suitable wife for you?"
Amber asked.

Duncan's eyes narrowed as he searched for any
hint of jealousy in Amber's voice. Erik might not be
drawn to Amber as a man is to a desirable woman,
but Duncan found it hard to believe that Amber
wasn't attracted to the handsome lord.

Yet no matter how carefully Duncan searched,
there was nothing in her voice and expression but
simple affection.

"No," Erik said. "It's difficult to find a girl who
fulfills the needs of both Scots and English kings."

The buried anger in Erik's voice was noted by
Duncan. It was an anger that appeared whenever
the proud young thane was brought up against the
reality of the power of Henry, King of England.

"What will become of Stone Ring Keep after you
marry?" Amber asked. "I can't imagine it without you."

"You will be safe enough with Cassandra and my seneschal in residence," Erik said.

"Ah, then you've finally chosen a seneschal?"

"No. I've found no one I can trust with a plum as rich as Stone Ring Keep. Until I do, or until I marry . . ." Erik shrugged.

"I'll miss you."

Amber's words were so soft that Erik almost didn't hear them.

Duncan did hear. The new evidence of affection between Erik and Amber irritated Duncan.

"I'll still live part of each year at Stone Ring and Winterlance," Erik said, "married or no."

Amber simply smiled, shook her head, and said, "You have done a grand job preparing Sea Home."

"Thank you. Talking to knights who came back from the Holy Land gave me many ideas."

"Not to mention the Normans," Duncan said. "They are masters of motte and bailey construction."

"Aye. I don't intend to lose my land to the Norman usurpers."

"Are you expecting trouble soon?"

"Why do you ask?" Erik said sharply.

"Your laborers have the look of a long, hard summer behind them."

Erik watched Duncan for the space of several breaths. There was nothing about Duncan's posture or eyes that suggested a man asking questions for a hidden purpose.

Far from it. Duncan was one of the most open men Erik had ever encountered. He would have staked a great deal on Duncan's basic honesty.

In fact, Erik already had.

Leaving Duncan with Amber had been a calculated risk, even with Egbert's constant presence. But in all the days of enforced closeness, Amber had learned nothing that suggested Duncan was a Norman wolf disguised as a nameless Saxon sheep.

"Of all my father's holdings, Sea Home is the most vulnerable to Norman interference," Erik said bluntly. "My cousins also covet it."

"Because it guards the sea approach to the Disputed Lands?" Duncan asked.

"Does it?" Erik asked gently. "Your eyes see very far in this stew of rain and cloud."

Amber gave Erik a wary look. Whenever he took that special, gentle tone of voice, wise men looked for a place to hide.

"There would be no other reason to have a keep here at the edge of unproductive salt fens," Duncan said. "There is no narrowing of the sea, no cliffs, no river passage, no natural ramparts, nothing to use against an enemy but what you build yourself."

"Apparently strategy was part of your learning in the time that you don't remember," Erik said.

"All leaders should know how to choose the time and the place of their battles."

"Were you such a man?" Erik asked softly. "Did you lead others rather than follow?"

Afraid not to speak, afraid *to* speak, Amber held her breath and waited for Duncan's answer.

"I think . . . yes," Duncan said.

"You don't sound certain," Erik retorted.

"It's difficult to be certain without memory," Duncan said crisply.

"If you remember, tell me. I have use for men who can lead others."

"Defending Stone Ring Keep?"

"Aye," Erik said. "The Norsemen covet it as much as they covet Winterlance."

"And Sea Home is coveted by Normans."

"So is Stone Ring Keep."

A chill came over Amber. The challenge in Erik's voice was subtle, but unmistakable. Memories of her conversation with Erik on the night that Duncan had been found echoed through her.

Then the rumor is true? A Norman granted his Saxon enemy the right to rule Stone Ring Keep?

Aye. But Duncan is no longer Dominic's enemy. The Scots Hammer swore fealty to Dominic at the point of a sword.

"Your father is lucky to have a strong son," Duncan said matter-of-factly. "It's the nature of men to fight for honor, God, and land."

"Especially land like Sea Home," Erik agreed. "It's the richest of my father's holdings. The pastures fatten many cattle and sheep. The sea yields fresh fish all year. The croplands are fertile. Waterfowl abound in the fens and deer are thick in the forests."

Duncan heard the clear love of land in Erik's voice and knew a swift stroke of jealousy.

"It would be a fine thing to have land," Duncan said softly.

"Oh, no," groaned Erik in mock despair. "Not another lout in armor pining to take Sea Home from me!"

"Sea Home? Nay," Duncan said, smiling. "The land around Stone Ring Keep is more to my liking. Higher, rockier, wilder."

Amber closed her eyes and prayed that Erik would see in Duncan only what she was seeing— a man speaking the truth among people he considered his friends.

"I prefer the salt wind and the cry of sea eagles," Erik said.

"You have them, and Stone Ring Keep besides," Duncan said.

"So long as I hold them, yes. In the Disputed Lands, a man's future is only as long as his sword arm."

Duncan laughed. "The gleam in your eye says you don't regret being tested."

"You have the same gleam in yours," Erik retorted.

Amber opened her eyes and let out her breath in relief. Erik was teasing Duncan as he would a friend.

"Aye," Duncan said. "I love a good fight."

"Nay," Amber interrupted firmly. "I'll not have it."

"Have what?" Erik asked with transparent innocence.

"You are planning to have Duncan join your battle games."

"Are you willing?" Erik asked Duncan.

"Give me a sword and I'll show you."

Fear lanced through Amber. Without thinking, she leaned forward and wrapped her fingers around Duncan's wrist. The warmth and sheer maleness of him swept through her. She ignored her response, for the fear that drove her was equally strong.

"No," Amber said urgently. "You nearly died in that storm. It's much too soon for you to fight unless there is real need."

Duncan looked down into her anxious golden eyes and felt something taut within him loosen. She had avoided his touch for days, yet she cared for him deeply. Her emotion was so clear to him that he barely refrained from kissing away the lines of fear around her full mouth.

"Don't worry, precious Amber," Duncan whispered against her cheek. "I won't be thrashed by ill-trained knights."

Duncan's humor, passion, and supreme self-confidence flowed through the touch to Amber. He wasn't the least afraid of testing himself against the best Erik had to offer.

In fact, Duncan was anticipating it with the pleasure of a hungry wolf looking over a sheepfold.

Reluctantly Amber loosened her hold on Duncan's wrist. Though she no longer held him, her fingertips lingered on his wrist with a hunger that was reflected in the shadowed depths of her eyes.

Duncan saw the yearning in her gaze and felt fire flare through his loins. His fingers curled over hers, holding them, needing the contact with a force he couldn't question.

Erik watched with a combination of wonder and unease.

"You told me," Erik said to Amber, "but I didn't truly believe. Touching him doesn't hurt you. It . . . pleases you."

"Yes. Greatly."

Erik looked from Amber's face, pleasure and unhappiness combined, to Duncan. There, defiance and pleasure were mingled, making him appear warrior and lover both.

"I do hope," Erik said distinctly to Amber, "that Cassandra finishes casting the rune stones before I'm forced to decide between what pleases you and the safety of the Disputed Lands."

Fear rippled through Amber. She closed her eyes and said nothing.

Nor did she pull her fingers away from Duncan's clasp.

A shout from one of Erik's knights came through the mist. As one, Erik and Duncan turned. Four knights were riding out from the stables toward the place where Erik waited. Three of the knights were familiar to Erik. The fourth wasn't.

Duncan straightened and leaned forward as though to see better through the seething mists. Three of the knights were unknown to him.

The fourth made shadows stir and condense into something that was neither memory nor forgetfulness.

6

CLOUDS separated, allowing pale gold sunlight to stream over the rain-drenched land. The green of grass and trees became incandescent. Pale stone gleamed like pearl. Bark was an ebony richness. Water drops gathered on every surface, making the land shimmer as though with secret laughter.

Amber shared none of the land's hidden amusement. She had felt Duncan's memories twitch and shiver, a dragon awakening deep within his shadows.

"Who is the fourth man?" she asked Erik.

"I don't know," he said.

"Find out."

The sharp demand in Amber's voice surprised Erik. What surprised Duncan was the feel of her nails digging into his wrist.

"Is something amiss?" Erik asked.

Belatedly Amber realized what she had done. If the fourth man was indeed from Duncan's past—and if Duncan was indeed the enemy she feared—she had put him in danger with her incautious demand.

"No," Amber said, making certain that her voice was calm. "I'm simply wary of new warriors in the Disputed Lands."

"So is Alfred," Erik said dryly.

Amber's smile was a brief shadow of her usual one, but only Duncan noticed.

Only he knew of her nails biting into his flesh.

"Who is Alfred?" Duncan asked.

"One of my best knights. He is the one on the white stallion, next to the stranger."

"Alfred," Duncan said, memorizing the man.

"Alfred the Sly," Amber corrected.

"You've never forgiven him for calling you a sorceress," Erik said wryly.

"He had the Church believing him."

Erik shrugged. "The priest was a fat old fool."

"That 'fat old fool' laid hands on me."

Erik turned toward Amber so quickly that his horse started in alarm.

"What are you saying?" he demanded.

"The priest sought an alliance with the devil through carnal knowledge of me," Amber said. "When I refused him, he tried to take by force what I wouldn't give."

"God's teeth," Duncan hissed.

Erik was too shocked to speak. Abruptly his features flattened beneath his beard, pulling his mouth into a thin line.

"I will hang that cursed priest where I find him," Erik vowed softly.

Amber's smile was chilling. "You won't find him this side of Judgment Day."

"What do you mean?"

"Several years past, the priest went to the Stone Ring with darkness in his mind. Lightning came. When it left, it took the priest to the very hell that so fascinated him. Or so Cassandra tells me . . ."

"Ah. Cassandra. A very wise woman indeed," Erik said, smiling like a wolf.

"The priest," Duncan said harshly to Amber. "He didn't harm you?"

"I used the dagger Erik gave me."

Duncan remembered the silver dagger she had used to cut his own bonds.

"I wasn't wrong to be wary of you, was I?" he asked dryly.

Amber smiled at Duncan, a smile as warm as her other one had been cold.

"I would never harm you, Duncan. It would be like harming myself."

"But I," Erik cut in, "have no such problem. I will most certainly 'harm' any man who forces himself on Amber."

Duncan looked past Amber to the cold wolf's eyes of the young lord.

"You will note, Sir Erik, who is holding and who is being held," Duncan said flatly.

Amber looked at her own hand, her fingers clenched on Duncan's wrist, her nails biting into his hard flesh.

"I'm sorry," she said, snatching her hand back.

"Precious Amber," Duncan murmured.

He held out his hand, smiling. Without hesitation, she put her fingers in his.

"You could stick silver daggers into me," Duncan said, "and I would ask only for more of your sweet touch."

Amber laughed and colored, ignoring Erik's look of concern and the disbelief on the faces of three of the four knights whose horses were trotting closer.

"Do you understand, now?" Duncan asked Erik.

There was a challenge in Duncan's voice that Erik could not mistake.

"You have no claims of family or clan or duty on Amber, nor any intent other than to see that she is protected," Duncan continued. "When my memory returns, I will claim the right to woo Amber for my wife."

"What if your memory doesn't return?" Erik asked.

"It must."

"Really? Why?"

"Until I know what obligations I carry from my past, I can't make new vows. And I find that I must."

"Why?"

"Amber," Duncan said simply. "I must have her. Yet I should not offer marriage until I know myself."

"Amber?" Erik asked, turning toward her.

"I have always been Duncan's. I always will be."

Erik closed his eyes for an instant. When they opened, they were clear and cold.

"What of Cassandra's warning?" he asked gently.

"There are three conditions. Only one has been met. Only one will be met."

"You sound very certain."

"I am."

Amber smiled with a bittersweet beauty that was haunting. She knew that Duncan wouldn't take her unless he remembered his past.

And if he did remember, she was afraid he wouldn't have her at all.

Enemy and soul mate.

"I wonder if prophecies can be so neatly divided and thereby neutralized," Erik muttered. "Or if it even matters."

"You speak in circles," Amber said.

"Both of you," said Duncan.

The other two ignored him.

"Death always flows," Erik said. "Rich life is always a possibility. Remember that, Amber, when you are offered a choice between a rock and a hard place."

With that enigmatic advice, Erik turned away to face the knights who were riding up alongside him.

Silently Duncan watched while greetings were exchanged among Sir Erik's knights. Three of the men he looked at briefly but without great curiosity.

The fourth man was different. Duncan stared at him intently, feeling almost certain that he had met the knight before. Almost certain, but not quite.

He would have questioned the knight, but a stark sense of danger sealed Duncan's lips. It was the second time since the Holy Land that Duncan had felt such a warning deep within himself.

Duncan couldn't remember what the other time had been, but he knew that it had occurred.

If the fourth knight recognized Duncan, he didn't show it. In fact, other than an incisive glance from eyes like black crystal, the knight had shown little interest in Duncan at all.

Duncan couldn't say the same. He kept staring at the knight's features half revealed beneath his helm. The blond hair and high, sharply carved cheekbones plucked at chords of memories within Duncan.

Candles and voices chanting.

A sword unsheathed.

No, not a sword. Something else.

Something living.

A man?

Duncan shook his head fiercely, willing memory to stay rather than to slip back among the shadows.

Green flames.

No, not flames.

Eyes!

Eyes as green as spring itself. Eyes burning with a thousand years of Glendruid hope.

And other eyes as well. A man's eyes.

Eyes black as midnight in hell.

A knife blade cold between my thighs.

A chill coursed through Duncan. It was a memory he could have died happy without ever recalling—the instant he had felt an enemy's knife blade

slide cold between his thighs, threatening to cas-
trate him if he so much as twitched.

Duncan's eyes narrowed as he looked at the
fourth knight. The man had eyes as black as midnight in hell.

Was he once my enemy?

Is he my enemy still?

Wary, motionless, Duncan strained to hear whatever message the shadows would grudgingly yield.
Nothing came to him but two conflicting certainties.

He is not my enemy.

He is dangerous to me.

Slowly Duncan straightened in his saddle, forcing
himself to look away from the unknown knight. As
Duncan moved, he realized that he was holding on
to Amber's hand as though to a sword on the brink
of battle.

"I'm sorry," he said in a voice that went no farther than her ears. "I've crushed your fingers."

"I'm not hurt," she whispered unsteadily.

"You're pale."

Amber didn't know how to tell Duncan that it
was the stirring of his memories rather than his
harsh grip on her hand that was causing her pain.
Her thoughts beat as frantically as birds caught in
a hunter's net.

Not now!

*Not with so many knights nearby. If Duncan is the
enemy I fear, he will be killed before my very eyes.*

And then I shall go mad.

Just before Duncan released Amber, he lifted her
hand to his mouth. When his breath and mustache
brushed over her sensitive fingers, it gave her a
pleasure so great that she trembled.

Amber didn't know that color returned to her
face in a rush and that her eyes suddenly burned
like candle flames caught within transparent gold-
en gems. Nor did she realize that she leaned toward

Duncan with unconscious longing as soon as his touch left her skin.

The fourth knight noticed everything and felt as though someone had slid a knife blade between his legs. Never would he have believed it if he hadn't seen it with his own eyes.

Long, powerful fingers flexed around the pommel of his sword while black eyes measured Duncan for a shroud.

"I've found two warriors for you, lord," Alfred said. "He and his squire are on a quest, but he is willing to stay and fight outlaws for a time."

Erik looked at the fourth knight.

"Two?" Erik said. "I see only one, though God knows he's big enough for two. How are you called?"

"Simon."

"Simon . . . I have two men-at-arms with that name."

Simon nodded. It was hardly an uncommon name.

"Who was your last lord?" Erik asked.

"Robert."

"There are many Roberts."

"Aye."

Erik turned to Alfred. The knight's features were as blunt as a fist, but he was a fine man in a fight.

"Not much for talk, is he?" Erik asked Alfred dryly. "Has he taken a vow?"

"He is talkative enough with that black sword he wears," Alfred said. "He had Donald and Malcolm on their backs before they knew what happened."

Erik turned back to Simon.

"Impressive," Erik said. "Have you been blooded?"

"Aye."

"Where?"

"In the Holy War."

Erik nodded, unsurprised. "There is a Saracen look to your blade."

"It drinks outlaw blood as readily as Turkish," Simon said calmly.

Erik smiled. "And Norse?"

"The blade cares not."

"Well, we have outlaws in plenty."

"You have three less than formerly."

Tawny eyebrows lifted in a combination of amusement and surprise.

"When?" Erik asked.

"Two days past."

"Where?"

"Near a lightning-struck tree and a stream coming from a cleft in the mountainside," Simon said.

" 'Tis the boundary of Lord Robert's lands," Erik said.

Simon shrugged. "It looked like no man's land to me."

"That will change."

In silence, Erik measured the knight for a long moment, taking in the well-used, well-made clothes and weapons, and the excellent lines of the horse Simon rode.

"Have you armor?" he asked.

"Aye. It is in your keep's armory." Simon smiled oddly. "It was that which made me stay."

"The armory? How so?"

"I wanted to know more about a lord who builds a secure well, barracks, and armory before he builds quarters for his own comfort."

"Your accent tells me you spent time in the Norman lands," Erik said after a moment.

" 'Tis hard not to. They rule so much."

Erik grimaced. "Too much. Why did you leave?"

"The continent is too settled. There is nothing for a landless knight to do but hone his sword and dream of better days."

Laughing, Erik turned to Alfred and nodded his acceptance of Simon.

"What of the other man?" Erik asked.

"The Norseman is tracking outlaws," Alfred replied.

"A Norseman?"

"He looks it, though he speaks our language. Pale as a ghost. Called Sven. Fights like a ghost, too. Never seen a man so hard to pin down, except maybe you."

"He can *be* a ghost for all of me," Erik retorted, "so long as he haunts outlaws rather than my vassals."

Alfred laughed and then nodded toward Duncan.

"I see that I'm not the only one who went fishing for warriors and came up with a prize."

A glance at Duncan was Erik's only response. Then he looked at Amber. Though he said nothing, she knew him well enough to understand that she wasn't to argue with whatever might happen next.

"He is an unusual man," Erik said calmly. "Almost a fortnight ago, I found him near Stone Ring."

A murmuring went through the knights, followed by a flurry of movement as they crossed themselves.

"He was sick unto death," Erik continued. "I took him to Amber. She healed him, but not without cost. He remembers nothing of his life before he came to the Disputed Lands."

Erik paused, then said distinctly, "Not even his name."

Simon's eyes became measuring black slits as he looked from Erik to Duncan, and from there to Amber. Against the hundred shades of gray that were the mist and clouds, she burned like a shaft of sunlight.

"Yet he had to answer to something," Erik continued. "Amber saw the marks of battle on him, knew the shadows veiling his mind, and named him 'dark warrior'—Duncan."

A subtle tension went through Simon, a tightening of the body as though for battle or flight.

None noticed but Duncan, who had been watching the fair-haired, dark-eyed stranger out of the corner of his eye. Yet Simon was looking not at him, but at Amber.

"Are you especially skilled with herbs and potions?" Simon asked her.

The question was polite and his tone was gentle, but the bleak midnight of his eyes was neither.

"No," Amber said.

"Then why was he brought to you? Is there no wise woman to heal men in the Disputed Lands?"

"Duncan wore an amber talisman," Amber said, "and all things amber are mine."

Simon looked puzzled.

So did Duncan.

"I thought you gave the talisman to me while I lay senseless," he said to Amber, frowning.

"Not I," she said. "Why do you think that?"

Duncan shook his head, baffled. "I don't know."

Without hesitation, Amber lifted her hand to his cheek.

"Try to remember when you first saw the pendant," she whispered.

Duncan went still. Pieces of memory tumbled in his mind, but they had no more form and substance than bright leaves torn from their moorings by a wild autumn wind.

Concerned Glendruid eyes.

A golden flash of amber.

A kiss brushed against his cheek.

God be with you.

"I was so certain a lass gave me the talisman . . ."

Duncan's voice trailed off into a muffled curse. His fist hit the pommel of the saddle with enough force to startle the horse.

"To be so teased and taunted by shadows is worse than no memory at all!" he said savagely.

Amber snatched her hand back from Duncan's skin. His rage was like a brand waved close to her flesh, hinting at the searing pain that waited for her if she continued touching him while he was so enraged.

Erik looked sharply at Amber.

"What is it?" he demanded.

She simply shook her head.

"Amber?" Duncan asked.

"A woman gave you the talisman," Amber said unhappily. "A woman with eyes of Glendruid green."

The word went through the knights like a fitful breeze through the marsh.

Glendruid.

"He has been bewitched!" Alfred said fearfully, crossing himself.

Amber opened her mouth to deny it, but Erik was faster.

"Aye, like enough," Erik said smoothly. "It would explain much. But Amber is certain that whatever spell Duncan was under in the past, he is free of compulsion now. Isn't he, Amber?"

"Aye," she said quickly. "He is not the devil's tool, or he couldn't wear the amber talisman at all."

"Show them," Erik ordered.

Without a word, Duncan unlaced his shirt and pulled out the amber pendant.

"There is a cross on one side in the form of a knight's prayer to God for safekeeping," Erik said. "Look at it, Alfred. Know that Duncan belongs to God rather than to Satan."

Alfred urged his horse forward until he could see the pendant dangling from Duncan's big fist. The incised letters of the prayer clearly formed a cross with a double bar. Slowly, painfully, Alfred spelled out the first words of the prayer.

"As you say, lord. 'Tis a common prayer."

"The runes on the other side are also a prayer for protection," Amber said.

Alfred shrugged. "The Church didn't teach me runes, lass. But I know you. If you say there is no evil in the runes, I believe it."

"Exactly," Erik said. "So greet Duncan as your equal. Don't fear him for what he has gone through. It is his future that matters, and that future lies with me."

There was silence while Erik looked from knight to knight. All knights save Simon nodded, accepting Duncan as Erik already had. Simon simply shrugged as though it were no great matter to him either way.

Amber let out a long, soundless sigh. She knew that rumors of a strange man under her care had rippled through the countryside in the past twelve days. Still, Erik had taken a great risk in springing Duncan's lost past on his knights so baldly. They might easily have turned against Duncan and driven him out as a tool of dark sorcery.

As though hearing Amber's fretful thoughts, Erik winked at her, silently reminding her that he was quite skillful at predicting how men would react.

"Let us see what we have in the way of fighting men," Erik said. "Alfred, have you tested Simon's skill yourself?"

"No, lord."

Erik turned to Duncan. "Would you like to hold sword in hand again?"

"Aye!"

"Nay!" Amber said just as quickly. "You are still healing from the sickness that—"

"Leave off," Erik interrupted curtly. " 'Tis no true battle I'm proposing, but merely an exercise."

"But—"

"My knights and I must know the mettle of the men who will fight by our sides," he said, ignoring her attempt to interrupt.

A look at Erik's topaz eyes told Amber that arguments would be futile. Yet she spoke again anyway.

"Duncan has no sword."

With a casual grace that spoke of skill and strength combined, Erik drew his own sword and offered it to Duncan.

"Use mine," Erik said.

It wasn't a request.

"It would be an honor," Duncan said.

The instant Duncan grasped the sword, a subtle change came over him. It was as though a veil had been lifted, revealing the warrior poised beneath the richly dressed exterior of the man. The weapon gleamed and sliced through the air with wicked sounds as Duncan tried the blade's balance and reach.

Erik watched Duncan and wanted to laugh aloud with sheer pleasure. Amber had been right. Duncan was indeed a warrior among warriors, first among equals.

"A fine weapon," Duncan said after a minute. "Quite the finest I've ever held. I shall try to do it honor."

"Simon?" Erik asked blandly.

"I have my own sword, sir."

"Then out with it, man. 'Tis past time to hear the music of steel on steel!"

Simon's blade-thin smile made Amber bite her lip anxiously. While Donald and Malcolm weren't as skilled as some of Erik's other knights, they were courageous, strong, dogged fighters.

And Simon had defeated both of them with ease.

"No blood, no broken bones," Erik said abruptly. "I simply want to see what manner of fighter you both are. Do you understand me?"

Duncan and Simon nodded.

"Shall we fight here?" Simon asked.

"Down there. And afoot," Erik added. "Duncan's horse is no match for yours."

The battleground Erik had chosen was a mead-ow whose autumn stubble had been softened by rain. Beneath the thickening clouds, mist flickered like silver flames.

Together, Duncan and Simon dismounted, cast mantles over their saddles, and walked to the mead-ow. The smell of sun-cured, rain-drenched stubble permeated the air. When they reached a relatively level, mud-free stretch of ground, they turned and faced each other.

"I ask forgiveness for any wound I might give," Simon said, "and offer the same for any I receive."

"Aye," Duncan said. "I ask and offer the same."

Simon smiled and unsheathed his sword with a feline grace and speed that was as startling as the black finish on the blade.

"You are very quick," Duncan said.

"And you are very strong." Simon smiled oddly. " 'Tis a battle I'm accustomed to."

"Are you? Not many men are as strong as I."

"My brother is. That is one of the two advantages I have over you today."

"What is the other?" Duncan asked, raising his blade to meet Simon's.

"Knowledge."

The blades kissed ritually with a muted metal cry, then slid away. Both men began circling and feinting, testing for weakness in the other.

Without warning, Simon made a catlike leap for-ward and sent the flat of his blade whistling toward Duncan. It was the same lightning attack that had felled Donald and Malcolm.

At the last possible instant, Duncan twisted and brought up his borrowed sword. Steel met steel with a horrible clash. Then Duncan whipped his blade back as though it weighed no more than a breath, leaving Simon only air to lean on.

Most other men would have gone to their knees at the sudden loss of balance. Simon managed to catch himself and simultaneously twist under Duncan's descending blade, delivering a blow to Duncan's legs at the same time with the flat of his sword.

Very few men could have remained standing after such an attack. Duncan was one of them. He grunted and pivoted on one foot, turning with the force of the attack. The turn took much of the power from the blow.

Before Simon could follow his advantage, Duncan made a backhanded slash with his heavy broadsword. The move was unexpected, for it required a sheer strength of arm and shoulder that was rarely found.

Simon slipped the attack with a cat's grace. Sword met sword with a force that clashed up and down the meadow. For long moments the swords stayed crossed, each man straining for the advantage.

Finally, inevitably, Simon gave way to Duncan's greater strength. One half step backward, then two, then more.

Duncan followed eagerly.

Too eagerly.

Simon twisted aside, leaving Duncan off-balance. He went down on one knee and then lunged quickly to the left, barely avoiding Simon's attack. Duncan scrambled upright just in time to lift his sword to meet Simon's attack. Steel clashed and screamed. The heavy blades crossed and held as though chained together.

For a brief time both men stood braced, breathing hard, their breath rising in silver plumes above the crossed swords. With each breath they took came the sharp fragrance of harvest past, wet earth, and cured grass.

"It smells like Blackthorne Keep's best hay meadow, doesn't it?" Simon asked casually.

Blackthorne.

The word went into Duncan like a dagger, slicing through shadows to the truth beneath. But before he could see that truth, the shadows flowed together over the wound, healing the tear in the darkness as though it had never existed.

Disoriented, Duncan shook his head.

It was all the advantage Simon needed. He twisted aside with the speed of lightning, unlocking the swords and delivering a blow to Duncan's body that knocked the breath from him. An instant later, Simon tripped Duncan and sent him to the cold ground.

Swiftly Simon knelt close to his fallen opponent. He bent over Duncan and spoke urgently, knowing it would be a very short time before the others came running to the stubble field to see how Duncan fared.

"Can you hear me?" Simon asked.

Duncan nodded, for he had no breath to speak.

"Is what the witch said true?" Simon demanded. "You have no memory of any time before you came here?"

Painfully, Duncan nodded.

Simon turned away, concealing his savage expression.

Pray God that Sven returns soon. I've found what we were seeking.

But he is still lost.

Cursed hell-witch. To steal a man's mind.

And smile!

7

"**A** MAN of your skill should not go unarmed," Simon said. "Surely there is a weapon in all this armory that Sir Erik could spare?"

Duncan rubbed his midriff ruefully. It still ached from the blow Simon had given him yesterday.

"Right now I feel about as skilled as a green squire," Duncan said.

Simon laughed.

After a moment, so did Duncan. He felt a kinship with the blond knight that was as unexpected as it was strong.

"I had the advantage in our battle," Simon said. "I've spent a lifetime battling a man of your strength. You've had little practice against a man of my quickness. Except, perhaps, Sir Erik? There is a lean grace about the man that makes me wary."

"I've never seen Erik fight. Or if I have, I don't remember it," Duncan added broodingly.

"If you haven't seen him fight since you awakened in the Disputed Lands, you haven't seen him fight at all," Simon said beneath his breath.

"What was that?"

"Nothing of importance," Simon said.

He looked around the armory, cataloging the weapons with reluctant admiration for Erik's foresight. The young lord would be a formidable enemy, if it came to that.

And Simon suspected that it would.

The sound of people walking toward the armory drifted like smoke through the half-finished stone keep. First came a man's deep voice, then a woman's musical laughter. Erik and Amber.

Duncan turned toward the doorway with an eagerness that made Simon both furious and deadly cold.

Hell-witch.

Duncan comes to her lure like a starving hound to a meal of garbage.

"There you are," Erik said to Simon. "Alfred said you were likely here, seeing to the repair of your arms."

"Just appreciating the skill of your armorer," Simon said, watching Amber run to Duncan. "Not since the Saracens have I seen such work."

"That is what I wanted to talk to you about," Erik said.

"The repairs made to my hauberk?"

"No. Saracen arms. Something you said yesterday about their archers intrigued me."

With an effort of will, Simon forced himself to concentrate on Erik rather than on the girl who looked so innocent yet who was so deeply steeped in evil that she could steal a man's mind with neither hesitation nor regret.

"What was that, lord?" Simon asked.

"Did their warriors truly shoot from horseback at a gallop?"

"Yes."

"Accurately? At good distance?"

"Aye," Simon said. "And as quickly as hail falling."

Erik looked into the darkness of Simon's eyes and had no doubt that whatever memories of war lay there were much of the reason for the man's bleak, chilling competence.

"How did they manage?" Erik asked. "A crossbow has to be armed by a man standing on the ground."

"The Saracen used a single bow. It was half the length of our longer English bows, yet shot arrows with a force like that of a crossbow."

"How can that be?"

"It was a question that D—" Simon covered his error by clearing his throat and quickly speaking again. "It was a question my brother and I often argued."

"What did you decide?"

"The Saracen curved and recurved their bows in such a way as to double or redouble their power without the penalty of heaviness that the crossbow bears."

"How?" Erik asked.

"We don't know. Every time we tried to make one for ourselves, we broke the bow."

"God's teeth, what I wouldn't give for a handful of Saracen bows!" Erik said.

"You'll need Saracen archers, too," Simon said dryly. "There is a trick to using the bow that non-Saracen warriors have trouble mastering. In the end, honest Christian swords and pikes carried the day."

"Still, think what an advantage those bows would be."

"Treachery is better."

Startled, Erik stared at Simon.

So did Duncan.

"My brother," Simon said, "often told me that there is no better way to take a well-defended position than by treachery."

"A shrewd man, your brother," Erik muttered. "Did he survive the Holy War?"

"Aye."

"Is he what you are seeking in the Disputed Lands?"

Simon's expression changed.

"Forgive me, lord," Simon said softly. "What I seek in these lands is a matter between me and God."

For the space of a breath, Erik paused. Then he smiled faintly and turned back to the hauberk that had recently been hung in the armory.

"A fine hauberk," Erik said.

"Your armorer repaired the chain mail so deftly that it is better than when new," Simon said.

"My armorer's skill is famed throughout the Disputed Lands," Erik said matter-of-factly.

"Justly so. Will he make Duncan a sword and dagger, and a chain-mail hauberk and hood to take into battle?"

"He will have to," Erik said in a dry tone. "There isn't a hauberk already made in all of the islands that will fit Duncan's breadth of shoulder."

"There is one," Duncan said absently.

"Oh?"

"Dominic le Sabre's," Duncan said.

Amber looked intently at him, but said nothing, for she feared the consequences if his memory returned.

Simon stared with equal intensity at Duncan, yet asked no questions for the same reason.

Erik, however, didn't fear Duncan's memory returning.

"Then you have seen the infamous Norman?" Erik asked.

"Yes."

"When?"

Duncan opened his mouth to answer before he realized that he didn't know.

"I don't know," he said in a clipped voice. "I simply know that I have."

Erik shot a quick glance at Amber. She looked back at him in silence.

"Is your memory returning?" Erik asked.

Simon and Amber held their breath.

"Fragments. No more," Duncan said.

"What does that mean?"

Duncan shrugged, winced at the discomfort to his bruised body, and prodded his chest with impatient fingers.

A pity that she isn't here to take the ache with her clever balms and lotions.

Then Duncan heard his own thoughts and froze, wondering who "she" was.

Green eyes.

The smell of Glendruid herbs.

Water warmed for bathing.

The scent of her soap.

"Duncan?" Erik pressed. "Are your memories returning?"

"Have you ever seen the moon's reflection in a still pond?" Duncan asked with buried savagery.

"Yes."

"Throw a bucket of stones in the pond and look at the moon's reflection again. That's what I have of my memory."

The bitterness in Duncan's voice made Amber long to touch him, to soothe him, to give him a sensual ease that would balance the ache of loss.

"So I remember that I have seen the Glendruid Wolf," Duncan said, "but I don't remember when or where or how or why, or even what he looked like!"

"Glendruid Wolf," Erik murmured. "So he is truly called that. I had heard rumors . . ."

"What rumors?" Amber asked, anxious to change the subject.

"That the English king's Sword has become the Glendruid Wolf," Erik said.

Amber looked baffled.

"One of Cassandra's prophecies was accurate. Again," Erik said.

"Which one?"

"Two wolves circling, one ancient, one not," Erik said. "Two wolves testing each other while the land held its breath and waited . . ."

"For what?" Simon asked.

"Death. Or life."

"You didn't tell me," Amber said quickly.

"You were having enough trouble with your own prophecy," he said dryly.

"Which wolf won?" Simon asked.

"Cassandra's prophecies aren't like that," Erik said. "She sees future crossroads, not which road is taken."

With a shudder, Amber turned away. She didn't want to hear about Cassandra's prophecies.

"Duncan?" she said.

He made a questioning sound, only half listening. One of the weapons hanging on the armory wall had caught his attention.

"Will you go with me to the Whispering Fen?" Amber asked. "Cassandra asked me to see if the geese have arrived."

Then Amber realized which weapon Duncan was staring at. Her heart turned over with raw fear. Quickly she stepped in front of him and put her hand on his cheek.

Bright pleasure leaped.

Dark memories writhed.

"Duncan," Amber said in a low voice.

He blinked and focused on Amber rather than on the weapon whose length of thick chain and heavy, bristling ball had made memories swirl and seethe in darkness.

"Aye, lass?"

Amber's lips trembled slightly, pleasure and pain in one. Her pleasure. His pain that was also hers.

"Go with me to Whispering Fen," Amber said softly. "You have had enough of battles."

Duncan looked past her bright golden hair to the gray steel chain draped along the wall.

"Aye," he said. "But have they had enough of me?"

Duncan reached over Amber's shoulder and took the weapon from its rest with an ease that belied the weapon's weight.

"I'll take this with me," he said.

Amber's teeth sank into her lower lip as she saw what lay in Duncan's hands.

Simon saw it as well. Quietly he began preparing for the battle that would come if the pond of Duncan's memory stilled long enough for the fragments of light to flow into a true image of the past.

Erik simply stared. He didn't realize he had drawn his own sword until he felt its cold, familiar weight in his hand.

"The hammer," Erik said in a neutral voice. "Why did you choose that from all the weapons in the armory?"

Surprised, Duncan looked at the weapon that felt so right in his hands.

"I have no sword," Duncan said simply.

"So?"

"There is no better battle weapon than the hammer for a man with no sword."

Slowly both Simon and Erik nodded.

"May I borrow it?" Duncan asked. "Or is it the special favorite of one of your knights?"

"No," Erik said in a soft voice. "You may keep it."

"Thank you, lord. Daggers are fine for close fighting or slicing roasts, but a man needs a weapon with reach for serious fighting."

"Are you planning to fight soon?" Erik probed.

Grinning, Duncan let the chain slip and rattle through his fingers, testing the hammer's weight and length.

"If I came upon some outlaws bent upon an early grave," Duncan said, "I would hate to disappoint them for lack of a weapon."

Simon laughed outright.

Erik smiled like the wolf he was reputed to be.

All three men looked at one another in silent recognition—and appreciation—of the hot fighting blood that ran through each of them.

Abruptly Erik clapped both Duncan and Simon on the shoulder as though they were brothers by blood as well as by inclination.

"With men like you at my side, I wouldn't fear taking on the Glendruid Wolf himself," Erik said.

Simon's smile faded. "The Scots Hammer tried. And failed."

For a moment Duncan became so still that it seemed as though his very heart had stopped beating.

Amber's had. Then it lurched and beat frantically.

"Duncan?" she asked, nakedly pleading. "Won't you come now with me to the fen?"

He didn't answer for the space of one breath, two breaths, three . . .

Then he made a low sound. His fingers clenched on the hammer until it seemed that steel must give way before flesh.

"Aye, lass," Duncan said in a low voice. "I will go with you."

"It may storm before sunset," Erik warned.

Smiling gently, Duncan touched a lock of Amber's hair.

"With Amber nearby," he said, "I never lack for sunlight."

She smiled in return, though her lips trembled with a fear for him that was so great she was afraid she would scream.

"Won't you leave that behind?" Amber asked, pointing to the hammer.

"Nay. Now I can defend you."

"It isn't necessary. There are no outlaws this close to Sea Home."

Ignoring the others in the room, Duncan leaned down until his lips all but brushed Amber's hair. He inhaled her scent deeply and looked into her anxious golden eyes.

"I won't take a chance with you, precious Amber," he murmured. "If someone cut you, I fear I would bleed."

Though the words were very soft, Simon heard them. He looked at Amber with an anger that was difficult to conceal.

Cursed hell-witch. To steal a man's mind and smile!

"Duncan," Amber whispered.

The sound was as much a sigh as a name. She took his hard hand between hers, ignoring the cold weight of chain.

"Let us hurry, my dark warrior. I have already packed a supper and sent word for two horses to be made ready."

"Three," corrected Erik.

"Are you going?" Amber asked, surprised.

"No. Egbert is."

"Ah. Egbert. Of course. Well, we shall just ignore him."

DUNCAN shifted carefully and then looked over his shoulder, not wanting to cause the nervous horse any alarm. They had crept away from the picnic, leaving Egbert asleep with his own horse and Duncan's grazing nearby. Amber had insisted that they take only her horse when they stole away to the fen.

The trail out of Sea Home's gentle fields had quickly become rugged, especially for a horse carrying double. There were places they had ridden over that had made Duncan blink. At first glance the way looked impassable. But a few steps aside from the obvious path, another look, and there was always a surprisingly easy course to follow.

It was enough to make a man nervous. Appar-

FORBIDDEN 111

ently the horse wasn't happy about it, either. Or perhaps the animal was simply uneasy about carrying two riders.

"No sign of him," Duncan said, looking forward once again.

"Poor Egbert," Amber said, but she sounded more amused than alarmed. "Erik will be quite put out."

" 'Poor Egbert' is asleep on the other side of that ridge," Duncan muttered. "He lies at ease in a field warmed by a sun that doesn't know summer has fled. Is that such a harsh fate?"

"Only if Erik discovers it."

"If the squire is half as clever as he is lazy, he won't tell Erik that he fell asleep."

"If Egbert were that clever, he wouldn't be that lazy."

Duncan gave a crack of laughter and tightened his right arm around Amber's supple waist. His left arm held the reins. Amber's hands rested on his arms as though she enjoyed the simple warmth of his body.

"In any case, we left your mount with him," Amber said. "And instructions to wait for us."

"Are you certain the lad can read?"

"Better than he can write, according to Cassandra."

"Does he write?" Duncan asked, surprised.

"Badly. Erik despairs of ever making him skilled enough to tally a keep's crops, animals, and taxes."

"Then why doesn't he send the boy back to his father?"

"Egbert has none," Amber said. "Erik found him by a cart road. His father had been killed by a falling tree."

"Does Erik make it a habit to pick up and care for stray people?"

"If they can't care for themselves, someone must."

"Is that why you cared for me?" Duncan asked. "Duty and compassion?"

"Nay."

Amber remembered what it had felt like when she first touched Duncan, a pleasure so great it shocked her into snatching her hand back. Then she had touched him again.

And lost her heart.

"It was different with you," Amber said in a low voice. "Touching you pleased me."

"Does it please you still?"

A telltale wash of color across her cheeks silently answered Duncan's question.

"I'm glad," he said. "Very, very glad."

With subtle pressures of his arms, Duncan gathered Amber even closer to his body. The hunger for her that was never far beneath his thoughts flooded his body with anticipation, even as his conscience railed him.

He shouldn't seduce her until he had more answers to the dark questions from his past.

Unknown vows haunted him.

And yet . . . and yet.

It was surpassingly sweet to ride through an autumn land with slanting yellow sunlight warming his face and an amber fairy relaxed within the circle of his arms.

"The sun," Amber murmured. "What an unexpected glory."

She lifted her arms and pushed the wool cowl from her head. The indigo cloth fell in folds over her nape and shoulders, allowing the gentle golden warmth of the sun to bathe her.

"Aye," Duncan said. "It is indeed glorious."

But it was Amber rather than the sunlight that Duncan praised.

"Your hair," he murmured. " 'Tis a thousand shades of golden light. I've seen nothing more beautiful."

Amber's breath caught as a fine shiver went over her body. The hunger in Duncan summoned her. She wanted nothing more than to pull his strength around her like a living mantle, shutting out the world, giving herself to him in a secret silence that no other person could violate.

Yet she must not give herself to him.

Heart and body and soul.

"Amber," Duncan whispered.

"Yes?" she said, stilling a shiver of response.

"Nothing. I simply like whispering your name against your bright hair."

Pleasure expanded through Amber. Without thinking, she lifted her hand to touch Duncan's cheek. The faintly rough texture of his skin where beard lay just beneath the surface pleased her. The strength of his arm around her waist pleased her. The heat and resilience of his chest pleased her.

Duncan pleased her to the center of her soul.

"There is no man like you."

Amber didn't know she had spoken the thought aloud until she felt a tremor ripple through Duncan's strength.

"Nor is there a woman to equal you," he whispered as he kissed the palm of her hand.

When Duncan bent to put his cheek against Amber's hair, the delicate scent of sunlight and evergreens swept through him. She smelled of summer and warmth, of Scots pine and a clean wind.

The fragrance was uniquely Amber. He could not get enough of it.

Amber heard the hesitation in Duncan's breathing, sensed the piercing pleasure that he took from her simple presence, and longed to be free of prophecy.

But she was not.

"A pity the warmth won't last," Amber said raggedly.

Duncan made a questioning sound as he nuzzled a wisp of hair that lay against her neck.

"Erik was right," she said, her voice quick, almost frightened. "A storm is coming. But it simply serves to make the sunlight more precious."

Reluctantly Duncan lifted his head and looked to the north. A thick line of clouds loomed there, held back by a southerly wind. Overhead, the sky was a sapphire bowl arching above fells whose rocky peaks wore a pearly cowl of cloud.

"It won't storm by sunset," Duncan said.

Amber said nothing.

"Perhaps by moonrise," he added, "but I think not."

Duncan looked over his shoulder once more. Behind them a narrow crease cut into the rugged highlands that rose between Sea Home and Stone Ring Keep. The crease was the beginning of Ghost Glen, named for the pale-barked trees clinging to its steep sides, and for the haunting wail of autumnal winds.

No other rider was following Duncan and Amber down the ridge they had just descended. No other rider was visible ahead, where land and sea mingled to make Whispering Fen. The way they would take to the fen was unmarked, known only to the amber girl who fitted so perfectly in Duncan's arms.

There had been no sign of habitation at all on this side of the ridge. No cart road, no smoke lifting above a clearing, no plowed fields, no drystone fences, no deer parks, no mark of axe on trees. Small, steep-sided, stitched together by the fey conversations of a brook, Ghost Glen held neither hamlet nor farm nor walking paths. It was a place of ancient forest and primeval silence.

The land was both savage and oddly innocent, removed from the strife of the Disputed Lands. Had Duncan not seen standing stones grouped in solitary glades, he would have sworn no other person had ever passed this way.

Yet people had lived here once. Some named them Druids. Some named them sorcerers. Some named them not men at all, but devils or gods.

And some—the few who might know—called those vanished people Learned.

"Egbert won't follow us," Amber said as she felt Duncan twist to look behind once more.

"How can you be sure? He is lazy, but not blind. We left a trail."

She hesitated, wondering how to explain to Duncan the combination of knowledge and instinct that made her so certain they were safe from intrusion here.

"Egbert can't follow us," Amber said. "Even if he weren't afraid, he wouldn't be able to see where we went."

"Why not?"

"He isn't Learned," she said simply.

"What does that have to do with it?"

"Egbert would see obstacles and turn aside, certain that no one could pass the way we did."

A cool breath blew down Duncan's spine as he remembered how impassable parts of the trail had looked . . . at first.

"That's why I made you leave your horse," Amber added.

"It wasn't Learned?" Duncan retorted dryly.

She laughed and shook her head, making sunlight gleam and run like liquid amber through her hair.

"Whitefoot is used to my ways," Amber said. "She goes where I guide her."

"You see a path," Duncan said.

It wasn't quite a question, but Amber answered anyway, shrugging.

"I'm Learned." Then she added with a sigh, "But, according to Cassandra, I'm not very Learned and never will be unless I settle to it and stop roaming the wild places."

"Like this one?"

"Aye."

Duncan looked at the smooth curve of Amber's cheek and wondered how he, who had never been taught, had managed to see both obstacle and trail. Before he could ask Amber, she was talking again.

"Despite my failings as a student, I have absorbed enough Learning to walk a few of the ancient trails. Ghost Glen is my special place. I've never shared it with anyone. Until now."

Her quiet words went through Duncan like distant thunder, as much felt as heard, a tremor of the earth itself.

"Amber?"

Duncan's voice was low, aching, nearly rough. She sensed the leap of sensual hunger in him. She also sensed a nameless yearning that pervaded him as surely as sun pervaded the day.

"What is it?" she whispered, turning to Duncan.

"Why did you bring me here?"

"To count Cassandra's geese."

Hazel eyes searched Amber's face.

"Geese?" he asked.

"Aye. They come here from the north in the autumn, pulling winter behind them like a bleak banner."

" 'Tis early for geese, isn't it?"

"Yes," Amber said.

"Then why are you looking for them?"

"Cassandra asked me to. The rune stones foretold an early, harsh winter. If the geese are here, we'll know Cassandra cast the stones correctly."

"What do your serfs say?" Duncan asked.

"They say the signs are mixed."

"How so?"

"The sheep are growing very thick coats, yet the birds still call from the trees. The sun is still warm, yet joints and old wounds ache. The good priests pray and dream their dreams, yet none agree as to God's answer."

"Signs. Prophecies. Priests. Dreams." Duncan grimaced. "It's enough to make a warrior's head ache. Give me a sword and a shield and I'll make my own way, come what will—or what *has*."

The open wound of Duncan's lost memory drew harsh brackets on either side of his mouth. Amber traced the lines with a fingertip, but she was unable to reach past Duncan's pain and anger.

Unhappily she turned away, facing the wild green glen once more. On both sides of the path, rowan trees clung to gray rock cliffs like fallen angels. The few berries that had been overlooked by birds glowed in ruby bursts at the ends of branches. Ghostly birches thronged in creases and crowded ridge lines. Their leafless branches lifted to the autumn sky in silent query about the lost summer and the winter to come.

Ahead and to the right, a low circle of reclining stones marked an ancient place. A larger, more ragged circle of standing stones loomed on an oddly flattened ridge line.

An eagle's high, untamed cry pierced the silence. The call was repeated one, twice, thrice.

Duncan tilted back his head and returned the wild whistle with uncanny accuracy.

The bird of prey wheeled aside as though reassured of Duncan's and Amber's right to be within the fey glen. As they watched, the eagle rode a transparent torrent of air to the far side of the ridge and disappeared.

"Who taught you to answer the eagle's question?" Amber asked softly.

"My mother's mother."

"She was Learned."

"I doubt it," Duncan said. "We had none we called Learned."

"Sometimes, in some places, it is safer to have no name."

Neither Duncan nor Amber spoke again until they had followed the hurtling silver creek into a small dale and down to the restless sea. The grasses of the marsh were equally alive, combed by a fairy wind.

For the man and woman poised on a low rise above the fen, the sound of wind and marsh was that of score upon score of people whispering, murmuring, sighing, confiding . . . a thousand hushed breaths stirring the air.

"I know now why it is called Whispering Fen," Duncan said quietly.

"Until the winter geese come, yes. Then the air resounds with their honking and whistling, and the fen whispers only in the smallest hours of the night."

"I'm glad to know it this way, with the sun turning the tips of marsh grass into candles. 'Tis like a church in the instants before the mass is chanted."

"Yes," Amber whispered. "It is exactly that. Filled with imminence."

For a few moments Duncan and Amber sat in silence, absorbing the special peace of the fen. Then Whitefoot stretched her neck and tugged at the bit, wanting the freedom to graze.

"Will she wander if we dismount?" Duncan asked.

"Nay. Whitefoot is almost as lazy as Egbert."

"Then we will rest her for a time before we start back."

Duncan dismounted and lifted Amber from the horse's back. When he set her on her feet, her fingers caressed his cheek and the thick, dark silk of his mustache. He turned his head and kissed her hand with a tender, lingering heat that shortened her breath.

When Amber looked up into Duncan's eyes, she

knew she should draw away. She didn't have to
be touching him to be certain that he wanted her
with a wildness that equaled the eagle's cry.

"We should start back very soon," she said.

"Aye. But first . . ."

"First?"

"First I will teach you not to fear my desire."

8

"THAT—that wouldn't be wise," Amber said raggedly.

"On the contrary, precious Amber. It would be the wisest thing I have ever done."

"But we shouldn't—we can't—"

The slow drawing of Duncan's fingertips over Amber's lips scattered her words and her thoughts. She could sense his desire so clearly that it made her tremble.

And even more clearly she sensed his restraint.

"Duncan?" Amber asked, confused.

"I won't take you," he said simply. "I don't know what I did to you in the past that you fear my desire now, but I do know that you fear it."

"It is not—what you—dear God—you must not take me!"

"Hush, precious Amber." Duncan sealed her lips with a gentle pressure of his thumb. "I won't take you. Do you believe me?"

Amber felt the truth in Duncan, a certainty even stronger than the passion that burned within him.

"Yes," she whispered. "I believe you."

A long, low breath that was almost a groan came from deep in his chest.

"Thank you," Duncan said. "In the past, no one would have questioned my oath. But here . . . here I must prove my worth and honor all over again."

"Not to me. I sensed your honor and your pride very clearly the first time I touched you."

Duncan gave Amber's mouth a tender, brushing movement of his lips that was almost too light to be called a kiss.

"Come," he said softly, holding out his hand. "Walk with me."

Amber laced her fingers through Duncan's and trembled at the banked fires of passion that burned so intensely in his body.

"Where are we going?" she asked.

"To find a place of shelter."

"The wind isn't cold."

"Not while we wear our mantles," he agreed.

What Duncan left unsaid rippled through Amber in a wave of unease and anticipation combined.

The murmuring of sea and grass and wind followed both of them to the base of a low rise. There man had once smoothed a circle to raise tall stones within. Though the builders had long since vanished, the grassy circle and stones remained.

"This place is sheltered," Amber said. "Unless you fear the stones?"

For a moment Duncan closed his eyes. Senses that slept within him until times of danger quivered to alertness at his prodding, found nothing of concern, and sank into timeless sleep again.

Amber, whose hand was still joined with Duncan's, watched him with amazement. Because of Cassandra's teaching, Amber knew that if ancient evil had ever lingered near the circle of stones, the evil had long since fled from the place.

And so did Duncan, who had never been taught.

He must be an unknown knight. I am silly to keep fearing he is the Scots Hammer, enemy of Erik.

"There is nothing to fear in the stones," he said after a moment.

"You are Learned," Amber said.

Duncan laughed. "Nay, my golden witch. I'm

simply a warrior who fights with everything available, including my head."

Amber started to quarrel about being named a witch before she realized that he had used the term with affection rather than with accusation. When she saw that Duncan was watching her with amusement and approval in his vivid hazel eyes, she decided that she liked being his "golden witch."

"That's what Learning is," Amber said absently. "Using your head."

"In that event," Duncan said, looking around the circle of stones, "I learned during the holy crusade what every hound is born knowing—danger has a special scent and feel."

"I think there is more to it than that."

"And I think there is less."

Duncan glanced sideways at Amber. She was watching him with luminous golden eyes and an intensity that made him want to ravish her both tenderly and very thoroughly.

"Come, my amber delight."

"Ah, so I'm a delight now rather than a witch. You must be Learned!"

The smile Duncan gave Amber was like a caress.

"Delightful witch," he said in a low voice. "Sit against this stone with me and we'll argue about what is Learned and what is simply common sense."

Smiling, Amber answered the tug on her hand by settling into the grass beside Duncan. The stone he had chosen to shelter them from the fitful wind was taller than a man. Its face was seamed by time and salt air. Within blade-thin crevices on the stone's surface grew gardens so tiny that a man could scarce see the moss bloom.

Yet bloom it certainly did. Growing things thrived on the surface of the stone, weaving a thick, vibrantly colored mantle over much of the ancient monolith.

Amber tested the moss with her fingertips, then closed her eyes and settled back against it with a sigh.

"How long do you think the stones have waited thus?" she murmured.

"Not half so long as I've wanted to do this."

Amber's eyes opened. Duncan was so close that she could feel the warmth of his breath and see the individual splinters of color in his hazel eyes. She drew back slightly, wanting to touch the clean line of his mouth beneath his mustache.

"Nay, lass," Duncan said. "There is nothing to fear."

"I know. I just wanted to touch you."

"Did you? How?"

"Like this."

Amber's fingertip traced the rim of Duncan's upper lip. The keen thrill of pleasure that coursed through him at her touch was as much a reward to Amber as the intimate rush of his breath caressing her fingertips.

"You like that," she said, delighted at the discovery.

Duncan's breath caught as another caress skimmed his lip, sending a tongue of fire through him.

"Aye," he said huskily. "I like that. Do you?"

"Like touching you? Yes. Too much, I fear."

"There is no place for fear between us."

The rush of Duncan's breath was replaced by the smooth heat of his mouth against Amber's. He felt the hesitation in her.

Then he felt the subtle yielding as she allowed the kiss. His heartbeat speeded as fire searched through his body.

Yet Duncan did no more than increase the pressure of his mouth on hers just a bit. It was barely enough to part Amber's lips for a skimming caress from the tip of his tongue. But it was enough to make her sigh and yield more of her mouth to the gentle kiss. Again he delicately traced her lips.

"Duncan," Amber whispered. "You are . . ."

His tongue moved again, this time more deeply.

Breath and words caught in Amber's throat. The gliding caress along the sensitive inner side of her lips was as delicate as a butterfly's wing. If she hadn't been touching Duncan, she would have thought that he was as gentle as a butterfly, too.

But she was touching him. She felt the banked heat of his fiery hunger. The contrast between his actions and his intense need should have frightened her.

Instead, it beguiled her as no caress could have.

"Truly I am safe with you," Amber whispered.

"Always, my golden witch. I would sooner cut off my own sword hand than harm you."

When Duncan's arms eased around her, Amber made no move to withdraw. He lifted and settled her across his thighs with a slow movement that was also a caress, telling her that he was frankly savoring her warm weight in his lap.

"Open my mantle and put your hands inside," Duncan said softly.

Amber hesitated.

"Do you not want to share my warmth?" he asked.

"I'm afraid to."

Duncan's eyelashes lowered. The sadness that went through him drew a low cry from Amber.

"You don't trust me," he said. "What did I do to you in the past that you so fear me now? Did I force myself on you?"

"Nay," she whispered.

Then she whispered it again and again, torn by his uncertainty and grief, the wound to his self-esteem that she did not believe his vow that she was safe with him.

She couldn't bear to hurt him so.

Unbidden, Amber's hands slid into the opening of Duncan's mantle. With a need she couldn't conceal, she fought through clothing until she could feel once more the living heat of his naked skin against her own. The small consummation drew a low cry from the back of her throat.

Baffled, Duncan looked at Amber's closed eyes and taut features as she experienced the textures of his body. When he realized that simply touching his naked skin was such a keen pleasure for her, he was both shaken and violently aroused.

"Amber?"

"Yes," she whispered. "It is myself I fear, not you."

She lowered her head against Duncan until her breath could bathe what her fingers were caressing.

"It is myself . . ."

Her whisper merged with the heat of her mouth against Duncan's throat. A current of fire ripped through him. The feel of Amber's tongue caressing his skin was so sweet and unexpected that it made him groan.

"Every touch I give you, even the least . . ." Amber whispered.

Her tongue stroked Duncan as delicately as a cat's. His whole body tightened in response.

"See?" she whispered. "I touch you and you burn. I feel you burning and I burn as well. Then I touch you again and the flames leap higher."

"By God's holy blood," Duncan said hoarsely, finally understanding the source of Amber's fear. *"You want me as much as I want you."*

Her smile was bittersweet. She let out a ragged breath.

"Nay, Duncan. I want you more. Your desire and my own combined."

"That's why you're afraid?"

"Yes. I fear . . . this."

Again Amber touched Duncan's flesh with the tip of her tongue, savoring the taste and warmth of his body, the smooth texture, and most of all the rapid, heavy beating of his blood just beneath his skin.

"Don't fear it," Duncan said, his voice low and almost rough. "Passion such as this is a gift from God."

She laughed sadly. "Is it? Is it a gift to see Paradise from afar, and know that you must never enter?"

One of Duncan's hands slid beneath Amber's cowl. His fingers eased into her loosely braided hair until he held her securely. A steady pressure of his palm turned her head up so that he could look into her golden eyes.

"We can taste Paradise without breaching its coral gates," Duncan said.

"Is that possible?"

"Aye."

"How?"

"Follow me. I'll show you."

Duncan closed the scant distance between their mouths. Amber's lips parted at the touch of his tongue. She felt again the delicious sensation as he skimmed the inside of her lips.

Then the touch of his tongue became firmer, more insistent, prowling the edges of her mouth, seeking entry to the warm darkness just beyond his reach.

"What do you . . . ?" Amber began.

She never finished asking what Duncan wanted, for his tongue glided between her teeth, taking her words and giving her fire in return.

The rhythmic slide and retreat and return of his tongue made fire lick unexpectedly through her body. Yet almost as soon as the heat bloomed within her, it faded, for the firm, provocative warmth of his tongue had been withdrawn.

The small sound that escaped Amber's throat flicked Duncan like a whip. The eager searching of her tongue for his was a stroke of pure flame in his loins. He laughed low in his chest and tightened his arms, drawing her even closer to the part of him that burned most hotly.

"Is this what you seek?" Duncan asked.

His tongue surged between Amber's teeth even as he rocked her hips against his. Her answering hunger made his head spin. She uttered a low sound and pressed even closer to the hot pleasures of his body. When he would have moved to bank the wild flames rising between them, her arms wrapped around his neck and her tongue sought his in a sensual duel that neither could lose.

Without releasing her mouth, Duncan lifted Amber and eased her down into the grass. Beneath her mantle, one of his hands tugged laces free. Suddenly he turned his head just enough so that his teeth could catch her lips in a series of gentle, burning bites.

A honeyed fire burst within Amber, dragging a moan from her. Duncan's teeth tenderly stinging her neck sent more heat through her flushed skin. When she felt him pulling her arms from around his neck, she protested.

"I know we must stop," Amber said, "but not yet."

"No, not yet," Duncan agreed. "We have much farther to go before we turn back at the final gate."

His mouth closed over hers once more. Gently, steadily, while his tongue teased and tormented her with promises of Paradise, he pulled her arms away from his neck and pressed them against her own body.

Amber didn't realize what Duncan wanted until she felt cool air wash over her breasts. Her mantle had been pushed to either side of her body, she was bare to the waist, and her arms were bound against her hips by half-shed clothing.

Duncan was no longer touching her. He was sim-

ply looking at her with eyes that blazed. She was
beautifully formed, neither too full nor too small,
warm and taut, with nipples the pink of wild rose-
buds. He ached to hold each bud in his mouth, to
caress it with his tongue, to test the creamy softness of her breasts with his teeth.

Between her breasts golden light pooled, caught
within timeless amber. The pendant shimmered and
rippled with radiance as though it were infused
with Amber's very life.

He touched the pendant in silent greeting. Then he
lifted his fingers and simply looked at the beauty that had lain hidden beneath heavy folds of
clothing.

"Duncan?" Amber whispered.

She looked into his eyes and trembled at what
she saw.

"Are you cold?" Duncan asked, seeing her shiver.

Amber trembled again, for his voice was like the
rasp of a cat's tongue. She tried to answer his question, but her mouth was dry and her heart was
beating frantically. Without Duncan's touch pouring his hunger into her, her own desire was being
quenched by unease.

"Dinna worry, golden witch," Duncan said thickly, bending down to Amber. "I will warm you."

The searing heat of Duncan's hands and mouth
on her breasts was both unexpected and fiercely
arousing to Amber. As he kissed first one pink
tip and then the other, they hardened magically.
His mustache caressed the sensitive flesh while his
tongue licked slowly, hotly.

Fire lanced through the center of Amber's body,
setting aflame places that had been secret even
from her.

Until Duncan touched her and she burned.

When he finally lifted his head, the breeze found
Amber's heated skin. He smiled to see her nipples

tighten even more. His fingertips closed over the flushed pink tips of her breasts. He rolled the velvet flesh lightly, pressed sensuously. When heat bloomed just beneath her creamy skin, he felt as though he were being stretched upon a rack of fire.

"How could I have forgotten your response to me?" Duncan asked wonderingly. "God must feel like this when he causes the sun to rise."

"We've never before—"

"Nay," he interrupted softly. "You would not fly so high, so quickly, unless you knew the lure of the hunt as surely as I."

Amber shook her head, the only answer she could make, for passion had stolen her voice.

"Don't be shy of the truth, precious Amber. Your response is a greater gift than any maidenly restraint."

She tried to answer, but all that came from her lips was a ragged cry. The passion she felt should have frightened her. But when he touched her, whatever virginal wariness and Learned caution she had were burned away in the overwhelming heat of Duncan's desire.

And her own. Duncan's desire and hers combined.

When he bent once more to draw one of her aching nipples into his mouth, Amber's breath came out in another low cry. When he shaped her with slow rhythms of his tongue, tender lightning burned from her breasts to her hips. Her back arched in abandoned response until she strained against the bonds of cloth holding her elbows to her sides.

Reluctantly Duncan lifted his head, wondering if the hungry intimacy of the caress had alarmed Amber.

"Don't struggle," he said gently. "I won't hurt you."

"I know. But I can't—'

She made a sound of frustration and jerked her arms. All she managed to do was tangle them more closely to her body.

"What can't you do?" Duncan asked.

The sweet swaying of Amber's breasts made sensual heat flush Duncan's body. The thought of her arching like that against his chest while he lay naked between her legs brought him to the edge of bursting.

"I can't touch you while I'm tangled in clothes this way," Amber said.

Duncan set his jaw against the temptation she was offering.

"I think that's just as well," he said raggedly.

"Don't you want me to touch you?"

He smiled at the confusion in Amber's eyes, even though the thought of feeling her hands on his body brought a leap of need so great that it was indistinguishable from pain.

"Aye," Duncan groaned, brushing his mustache over one taut nipple. "And aye"—he brushed again—"and aye, and aye one thousand times more!"

The sound Amber made could have been pleasure or fear. Even she couldn't have said which. She had never felt anything as powerful as the combination of her own untried sensuality, Duncan's torrential need, and the fierce restraint he exercised on his passion.

"But if you touch me . . ." he said hoarsely.

The words became lost in the ripple of sound Duncan drew from Amber as his teeth raked with exquisite delicacy over her nipple. Smiling darkly, he turned to her other breast and repeated the primitive caress.

"If you touch me," Duncan whispered, savoring Amber's unbridled response to him, "I shall be much less certain of my own control."

Beneath the words was Duncan's own growing doubt that his restraint was equal to Amber's sweet and abandoned response. He had never known a woman could want him so much, so deeply, without coyness or calculation.

"Dark warrior," Amber said, "you would never break your vow to me."

The certainty in Amber's voice was repeated in the clarity of her eyes watching him. Duncan saw himself reflected darkly in her luminous depths and at the same time he saw her absolute trust in him.

"You humble me," Duncan said.

"Then don't raise me so high," she whispered, smiling.

"Shall I free your arms?"

Though Amber knew she could free herself if she had the patience, she wanted it to be Duncan who released her. She wanted him to understand the completeness of her trust, as she understood the intensity of his promise not to take her.

He was a man of honor. Honor was the very core of his pride and strength. Honor was what had made him the man he was.

"Yes," Amber whispered. "Free me."

Yet still Duncan hesitated.

"I promise I won't be too forward," Amber said, trying and failing to hide her smile.

The smile Duncan gave Amber then was the one that called meadowlarks from a midnight sky.

"That would be very disappointing, sweet witch."

Slowly Duncan lowered his head to Amber's breasts, tantalizing her with the warmth of his breath while he teased her with silky touches of his mustache and tongue. His reward was a series of broken sighs and tiny sounds as she twisted against the cloth binding her elbows.

"You tempt me," Duncan said.

"And you torment me."

"A sweet torment?"

He cupped his hand around one of Amber's breasts, lifting and caressing, testing the tight peak.

"Aye," she said. "Very sweet."

"Not as sweet as these pink buds."

Amber drew her breath in swiftly. She could feel the passion sweeping through Duncan in hot pulses as he looked at his fingers on her breasts.

"Nor as sweet as making you moan beneath my mouth," Duncan added, bending down to Amber once more.

"My arms," she said.

And it was all Amber could say, for Duncan's powerful forearm was beneath her shoulder blades, arching her back, and his mouth was on her naked breasts. With a ragged sound of pleasure, she gave herself to his caresses, hiding nothing of her own response.

It wasn't until Duncan lifted his head that Amber realized he had unfastened her clothes completely. He sat up and pulled the long sleeves down over her wrists one at a time. Then he eased her clothing farther down her body, revealing more creamy skin and the long, inward curving lines of her torso.

Though Duncan wanted to keep undressing Amber more than he wanted air itself, he forced his hands to stop at her waist. He kneaded her resilient flesh lightly, hungrily.

It wasn't enough for either of them. With a quick, graceful movement, Amber sat up. The rush of cool air made her shiver. Instinctively she shrugged the folds of her mantle forward, covering her shoulders even as she reached for the laces at the front of Duncan's shirt.

"Be as I am," Amber said, pulling laces free. "Naked but for the mantle."

"And if I take chill?" he asked, smiling slightly.

"Why, I will warm you, of course."

Duncan's smile widened. He threw off his mantle. His shirt soon followed. With a slow care that was both torment and pleasure, Amber drew the mantle back around Duncan's shoulders and fastened it at the side.

The amber talisman he wore shimmered with an uncanny light, as though infused with Duncan's own immense vitality. Amber bent her head and brushed her lips over the ancient talisman in silent greeting.

Only then did she give in to the temptation that haunted her, running her fingers through the cloud of dark hair on his chest. Eyes closed, smiling, kneading him as a contented cat would, she tested the muscular flesh of Duncan's torso with fingernails like delicate, unsheathed claws.

"I love the feel of you," Amber said softly. "When you slept so unnaturally, I spent many hours rubbing oil of amber into your skin to keep away fever."

"Did it work?"

"Of course. Amber is noted for its ability to take fire from a body."

"It wouldn't work on me now," Duncan said.

"Why not?"

"Your hands bring me fever."

Amber didn't doubt it. She could feel the passionate heat radiating from Duncan's body.

And if that wasn't enough, she had the truth of his words pouring into her through the medium of touch.

" 'Tis like bathing in a magical fire," she whispered.

"What is?"

"Touching you. Feeling your passion."

The smile Duncan gave Amber was rather fierce, but she didn't care. She felt the truth of him, and that truth was his restraint. He had given his vow, and he was a man who would die before he was forsworn.

"But I must confess something to you," she whispered.

"Why? Do I look like a priest?"

Amber laughed. "Nay. You look like what you are, a warrior both fierce and sensual."

"Then why confess to me?"

"Because I only now realized that I smoothed oil over you long after the danger of fever was past."

Duncan's breath caught. "Did you?"

"Yes," she admitted.

"Why?"

"For the forbidden pleasure of touching you."

One of Amber's fingertips brushed over a male nipple. The sudden surge of pleasure that went through Duncan was as clear to her as a cry. Her fingers returned, lingered, and teased with a skill far beyond her experience, for his response was her unfailing sensual guide.

"But touching me isn't forbidden now?" Duncan asked almost roughly.

"No. 'Tis foolish," Amber whispered, "but not forbidden."

"Why not?"

She bent her head and kissed first one, then the other, nipple. When she drew her tongue slowly over him, his whole body tightened with a pleasure that was nearly violent.

"Because you promised that I would be safe here with you," Amber whispered.

"Today," he said, doubting he would ever be able to withstand such temptation again.

"Yes, today, now," she said, "in this place where ancient stones watch over the sea."

Duncan framed Amber's face with his hands, then took her mouth with a hunger that was like nothing he had ever felt before. The kiss was deep and powerful, urgent with the rhythms of the joining that he would not permit, for he had given his vow.

Amber yielded her mouth and took his at the same time, glorying in the heat and strength of the man holding her. The pricking of her nails against his skin made him groan with pleasure. Hearing his passion, feeling it, tasting it, Amber raked slowly over his muscular back again.

"You will make me wild," Duncan said against her mouth.

"I feel wild," she admitted, "but 'tis your doing."

He bit her lower lip with savage care.

"How wild do you feel?" he asked. "Enough to be naked to my hands and eyes? Enough to let me caress you in new ways?"

The violence of the hunger that went through Duncan as he spoke told Amber that he wanted her to say yes so much that he was shaking with it.

Knowing that, touching him, trusting him, it was impossible for her to say no.

"Yes," Amber whispered.

Duncan's arms tightened until she could barely breathe. Slowly he pressed her back until she lay once more on the ground. Her mantle fell away, revealing the pale curves and pink buds drawn tight by his mouth.

"Lift your hips."

Duncan's voice was hardly recognizable. The anticipation pouring through him as he looked at Amber's half-nude body was so great that it almost overwhelmed her. She could barely breathe, much less move.

Amber didn't know what Duncan was going to do next. She knew only that waiting for it was piling fresh fuel on the wildfire of his passion.

"Duncan?" Amber whispered.

"Lift yourself," he said. "Let me see the flower whose heart I foolishly vowed I would not take. Today."

Trembling with conflicting emotions, Amber did as Duncan asked. As her hips lifted, clothes slid down her body, urged by his strong hands. When he was finished she was naked but for the mantle at her back and the bright stockings on her legs. The feeling was both shocking and erotic.

"You are beautiful beyond words," Duncan said hoarsely.

He was no longer touching Amber, leaving her suddenly vulnerable to her own innate shyness and unease. With a muffled cry she reached beneath herself and jerked a corner of the mantle over her hips. When he moved to pull the mantle aside, she resisted.

"Don't be shy," Duncan said. "You are more beautiful than any flower in a sultan's garden."

As he spoke, his hand slid beneath the mantle.

The instant Duncan touched Amber, his desire arced through her. It was like being ravished by lightning both gentle and fierce.

Fingers spread wide, he put his palm low on her body and spanned her pelvic girdle with a hand that trembled very slightly from passion and restraint. Then his hand turned and his smallest finger eased through the silky warmth of her hair to find even warmer, silkier flesh beneath.

The unexpected caress sent a cascade of heat through Amber. The ragged sound of her breath breaking made Duncan smile. Seeing the centers of her eyes darken and expand in passionate response made blood pool even more hotly between his thighs until his hardened flesh leaped with every beat of his heart.

Feeling the tight, sultry petals brushing against his finger tempted him mercilessly. With every breath he took he regretted the vow he had given.

Duncan's hand shifted again. Tenderly, insistently, watching Amber's eyes, he caressed her.

"Duncan," she said. "What—"

Then Amber could say no more. He had discovered the sleek, sensual knot concealed within her closed petals. A sound of surprise was dragged from her as golden pleasure pulsed.

As though Duncan felt Amber's pleasure as clearly as she did, he groaned. His finger teased the bud again, calling forth another shimmering pulse, then another. Each time he caressed her, the shivering, sultry heat of her response licked over his fingers.

Yet when he tried to slide his fingers between her sleek petals, her legs were too tightly held.

"I won't force you," Duncan said in a low voice, "but I shall die if I can't at least touch you. Open your warm keep to me. I shall be a most gentle guest."

"I shouldn't. We shouldn't. It is too much to ask of you," Amber said. "To come so close and yet not take me . . ."

"Yes. Ask it. Please."

"But I'm afraid."

Duncan laughed softly as he rubbed over the bud once more, drawing another pulse of pleasure.

"Nay, golden witch. That isn't fear I feel licking over my fingertips. It's passion, hot and sweet and pure."

Fingers plucked and pleasure surged. Amber's hips lifted in unwitting response. His hand moved again. Sensual lightning stabbed. Another caress and another urgent movement, another fiery response.

"Dear God," Amber whispered.

Duncan wanted to shout his triumph as he stroked and another wave of pleasure swept visibly through Amber. With a broken sigh, she closed her eyes and yielded yet more of herself to him, hot petals opening to his touch.

By the time Duncan slid the mantle covering Amber aside, she no longer cared. All that mattered to her was that the sweet torment continue.

When his hand pressed against her legs, she gave him what he sought, opening herself so that he could touch her in any way he pleased.

Deliberately Duncan drew his fingertips over the petals that were slowly opening to him. He caressed Amber in a taut silence that was heightened by the rapid, broken sound of her breathing. She no longer sensed his leashed passion, for her own had become overwhelming.

Without warning, ecstasy burst, ravishing Amber's senses. Her shivering cry and the hot, helpless rush of her response told Duncan just how much she had enjoyed his caresses.

Despite the savage thrust of his own unanswered need, Duncan smiled. Even after the last tremors of pleasure no longer shook Amber, he was reluctant to leave off caressing the sultry flower he had so recently coaxed into opening.

But he knew he must stop.

If he kept caressing her, he might very well throw his vow to the sea winds and sink his hungry flesh into the place that was so fully prepared to receive him. With a difficulty that was in itself a warning, he forced himself to release the tender flower.

Yet even then, Duncan couldn't make himself retreat entirely. His hand remained between Amber's legs, close enough to feel her warmth, but not touching her.

Amber's eyes opened and she knew herself naked with Duncan's hand lying intimately between her legs. She flushed and reached for the mantle to cover herself once more.

"Nay," Duncan said thickly. "Don't hide. You are even more beautiful in full bloom than you were unopened."

As he spoke, his fingertip skimmed her still sensitized flesh. She cried out as the violence of his hunger and restraint poured through her, shaking her.

"It isn't enough!" Amber said. "You are in pain."

"Aye. And this," Duncan said, caressing her slowly with his fingertip, "is salt in the raw wound of my need."

With a harsh word he closed his eyes.

Into the silence came a rustle and murmur, a whispering of wind, grass, and the distant voice of winter. The sound increased until it grew greater than the rush of breath from Duncan's harshly restrained body.

A distant part of Amber's awareness registered the fey, growing sound, but she ignored it. Duncan was all of the world she cared about.

And she had hurt him without even knowing what she had done.

"Duncan," she said huskily.

When Amber's fingers touched his bare flesh, he flinched as though she had taken a whip to him.

"Nay," Duncan said in a raw voice. "Don't touch me."

"I want to ease you."

"Breaking my vow won't ease me."

Amber took a deep, shaken breath. What she was going to do was dangerous, two parts of the bleak prophecy fulfilled. Yet she could not endure Duncan's pain any longer, not when the means to banish it lay within her.

"I release you from your vow," Amber whispered.

Duncan surged to his feet.

"Don't tempt me, golden witch. I already wear the fragrance of your passion. 'Tis like breathing fire. I can't take much more."

The silence that followed Duncan's words was filled by distant rustles and murmurs and eerie cries that swelled until they were a breaking wave of sound pouring across the fen. Air whistled through thousands upon thousands of wings as skeins of wild geese spiraled down, their bodies dark against the falling sun, their voices calling in autumnal urgency, crying of untimely winter.

Death will surely flow.

Death will surely.

Flow.

Death will.

Surely.

Amber put her hands over her ears to stop the sounds of a terrible prophecy coming true.

9

ERIK waited for Duncan and Amber in a chair of riven oak whose seat was softened by a loose cushion. Despite luxurious wall hangings and a roaring fire in the central hearth, the great hall of Sea Home's manor house was cold. Each time a violent gust of wind forced icy air through chinks in the manor's thick timber walls, the tapestries stirred. Though the carved wooden screens were placed so as to turn the drafts from the manor's main door, torch flames leaped and wavered when the door opened, as it just had.

The flames of the central fire bent and whipped in the draft. Their dance was reflected many times over in the eyes of the rough-coated wolfhounds that lay at Erik's feet, in the peregrine's unflinching glare from the perch behind the oak chair, in Erik's own eyes . . . and in the ancient silver dagger that he was turning slowly in his hands.

A door bar thumped home as the main door was shut once more. Moments later the leaping flames shrank to their accustomed size. Sounds of hurrying footsteps accompanied the low urging of Alfred's voice as Erik's knight approached the great hall.

Without a word, Erik stared at the three people who had barely beaten moonrise back to the keep. Egbert looked sheepish. Amber appeared flushed

141

with more than the cold wind that had sprung up. Duncan looked like what Amber had named him— a dark warrior.

In the silence that stretched and stretched, Erik watched the three people, ignoring Alfred entirely. In defiance of Erik's usual good manners, he invited no one to sit on the chairs that had been dragged close to the fire for warmth and ease.

It was very clear to Amber that Erik was holding on to his temper by a bare thread.

"You seem to have brought winter with you," he said.

Despite Erik's nearly tangible anger, his tone was mild. The contrast between his voice and the dagger gleaming wickedly in his hands was alarming.

"The geese," Amber said. "They have just come to Whispering Fen."

The news did nothing to soften Erik's expression. Yet his tone remained the same, calm to the point of flatness.

"Ahhhh. The geese," Erik murmured. "Cassandra will be pleased."

"By an early winter?" Duncan asked.

"It must be reassuring to have one's every thought turned to truth," Erik said without looking away from Amber, "while mere mortals must depend upon such slender reeds as trust and honor."

The blood left Amber's face. She had known Erik for her entire life, yet she had never seen him quite like this. She had seen him angry, yes, for he had a volatile temper. She had even seen him in a cold fury.

But never with her.

And never this cold.

"You may retire now, Alfred," Erik said.

"Thank you, lord."

Alfred vanished with the alacrity of a man fleeing demons.

"Egbert."

Erik's voice was like the flick of a whip. The boy jumped.

"Yes, lord?" he said hurriedly.

"As you slept the afternoon away, you will have guard duty tonight. Go to it. Now."

"Aye, lord!"

Egbert left with impressive speed.

"I believe," Erik said thoughtfully, "that I've never seen the boy move so quickly."

Amber made a sound that could have meant anything or nothing at all. She was still absorbing the fact that Erik knew Egbert had spent much of his time asleep.

She wondered if Erik also knew that she and Duncan had ridden off alone.

"He is frightened of you," Amber said.

"Then he is smarter than I guessed. Smarter than you, certainly."

Amber flinched.

Duncan took a step forward, only to stop when Amber grasped his wrist in an unspoken plea.

"How was your ride?" Erik asked silkily. "Chilly?"

"Not at first," Duncan said.

"The day was beautiful," Amber said quickly.

"And how was your special place, Learned maid? Was it beautiful, too?"

"How did you know?" she asked in a strained voice.

Erik's smile was that of a wolf just before it leaps.

Abruptly Duncan wished he were wearing a sword or carrying the hammer. But he had neither weapon. He had only the certainty that Erik, for all his moments of charm and laughter, could be a deadly enemy.

With careful movements, Duncan took off his mantle and draped it on a trestle table to dry.

"May I?" he asked, reaching for Amber's mantle.

"No. I—that is, I'm—"

"Afraid your laces aren't fully tied?" Erik finished gently.

She gave him a fearful look.

The expression that came over Erik's face didn't make Amber feel any more easy. He was in a savage humor.

"What, no protestations of innocence?" Erik asked in a soft voice. "No reassurances that you didn't leave Egbert sleeping in a field while two horses cropped grass nearby?"

"We—" Amber began, but Erik's voice overrode hers.

"No soft cries that honor hasn't been outraged and trust breached, along with your maidenhead? No blushes—"

"Nay, that's not—"

"—and stuttered little pleas that—"

"*Enough.*"

The flat promise of violence in Duncan's voice shocked Amber.

The hounds around Erik's chair came to their feet in a bristling, snarling rush. The peregrine's hooked beak opened in a shrill, savage cry. Unknowingly, Amber's nails dug into Duncan's wrist.

"Leave off harrying her," Duncan said, ignoring the threatening animals.

He opened his mouth to add that discussing Amber as though she were a virgin was ridiculous, and nobody knew it better than Duncan. But a look at Erik's feral, wolflike eyes convinced Duncan to be careful how he stated the truth.

"Amber's maidenhead is as intact now as it was this morning," Duncan said flatly. "You have my vow on that."

In a silence outlined by the leap of flames, Erik turned the dagger over and over in his hand while he studied the dark warrior who loomed in front of him, ready for battle.

Yea, even eager for it.

Abruptly Erik understood. He threw back his head and laughed like a tawny devil.

The hounds settled their ruffs, stretched, and sprawled at ease once more, yellow eyes reflecting fire. A sweet whistle from her master cooled the peregrine's ire.

When quiet had been restored, Erik gave Duncan a look of masculine sympathy.

"I believe you," he said.

Duncan nodded curtly.

"You don't have the relaxed air of a man who has spent the afternoon—and himself!—lying between a woman's soft legs," Erik added.

Duncan said something profane beneath his breath.

"Come to the fire, warrior," Erik said, struggling not to show the smile concealed within his beard. "You must be stiff as a sword with chill. Or is that the only part of you still warm?"

"Erik!" Amber said, embarrassed.

He looked at her bright cheeks and smiled with a combination of affection and amusement.

"Little Learned innocent," Erik said gently, "there isn't a man or woman in the keep who doesn't know where Duncan looks—and who looks back at him."

Amber put her hands to her hot cheeks.

" 'Tis a source of much betting among the men," Erik said.

"What is?" Amber asked faintly.

"Whether you or he will break first."

"It won't be Duncan."

Amber didn't understand how much the tartness in her voice had given away.

Erik understood immediately. So did Duncan. While Erik gave in to laughter, Duncan went to

Amber and hid her flaming face against his chest.

The contradictory currents Duncan's touch revealed—prowling hunger, rue, laughter—were oddly comforting to Amber. But nothing was as reassuring as knowing that Duncan again welcomed her touch.

He had all but turned himself inside out to avoid contact with her on the way back to Sea Home.

With a sigh, Amber leaned against Duncan. Silently she drank the heady wine of his presence, letting it drive out the cold that had come over her when she heard the geese descending.

"Touching," Erik said dryly. "Literally."

"Leave off," Duncan retorted.

"I suppose I must, but I haven't been quite this amused since you accused me of wanting Amber for myself."

Her head snapped up. She looked at Duncan, startled.

"You didn't," Amber said.

"Oh, but he did," Erik countered.

Amber made an odd sound.

"Are you laughing?" Erik asked.

"Ummm."

He frowned at her.

"Do you think it so unreasonable that a maid might be drawn to me?" Erik asked, offended.

"Nay," Amber said quickly.

Erik raised his eyebrows.

After a moment Amber lifted her head and looked at the dark warrior who held her quite gently.

"But," Amber added, " 'tis absurd to believe that this maid would ever allow any man to touch her, save one."

"Duncan," Erik said.

"Aye. Duncan."

"That is to be expected between a man and his betrothed," Erik said matter-of-factly.

As one, Duncan and Amber spun and stared at Erik.

"My betrothed?" Duncan asked carefully.

"Of course," Erik said. "We will announce it tomorrow. Or did you expect to seduce Amber with no thought to her honor—and mine?"

"I have told you," Duncan said. "Until my memory returns, I can't ask for Amber's hand."

"But you can take the rest of her, is that it?"

Duncan's face darkened.

"The people of the keep are whispering," Erik said. "Soon they will be talking openly about a foolish maid who lies with a man who has no intention of—"

"She has not—" Duncan began.

"Leave off," Erik snarled. "It will come as surely as sparks fly upward! The passion between the two of you is strong enough to taste. I've seen nothing like it in my life."

Silence was Duncan's only response.

"Do you deny this?" Erik challenged.

Duncan closed his eyes. "No."

Erik looked at Amber. "I needn't ask you about your feelings. You look like a gem lit from within. You burn."

"Is that such a terrible thing?" she asked painfully. "Should I be ashamed that I have finally found what every other woman takes for granted?"

"Lust," Erik said bluntly.

"Nay! The profound pleasure of touching someone and not feeling pain."

Shocked, Duncan looked at Amber. He started to ask what she meant, but she was talking again, her words urgent, driven by the tension that vibrated through her.

"Passion is part of it," Amber said. "But only part. There is peace as well. There is laughter. There is . . . joy."

"There is also prophecy," Erik shot back. "Do you remember it?"

"Better than you. I remember that prophecy said he *might* claim rather than he *will*."

"What are you talking about?" Duncan demanded.

"A woman's heart and body and soul," Erik said. "And the catastrophe that will—"

"*Might*," Amber interrupted fiercely.

"—come if she is foolish enough to give all three to a man with no name," Erik finished coldly.

"You make no sense," Duncan said.

Erik's smile was as savage as the yellow of his eyes.

"Have you remembered anything more of your past?" he asked Duncan bluntly.

"Nothing useful."

"Are you the best judge of that? You who have neither memory nor name?"

Duncan's mouth thinned and he said nothing at all.

"God's teeth," Erik hissed.

For a time there was a taut silence.

"What have you remembered, useful or not?" Erik asked Duncan.

"You heard before I fought Simon."

"Tell me again."

"Green eyes," Duncan said curtly. "A smile. The scent of spices and herbs. Hair the red of flames. A kiss and a wish for God to be with me."

Erik glanced quickly at Amber, who was still standing close to Duncan.

Touching him.

"Ah, yes," Erik said. "The Glendruid witch who cursed you."

"Nay," Duncan said instantly. "She didn't curse me."

"You sound very certain."

"I am."

"Amber?" Erik asked softly.

"He is telling you the truth."

Duncan smiled slightly as he smoothed a wisp of Amber's golden hair back from her face.

" 'Tis sweet to be championed by you," Duncan said, smiling down at Amber. "Your faith in my honesty is humbling."

"What she has is more certain than faith," Erik said flatly. "Scrying truth by touch is Amber's gift."

"And curse," she whispered.

"What do you mean?" Duncan asked.

"Just what I said," Erik retorted. "If I question a man while Amber touches him, the truth is clear to her no matter what lies he may speak aloud."

Duncan's eyes widened, then narrowed thoughtfully. "A useful gift."

"It is a sword with two edges," Amber said. "Touching people is . . . uncomfortable."

"Why?"

"Why does the moon shine less brightly than the sun?" she asked bitterly. "Why is the oak mightier than the birch? Why do geese cry out the coming of winter?"

"Why are you distressed?" Duncan countered, his voice gentle.

Amber looked away from him to the hounds gathered with eyes of fire around Erik's feet.

"Amber?" Duncan asked softly.

"I—I'm afraid you will be put off by my—by what I am."

He caressed Amber's cheek with the backs of his fingers, turning her face toward him again.

"I told you once that I had a penchant for witches," Duncan said. "Especially beautiful ones. You're touching me now. Have I told you true?"

Amber's breath caught as she looked into the smoldering hazel of Duncan's eyes.

"You believe what you are telling me," she whispered.

Duncan's smile made Amber's heart turn over with joy. He saw the change in her expression and bent down to her without realizing what he was doing.

"Erik is right," Duncan said. *"You burn."*

Erik came to his feet in a surge that scattered hounds left and right.

"It's a pity you don't remember your past," Erik said distinctly. "It will make life a foretaste of hell for Amber."

"For Amber?" Duncan said. "How so?"

"Do you think she will enjoy being your leman rather than your wife?"

"She isn't my leman."

"God's blood," Erik exploded, "do you think I'm as big a fool as you?"

"Erik, don't," Amber said urgently.

"Don't what? Tell the truth? Your dark warrior won't marry you until he remembers his past, and he can't keep his hands off you longer than it takes to swallow. You'll be his whore before the first snow falls!"

Abruptly Duncan dropped his hands to his side.

Erik saw and laughed harshly.

"That's fine for now," he said in a scathing voice. "But the next time she offers herself, can you promise you won't take what she is so willing to give?"

Duncan opened his mouth to promise, but knew before the first word was spoken that he would be forsworn. Amber was a fire in his flesh, in his blood, in his very bones.

"If I take Amber's *maidenhead*," Duncan said tightly, "I will marry her."

"With or without your memory?" Erik demanded.

"Aye."

Erik sat back in his chair and smiled in the manner of a wolf that has just harried its prey into a trap.

"I will hold you to your vow," Erik said softly.

Amber let out a long breath and relaxed for the

first time since she had seen the feral blaze of Erik's eyes.

Then Erik fixed his gaze on Amber and she wondered if perhaps she hadn't relaxed too soon.

"This Glendruid witch . . ." Erik said musingly.

Breath held, Amber waited. She had wondered when Erik would connect Glendruid with Dominic le Sabre.

And what he would do when he did.

"Do we have one like her among the Learned of the Disputed Lands?" Erik asked.

With an effort, Amber managed not to show her relief.

"Like her?" she asked. "In what way?"

"Red hair. Green eyes. A woman whose gift would tell her to send Duncan out with an amber talisman around his neck."

"I know of no one like that."

"Nor does Cassandra," Erik said.

"Then no such woman lives among the Learned of the Disputed Lands."

Thoughtfully Erik tested the edge of the silver dagger with his thumb. The runes inscribed on the blade rippled with each motion as though alive, restless.

"Cassandra's prophecy at your birth is well known in the Disputed Lands," Erik said.

"Yes," Amber said.

Duncan looked at her in silent question.

She didn't glance away from Erik. For the moment, she was focused entirely on the golden knight who had pulled his Learning about him like a cloak of fire, giving him a power that transcended even his position as Lord Robert's heir.

"Your affinity for amber is also well known," Erik said.

Amber nodded.

"Glendruid's gift is that their women see into a man's soul," he continued.

As Erik spoke, he looked at Duncan as though for confirmation.

"Aye," said Duncan. "They are known for that very thing."

"Indeed," Erik murmured. "Where did you learn this?"

" 'Tis well known."

"Where you came from, perhaps. But not here." Erik's dark gold glance flicked back to Amber.

"So tell me," he said softly, "who among the Learned of the Disputed Lands has Glendruid's gift of seeing into a man's soul?"

"I do, in a small way."

"Yes, but you didn't give Duncan that amber talisman to wear, did you?"

"No," Amber said softly.

"A Glendruid witch did," Erik said, looking to Duncan again.

Duncan nodded his head.

Erik flipped the dagger casually, sending the silver blade end over end into the air, then catching the haft with a deft movement before sending the dagger into the air again.

Amber barely concealed a shiver. Like the sun after a winter ice storm, Erik burned.

Coldly.

"Where did you find this Glendruid witch you spoke of?" Erik asked Duncan.

"I don't remember."

"The Scots and Saxons are said to have a few such women," Amber said quickly.

The knife spun with lazy grace before Erik plucked it out of the air with a speed that made Duncan blink.

"Simon," Duncan said before thinking.

"What?" asked Erik.

"I believe you are as quick as Simon."

Erik's golden eyes became hooded. He slid the dagger into its sheath with careless skill.

"That won't be put to the test," he said softly. "Simon has left us."

"But why?" asked Duncan, surprised.

"Simon told Alfred that he felt he must resume his quest. He left immediately."

Absently Duncan rubbed his body, remembering Simon's blow.

"Despite my aching ribs," he said, "I liked the man."

"Aye," agreed Erik. "It was almost as though you knew one another."

A chill went over Amber that had nothing to do with the drafts in the room.

"He looked familiar to me," Duncan admitted.

"Is he?"

"If he is, I have no memory of it."

"Amber."

Though Erik said no more, Amber knew what he wanted. She laid her fingers on Duncan's wrist.

"Was Simon known to you?" Erik asked Duncan.

Angrily, Duncan looked from Amber's hand to Erik.

"You question my word?" Duncan asked savagely.

"I question your *memory*," Erik answered. "An understandable precaution, surely?"

Duncan let out a long, hissing breath. "Aye. That is understandable."

"And?" Erik prompted gently.

Amber winced. She knew Erik was at his most dangerous when he appeared most gentle.

"When I first saw Simon," Duncan said, "I sensed danger like the shadow of a hawk."

Swiftly Amber drew in her breath.

"In my mind I heard voices chanting and saw candles," Duncan continued.

"Church?" Erik asked.

But it was Amber he asked, not Duncan.

"Yes," she said. "It has the feel of church."

"What else do you sense?" Erik asked curiously.

"Duncan's memories stir, but not strongly enough to win free of the shades of darkness."

"Interesting. What else?"

Amber glanced sideways at Duncan. He was watching her with an expression of growing disbelief.

"Think of the church, dark warrior," she said.

The taut line of Duncan's mouth was his only answer. Amber took in a ragged breath.

"I gather that whatever happened in the church was a special occasion rather than an ordinary mass," she said faintly.

"Funeral? Wedding? Baptism?" Erik prodded.

Amber simply shook her head. "He doesn't know."

Duncan gave Amber a long look.

Subtle tension overtook her, drawing her mouth into a taut line.

"What is it?" Erik asked.

"Duncan resents me," Amber said.

"Quite understandable," Erik said in a dry voice. "I don't hold it against him."

"But he holds it against me. It is like grasping nettles," Amber whispered. "May I release him?"

"Soon. Until then," Erik said, switching his glance to Duncan, "you might consider that Amber is your best hope of piercing the darkness of your past."

"How so?" Duncan asked coldly.

"I should think it would be obvious," Erik retorted. "Apparently she can sense things in your thoughts that you miss."

"Is that true?" Duncan asked Amber.

"With you, yes. With others, never."

Duncan looked down at Amber. The unhappiness in her expression told him that she disliked the process of questioning him through touch as much as he did.

"Why am I different?" he asked. "Because I have no memory?"

"I don't know. I know only that we're joined in ways I don't understand."

For a long moment Duncan simply looked at Amber. Then his breath sighed out. He picked up her fingers and gave them a kiss. Holding her hand between his own, he began speaking softly.

"When I first saw Simon, I sensed danger, voices chanting, candles," Duncan said. "Then I remembered the feel of a cold knife blade between my thighs."

Amber made a shocked sound.

"Not a comfortable memory," Erik said, smiling thinly.

"Aye."

Duncan's voice was as sardonic as Erik's smile.

"Go on," said Erik.

"There's little more to it," Duncan said, shrugging. "I remember a man watching me with eyes as dark as midnight in hell."

"Simon," Erik said.

"At first I thought so. But now . . ." Duncan sighed.

"Amber?" Erik asked.

"Why did you decide it wasn't Simon?" she asked Duncan.

"Because he didn't recognize me. If I had held a blade between a man's thighs, I would certainly recognize him and know the reason for our enmity."

Amber stiffened.

"What is it?" Erik asked softly.

"The church," Amber said. "It was a wedding."

"You're certain?" Duncan and Erik asked as one.

"Aye. The feel of an embroidered shoe—" she began.

"In my hand! Yes!" Duncan interrupted triumphantly. "Her shoe was silver, as delicate as frost! I remember it!"

Tears stood in Amber's eyes, then slipped sound-lessly down her cheeks.

"Is there anything else, Amber?" Erik asked.

His voice was truly gentle this time, for he had seen her tears and guessed the reason why.

Abruptly Duncan realized that he was holding very tightly to Amber's fingers.

"Did I hurt you?" he asked.

Amber shook her head but would not meet Duncan's eyes. Long fingers tilted her face up to his with a strength that would not be denied.

"Precious Amber," Duncan said. "Why do you cry?"

Her lips parted but no words came out. Her throat was too filled with tears for her to speak.

"Is it something in my memories you see that I don't?" he asked.

Amber shook her head and tried to pull away from Duncan. His hands tightened, holding her.

"Is it—" he began.

"Leave off," Erik interrupted curtly. "Release her from your touch. Let her find what peace she can."

Duncan looked beyond Amber to the man whose eyes were like those of his wolfhounds, gleaming with reflected fire.

"What's wrong?" Duncan demanded. "Is it a Learned matter? Is that why she won't tell me?"

"Would that it were," Erik muttered. "Learned matters respond to intelligence. Matters of the heart do not."

"Talk sense!"

" 'Tis quite simple," Erik said. "You stood in church with a woman's shoe in your hand."

"What has that to do with Amber's tears?" Duncan asked in exasperation.

"She has given her heart to a man who is already married. Surely that is cause for tears?"

At first Duncan didn't understand. When he did, he gathered Amber into his arms and laughed. After an instant, so did she, sensing the truth that Duncan had just discovered.

"I was giving the shoe to another man, not taking it from him," Duncan said. "It was he who married the shoe's owner, not I!"

The wolfhounds came to their feet, threw back their heads, and howled with an elemental triumph.

Duncan stared at the hounds, wondering what possessed them.

Amber stared at Erik, wondering why he felt a triumph so great that his hounds cried it to the night.

10

"YOU sent them alone to the sacred Stone Ring?" Cassandra asked, horrified.

"Yes," Erik said. "Duncan wants to find his memory before he finds himself lying between Amber's legs. I would rather the reverse were true."

"You take too much upon yourself!"

"As you taught me," Erik said softly, "without risk there is no gain."

"This isn't risk. This is madness!"

Erik turned away from Cassandra and looked out over Hidden Lake and its wild fens where myriad waterfowl glided and fed. A lid of clouds concealed the highest reaches of the fells. Below the clouds, the glen was tawny and black, evergreen and bronze, a painted bowl waiting to be filled with winter.

Though Erik couldn't see the top of Stormhold, he knew that the high peak would soon be veiled with glittering snow. The geese and Cassandra had been right. Winter was bearing down on them, wearing a cloak of icy wind.

The peregrine on Erik's wrist moved uneasily, disturbed by the currents of emotion seething beneath the man's calm surface. Warily Cassandra eyed the falcon, knowing that only his wolfhounds were more sensitive to Erik's emotions.

"This 'madness,' as you call it," he said quietly, "is my best chance of keeping the southern estates until I can find more good knights to take service with me."

"Your father has many other holdings," Cassandra countered. "Tend them instead."

"What are you suggesting, Learned? That I cede Stone Ring Keep to Dominic le Sabre without a battle?"

"Yes."

The peregrine flared its wings and uttered a sharp cry.

"What of Sea Home?" Erik asked gently. "Shall I give that to the Norman bastard as well? And Winterlance?"

"There is no need. Stone Ring was the only keep mentioned by the English king—and agreed to by the Scottish king, I might add."

"For the moment, yes."

"The moment is all we have."

The falcon shifted restlessly against the leather gauntlet Erik wore. Wind tugged Erik's rich bronze mantle, sending cloth swirling, revealing the indigo wool tunic he wore beneath. The pommel of his sword gleamed like silver lightning.

"If I hand over Sea Home like a woman's shoe at a marriage ceremony," Erik said finally, "then every outlaw in the Disputed Lands will descend in hope of spoils."

Cassandra shook her head. "I've had no vision of such a thing."

"Nor will you," Erik retorted. "I will fight to the last drop of blood before I hand Stone Ring Keep over to Dominic le Sabre!"

Unhappily Cassandra looked down at her hands, which were all but hidden by long, full scarlet sleeves. Rich embroidery in blue and green glistened like water threading through fire.

"I have dreamed," she said simply.

Impatience showed in Erik's glance.

"Of what?" he asked in curt tones. "Battles and blood and keeps falling stone by stone?"

"Nay."

Erik waited.

Cassandra looked at her long, carefully tended fingers. A large ring set with three gems shone as brightly as the embroidery. Sapphire for water. Emerald for living things. Ruby for blood.

"Tell me," Erik commanded.

"A red bud. A green island. A blue lake. Together as one. And in the distance, a potent storm waiting."

The peregrine opened its beak as though the day were too hot rather than decidedly chill. Absently Erik soothed the bird without taking his eyes from Cassandra's ageless face.

"The storm swirled out and touched the red bud," she said. "It bloomed with great beauty . . . *but it bloomed within the storm.*"

Erik's eyes narrowed.

"The green island was next to be touched," Cassandra said. "The storm surrounded it, caressed it, possessed it."

Tawny eyebrows lifted, but Erik said nothing. He simply continued stroking the restless falcon with slow, calming sweeps of his hand.

"Only the deep blue water of the lake remained untouched," Cassandra said. "But it yearned toward the storm, where the flower bloomed in scarlet riches and the island glowed in shades of green."

The wind flexed, tugging at Erik's mantle and the long red folds of Cassandra's clothes. The falcon whistled and resettled its wings, watching the sky with hungry eyes.

"Is that all?" Erik asked.

"Is that not enough?" Cassandra retorted. "Where the heart and body go, the soul will soon follow.

Then rich life might come, but death certainly will flow!"

"The amber prophecy," Erik said beneath his breath. "Always that cursed prophecy."

"You should have left Duncan to die in the Stone Ring."

"Then the bud would never have bloomed and the island would never have glowed in shades of green. Of *life*."

"But that's not—"

"Your dream describes rich life, not death," Erik continued ruthlessly. "Is that not worth a few risks?"

"You are risking catastrophe."

"Nay," Erik said savagely. "Catastrophe is already upon me! My father is so tangled in clan rivalries that he refuses to spare warriors for his outlying estates."

"It was ever thus."

"I must have warriors," Erik said. "Powerful warriors. Duncan is such a man. With him I can hold Stone Ring Keep. Without him, it is lost."

"Then let it go, and Duncan with it!"

"Whoever holds those estates holds the key to the Disputed Lands."

"But—"

"Whoever holds the Disputed Lands," Erik continued without pause, "holds a sword at the throat of the northern lords from here to Dun Eideann's stony knobs."

"I have dreamed of no such war."

"Excellent," Erik said softly. "That means great risk will indeed be rewarded by great gain."

"Or great death," Cassandra retorted.

"It takes no prophetic gift to see death. 'Tis the common end of living things."

"Stubborn lordling," she said angrily. "Why can't you see the danger of what you're doing?"

"For the same reason that you can't see the danger of doing nothing!"

With a muscular thrust of his arm, Erik launched the falcon. Her painted jesses gleamed and her elegant wings beat rapidly. She mounted the wind with breathtaking ease, riding the wild, transparent beast higher and higher into the sky.

"If I do nothing," Erik said, "I will surely lose Stone Ring Keep. If I lose Stone Ring Keep, Sea Home becomes as exposed and naked as a newly hatched chick."

Silently Cassandra watched the peregrine.

"Winterlance will be little better off," Erik continued relentlessly. "What the outlaws don't seize, my cousins or the Norsemen will take. Do you deny this?"

Cassandra let out a sigh. "No."

"A weapon has been given to me."

"Double-edged."

"Aye. The weapon requires careful handling. But better it be in my hands than in Dominic le Sabre's."

"Better you had left Duncan to die."

"Hindsight or prophecy?" Erik asked sardonically.

Cassandra said nothing.

"He wore an amber talisman and slept at the foot of the sacred rowan," Erik said after a moment. "Would *you* have left him to die?"

Again Cassandra sighed. "No."

Erik narrowed his eyes against the brilliant silver of a cloud-chasm where the sun threatened to burn through. The peregrine was well up into the sky, scouting the marshy edges of the lake with matchless eyes, questing for waterfowl.

"But what if he remembers before he marries?" Cassandra asked quietly.

"That isn't likely. The storm is as hungry for the possession as the bud, the island, and the lake put together. He will have her before the week is out."

Scarlet sleeves whipped in a burst of wind, revealing Cassandra's tightly clenched hands.

"It won't be rape," Erik said. "In Duncan's presence, Amber burns as though lit from within."

For a time the only sound that came was the muted rattle of marsh grasses combed by the wind.

"But if Duncan remembers first?" Cassandra repeated.

"Then he will try his strength against my quickness. And he will lose, as he lost to Simon. But with a difference."

"Duncan will die."

Erik nodded slowly. "It is the only defeat he would accept."

"What, then, of Amber?"

A falcon's wild, mournful cry keened through the wind, answering Cassandra before Erik could. She turned, saw his face, and knew why the falcon had screamed.

Cassandra's eyes closed. For long moments she listened to the inner silence that spoke most clearly of crossroads and coming storms.

"There is another possibility," she said.

"Aye. My own death. Having seen how Duncan fared against Simon, I don't hold it likely."

"Would that I had met this Simon," Cassandra said. "Any man who could defeat Duncan easily would be a warrior worth knowing."

"It wasn't an easy victory. Despite Simon's catlike speed, Duncan nearly caught him twice."

Cassandra's eyes darkened, but she said nothing.

Erik drew his bronze mantle more closely around his shoulders. Through long habit, he made certain that the folds of cloth didn't foul the sword he wore along his left side.

"If truth be known," Erik said, smiling slightly, "I'm hoping not to face Duncan over drawn swords. He can be devilish quick for a man his size."

"You're hardly smaller. Nor was Simon."

Erik said nothing.

"If you die on Duncan's sword, you won't go into the darkness alone," Cassandra said softly. "I will send Duncan after you with my own hands."

Startled, Erik looked at the serene face of the woman he thought he knew.

"Nay," he said. "That would bring a war Lord Robert couldn't win."

"So be it. It was Lord Robert's arrogance that caused much of what might come. He is overdue to sleep on a bed of thorns and regrets."

"He wanted only what all men want. A male heir to hold his lands undivided."

"Aye. And he would have set aside my sister to achieve it."

For a moment Erik was too surprised to speak.

"Your *sister*?" he asked.

"Aye. Emma the Barren."

"Why wasn't I told?"

"That I'm your aunt?" Cassandra said.

Erik nodded curtly.

"It was part of the bargain Emma and I struck," she said. "Lord Robert fears the Learned."

Erik wasn't surprised. The breach with his father that had come over Erik's pursuit of Learning had never been healed.

"Once Emma married Robert," Cassandra said, "he barred me from her presence. He lifted the ban only once, when she came to me as Emma the Barren."

"And went home to conceive soon after," Erik said dryly.

"Yes." Cassandra's smile was as chilly as the day. "It was my great pleasure to give Robert the Ignorant a Learned sorcerer for a son and heir."

The smile changed as Cassandra looked at Erik, permitting herself to show the love she always felt and rarely revealed.

"Emma is dead," she said quietly. "I owe nothing to Robert but my contempt. If you die at Duncan's hands, I will declare a blood feud."

For once Erik didn't know what to say. Of all the patterns and possibilities he had foreseen, this hadn't been one.

Wordlessly he opened his arms to the woman who had been his mother in spirit if not in flesh. Cassandra returned the hug without hesitation, savoring the strength and vitality of the man whose birth wouldn't have been possible without her Learned intervention.

"I would prefer a different monument to my passing than the beginning of a war only my enemy can win," Erik said after a few moments.

"Then examine your enemy with an eye to future good. Dominic le Sabre might make a better ally than your cousins do."

"Satan himself would make a better ally than my cousins."

"Aye," Cassandra said ironically. "It is a thing to think upon, is it not?"

Erik gave a crack of laughter and released Cassandra.

"You never give up," he said, smiling, "yet you call me stubborn."

"You are."

"I am merely following my gift."

"Stubbornness?" she asked dryly.

"Insight," he retorted. "I see the means to success where others see only the certainty of failure."

Cassandra touched Erik's forehead with her fingertips as she looked into his clear, tawny eyes.

"I pray that clarity rather than arrogance will be your guiding star," she whispered.

DISTANT thunder rumbled over Duncan and Amber as they rode their horses toward Stone Ring and the sacred, unblooming rowan. Uneasily Duncan turned toward the grumbling sound and wondered if the storm would break near or far away.

The clouds that had formed a lid over the fells were flowing lower and lower, dragging a thick mist with them. Yet it wasn't the damp weather that prickled coolly down Duncan's spine. He sensed the possibility of danger, yet all about him seemed safe.

Absently he checked that the hammer he had taken from the armory lay ready to hand.

"Stormhold," Amber said.

Duncan turned toward her quickly. "What?"

" 'Tis just Stormhold purring like a great, contented cat now that winter is on the way."

"Then you think the fells love the storms?" he asked.

"I think they were born for one another. The storms reach their greatest glory in the fells. The fells are never more magnificent than in the fierce grasp of a storm."

"Dangerous, too," Duncan muttered.

The whisper of peril came again to him. Again he looked around, but saw nothing moving except the silent, sweeping veils of mist.

"Danger whets beauty," Amber said.

"Does peace dull it, then?"

"Peace renews beauty."

"Is that part of your Learned teachings?" Duncan asked dryly.

" 'Tis part of common sense, and well you know it," she retorted, rising to the bait.

Duncan laughed, enjoying Amber's quickness even though it made him ache to touch her again. Despite his hunger, he made no move to reach for her. He wasn't certain why she had carefully avoided touching him since Whispering Fen, but he was certain that she had.

Smiling, Amber turned her face to the wild, seething sky. Against the violet folds of her cowl and mantle, her skin had the glow of a fine pearl. The deep rose of the mantle's lining was repeated in her lips. When the cowl fell back, it revealed the circlet of silver and amber holding her loosely braided hair.

Gems of amber were everywhere on her. Bracelets of clear, golden pieces of amber circled her wrists, gleaming with every movement she made. The silver dagger at her waist was set with a single red amber eye. The hand-sized silver pin that fastened her cloak was set with translucent amber gems in the shape of a phoenix, symbol of death and rebirth through fire. A necklace of amber pieces hung around her neck, as did the pendant in whose golden depths Amber could sometimes see shadows of the past.

Yet as Duncan watched her, it wasn't the fortune in costly gems he saw. He saw the thick fringe of her eyelashes and the wild roses blooming in her cheeks. He ached to taste the chill of the wind on her skin, and then to drink the warmth behind her rosy lips.

He wished she were riding in front of him rather than on her own horse. If she were in front of him, he could gather her close, slide his hand into the opening of her mantle, and caress the soft warmth of her breasts. Then he would feel the softness change as her nipples tightened, pouting for the heat of his mouth.

Duncan's thoughts had an immediate effect on his body. The rushing, flooding heat and the hardening of his flesh was something he was becoming accustomed to around Amber. What he wasn't accustomed to was a small, quiet voice warning him that he must not take her.

It would be wrong.

Yet as soon as the thought came, Duncan disputed it.

She isn't betrothed. She isn't married. She isn't vir-

gin, despite Erik's protestations. She and I have known one another. I'm certain of it.

And she is willing.

What can be wrong with that?

Nothing answered Duncan's inner questioning except the stubborn silence of the darkness where memories lay beyond his reach.

Am I married? Is that what the cursed silence is trying to tell me?

No memory came, yet Duncan felt certain he was not married. He couldn't say why, but the feeling remained unshakable.

"Duncan?"

He turned toward the girl whose eyes were even more beautiful than the amber gems she wore.

"We are nearing the Stone Ring," Amber said. "Does the countryside look familiar to you?"

Amber reined in her horse at the top of a low rise. Duncan urged his horse alongside before he stopped and stood in the stirrups to get a better look at the land.

It was a glorious, hushed country of mist-wreathed trees, random outcroppings of stone, and steep-sided hills whose tops were lost in silvery cloud. A brook gleamed darkly among mossy rocks and fallen leaves, its voice hardly greater than that of the water drops slowly sliding from naked oak branches to the ground.

Anxiously, Amber waited, watching Duncan's face for the recognition she both feared and prayed would come.

The fear was for her own happiness.

The prayer was for Duncan's.

"It looks much like the trail to Ghost Glen," Duncan said finally. "Would that Whispering Fen lay beyond."

A small smile played beneath his dark mustache as he spoke. Color that had nothing to do with the cool day rose in Amber's cheeks. When Duncan saw her blush, his smile widened into a frankly sensual grin.

"Are you remembering what it was like to feel my mouth upon your breasts?" he asked.

The color in Amber's cheeks deepened.

"Or are you remembering the lush blooming of the flower?" Duncan asked.

Her breath hesitated.

Watching Amber, Duncan added softly, "I dream of the flower's sleek, hot petals and wake up in a fever."

Amber could no more conceal the sensual shiver that went through her body at Duncan's words than she could take the high color from her cheeks.

"Tell me you remember," Duncan coaxed in a low voice. "Tell me that I'm not alone in my fever."

"I'll die remembering," Amber said, her eyes half closed. "You gave me . . . Paradise."

The sensual catch in her voice sent a stroke of heat through Duncan's body.

"You delight and tempt me beyond endurance," he said huskily.

A sad smile curved Amber's lips.

"I don't mean to," she said. "I've tried not to, now that I know."

"Know what?"

"The power of what draws us together."

"Is that why you've avoided touching me as though I were somehow unclean?"

Amber gave Duncan a quick, sideways look. "I thought it would be easier for you that way."

"Is it easier for the falcon to have broken wings?"

"*Duncan*," she said, stricken. "I never meant to hurt you. I thought—I thought if I weren't always in your sight or within your reach, you would want me less."

"Do you want me less now than yesterday or the day before?"

Her eyes closed as she made a despairing sound.

"Amber?" Duncan pressed.

"I want you more, not less," she said in a low voice.

Duncan's smile flashed. Then he saw the tears slipping from beneath Amber's closed lashes and the smile vanished as though it had never been. He urged his horse closer to hers.

"Why do you cry?" he asked.

Slowly Amber shook her head. Warm, hard fingers tilted her chin up.

"Look at me, precious Amber."

A torrent of Duncan's emotions poured into Amber with his touch. Even as she drank them, she knew she must stop. The longer she knew Duncan, the more she understood what taking her would cost him.

His honor.

"Won't you tell me why you cry?" Duncan asked.

Amber's tears simply fell more rapidly as she sensed his concern.

"Do you feel I dishonored you with my touch?" he asked.

"Nay," she said.

The sound of Amber's voice was thinned by the restraint she had to exert to keep herself from fleeing Duncan.

Or from throwing herself into his arms.

"Are you afraid I will take you?" he asked.

"Yes," she whispered.

"Would giving me the Paradise within your body be such a terrible thing?"

"No."

Amber took a deep, aching breath and opened her eyes. Duncan was watching her with such tender concern that she longed to reassure him.

"For me it would not be a terrible thing," she said in a shaking voice. "For you . . . ah, dark warrior, for you I fear it would be the beginning of Hell rather than Paradise."

Duncan smiled. "Fear not. You will please me to the soles of my feet. I know it as surely as I know the hammering of my own blood at the thought."

The sound Amber made was half laugh, half cry of despair.

"And then what?" she asked. "What if I am the maiden you don't believe I am?"

"I will keep my vow."

"We will marry?"

"Aye," he said.

Amber took another deep breath. "And in time you will hate me."

At first Duncan thought she was teasing him. Then he realized she was not.

"Why would I hate the girl who is sweeter to me than I ever dreamed a woman could be?" he asked.

"Dark warrior," Amber whispered.

Her voice was so soft he could barely hear it, just as the brush of her lips over his hand was so light he could barely feel the caress.

"Tell me," Duncan coaxed, "what saddens you so?"

"I feel the restlessness in you," Amber said simply.

He smiled. "The cure for it lies within your warmth."

"For the prowling hunger, yes. For the part of you chained within shades of darkness, unsettled, troubled, hungering for a life that is no more . . . I have no cure for that."

"I will remember someday. I am certain of it."

"And if we are married before that day? What then?"

"Then you'll have to call your husband by another name in public," Duncan said, smiling, "but in the bedchamber I will remain your dark warrior and you will be my amber witch."

Amber's lips trembled in an attempt to smile.

"I think—I fear you would be my enemy if you remembered."

"And I think you are a girl who fears that I will force the gates of Paradise."

" 'Tis not—" Amber began.

Her words ended in a startled sound as Duncan lifted her from the saddle and settled her across his lap. Even through the thickness of her mantle, she felt the hard, blunt ridge of his desire pressing against her.

"Fear not," Duncan said. "I won't take you until you ask for it. Nay, until you beg for it! Bringing you to that pitch will be a sweet, agonizing delight."

Duncan's smile was both tender and hot with sensual anticipation. It made Amber's heart turn over with emotions she was afraid to name, much less to speak of aloud.

"I have neither family nor high station," she said desperately. "What if you have both?"

"Then I shall share them freely with my bride."

Hearing her dream spoken aloud did nothing to stem the hot glide of tears down Amber's cheeks.

Is it possible? Can Duncan come to love me enough to forgive me if his memory returns?

Can such a rich life come from such a dark beginning?

Duncan leaned forward and caught tears from Amber's eyelashes with tender kisses. Then he brushed his lips across hers in a kiss that was surprisingly chaste.

"You taste like a sea wind," he said. "Cool and faintly salt."

"You taste the same."

" 'Tis your tears on my lips. Will you let me taste your smile, too?"

Amber could no more help smiling than Duncan could keep from sealing his mouth over hers in a kiss that was as deeply seductive as his first kiss had been restrained. When he lifted his head, she was flushed, trembling, and her mouth followed his blindly.

"Aye, lass. That is how it will be. Your lips parted, full, flushed with hunger for me."

Duncan was bending down to Amber again when the outlaws struck from all sides.

$\mathcal{2}$ 🍀 11

THE men were armed with knives, wooden staffs, and a makeshift pike. Hampered by having Amber in his lap, Duncan wasn't able to fight effectively. Leaping and snarling like wolves, the outlaws dragged Duncan from the horse, and Amber with him.

When one of the outlaw's hands closed around Amber's arm while he clawed at her valuable necklaces, she gave a terrible cry. Part of her hoarse shout came from pain at being touched. Much of it came from pure rage that an outlaw would dare to take the sacred amber pendant from her neck.

The flash and slice of Amber's dagger drew an answering scream from the outlaw. He jerked his hands away from her, but only for a moment. She saw his fist coming and managed to turn aside as it struck. Despite her quickness, she was so dazed by the blow that she fell full-length on the ground.

The second time it was a dagger rather than a fist that the outlaw raised against Amber. Even as she gathered herself to turn aside from the attack, she heard the eerie steel moan of a war hammer slicing circles from the air. There was an awful crack as steel met flesh. The outlaw fell like a stone.

When his limp hand touched Amber, she felt nothing at all. The man was quite dead.

She jerked her hand back and began scrambling

to her feet. An unexpected shove kept her flat, but no pain came from the contact. It was Duncan's hand that had touched her.

"Nay!" he ordered, standing astride Amber. "Stay down!"

She needed no explanation of why the ground was safer for her at the moment. The hammer's deadly humming had begun once more.

Through a veil of her own hair, Amber watched outlaws surge forward again in a ragged charge, their staffs held like lances. Stout wood splintered as though it were charcoal. The single pike was destroyed. Another outlaw fell. He neither moved nor made a sound.

The heavy war hammer was a lethal steel blur circling Duncan's head. The remaining outlaws hesitated, then gathered themselves for another overwhelming rush such as they had used to drag Duncan and Amber to the ground.

With no warning, Duncan leaped forward. The hammer became a lightning bolt, striking in the blink of an eye. The outlaws yelled in outrage as another of their own fell and didn't rise again.

Duncan leaped back, standing astride Amber once more, protecting her in the only way he could.

"Get behind him," shouted one of the outlaws. "He won't leap so high-and-mighty with his hamstrings cut!"

Three outlaws broke from the pack and began moving to Duncan's rear, careful to remain beyond the deadly reach of the hammer. Duncan couldn't watch the circling outlaws and the men in front at the same time.

"Duncan, they will—" Amber began.

"I know," he interrupted roughly. "By all that's holy, *stay down!*"

Amber clenched the dagger in her hand and prepared to defend Duncan's back as best she could. The dagger's red eye glowed balefully as she shifted the blade, following the progress of the closest outlaw.

As the hammer wailed of coming death, Amber's voice rose in eerie consonance, cursing the outlaws in a language forgotten by all but a handful of Learned.

One of the outlaws stared at Amber in sudden horror, understanding too late whom he had dared to attack in his greed for wealth. He dropped the splintered end of his staff and ran.

The remaining outlaws paused in their ragged charge, but only for an instant. The men standing in front of Duncan feinted with staffs, seeking an opening in the deadly circle made by the hammer's swift, vicious flight. Other men moved well away from Duncan, angling toward his back.

Suddenly two men rushed in from the rear.

"Duncan!"

Even before Amber's cry left her lips, Duncan leaped and turned about in midair. So great was his strength and his skill with the hammer that the weapon's deadly hum never hesitated during his turn.

The hammer swept around in a savage arc, bringing death to the two outlaws who had thought that Duncan's back made a safe target. Before the other outlaws could take advantage of his turn, he had leaped and faced about to confront them again.

The hammer hummed once more its song of death, whipped in circles by Duncan's tireless arm.

His shocking skill with the weapon broke the outlaws' will. One of the men made a lunge for Whitefoot, but gave it up when the mare shied violently away. The remaining men turned and ran for the cover of the surrounding mist and forest, leaving their dead behind.

Duncan watched for the space of a few more breaths before he allowed the hammer to fall silent. A flip of his wrist slackened the chain. Instead of flying in deadly arcs, the hammer came obediently to rest. He slung it over his shoulder, balancing the weight of the ball in back with that of the chain in front. Should he need the weapon again, it would instantly be ready.

And deadly.

With shadowed golden eyes, Amber watched the man with no name who had come to her in shades of darkness ... and whose true name she had just discovered, her greatest fear come true.

Duncan of Maxwell, the Scots Hammer.

"Are you hurt?" Duncan asked. "Did those carrion eaters touch you?"

The caress of his fingers on Amber's pale cheek made her want to weep for all that could never be.

Soul mate and enemy in one.

Her beloved foe kneeling next to her, concern darkening his eyes while currents of warmth and pleasure coursed through her at his simple touch.

"Amber?"

The last frail reed of hope was splintering in front of her eyes. Though Duncan had shown traits of Learned schooling, and the Scots Hammer had never been Learned, she could hardly deny the deadly skill with which Duncan had wielded the hammer.

There could be no more doubt, no more denial, no hope of error, no excuse not to tell Erik that he had saved the life of his greatest enemy and brought that enemy to Amber.

Who had then betrayed Erik by keeping her deepest fears of Duncan's identity secret.

I can betray Erik no longer.

But how can I betray Duncan, my love, my enemy, the very blood in my veins ...

Powerful arms lifted Amber. Gentle lips brushed her cheeks, her eyes, her mouth. Each caress was a separate knife turning in her soul.

"I am . . . unhurt," Amber said raggedly.

"You're very pale. Have you never seen battle before now?"

She fought for breath, saying nothing.

"Dinna worry, precious Amber," Duncan whispered against her cheek.

Unable to speak, she simply shook her head.

"You aren't frightened, are you?" he asked. "I can protect you from worse than that worthless lot of outlaws and thieves. You know that, don't you?"

Amber laughed almost wildly. Then she turned her face into Duncan's chest and wept.

Duncan of Maxwell, the Scots Hammer. Aye, I know all too well that you can protect me.

From everything except the prophecy.

And from myself.

That most of all. How can you protect the heart from the very flesh surrounding it?

Soul mate.

Foe.

Lightning split the day from sky to ground. A savage peal of thunder came right behind.

"The horses," Amber said.

"Stay here," Duncan said, setting her down. "I'll get them."

As Duncan turned away, Amber saw a patch of red on his tunic.

"You're wounded!" she said.

He kept walking.

"Duncan!"

Heart beating frantically, Amber ran after him.

"Easy, lass," he said, catching her up in his arms. "You'll scare the horses."

"Put me down! You'll hurt yourself more!"

Duncan's smile flashed whitely beneath his mustache as he saw the concern in Amber's eyes. He set her on her feet, took a few quick steps, and grabbed Whitefoot's rein.

The mare minced nervously but didn't fight Duncan's hand. He turned, lifted Amber, and set her astride her mare in a single easy motion. Then he smiled up at her.

"Simon's blow hurt more than—" Duncan began.

"But you're bleeding," Amber interrupted.

"I've let more blood to a leech than to that outlaw's pig sticker."

Before Amber could say anything more, Duncan turned, caught up his own horse, and mounted it with muscular ease. His actions belied the red stain on his tunic.

"Which way to the Stone Ring?" he asked. "Yonder?"

Amber didn't even look which way Duncan was pointing. Her only thought was to get his wound cared for.

"The keep is that way," she said, pointing.

Lightning cracked and thunder shook the earth.

"The storm is that way, too," Duncan said. "Is there any shelter nearby?"

"Stone Ring has a mound at the center and a room inside."

"Lead us there."

For a moment longer Amber hesitated, watching the sky with uneasy eyes. The sense of imminence that she had often known in Ghost Glen or other sacred places was growing within her now.

Yet she wasn't standing within an ancient place where stones had been placed by hands long since dead.

"Amber? What is it? Don't you know the way?"

A dazzling bolt of lightning sliced through the day, brighter than a hundred suns. Thunder split the sky and rolled like an avalanche through the glen.

The hairs on Amber's nape stirred. The lightning

had struck near the path back to the keep, as though in warning against going back.

But we must go back! Duncan is hurt.

Another bolt lanced down, closer this time.

Amber felt herded, harried, prodded like an animal into the mouth of a funnel whose narrowing walls she could sense but not see. The feeling of imminence grew and grew in her until she felt she would burst.

"We must run for the keep!" Amber said, setting her heels to Whitefoot.

Lightning lanced down directly ahead. Whitefoot took the bit in her teeth and bolted in the opposite direction while thunder rolled behind.

At first Amber fought the horse for control. Then she gave in to the animal, accepting what she couldn't change. A glance over her shoulder told Amber that Duncan's mount was following at an equally frantic pace.

Stone Ring was upon them before there was any chance to turn aside or choose another path. Whitefoot raced between the outer ring of stones, not slowing until the inner ring was reached. There the horse calmed immediately, as though flight was suddenly the last thing on its mind.

Amber dismounted in a rush, picked up her skirts, and ran back to the outer ring. As she had feared, Duncan's mount had balked at the ragged outer circle of stones. He spurred the horse once, then again with greater force, but the animal only backed away more urgently.

"Wait!" Amber called. "He can't see the way!"

"What are you talking about?" Duncan shouted. "There's enough room between these stones to run five abreast!"

"Aye, but he can't see it!"

Cowl awry, hair disheveled, Amber ran to the outer ring. There she took the horse's bridle and spoke soothingly to it. When the animal was calmer,

Amber put one hand on the horse's muzzle and the other on the rein.

A gentle tug, a low word of encouragement, and the horse stepped forward. The mincing wariness of its gait told how little the animal liked the place. Ears flicked nervously in all directions until the inner ring was reached. Then the animal snorted and let down its guard, visibly at ease again.

Duncan looked around, wondering what the horse sensed that told it safety lay here.

"What did you mean that my horse couldn't see the way?" Duncan asked.

"Your mount has never been into the Stone Ring before," Amber explained.

"Why should that matter?"

"In order to enter sacred sites, Whitefoot had to learn to trust my guidance rather than her eyes in certain places."

"Such as the way to Ghost Glen?" Duncan asked.

Amber nodded. "But your horse hasn't learned to trust you in the same way. Nor has it ever been inside Stone Ring before, so it couldn't find the way by itself."

Thoughtfully, Duncan looked around the ancient ring. Like the horse's, Duncan's senses told him there was more to the place than his eyes could see.

And like the horse's, Duncan's inner sense of danger no longer stirred. Rather, it slept, as though certain of safety.

"Remarkable," Duncan said. "The place is enchanted."

"Nay. It is simply different. There is peace here, for those who can see through the stones."

"Learned."

"Once I would have said aye. But now . . ." Amber shrugged.

"What made you change your mind?"

"You."

"Maybe I was Learned in the time I don't remember," Duncan said.

Amber's smile was bittersweet. She knew that the Scots Hammer wasn't Learned.

"Maybe," she said quietly, "you are simply a man with an unused gift for Learning."

Duncan smiled slightly and began reconnoitering the haven that lay within Stone Ring while a wild storm broke over the trail they had just ridden.

The central mound of the Ring was fully thirty strides in length and half that in height. The mound itself had once been completely surfaced with a paving of stones. Time, storm, and sunshine had changed all that. Now the mound grew a veritable garden of plants both common and rare between widening cracks in the stone paving.

Other than the mound, the circle was much too open to suit Duncan. There was no place to hide, much less a place suited to defense. Though there was forest just a few yards away from the outer stones, the interior of the circle was like a meadow. Only one tree grew inside, and that tree was hardly sturdy enough to provide shelter from a storm.

Despite that, Duncan's eyes kept coming back to the tree. Graceful, elegant, the rowan stood like a dancer at the highest part of the mound.

"What is it?" Amber asked, seeing Duncan's stillness.

"That tree. I feel that I . . . know it."

"You may. Erik found you beneath the rowan."

Duncan turned and looked at Amber with eyes in which both shadows and memory stirred.

"It guarded me while I slept," Duncan said slowly. "I'm as sure of it as I am that you are standing there. *The rowan guarded me.*"

Duncan dismounted and strode up the mound toward the rowan. Fear squeezed Amber's heart. Not wanting to, knowing that she must, she followed him. By the time she caught up, he was already standing beneath the tree, fists on his hips, studying the rowan as though it might be either foe or friend.

"Are you remembering?" Amber asked quietly.

At first Duncan didn't answer. Then he slowly uncurled one fist and held his hand out to her.

"Am I remembering?" Duncan asked.

The instant Amber's hand rested in his, the complex emotions, dreams, fears, and hopes that were Duncan of Maxwell poured through the touch. Never had the contact been so vivid.

Exhilaration after the victorious battle.

Fear for Amber's safety in the coming storm.

Determination to remember the past.

Rage at whatever had taken his memory.

And then, when the warmth of her flesh registered on his, there came a wave of desire so great that it all but brought Amber to her knees. She could feel nothing but Duncan's passion for her, see nothing, sense nothing. He flooded her mind and body with a sensual hunger that was like nothing she had ever felt before.

Duncan.

Though Amber hadn't said the name aloud, he opened his eyes and looked at her with eyes that blazed.

Duncan's fingers circled Amber's wrist like steel bands. He pulled her closer with a force that would have been impossible to resist. Nor did she want to resist. She wanted only to answer the elemental need that cried out to her from every fiber of her dark warrior's being.

When Duncan's arms wrapped around Amber, she made no objection, even though he held her so tightly she became light-headed from lack of breath.

Though she said nothing, Duncan knew.

"I'll breathe for you," he said in a low voice.

He brought his mouth to hers in a kiss that would

have been harsh had she not been fighting to get even closer to him, to taste him more deeply, to get inside his very skin.

It was the same for Duncan, fighting to get closer to Amber, to feel yet more of her sweet flesh against his, to slake the savage hunger of his body for her in the only way possible.

Distantly Duncan realized that he had dragged Amber down to the ground and that her hands were struggling against him.

"Please," he said, "*I need you.*"

A sound that was neither aye nor nay came from Amber's throat. With an effort that left him shaking, Duncan managed to let go of her.

The instant Amber was free, she cried out as though at a blow. Duncan reached for her to comfort her, then realized he didn't trust himself.

"Duncan?" Amber said.

Her voice trembled, as did the hand she held out to him.

"You're a fire in my blood, in my flesh, in my soul," Duncan said savagely. "If I touch you again, I'll take you."

"Then touch me."

"Amber—"

"Take me."

For a long moment Duncan looked at the golden eyes and outstretched hand of the girl he wanted more than he wanted life itself.

Then he touched her, felt her burning, saw the wildfire of his own need blaze in her eyes.

Duncan's torrential male hunger poured over Amber in a river of fire. She was a spark caught in a whirlwind, recklessly burning, helplessly spiraling upward to an unknown destiny. With a woman's instinct, she sought Duncan's flesh both as haven and as fuel for an even greater fire.

Duncan pulled Amber close with a strength he could barely control. The feel and taste of her mouth

made him groan with redoubled need. His body
chained hers to the ground as his tongue shot
between her teeth, claiming her mouth in urgent,
elemental rhythms.

With a wildness that equaled Duncan's, Amber
fought to get closer to him, to ease the torment of
his arousal and her own, a suffering that was also a
savage pleasure. Her hands searched over his body,
seeking ways through and beneath his clothing.

The feel of Amber's hands on his face, his chest,
his breeches, was heaven and hell combined for
Duncan. When she found the aching source of
his need, the pleasure nearly undid him. His hips
thrust suddenly against her, once, twice, thrice,
and a groan was dragged from the depths of his
passion.

Amber felt both Duncan's pleasure and his driving, unfulfilled need. However great his enjoyment
of her hand caressing him, it wasn't enough. She
could feel the savage heat of him, taste the salt
of his passion on his neck, and she knew that she
was pouring oil rather than water on the fire of
his need.

"Show me how to ease you," Amber said urgently. "I can't bear the hunger tearing at you!"

The sound Duncan made then was indeed that of
a man in torment. His hands swept down Amber's
body to her hips. Strong fingers clenched there for
an instant, sending pleasure lancing through her.
Before she could do more than take a swift breath,
his hands were sweeping down her legs to her feet
and then back up again.

Amber hardly noticed the cool bite of autumn
on her legs, for the anticipation in Duncan was
spinning through her, driving out all else. When
his hand pressed between her legs, tested the liquid heat of her body, and found it ready, his wild
elation speared through her.

With it came a piercing pleasure that was hers,

for in the act of withdrawing his touch, he flicked over the aching nub of her own need. Instinctively she sought another such caress, twisting beneath Duncan in silent demand.

"Aye," he said savagely. "I can wait no longer either."

His hands clamped on Amber's thighs, stilling and opening her at the same instant. In the next instant he drove into her.

A searing pain clenched Amber's body, only to be burned away by the fierce pleasure that pulsed through Duncan as he felt himself fully sheathed in her. Then came a moment of utter stillness and disbelief.

Duncan struggled to control the wildness hammering in his blood, but it was impossible. Amber was a velvet fire surrounding him tightly, caressing every bit of his aching length. With a broken sound, he began to move, driving for completion within her body.

His release broke over Amber like a storm. She let out a long, ragged sigh and closed her arms around him, feeling both the ecstasy and the wildness pulsing through him into her.

Yet as soon as the last pulse was spent, there came not peace, but unhappiness. Duncan rolled aside and saw what he feared he would—his lover's blood bright on his body.

"*I hurt you*," Duncan said through his teeth. "God's wounds, I never meant that! What is wrong with me? I've never been like that with a woman!"

"Nay," Amber said, touching Duncan's cheek. "I'm not hurt."

"You're bleeding!"

"Of course. 'Tis the nature of virgins to bleed when they first take a man into their body."

The look on Duncan's face would have been amusing, if he hadn't been so clearly horrified.

"You were a virgin?" he asked roughly.

"How can you doubt it?" Amber asked, half smiling. "You wear the truth of it like a crimson banner."

"But you responded so quickly, so wildly, like a falcon that has been flown many times."

"Did I?"

"God's teeth, yes!"

"I wouldn't know," Amber said simply.

Duncan closed his eyes and measured the extent of what he had done. She had been a virgin, she had given herself to him . . . and he had given her nothing in return but pain.

He was certain of it. He had felt the tearing instant as clearly as she must have, but he had denied it even as he had felt it.

If I take Amber's maidenhead, I will marry her.

With or without your memory?

Aye.

I will hold you to your vow.

With fingers that trembled, Duncan pulled Amber's clothing into place so that she was fully covered.

She watched with troubled eyes, not understanding. His touch told her that he was angry and sad and disgusted all at once, but touch alone couldn't tell her why.

"Duncan," Amber whispered. "What is wrong?"

He looked at her with eyes that were more dark than light, more shadowed than she had ever seen them. His mouth was twisted with the same dark emotion.

"You were untouched," Duncan said harshly, "and I rutted on you like an animal. God's teeth, I should be whipped!"

"Nay! You didn't force me."

"I didn't pleasure you, either."

"What do you mean?"

Amber's look of confusion did nothing to restore Duncan's self-respect.

"The pleasure you knew in Ghost Glen," he said, "you knew none of it today."

"I knew *your* pleasure most keenly today. Is that wrong?"

Duncan made a growling sound of disgust and turned away, unable to bear the sight of himself reflected in her anxious golden eyes any longer.

"Dark warrior?" Amber whispered.

The raggedness of her voice haunted Duncan. The merest touch of her fingers on his wrist chained his great strength.

"Tell me what I've done wrong," she said.

"You've done nothing wrong."

"Then why do you turn away from me?"

"It is myself I turn away from," Duncan said savagely, "but wherever I turn, I find I am already there. Leave me be."

When Amber lifted her hand, Duncan surged to his feet. He arranged his clothing with a few curt motions and stood with his fists clenched at his sides.

"Can you sit a horse?" he asked through clenched teeth.

"Of course."

"Are you certain?"

"Duncan," Amber said in exasperation, "I rode here with you, remember?"

"And then I tore at you until you bled. I ask you again: can you ride?"

"And I say again: aye!"

"Good. We must go quickly to the keep."

"Why?"

No answer came.

Amber looked up at the sky. What had once been wildly threatening and riven by lightning was now the pearly gray of a dove's breast.

"Look," Amber said wonderingly. "The storm is fled!"

Duncan gave the sky a single, savage glance.

Broodingly he turned and looked at the rowan that stood guard over the mound's eternal sleep.

Are you pleased, rowan?

Better that you had let me die than live to become a warrior with no self-control, a defiler of virgins.

The bitterness of Duncan's thought wasn't lessened by the realization that he would have to endure Erik's displeasure that his vassal was a virgin no longer.

Duncan had taken that which was clearly forbidden. Now he must bear the consequences.

And he must pray that in keeping one vow, he would not forswear another, unremembered vow.

"Come," Duncan said flatly, starting toward the horses. "There is a wedding to be arranged."

12

"LORD, a weasel-eyed pilgrim demands to see you," Alfred said.

Erik looked up from his contemplation of a manuscript that consisted largely of enigmatic, elegant runes. The large, rough-coated wolfhounds at his feet looked up as well. The orange flicker of hearth fire leaped redoubled in their eyes.

"A pilgrim," Erik said neutrally.

"Aye. So he says."

If the knight's words hadn't made his contempt clear enough, his voice and posture did. He fairly vibrated with disdain.

With a last, lingering glance, Erik set aside the parchment he had been studying.

"To what purpose does he wish to see me?" Erik asked.

"He claims to have knowledge of the Scots Hammer."

The falcon above Erik's chair sent a sharp cry through the room.

"Does he really," Erik murmured. "How intriguing."

Alfred looked sour rather than intrigued.

"Where?" asked Erik. "When? Under what circumstances? And is he certain the man was indeed the Scots Hammer?"

"The churl said only that he must speak to you

alone, in a privacy greater than that of the confessional."

Erik leaned back in his riven oak chair, picked up his silver dagger, and began running his fingertips over the flowing runes inscribed on the blade.

"How odd," Erik said.

Alfred grunted.

The falcon's hooked beak followed each motion of Erik's fingers, as though in expectation of blood sport at any moment.

"Bring him."

"Yes, lord."

As Alfred turned to leave, he eyed the peregrine warily. She had been known to fly at men rather than at feathered prey, and she suffered no leash such as other falcons wore while on their household perches.

A soft whistle from Erik's lips soothed the fierce bird. She flared her wings, folded them neatly at her sides, and resumed watching with unblinking intensity as Erik's fingers caressed the dagger's gleaming blade.

A distinct odor preceded the pilgrim's arrival to Stone Ring Keep's great hall. The smell was a compound of greed, fear, eagerness, and a body that hadn't known the kiss of water since baptism.

"Did you find it in a hen roost?" Erik asked idly of Alfred. "Or was it buried beneath a pile of dead fish, perhaps?"

Alfred snickered. "No, lord. It came walking up to me all of its own."

"Ah, well," Erik murmured, "not everyone has a Learned appreciation of the solace of a warm bath."

The pilgrim shifted uncomfortably. Though the clothes he was wearing were made of fine cloth, they fit badly, as though cut for another man. Or several men. His hair would have been flaxen, if clean. He took in the great hall with pale, darting glances, as though afraid to be caught looking at the gold and silver plates displayed in their accustomed tiers near the lord's dais.

Erik caught the direction of the pilgrim's glance. The lord's mouth curved. It wasn't a pleasant smile.

When the pilgrim saw Erik's expression, the odor of greed gave way to the acrid scent of fear. The hounds stirred and snarled softly among themselves. The biggest of them stood and stretched, yawning widely, giving the nervous guest an excellent view of teeth sharply gleaming.

"Stagkiller," Erik said, "quit teasing it."

The hound's jaws snapped shut. He scratched at the fragrant rushes with long, strong nails, turned around three times, and lay down.

"Great lord," the pilgrim said, stepping toward Erik.

The hounds came to their feet in a single, lithe rush.

"Come no closer," Erik said calmly. "They smell fleas on you. They can't abide the creatures."

Alfred began coughing, only to stop at an incisive glance from Erik.

"Speak," Erik said to the pilgrim.

"I hear there be a reward for knowing of the Scots Hammer," the man said.

Erik nodded.

The pilgrim darted a quick glance at Alfred.

"You may leave," Erik said to his knight.

Alfred, on the edge of objecting, caught a slight motion of Erik's dagger.

"Yes, lord."

When the sound of Alfred's boots had faded from the great hall, Erik gave the pilgrim a hooded glance that was chillingly like that of the peregrine.

"Speak quickly and to the point, *pilgrim*."

"I be in the forest and hear a scream," the man said in a rush, "and I run to see what passes and—"

"In the forest?" Erik interrupted. "Where?"

"Yonder a few hours' walk."

Erik followed the direction of the man's dirty finger.

"Near the Stone Ring?" Erik asked.

The pilgrim crossed himself nervously and started to spit on the floor, then thought better of it.

"Aye," he muttered.

"What were you doing on my estate? In the *forest*. Have you a taste for venison, perhaps?"

The smell of fear redoubled, making the hounds stir.

"I be a pilgrim, lord, nae a poacher!"

"Ah, you were on God's mission, then," Erik said gently.

"Aye!" the man said, obviously relieved. "I be a right reverent son."

"Excellent. I'm always pleased to have reverent pilgrims on my estates rather than poachers or outlaws."

As Erik spoke, the falcon cocked her head and watched the man with unblinking, predatory eyes.

"Continue," Erik said. "You were in the forest, heard a scream, and ran to see what was happening?"

"Uh, yes."

"And what was happening?"

"Some ruffians come upon a man and a maid. They be checking the fit of the other's stockings, if you take my meaning."

Tawny eyebrows lifted. "Aye."

"The ruffians sees the maid's amber gems all shiny and—God's bleeding wounds!"

The peregrine's shrill whistle had cut off the pilgrim's words and brought the hounds to their feet.

"The maid," Erik said very gently, not looking away from the dirty guest. "Was she hurt?"

"Nay, lord," the man said hurriedly. " 'Tis what I be trying to tell you."

"Did an outlaw lay hands upon her? Was she *touched*?"

"Uh...I..." The man swallowed. "She be dragged from her horse and cuffed a bit for sticking a dagger in the one what be taking her jewelry, 'tis all."

Erik closed his eyes for an instant, afraid that the false pilgrim would see what lay inside and flee before he finished his tale.

"She was dragged from her horse," Erik said with great gentleness. "And then?"

"The man be dragged with her, but he lands on his feet and starts to swinging a hammer."

A cold smile etched the line of Erik's mouth.

"God blind me, but he be a wizard with that hammer," the false pilgrim continued. "I sees right soon that I—er, the ruffians—be overmatched no matter that they be ten to his one."

Erik's smile widened but became no warmer.

"Then the maid sets to cursing in a heathen way and I sees that the ruffians got themselves that amber witch I hear talk of, the one what lives nearby this keep?"

A nod was Erik's only response.

The outlaw let out a silent sigh of relief that the lord wasn't going to ask any more uncomfortable questions.

"Some of the ruffians goes around the man's back to get under the hammer," the false pilgrim said quickly. "Just before they has him, the witch yells and the warrior give a great leap up and turn around in the air and come down facing what his back be facing before and the hammer keep humming without a hitch and it all happen quicker than I be able to blink twice."

Erik waited.

"Only one man be able to do that," the outlaw explained.

"Aye," Erik said.

He knew from experience that that particular fighting maneuver was more often talked about by knights than done successfully. In fact, Erik knew of only one warrior who could be depended upon to show such a combination of strength and skill. It was how the knight had received his name.

The Scots Hammer.

"I would like to have seen that," Erik said.

And meant it.

The false pilgrim grunted. His expression suggested that he could have lived and died very well without seeing the Scots Hammer at work.

"Then what happened?" Erik asked.

"The ruffians that still be able, they run like deer. The witch and the Scots Hammer rides off at a gallop."

"Toward this keep?"

"Nay. Away from it. I run here quick as I can, to tell you I see the Scots Hammer and get the reward."

Erik looked at the blade of his dagger and said nothing.

"Do you nae believe me?" the outlaw said anxiously. "It be the Hammer. Bigger by half than most men, dark of hair and light of eye, strong as an ox."

The dagger glinted as it turned idly in Erik's long fingers.

"It be not the first time I see the Hammer," the outlaw said quickly. "I be in Blackthorne on my, er, pilgrimage, when the Hammer be fighting Dominic le Sabre. I be as certain as sin of it."

"Yes," Erik said, "I believe you saw the Scots Hammer."

"The reward, lord?"

"Aye," Erik said very gently. "I shall give you a suitable reward for your day's work."

The peregrine's wings flared abruptly, startling the outlaw into backing up. His sudden motion brought the heads of all seven wolfhounds around to watch him.

The outlaw froze.

"Alfred," Erik said, pitching his voice to carry down the length of the great hall.

"Aye, lord!"

"Bring thirty pieces of silver."

"At once, lord!"

Erik watched the outlaw with an unblinking gaze. The man shifted unhappily.

"One small thing, my good pilgrim," Erik said softly.

"Aye?"

"Empty your purses."

"What?"

"You heard me. Do it. Now."

The gentleness of Erik's voice never varied, but the outlaw finally understood what lay behind the fine manners. It was no precious lordling he confronted, but a warrior in whose yellow eyes the fires of hell burned. With jerky motions, the outlaw began emptying the purses he had tied beneath his clothing.

The tip of Erik's dagger pointed to a table standing near the man.

Sullenly, the outlaw put the contents of the first purse on the table—two daggers with silver handles and steel blades. The stain on the blades spoke silently of blood.

The next purse revealed three combs of silver whose delicate designs suggested that they had once adorned the heads of fine ladies. A long, pale lock of hair was tangled in one comb, as though it had been ripped from a woman's head.

Erik watched with apparent indifference, but his eyes missed nothing.

Bread, meat, cheese, and a handful of copper coins appeared on the table. The outlaw looked up, saw Erik's baleful eyes, and cursed beneath his breath. Another purse spilled its contents onto the table. This time there was a gleam of silver and a single flash of gold.

"That be all," the outlaw muttered.

"Not quite."

"Lord, I be empty as a widow's womb!"

Erik came out of his chair with a speed so great that the outlaw had no time to flee. One instant Erik was sitting at ease. The next instant he had one hand buried in the outlaw's filthy hair and the point of a silver dagger resting against his dirt-caked throat.

"Do you wish to die unshriven with a lie still fresh on your lips?" Erik asked gently.

A single look into Erik's eyes convinced the outlaw that he would rather trade glances with Satan himself than with the sorcerer who was watching him right now.

"I—I—" stuttered the outlaw.

"The amber. Fetch it out."

"What amber? I be not rich enough to—aiee!"

The lies stopped as the dagger's tip bit delicately into flesh. The outlaw's hands dug frantically beneath his mantle. A purse appeared. A string was yanked. A broken bracelet fell out onto the table and gleamed in shades of gold.

Amber, pure and transparent, valuable beyond the means of any but a wealthy lord.

Into the silence came the sounds of Alfred hurrying up the great hall. There was a hesitation in his steps when he saw the point of Erik's dagger pricking the outlaw's throat. An instant later, a large battle dagger flashed in Alfred's hand.

"Have you the silver?" Erik asked.

The gentleness of Erik's voice made Alfred wish to be elsewhere.

Instantly.

"Aye. Thirty pieces."

"Excellent. Give them to this 'pilgrim.' "

Alfred dropped the coins into the outlaw's shaking hand.

"Do you have a name?" Erik asked the man.

"B-Bob."

"Bob the Backstabber, perchance?"

The outlaw went pale. Sweat stood visibly on his face.

"It is known throughout the Disputed Lands," Erik said softly, "that the maid from whose wrist that bracelet came is under my protection."

"She be safe, lord, I swear it on my mother's soul!"

"It is also known what punishment will come to any man who lays hands upon Amber the Untouched."

The outlaw started to speak, but Erik was still talking softly, implacably.

"Alfred, take Bob to a priest. Shrive him. Then hang him."

The outlaw turned and tried to flee. Erik's foot lashed out with the speed of a snake striking. The outlaw sprawled in a smelly heap at Alfred's feet.

"Do not make me regret my mercy," Erik said.

"Mercy?" the outlaw asked, dazed.

"Aye, creature. Mercy. Under the law, I could have your hands, your testicles, and the skin from your back before I drew your guts through your navel, quartered your body, and left your sorry, unshriven soul for the Devil to feed on until the Second Coming of Christ."

The outlaw made a low sound.

"But I am merciful," Erik said distinctly. "I will see you shrived and hanged with a shrewd knot, which is more decency than you showed the maid whose hair hangs from a silver comb and whose blood lies black upon yon dagger."

Fear shook the outlaw. "Ye be a sorcerer! Naught but such a man can know that!"

"Give the silver and the rest of this creature's goods to the chaplain for the poor," Erik said to Alfred.

"Aye, lord."

Alfred bent and began dragging the outlaw away. Just before they reached the doorway out of the great hall, Erik called out.

"Alfred!"

The knight stopped and looked over his shoulder. "Aye, lord?"

"When it is done, burn the rope."

AMBER dismounted before Duncan could come around his horse to help. Her knees gave a bit, then took her weight without further protest.

Duncan's mouth flattened beneath his mustache at the evidence that Amber no longer sought his touch. Not that he blamed her. What should have been a sweet initiation into the mystery of sex had been accomplished with all the finesse of a bull mounting a cow.

"Thank you, Egbert," Amber said when the squire stepped forward to take the reins. "Has Erik returned from Sea Home?"

"Aye. He is waiting for you in the lord's solar. Do hurry, maid. He is in a rare mood."

Duncan turned and regarded the squire with speculative eyes.

"How so?" Duncan asked.

"He had a man hanged not an hour ago."

Amber turned toward him so quickly that her cowl fell away, revealing her disheveled hair.

"Why?" she asked starkly.

"The fellow had an amber bracelet in his purse. Rumor says it is yours."

A quick glance at her left wrist confirmed Amber's fear. Where three strands of amber had been, now there were only two. In the turmoil of the battle—and of what followed—she hadn't noticed the bracelet's loss.

"I see," Amber said in a low voice.

She picked up her skirts and began walking quickly across Stone Ring Keep's small bailey to the forebuilding. The door stood open, as though someone inside were impatient to see her.

Duncan caught up with Amber before she reached the entrance to the great hall. They entered the solar together.

The sight that greeted them wasn't reassuring. Though only one wolfhound and the peregrine were permitted into the solar's warmth, their restlessness boded ill for Erik's temper.

"What is this I hear about an outlaw being hanged?" Amber said before Duncan could speak.

After a moment, Erik set aside the manuscript he had been reading. He looked first at Amber, then at Duncan.

"Hanging," Erik said distinctly, "is the punishment for any man who dares to touch that which is forbidden."

Amber's breath was drawn with a soft, ripping sound. Duncan had done a great deal more than touch her.

And somehow Erik knew it.

Erik reached beneath the manuscript and pulled out an amber bracelet. He held the gleaming jewelry out to her.

"Yours, I believe?" he asked.

Amber nodded.

The enigmatic, tawny eyes switched to Duncan.

"I hear you fought well," Erik said. "You have my gratitude."

"They were but ruffians," Duncan said.

"They were ten to your one," Erik said. "With wooden staffs and daggers and the cunning of wolves. They have defiled and killed at least one gentlewoman, and overcome three lone knights. Again, I thank you."

"May I speak with you alone, lord?" Duncan asked.

"The last man who made that request came to an unhappy end," Erik said, smiling slightly. "But I hold you in much higher regard. Warriors of your skill are very rare."

Duncan turned and looked at Amber, plainly expecting her to leave. She looked back at him and moved not one step toward the door.

"Amber?" Erik asked calmly. "Will you leave us?"

"I think not. What will be said here concerns me as much as anyone."

Erik raised his eyebrows and looked at Duncan, who didn't notice. He was watching Amber with unhappy hazel eyes.

"I wanted to spare you this retelling," Duncan said in a low voice.

"Why? It was a thing done by two, not one."

"Nay," he said bitterly. "It was done by one to another."

Before Amber could open her mouth to argue, Duncan turned to face Erik.

"I ask for the hand of your vassal in marriage," Duncan said grimly.

The peregrine gave an odd, trilling cry. The joyous sound rippling from the raptor's hooked beak was quite startling.

"Granted," Erik said immediately.

"Am I not to be asked?" Amber said.

An amused smile softened the line of Erik's mouth. "You have already given your permission."

"When?" Amber challenged.

"When you lay with Duncan," Erik retorted.

She went pale, then flushed.

Duncan stepped forward, standing protectively between Amber and Erik.

"It was none of her doing," Duncan said.

The smile vanished from Erik's face as though it had never been.

"Amber," he said distinctly. "Did Duncan force you?"

"Nay!"

"She was innocent," Duncan said. "I wasn't. The blame for what happened lies with me."

Erik hid a smile behind his beard as he made an unnecessary production out of replacing a loose manuscript page.

"I will hear no talk of blame," Erik said after a moment, looking up once more. "I will make no recriminations."

"You are generous," Duncan said.

"You want Amber. Amber wants you." Erik shrugged. "There is no reason against the match and a great deal to recommend it. You will be married immediately."

Shadows shifted and writhed within Duncan, half-remembered voices calling, telling him that he must not, he could not—he would be forsworn if he married Amber.

And he would be forsworn if he did not. He had given his word to Erik.

If I take Amber's maidenhead, I will marry her.

Duncan closed his eyes, fighting against the part of himself that insisted there was an urgent reason *not* to marry.

A name formed like bright, moon-washed water in his mind, glittering in the darkness of his memory, shining among shades of darkness that flowed and shifted, concealing and then revealing . . .

Ariane.

Just that. No more. A name from his cursed, unremembered past.

A name, an urgency, a reason not to marry.

But it was a reason and an urgency and a name from the time before Duncan had taken Amber's innocence and given her only pain in return.

Fingers cold with more than the autumn chill fastened around his wrist. Amber's hand. Duncan looked down into her shadowed eyes and felt a chill condense along his spine.

She was frightened.

Of him?

"Amber," Duncan said in a low, ragged voice, "wed or not, I won't touch you again unless you ask me plainly. I swear it!"

Tears stood in her eyes, magnifying their sadness and beauty. When she shook her head slowly, the tears spilled in brilliant silence down her cool cheeks.

Amber wanted to tell Duncan that she welcomed his touches, but she couldn't. If she opened her mouth, she was afraid all that would come from her throat would be a keening sound of sorrow.

She had heard a woman's name whispered in the shadows of Duncan's mind, an echo turning and returning from the unremembered past, tearing at her heart.

Ariane.

"Amber?" Erik said.

He was watching her with an intensity that burned as clearly as the hearth fire.

Amber closed her eyes and released Duncan's wrist. Yet in the very act of letting go of him, her fingertips caressed the veins where the force of his life surged just beneath his skin.

Erik sensed Amber's sorrow as clearly as he sensed her love for the dark warrior who watched her with haunted eyes.

"Duncan," Erik said, "leave us."

"Nay," Duncan said savagely. "I'll not have you shame Amber for what wasn't her fault."

Erik looked directly into Duncan's eyes and knew that the other man was walking on a knife-edge of control. Erik wondered what memories were returning, how quickly; and how much time he had before

Duncan awakened and knew himself as the Scots
Hammer.

Erik's enemy.

Amber's lover.

Betrothed to a Norman heiress whom he had
never seen.

Vassal to Dominic le Sabre.

A savage impatience flattened Erik's mouth as
he thought of how little time remained, how much
could go wrong, and how great the stakes were.

They must wed.

Immediately!

"I would no more humiliate Amber than I would
my own sister," Erik said carefully. "She is much
cherished by me. She is also well known to me."

He turned to Amber. "Do you wish Duncan
to stay while we talk about . . . wedding arrange-
ments?"

Amber's smile was even sadder than her tears.
Slowly she shook her head.

Without a word Duncan turned on his heel and
left the lord's solar.

Erik waited until the last harsh echo of Duncan's
footsteps had faded into the hiss of the fire. But
even then Amber didn't speak. She simply stood
unmoving, slow tears turning her pale cheeks to
silver.

Uneasiness rippled through Erik. He had seen
Amber many ways, in many moods, but never had
he sensed such unremitting sorrow in her.

As though something cherished had died.

"If it wouldn't cause you pain," Erik said, "I
would take you onto my lap and rock you like a
child."

Amber's laugh was little different from a sob.

"There is only one person who can hold me thus
without discomfort," she whispered.

"Duncan."

A look of profound loss shadowed Amber's face.

"Aye," she whispered. "My dark warrior."

"You will be wed to him before the chaplain chants morning mass," Erik said. "Why, then, do you grieve?"

"I cannot marry Duncan."

"God's blood, was he that great a swine with you?"

At first Amber didn't understand. When she did, a blush tinted her pale cheeks.

"Nay," she said.

Her voice was so soft that Erik could barely hear it.

"Are you certain? Some men are vicious when lust takes them," Erik said bluntly. "No matter how badly I need Duncan as my own, I'll not condemn you to spend your life lying beneath a rutting beast who is twice your size."

Amber put her hands to her suddenly hot cheeks. "Stop!"

Erik cursed beneath his breath, stood abruptly, and came to stand as close to Amber as he could without touching her.

"Look at me, Amber."

A combination of regret, tenderness, and concern was mixed together in Erik's voice and in the expression on his face.

"Did Cassandra never talk to you about the ways of men and maids?" Erik asked.

Amber shook her head.

Erik sighed. "It must be that she believed you would never be able to touch a man's hand without pain, much less hold part of his body within you in the marriage bed."

A small sound escaped Amber as she looked away from the tall lord she had known all her life.

Yet never had they talked like this.

"Nay," Erik said. "There is no need to be embarrassed about the way in which men and women unite. It is a gift of God. Did you find it . . . distasteful?"

Amber shook her head.

"Hurtful?" he asked.

She shook her head again.

"Then he didn't take you too quickly?" Erik pressed. "He's not unskilled?"

"Erik," Amber said faintly. "We should not talk of such things!"

"Why not? You have neither mother nor sister, and Cassandra has never experienced a man. Or would you rather talk about such things with a priest who has never experienced a woman?"

"I'd rather not talk about it at all," Amber muttered.

The returning life in her voice sent a surge of relief through Erik. He didn't know what would happen to Amber if she believed Duncan lost to her.

Nor did Erik want to know.

"You must talk about it," he said, "if only this once."

A sideways look convinced Amber that Erik wasn't going to be turned aside. Reluctantly, she nodded.

"If Duncan is unskilled in the arts of love," Erik said matter-of-factly, "it can be remedied. If he is a brute, there is no remedy."

"He is neither unskilled nor a brute," Amber said.

A long breath of relief was Erik's first response. Then he smiled.

"I begin to understand," he said.

"I'm glad one of us does."

Erik hid his smile.

"I'm told that a maid's first time is rarely her most, ah, memorable," he said.

"Nay," Amber said huskily. "I shall remember it until the day I die. Feeling ecstasy pulse through my dark warrior into me was . . . extraordinary."

A hint of color that had nothing to do with the hearth fire showed on Erik's high cheekbones. Then he tilted back his head and laughed.

"You give as good as you get, lass," Erik said.

At first Amber didn't understand. When she did, she laughed despite the color burning on her cheeks.

"I didn't mean to embarrass you," she said.

"I'll survive," he said dryly. "Now set your hair and clothes to rights before I call the priest to the solar. You will marry at a midnight mass."

Amber's smile faded. "That cannot be."

"Why?"

"Duncan has remembered a woman's name."

"Ariane?" Erik asked casually.

For a moment, Amber was too shocked to say anything.

"You knew?" she asked, whispering.

Erik nodded.

"How?" she demanded.

"Because your dark warrior is Duncan of Maxwell, the Scots Hammer."

Amber swayed as though she had been struck.

"You knew?" she whispered.

"I wondered. Then I hoped. Then I knew."

"Then you also know why I can't marry Duncan," she said.

"I know no such thing."

"Duncan is married to this Ariane, despite his certainty that he has never married."

"Nay. He is betrothed to a Norman heiress whose face he has never seen and whose name he has heard but once, when Dominic le Sabre informed Duncan of the arrangement."

"Duncan is vassal to Dominic le Sabre," Amber said in a shaking voice. She closed her eyes. "To marry me would be a betrayal of his vow of fealty."

"God's wounds," Erik snarled, his voice like a whip. "How can you be so blind? Wipe the tragedy from your eyes and look at me!"

The cold authority in Erik's voice shocked Amber as nothing else could have.

"God has sent you the one man whom you may touch without pain," Erik said. "God has sent me the one man whom I need to hold on to Lord Robert's besieged estates."

"But—"

"And God has sent the means of transforming a foe into an ally," Erik continued relentlessly. "Wed to you, Duncan will be *my* vassal, not Dominic le Sabre's!"

The silence stretched until it vibrated like the string of a bow too tightly drawn.

"It is wrong," Amber said. "Duncan came to the Disputed Lands a knight with wealth of his own, a promise of an estate, and a noble wife to bear him heirs."

"Not so," Erik countered savagely. "Duncan came to Stone Ring Keep more dead than alive, with no more memory than a babe, and you saved his life. He is newly born, and he is *mine*."

"His memory is returning," Amber said unhappily. "Piece by bright piece, the shadows are diminished."

"Aye." Erik's smile was grim. "That is why you will marry by midnight."

"Nay. The prophecy—"

"Hammer the prophecy," Erik said harshly. "You've made your bed, now you will lie in it as Duncan's wife."

"Cassandra will—"

"Accept what she can't alter," Erik said ruthlessly, cutting across Amber's protests again.

"Two parts of the prophecy have been fulfilled. Does that mean nothing to you?"

"It means you had better guard your soul most carefully."

There was a taut silence before Amber shook her head.

"I cannot," she said. "I cannot betray my dark warrior thus."

Erik's face changed, all softness gone. The topaz blaze of his eyes was colder than a winter sunset.

"You will marry the Scots Hammer at midnight—"

"Nay!"

"—or before the twelfth hour is struck, *you will see Duncan hanged.*"

13

"Y ou look downcast for a maid who just became her lover's wife," Cassandra said, pitching her voice to be heard above the feast's noise.

Amber said nothing. Her golden eyes were fixed on Duncan, who stood on Erik's right, receiving the congratulations of the assembled knights. Even among fighting men, Duncan stood out, taller than most, harder, yet with a laugh that no one could hear without laughing in return.

Many toasts had been drunk, many stories told, and much food eaten. Now jugglers and rhymers moved among the people, entertaining them with clever hands and ribald verses on the subject of wedding and bedding.

Erik's wolfhounds foraged in a furry, toothed turmoil beneath tables that were all but swaybacked from the burden of food, silver and gold plates, and goblets set with precious stones. Prized hawks sat above the party on wall perches, watching every motion with unnerving interest.

Cassandra watched Amber with the same kind of interest. No sooner had the wise woman returned from a birthing than she discovered a keep seething with excitement. A man hanged. A maid to be wed. Norse raiders rumored at Winterlance.

And, perhaps, the memory of a great warrior stirring, waking, looking around at a world with the eyes of a bird of prey.

There had been no time for Cassandra to protest, to agree, or to do anything except witness a marriage that never should have taken place.

There certainly had been no opportunity to talk to Amber in private, to ask her why she was risking so much when the gain was so unlikely, to ask her why she had allowed her body to follow her reckless heart, given over to a man who had come to her in shades of darkness.

Would that he remained that way.

But Cassandra's rune stones said that he would not. Duncan would awaken and then death rather than life would flow.

"Have you told Duncan yet?" she asked.

There was no need for Amber to ask what Cassandra meant. Amber knew. She had spent the hours before her marriage in solitude, asking questions of her amber pendant.

The answers that came back to her were always the same.

A choice of evils.

"No," Amber said.

"Soon or late, someone will recognize him," Cassandra said.

"Yes."

"What will you do then?"

"Whatever I must."

"It would have been better to let Erik hang him before the third aspect of the prophecy is fulfilled."

The look Amber gave Cassandra held the same tawny fires of hell that Erik's eyes sometimes did.

"I see." Cassandra's smile was real, and sad. "Heart and body are his. The soul is swiftly following."

"Other than see my dark warrior hanged," Amber said coldly, "what would you have me do?"

A toast was shouted by one of the knights. "Long life, wealth, and many sons!"

Goblets were lifted high. Amber smiled as was expected and saluted with her own goblet before she took a sip.

"Guard your soul," Cassandra said.

"How?"

As Amber spoke, she watched Duncan's hand. Strong, scarred, it made the heavy goblet he held appear almost delicate. After he set the goblet down, his fingertips roamed lightly over the gold design, testing its variations and textures.

Amber would have given a great deal to have his hand caressing her rather than cold metal. She longed for him in a way that frightened her even as it set her afire.

Then Duncan turned and saw Amber watching him. In the candlelight his eyes appeared more gold than hazel.

And like candles, they burned.

"Stay out of his bed, for one," Cassandra said dryly.

"What?" Amber said, looking at the other woman.

"Each time you touch Duncan, you give him more of yourself. If you wish it to stop, then you must withhold yourself from the marriage bed."

"That is against God's law."

"And your own desire."

Amber didn't bother to deny it.

"Erik knew the risk," she said.

"I wonder," Cassandra muttered.

"Be at rest," Amber said dryly. "Erik's gift is kin to yours, but is done without scrying stones. He sees—"

"Opportunity for gain where others see only defeat," Cassandra interrupted in a cold voice. "He is, however, human."

"So are all of us. Even you. In any case, Erik

believed the gain to himself, the vassals, and the land was worth it."

"To himself?"

"Yes. Why do you think he made Duncan steward of Stone Ring Keep?"

"To give you a husband of reasonable wealth," Cassandra said simply.

"That is a result, not a reason."

Cassandra gave the younger woman a look from clear, rain-colored eyes.

"Erik knows Duncan will be able to hold the keep," Amber said, "freeing Erik to fight the Norse raiders at Winterlance."

"Ah, yes. The Norsemen."

Death will surely flow.

Cassandra closed her eyes. "The Norsemen, too, know that a harsh winter is coming."

"Yes," Amber said. "The messenger from Winterlance said that the raiders were but two days away."

"Did he say how many ships were sighted?"

"One vassal saw four," Amber said. "One saw two. One saw seven."

Another toast was shouted. Again Amber raised her smile and her goblet, sipped, and returned to watching her husband.

"When does Erik leave?" Cassandra asked.

"At dawn."

"How many knights is he taking?"

"All but one," Amber said.

"Alfred?"

"Nay. Duncan."

"Even the Scots Hammer can't defend a keep by himself," Cassandra muttered.

"Four men-at-arms will remain."

"A risk, nonetheless."

Amber's mouth turned down in a melancholy smile.

"Is it?" she asked. "Duncan of Maxwell, lord of

an unclaimed keep and vassal of Dominic le Sabre, was Stone Ring Keep's greatest threat."

"And now Duncan is its seneschal, vassal of Erik the Undefeated," Cassandra said. "Is that how Erik's reasoning goes?"

"Yes."

The older woman shook her head with a mixture of rue and admiration for Erik's boldness.

"Still, 'tis an appalling risk," Cassandra said. "When Dominic le Sabre hears—and be certain that he will—he will attack Stone Ring Keep himself."

"There is no time to mount an attack before winter itself defends the land."

"There is always spring or summer," Cassandra said simply.

"By then, the Norse raiders will no longer threaten Winterlance. Erik can concentrate his knights here."

Cassandra let out her breath in a long, hissing sigh. She had never seen Amber like this, both sad and fierce, haunted and bold, vibrant and shuttered.

"Or perhaps by next spring or summer," Amber said, watching Duncan, "Lord Robert will finally realize that Erik must have more knights. Or perchance Erik will arrive at some understanding with Dominic le Sabre. 'Tis said he prefers peace to war. A true Glendruid Wolf."

" 'Tis also said he asks no quarter—*and gives none.*"

"The same has been said of Erik."

"Sometimes it's true," Cassandra said.

"And sometimes it isn't."

Laughter erupted from the knights at some sally neither woman had heard. Nor could anyone overhear them. The babble of festivities provided a haven for private conversation.

Cassandra meant to take full advantage of the opportunity. She had cast the stones for a fortnight, and for a fortnight the answer had come back the same.

A choice among evils.

"What," Cassandra asked carefully, "does Erik believe will happen when Duncan discovers his true name?"

"If Duncan is simply told, he will know it, but he won't feel it. He will be angry, but his feeling for me will outweigh his anger."

Amber's words were uninflected, the monotone of someone repeating an answer that was memorized rather than understood or believed.

"Do you think that?" Cassandra asked.

No answer came from Amber.

"What *do* you believe?" Cassandra asked in a clipped voice.

"I believe I love the man who came to me in shades of darkness," she whispered. "I believe he desires me all the way to his very soul. And I hope . . ."

Amber's voice faded.

"Tell me," Cassandra said, but her tone was as compassionate as it was insistent.

Long, dark gold eyelashes swept down, concealing eyes that held more shadows than light. When Amber spoke, her voice trembled with the force of her tightly held emotions.

"I hope and I pray that Duncan will learn to love me before he knows his true name," she said. "Then, perhaps . . ."

Amber's voice splintered. Hidden beneath the table, her nails dug heedlessly into her palms.

"Perhaps?" Cassandra asked.

A visible tremor went through Amber.

"Perhaps he will be able to forgive me for not telling him," she said.

"That is why you will go to the marriage bed," Cassandra said, understanding at last. "You hope to win him there."

"Yes."

"You go knowing that you will give more of yourself each time he touches you."

"Yes."

"You go knowing that you will likely wake one day and find yourself hated by the very man to whom you gave your heart, your body . . . and your soul."

"Yes."

"Do you know what will happen then?"

"Yes."

"You agree so easily," Cassandra said. "Look at me. Do you truly *know*?"

Slowly Amber's eyes opened and she turned to face the woman who was watching her with Learned eyes. The turmoil of the wedding feast receded as gray eyes searched golden ones for the space of one breath, two breaths, three. Four.

Abruptly Cassandra looked away, for her Learned discipline was being eroded by the bleakness that lay within Amber's eyes.

"Aye," Cassandra said raggedly. "You *know*. I salute your courage."

"While you deplore my common sense?" Amber asked.

Cassandra looked back at the girl who was her daughter in all but birth. Tears glittered like ice in Cassandra's eyes.

Amber was too stunned to speak. Never had she seen the Learned woman weep.

"I deplore only that God has asked this of you rather than of me," Cassandra said in a low voice. "I would rather the suffering be mine."

Before Amber could answer, another toast came from the knights. She raised her goblet, smiled rather fiercely, and drank a small swallow.

When she put down the heavy silver goblet, Duncan was standing in front of her. He held out his hand. She rose as gracefully as flame and went to him, putting her hand in his.

The moment Duncan's flesh met Amber's, pleasure rippled through her. The lines of strain that had drawn her smiles as fine as a knife's edge vanished like mist beneath a fiery sun. Her mouth softened, shadows retreated from her eyes, and she gave Duncan a smile that squeezed Cassandra's heart.

"Now do you understand?" Erik murmured in Cassandra's ear. "She needs her dark warrior even more than I do."

"I understand everything save what you will do when he awakens Duncan of Maxwell and kills her—"

"Nay," Erik interrupted in a low voice.

"—touch by touch, her heart bleeding—"

"Silence!" he hissed.

"—from ten thousand cuts no one else would have felt," Cassandra finished relentlessly. "What will you do then, mighty lord?"

"Duncan will love her in spite of all! How could a man not love a maid who looks at him with such transparent joy?"

" 'He will love her in spite of all,' " Cassandra mimicked with icy sarcasm. "This from the sorcerer who believes only in lust between a man and a woman? I would laugh at you, but I fear my soul would break at the sound."

"Duncan will love her. He *must*."

"Could you love a woman who had betrayed you?"

"I am not Duncan."

"You are a man. So is Duncan. When he understands how much Amber has cost him, he will hate her."

"What would you have done in my place?" Erik demanded in a low voice.

"I would have surrendered Stone Ring Keep to Dominic le Sabre."

"Never," Erik said flatly.

"That is pride speaking."

"What good is a man with no pride?"

"Ask Duncan," Cassandra said scathingly, "for you seem to believe he has none."

A chorus of shouts made Erik turn toward the revelers. Amber had one hand around Duncan's neck and she was whispering in his ear. Whatever she was saying made Duncan smile with a sensual heat that blazed as brightly as the fire.

Then Duncan lifted Amber's hand from his neck, kissed her fingers tenderly, and smiled at her once more. It was a different smile, for it promised safety as well as passion, caring as well as burning, peace as well as ecstasy.

"Look at them," Erik demanded in a low voice. "Look at them and tell me how I could have kept them apart short of death."

There was a savage silence followed by a sigh. Cassandra's fingers touched Erik's clenched fist.

"I know," she said softly. "That is why we rage at each other. It gives us the illusion we were once in control of Amber's destiny—and we chose wrongly—when in truth we never had that kind of control at all."

Hand in hand, Duncan and Amber approached Erik.

"We ask your leave, lord," Duncan said, "to seek our rest."

A roar of laughter went up from the knights.

"Rest?" Erik asked, covering his smile by smoothing his beard with his hand. "By all means, Duncan. If you aren't to bed soon, the cock will be up well after dawn."

More laughter gusted through the knights.

Erik's smile changed as he looked at Amber. He reached out to her, but stopped just short of touching her cheek.

"Be joyful in your marriage," Erik said.

Amber's smile was incandescent. It didn't dim even when she deliberately turned her head so that her cheek brushed against Erik's fingers.

The surprise that murmured through the gathered knights was reflected in Erik's expression.

"Thank you, lord," Amber said softly. "Your kindness to me has been that of amber itself, pieces of sunlight shining no matter how dark the day."

Erik's smile was both sad and so beautiful that Cassandra felt pain twist through her. The love Erik had for Amber was as clear as the tawny color of his eyes. Yet it was a love that held no sexual desire, despite Amber's beauty and Erik's forthright masculinity.

Abruptly, fear replaced pain in Cassandra.

He knows. By all that's Learned, he knows!

Is that why he risked so much? Is he trying to repay her for what was taken from her at her birth?

No answer came from within the well of serenity that held Cassandra's Learning.

"Will you give me your good wishes?" Amber asked, turning to Cassandra.

"You are my daughter in every way that matters," Cassandra said. "I would give you Paradise if I could."

Smiling, Amber glanced at her husband from beneath her long lashes. Though she said nothing, the fire reflected in Duncan's eyes burned higher.

"Thank you," Amber said, looking at Cassandra again. "Your good wishes mean a great deal to me. I love you as a daughter would."

With her free hand, Amber touched the other woman's cheek. The murmur of surprise was repeated throughout the gathered knights and ladies. Despite the clear affection between Amber, Erik, and Cassandra, never had the people of the keep seen Amber touch the lord or the Learned woman.

Tears glittered once more in Cassandra's eyes. She turned to look long and hard at the dark warrior whose fingers were interlaced with Amber's.

"You have been given a gift beyond price," Cassandra said distinctly. "Few men are privileged to know its like."

The splinters of darkness that lay deep within the clarity of Cassandra's eyes made coolness ripple down Duncan's spine. His instincts stirred, warning him that danger lay within this woman as surely as night lay within sunset's vivid colors.

Then realization came. It wasn't menace that lay darkly within Cassandra. It was knowledge.

And it was dangerous.

"May I embrace the husband of my daughter?" Cassandra asked.

If Duncan was surprised, the rest of the people were shocked, including Erik.

"Of course," Duncan said.

Cassandra stepped forward. Full scarlet sleeves rippled and flared over the forest green of Duncan's shirt as she placed her hands on his shoulders. Though Cassandra was a tall woman, she had to stretch on tiptoe in order to bring her face close to Duncan.

"This is the truth of the past," Cassandra said, kissing his left cheek.

A moment later she kissed his right cheek.

"This is the truth of the present," she said.

Then Cassandra's palms rested on Duncan's cheeks, holding him as surely as chains.

"Your life lies stretched between past and present," she said in a low, distinct voice.

Intently Duncan watched the Learned woman, feeling her cool hands like brands on his face while her silver eyes compelled everything within him to listen to her. Even the shadows.

Especially the shadows.

"To deny the truth of the past or the present will destroy you as surely as cleaving your head in two with a sword," Cassandra said.

A ripple of movement went through the knights as they crossed themselves.

"Remember what I have said when the past returns and seems to make a lie of the present," Cassandra commanded. *"Remember it."*

When she would have withdrawn, Duncan's hand chained one of her wrists.

Instantly Erik stepped forward, only to be warned off by a glance from clear silver eyes.

"What do you know of my past?" Duncan asked in a low voice.

"Nothing that would bring you ease."

Duncan glanced toward Amber. Though he said not one word, she put her hand on Cassandra's captive arm.

"What do you know of my past?" Duncan demanded again, softly.

"Nothing that would bring you ease," Cassandra repeated.

Duncan waited.

"She speaks the truth," Amber said.

Duncan's hand opened, freeing Cassandra.

The smile she gave him was both compassionate and coolly amused at his arrogance in questioning a wise woman's honesty.

"You are canny to listen to your wife," Cassandra said bitingly. "See that you remain so when past and present are both known."

Cassandra looked at Erik.

"With your permission, lord," she said, "I have a newly born babe who needs me more than a newly wed couple."

"Of course, Learned one," Erik said. "You need not ask my permission."

"Ah, but I enjoy doing so."

"Do you?"

"But of course," Cassandra said dryly. " 'Tis the only time you listen to me."

Laughter rose like a shout, for it was well known among the knights that their young lord was as headstrong as an unbroken stallion. Erik laughed the loudest of them all, for he knew himself better than they did.

Under cover of the laughter, Duncan bent down and spoke for Amber alone.

"Do you know what Cassandra knows?" he asked.

"Of your past?"

"Yes."

"I know that she is rarely wrong."

"Meaning?" Duncan asked.

"Meaning there is nothing in your past that will make you happy in the present."

"Are you certain?"

"Ask yourself, not me," she said.

"But I know nothing."

"Nor do you wish to. Not now. Not when you are married."

Duncan's eyes narrowed. But before he could speak, Amber did.

"Do you want to spend your wedding night asking questions whose answers are sure to make you unhappy?" she asked.

"Are they?"

"Aye."

The bleak certainty in Amber's eyes sent another wave of coolness washing over Duncan's spine.

"Amber?"

She put her fingertips over his lips, sealing in all the questions he hadn't asked and she didn't want to answer.

"Instead of asking questions neither of us wants to hear," Amber whispered, "wouldn't you rather take your bride to the privacy of the bedchamber and begin our future?"

🌿 14

WHEN Duncan led Amber into the room that had been hastily, yet thoroughly, arrayed for their wedding night, she made a sound of pleasure and surprise.

"It is quite wonderful," she said.

The chamber had been built for the lady of the keep and never occupied, for Erik had yet to take a wife. The exotic fragrance of myrrh pervaded the room, rising from the oil lamps whose bright, unwavering flames turned darkness into golden light. The hearth along the far wall burned with wood so hard and dry that there was barely any smoke to curl upward into the clever, narrow vent behind the logs.

"And quite grand!" Amber added.

Laughing, she turned around swiftly, making her gold dress lift and ripple as though alive.

With an effort, Duncan didn't reach out to the graceful amber girl who burned more brightly in his blood than any fire. He knew he shouldn't look at her, much less gather her close and bury his hard flesh within her softness again.

It was too soon. He was too harsh, too much a warrior for Amber's delicate flesh to take. If he took her again, and again saw her blood bright on his body, he didn't know what he would do.

Duncan's silence and grim expression dimmed Amber's pleasure in the luxurious room.

"Do you dislike it?" she asked anxiously, waving her hand around.

"No."

"You look so harsh. Is it . . . are you remembering?"

"Aye."

A lance of fear impaled Amber.

It is too soon! If he remembers now, all will be lost. And I will be lost with it.

"What are you remembering?" she asked in a low voice.

"The sight of your blood on my body."

Her relief was so great that Amber felt dizzy.

"Oh, that," she said. "It was nothing."

"It was your maidenhead!"

"I've given more blood to a leech," Amber said, smiling as she remembered Duncan's dismissal of his own wound. "And so have you, dark warrior. You told me so yourself."

Unwillingly, Duncan smiled in return. Saying nothing, he looked around the room, but his eyes kept returning to the marriage bed.

It was big enough for a man of Duncan's size—or Erik's. The bed was canopied and curtained with rich cloth in shades of gold, green, and indigo. A luxurious fur blanket lay over sheets of linen so fine that they were softer than the down that filled the mattress. The border of lace on the sheets was extraordinarily fine, as though countless snowflakes had been woven into a pattern that no hearth fire could melt.

"Have you ever seen such finery?" Amber asked, noting that Duncan was looking at the bed.

The instant the words were out of her mouth, she wanted to call them back. The last thing she wished to discuss now was Duncan's memory.

Or lack of it.

" 'Tis very rich," Duncan agreed. "Erik is a generous lord. This room is more suited to the lord's quarters than to those of his seneschal."

"Erik is pleased by our marriage."

"Aye. 'Tis a good thing."

"Why?" she asked, startled by the thread of steel in Duncan's voice.

"Because I would have married you with or without his leave, with or without my vow concerning your maidenhead. And he knew it. He could fight me or he could give you into my care."

Duncan turned away from the bed in time to see the stricken look on Amber's face. The pallor of her skin was such that not even golden lamplight could disguise it.

"You must not even think of fighting Erik," she said.

"Do you believe me such a poor warrior, then?"

"Nay!"

Eyes narrowed, Duncan waited.

"I love both of you," Amber said. "If you fought one another—nay! It must never happen!"

Duncan closed the distance between himself and his bride with a swiftness that was startling. He stood so near that he could smell the unique fragrance of resin and roses that was hers alone.

"What did you say?" he asked in a deep voice.

"If you fought—"

"No," Duncan interrupted. "Before that."

"I love both of you."

"Closer, but not quite."

For an instant Amber was confused. Then she understood.

"I love Erik," she said, hiding her smile.

Duncan grunted.

"And," she whispered, "I love you, dark warrior. I love you so much I am full to overflowing with it."

The smile Duncan gave Amber made her knees

weaken. He lifted her up in his arms, hugging her close. The relief that swept through her was her own and his combined.

But the surprise her words had caused was Duncan's alone.

Amber pulled back far enough to see his eyes. "Why are you surprised?"

"I didn't think an innocent maid could love a man who was so clumsy with her body," Duncan said.

"You aren't clumsy."

"I was a rut—"

Whatever he had meant to say was lost in the sudden pressure of Amber's mouth over his.

The fierce, unschooled kiss sent a torrent of fire through Duncan. For a hungry instant he permitted the sweet taste of Amber to fill his senses. Then he gently, implacably, separated his mouth from hers.

"Duncan?" Amber asked. "Don't you want me?"

He let out a harsh breath.

"You're touching me," Duncan said ironically. "You tell me. Do I want you?"

Amber closed her eyes as she felt the desire in him drench her senses.

"Aye," she whispered. "It is a river of fire pouring through me."

Duncan's eyes closed as a shudder of response shot through his whole body.

"Yes," he said roughly. "A river of fire."

His eyes opened, but even before Amber saw their darkness, she felt his icy restraint freezing the hot flames of desire.

"And you," Duncan said, "are a delicate amber fairy who hasn't even healed from the first time I held you down and ripped through your maiden-head."

"It wasn't like that!" Amber protested. "You didn't force me to—"

"I know what I did and didn't do," Duncan interrupted ruthlessly. "God's blood, my palms can still feel the heat and softness of your thighs as I spread them and thrust into you as though you were an enemy to be killed."

"Stop! I wanted you just as much as you wanted me. Why can't you believe that?"

Duncan's laugh was as rough as his eyes were bleak.

"Why? Because I've never wanted a woman like that. I didn't even know such passion was in me! How could an innocent feel anything close to it?"

"Duncan," Amber said, kissing his chin. "When I touch you, *I feel what you feel.*"

Her teeth closed delicately on his neck.

"Dear God, yes," she whispered. "I *feel* your breath break even as I hear it. I *feel* your heartbeat speed. I *feel* your blood rushing and quickening your flesh, making you ready to lie within me."

With a groan, Duncan pushed away the fine cowl that framed Amber's face. He fitted his hands against Amber's cheeks, savoring the smooth, soft heat of her skin.

The leap of his hunger was like wine to Amber. While she shivered beneath the claiming of his hands, her soft words incited him, pouring fire over him even as the heat of his desire poured over her.

"I can feel your hunger gathering like a storm," she whispered. "I can't feel the sword emerging from its sheath, but I can sense *you* feeling your own maleness sweep through you."

"Amber," Duncan said hoarsely.

"And I can feel my own body crying out to know the sweet stabbing of the sword within the sheath."

"No more, witch," Duncan said heavily. "You have me full to bursting already."

"I know."

A look into the golden fire of Amber's eyes told

Duncan that she did indeed know what her words had done to him.

And she liked it.

"Can I undo you with only my words?" Amber asked.

The combination of curiosity and sensuality in her eyes almost pushed Duncan over the edge.

"Enough," he said in a hoarse voice.

"Why?"

" 'Tis unseemly for a man to lose control."

"Even in the marriage bed?"

"We're not in bed," he retorted.

"Aye. And you have no intention of lying there with me, do you?"

" 'Tis too soon."

" 'Tis a great pot of slops!" Amber retorted. "Well, sir, if you won't take me, I shall just have to take you."

Duncan gave Amber a shocked look. Then he laughed at the thought of such a slender girl physically besting a man of his size and strength.

"Are you going to hold me down and ravish me, little fairy?"

"I don't think you would lie still for it."

"Not tonight," he agreed. "But the thought appeals."

" 'Tis deeds I want, not thoughts. As I am weaker than you, I must use the only weapon I have to ravish you."

"And that is?"

"My tongue."

The surge of fire that hardened Duncan's whole body was transmitted to Amber so clearly that she stiffened as though a whip had been laid across her back. An image condensed in her mind, a beautiful girl whose golden hair seethed in a fragrant, burning cloud over Duncan's loins as her tongue brushed fire over his rigid sword.

"Ah," Amber said. "Does my hair truly burn you

so sweetly? Then I give it to you, husband."

Before Duncan could say anything, her hands lifted quickly and bright combs scattered to the floor. Knowing he shouldn't, unable to stop himself, Duncan thrust his hands deeply into Amber's hair until cool, soft strands caressed the sensitive skin between his fingers.

A shiver of pure pleasure cascaded through Amber. Watching Duncan's eyes, she moved her head slowly, increasing the beloved pressure of his hands.

"Do you like that," he asked, "or is it my pleasure you're responding to?"

"Both," she said huskily. "I like your hands caressing me. I like knowing that caressing me gives you pleasure."

"Amber . . ." Duncan said, but he could say no more.

"Would it truly give you such great pleasure to feel my tongue tracing your sword?"

Duncan's hands clenched in Amber's hair. It would have been painful to her had she not felt his violent response to her words burn through her like wildfire.

"You are unraveling me," he said hoarsely. "Where did an innocent like you learn the tricks of the harem?"

"From you."

"Nay. I've never known a woman's mouth in that way."

"Yet when I said I would ravish you with my tongue, you saw my hair all wild over your naked loins and my tongue was a pink flame licking over you."

The desire that hammered through Duncan nearly brought both of them to their knees.

"Amber, you must stop!"

The roughness in Duncan's voice was another rush of desire through her.

"Nay," she whispered. "I find I am most curious to know what it is like to ravish you with my tongue. And, perhaps, my teeth?"

Duncan groaned and his fingers clenched again.

Amber made a ragged sound of pleasure as her words returned to her in an outpouring of his passion.

"Don't say such things," he muttered. "You will make me lose all control."

"But I like feeling fire sweep through you."

Abruptly, Duncan let go of Amber and stepped back so that he wasn't touching her.

"That's just it," he said, his voice tight. "The fire is going through me, not *you*."

The lack of Duncan's touch was like being dropped into an icy stream. Amber staggered, off-balance, lost.

"Duncan?" she said, reaching for him

"No," he said, stepping back even farther.

"I don't understand."

"Exactly. All you have ever known is a warrior's hunger hammering you until you bled. You've never known your own sweet desire."

"That's not true. Your desire and mine are different faces of the same coin."

Duncan raked his hand through his hair, then unfastened his rich mantle and tossed it aside.

"No," he said, turning back to her. "My desire drowns yours. It would be the same for you with any man."

At first Amber didn't understand.

When she did, she was furious. Her eyes narrowed to slits.

"You believe I have no passion that isn't secondhand, is that it?" she asked carefully.

He nodded.

"You believe that any man who touched me with passion would set fire to me."

Duncan hesitated, then nodded again.

"You shame both of us," Amber said icily, making no attempt to conceal her rage.

He started to speak, but she overrode him, clipping each word as though it were thread in a finished weaving.

"Thrice in my life I have felt a man's passion. The first time I ran like a deer until I was safe. Then I knelt and vomited until I was too weak to stand."

"How old were you?"

"Nine."

Duncan said something vile beneath his breath.

"At that age, you were too young to respond to passion," he said. "But now that you are old enough—"

"The second time," Amber interrupted, "I was nineteen. More than old enough to respond to passion, wouldn't you agree?"

Duncan shrugged.

"Wouldn't you agree?" she persisted.

"Yes," he said, his voice harsh. "And you did, didn't you?"

"Respond with passion?"

He nodded curtly.

"Oh, yes," Amber said. "I was consumed by passion—"

Duncan's mouth flattened.

"—if you concede that anger and loathing are passions," she said sardonically. "I drew my dagger, stabbed the hand that was groping under my skirt, and ran until I was safe. Then I vomited until I was too weak to swallow."

"Who were those animals?" Duncan demanded.

"The third time I felt a man's passion," Amber continued, ignoring Duncan's question, "a stranger's hand was tangled in my hair and chills of golden pleasure coursed through me."

"A stranger?"

"You."

"I don't understand," Duncan said.

"Neither do I, but 'tis true just the same. The first time I touched you, I felt a pleasure so keen that I cried out."

"It was my desire you were feeling, not your own."

"You were senseless at the time," Amber retorted.

Duncan's eyes widened. The reflected leap of candle flame made them appear almost as golden as Amber's eyes.

"What are you saying?" he whispered.

"I touched you, I *knew* you, and I wanted *you*. You were senseless, knowing nothing, remembering nothing, and fire curled through me when I ran my hands over your chest."

The sound Duncan made could have been Amber's name or a low sound of hunger, or both urgently mingled.

"I was made for you," Amber said, unfastening her mantle. "You and you alone. Won't you take what is yours and give me what is mine?"

"And what is that?" Duncan said.

But his smile and the thickening of his voice told Amber that he knew very well what was hers.

"We are joined in our souls," she said softly. "Can our bodies do less?"

"Turn around, precious Amber."

Uncertainly, she turned her back to Duncan. The feel of his fingers on her laces sent both desire and relief through her.

For a time there was no sound but the whisper of candle flames and the sigh of clothing as it was smoothed down warm flesh to fall in bright pools on the floor. Finally Amber wore nothing but her own warmth and firelight flickering over her skin.

Duncan's finger traced the length of Amber's back from nape to the shadowed cleft at the base of her spine. She held her breath.

"Do you like that?" he asked.

"Yes."

His fingertip traced again, sliding slowly down until it must stop or be caught between lush, alluring curves. The trembling of Amber's body and the raggedness of her breathing told Duncan that she did indeed enjoy the caress.

"Because I like it?" Duncan asked. "Is it my pleasure that makes your breath break or is it yours?"

"Both," Amber said in a husky voice. "Your pleasure and mine combined."

Again Duncan caressed the feminine line of back and hips, sliding more deeply into the shadow that tempted him mercilessly. He knew if he followed that dark curve he would find a place that was even softer than his dreams, hotter than his desire.

"I would like to feel that," Duncan murmured.

"What?"

He smiled slightly. "My desire and yours combined."

"Then take the gift of my body. Give me the gift of yours in return."

"You have the poorer of the bargain."

"Only because I am naked and you are clothed."

The combination of tartness and passion in Amber's voice made Duncan laugh softly.

"I will stay clothed for a while yet," he said.

"Why?"

"Because that way, I might be able to keep from taking you like a green squire who can't hold his seed long enough to see to his partner's pleasure."

Amber made a startled sound as Duncan bent and lifted her into his arms like a child. For one searing moment she felt the depth of his hunger. The next thing she knew, the fur bed cover was sleek and cool against her naked body and Duncan was no longer touching her.

When Duncan stretched out beside her, he was careful to ensure that there was no contact between them. Yet the fire in his eyes made Amber's heart turn over. She became intensely aware that her nakedness was beautiful to him.

"You have me at a disadvantage," Duncan said in a low voice.

"How so? You are clothed and I am not."

"Ah, but you touch me and you know how I feel. I touch you and know only how *I* feel."

His hand reached out. A single fingertip circled one of Amber's breasts at the exact point where smooth, pale skin gave way to velvety pink. Her breast tightened, sending streamers of fire to the pit of her stomach and beyond.

Smiling, Duncan watched Amber's body change to meet his touch, her nipple gathering into a peak that was as tempting as wild strawberries to his tongue.

"I know how that affects me," he said, "but I don't know how it feels to you."

A shiver of pleasure was Amber's only answer.

"Tell me, golden witch. Tell me what my touch does to you."

"It casts a net of fire over me."

"It hurts you, then?"

"Only when you look at me and I know what we both want and you withhold it," Amber said.

"What do we both want?" Duncan said. "This?"

He bent forward until his mustache almost grazed the tight crown of her breast. Almost, but not quite.

The difference was a lightning stroke of hunger going through Amber.

"Why do you tease me so?" she whispered.

"When I touch you, you feel my desire. If I'm not touching you, the only desire you feel will be your own."

The warmth of Duncan's breath washed over

Amber's sensitive skin. She arched upward only to have him evade her.

"Lie still, precious Amber. Or shall I do as you once did to me?"

"What?"

"Bind you with cords so that you can't move."

"You wouldn't."

Duncan's smile was dark and a bit wolfish.

"I am your husband. Under the law of God and man, I may do as I wish with you."

"And you wish to torture me," Amber muttered.

"Very sweetly," he agreed. "And very thoroughly."

Amber was smiling as she settled back onto the fur cover. The leashed passion in her husband's eyes intrigued her, as did the heightened awareness of her own body.

Saying nothing, Duncan gathered a handful of Amber's long hair. Letting it trail like a scarf from his hand, he teased her breasts until both nipples were drawn into tight buds.

"Beautiful," he said softly. "I ache to taste them, to feel them change with each stroke of my tongue. Do you remember how that felt?"

Fire splintered through Amber. She moved restlessly, wanting more than Duncan's words and the tantalizing caresses that weren't quite his flesh on hers.

"Do you remember?" Duncan asked again.

"Aye," Amber whispered. "Like fire and warm rain together."

Hair slid and stroked and teased Amber's breasts until she made a small sound with each breath she took. Smiling, Duncan caressed down the center line of her body until long golden hair met hair that was darker, a warm thicket protecting the vulnerable flower within.

When the caress moved on, teasing the pale curves of her thighs, Amber's fingers curled deeply into the fur. A tremor went through her, followed by another and another, until one knee flexed in helpless response.

"What do you feel?" Duncan asked.

"A chill that is hot rather than cold," she whispered. "It makes me want to—"

Amber's voice broke as the caress moved back up to the apex of her thighs, ruffling the hair so tenderly that she wanted to cry out her frustration.

"What do you want to do?" Duncan encouraged.

"Bite your hand for teasing me."

He laughed and bent down, blowing against her belly and then her loins, teaching her that she hadn't known what teasing was until that moment. The warm wash of his breath between her thighs sent flames searching through her body.

"Duncan, *please*."

"Please what? You have to tell me, precious Amber. I'm not a sorcerer to know your soul at a touch."

"I ache," she said.

"Where?"

"Where you are teasing me."

"And where is that?" he asked.

"Between my . . . my legs."

"Ah."

Smiling, Duncan shifted down the elegant length of Amber's legs until his breath bathed her ankles.

"Better?" he asked.

Amber made an inarticulate sound that still managed to convey a resounding negative.

"No?" He smiled secretly. "Maybe it is here you ache."

The warm, teasing exhalation of Duncan's breath caressed Amber's knees.

"There?" he asked.

"No," she said huskily.

But Amber, too, was smiling, for in shifting position Duncan had brushed accidentally against her.

Though the contact was barely more distinct than a breath, it swept through her like dawn through night, touching every part of her, teaching her about her husband and herself.

Duncan was enjoying his bride in ways that surprised even him. Though his hunger was a savage ache, it was chained by a greater need to explore the sensuous witch who lay watching him with smoldering eyes.

Knowing that, Amber felt less anxious about playing a lover's game whose rules were unknown to her. Nor did she fear any longer that Duncan wouldn't take her.

The need in him was all the greater for being so fiercely chained.

"Are you certain this isn't the place?" Duncan asked. "I'm told a woman's knees are quite sensitive."

The words were accompanied by another immaterial caress that made Amber gasp, for she distinctly felt Duncan's mustache as well as his breath between her knees.

"Did you like that?" he asked.

Amber nodded, making candlelight twist and twine like a lover in her long hair.

"I can't hear you," Duncan said.

"And I can't feel you," she said, watching him through half-lowered eyelids.

"Are you bargaining with me, wife?"

"Aye."

"Then tell me precisely where you ache and I shall soothe you."

Amber started to speak but her voice dried up.

"I . . . cannot," she whispered.

Duncan saw the color rising from her breasts to her cheeks and understood.

"I keep forgetting," he said in a low voice. "You fly so high, so quickly, yet you were a virgin only hours ago. Forgive me."

"Only if you touch me."

Duncan's head came up. He looked into his bride's eyes and saw his own hunger reflected.

Yet he wasn't touching her.

"You want me," he said.

The surprise in Duncan's voice made Amber want to laugh and pummel him at the same time.

"Haven't I been telling you just that?" she asked.

"But I thought it was my desire coursing through you."

"Sometimes, dark warrior, you have a very thick skull."

Duncan smiled and skimmed the back of his hand lightly over the triangle of dark golden curls.

"Is this where you ache?" he asked huskily.

The sound Amber made was ragged. The flexing of her knee was a silent invitation for greater intimacy.

Yet Duncan wanted more. He needed it. He had to be certain to his very core that Amber was seduced by her own desire rather than overcome by his.

"If you want me within your warm keep, you must open the gate yourself."

There was a hesitation, a broken sigh, and Amber shifted her legs.

Duncan unfastened his mantle and cast it aside.

"More," Duncan whispered.

Amber moved again, though a flush of color was once more climbing up her cheeks.

With swift, impatient movements, Duncan undid his shirt and dropped it onto the floor. The hungry, approving look he received from his bride did nothing to cool the hot race of blood through his body.

Nor did the sight of his bride lying half opened before him, her skin gleaming like a pearl against the fur.

But it wasn't enough.

"Still more," he coaxed.

"Duncan . . ."

The word was half protest and half demand that he cease teasing her.

She shifted slowly, legs pale and elegant, trembling as she felt herself becoming more and more vulnerable with each motion of her legs.

Just as Duncan bent down to caress Amber, he saw faint marks on the otherwise flawless skin of her inner thighs. When he realized how she had come by those marks, his mouth flattened into a bitter downward curve.

"Your keep is still too well defended," Duncan said. "The gate must be open wide. Very wide."

Amber's cheeks were fiery now.

"Why?" she whispered.

"Last time I forced your legs apart," Duncan said in a low voice.

"Nay," she said.

"Aye!" he countered savagely. "I can see the marks left by my hands."

"But—"

"If you would have me lie between your legs, you must make room for me willingly, knowing only your own desire."

Passion raked over Amber at the idea of once more having Duncan lie between her legs, of feeling ecstasy ravish him as he spent himself inside her.

A pulse of pleasure leaped and burst within Amber at the thought. Heat radiated up through her whole body as a secret rain softened her. With an inarticulate sound she opened herself fully, knowing only her own desire.

The blaze of Duncan's eyes was an intimate caress. She made an odd sound as the net of fire tightened throughout her whole body, changing it to receive him. Her legs moved again, as though Duncan were inside her, sharing his body with her.

"You are more beautiful than I have words to tell you," Duncan whispered.

"Then touch me and I shall know."

"Aye. And so shall I."

As Duncan spoke, his hand moved and a long finger slid smoothly, deeply, inside Amber, testing the truth of her desire. She stiffened and whimpered as though he had taken a whip to her.

But it was pleasure rather than pain Duncan had called from Amber, and he knew it as surely as she did. A delicious heat welled up around his caressing finger and spilled into his palm.

Her desire, her response, her need.

Hers, not his.

Duncan made a hoarse sound of hunger and relief. Slowly he withdrew from Amber's willing body.

"No," she said. "Duncan, I—"

Her voice broke as he traced the soft petals that were no longer concealed by golden curls. She had opened for him like a flower, and like a flower she was beautiful to him. The scent and textures of her desire enthralled him. He probed again, and again knew the liquid fire of her response.

Then Duncan's touch was gone and Amber was alone, drawn on a rack of unfulfilled desire. She cried out in protest.

"Patience," he said in a low voice. "I want to be as naked as you."

But Duncan's hands showed little patience as they stripped away his remaining clothes, watched by eyes as yellow as flames.

Amber's eyes widened as he turned back to her. He was fully aroused, overwhelmingly male, and his powerful body gleamed with hunger for her.

"Amber?"

"Were you like this in the Stone Ring?" she asked faintly.

"Aye."

She let out a breath she hadn't been aware of holding.

"I see. Then we shall fit together very well this time, too." Then Amber added beneath her breath, "Though I don't see how."

With a sound that could have been a laugh or a groan, Duncan lowered himself to the bed.

"I shall see to the fit," he said. " 'Tis a poor warrior who can't slide a sword properly into its sheath."

As Duncan settled between Amber's legs, brushing against her, the heavy currents of his passion poured over her, making her tremble.

"Are you frightened?" he asked.

"Touch me and find out."

Duncan reached down between their bodies, but it wasn't his hand that parted the soft petals of Amber's desire. The sleek heat that he discovered made his heartbeat double.

"You must tell me if I hurt you," he said huskily.

The only response possible to Amber was an upwelling of heat, a bud of passion swelling until it burst. Liquid fire washed over him, telling him silently of her welcome.

Duncan let out a breath that was also a groan and eased into her a bit more.

Amber's breath tore. The feel of her own body stretching to accept his presence was exquisitely exciting. The feel of Duncan's harshly leashed passion was a sweet torment. He was taking her so slowly, as though to assure her and himself that there would be no pain in this joining.

"Am I hurting you?" Duncan asked as he pressed just a bit more deeply into Amber.

"Nay," she said raggedly. "You are killing me so sweetly."

"What?"

"Dear God," she whispered.

Duncan felt the sensuous shivering deep within

Amber, knew the hot rain of her passion licking over him, and fought not to lose control. Sweat gleamed from his forehead to his heels, yet he did not speed his slow claiming of her body by one whit.

Another delicate shudder took Amber, giving her to the dark warrior who was seducing her into a passion she hadn't believed possible.

Yet even that wasn't enough. She needed Duncan. All of him. And she needed him right now.

Heedlessly her nails dug into his hips, demanding a deeper joining.

"Do you want more of me?" he asked.

"Yes," she said, "yes and yes and yes. Duncan, *please.*"

He smiled darkly and pressed deeper.

Slowly.

A low moan was torn from Amber's throat. Her hips moved in a seeking as old as Eve. The scent and silky fire of her passion caressed Duncan. He could not contain a single, burning pulse of response. She was so hot around him, so welcoming, so tight.

And he had not yet finished his claiming.

"Are you certain I'm not hurting you?" Duncan asked hoarsely.

A broken sound of pleasure was the only response Amber could make.

"Look at me," he said.

Amber's eyes opened slowly. They were golden, smoldering, almost wild. The sight of them drew another hot pulse from Duncan. She felt it as clearly as he did.

"Can you take more of me without pain?" Duncan asked.

"There is no pain when you lie within me, only pleasure."

The husky whisper of Amber's voice was as sweet to Duncan as the secret movements of her body and

the heady scent of her passion, more exotic than
sandalwood and myrrh.

"Lift your legs and wrap them about me," he
said in a low voice.

When Amber did, the pleasure heightened.

"Hold on to me," Duncan said. "Hold tightly and
hard."

Amber started to ask why, but the feel of him
slowly, completely, filling her body took away
words, took away thought, took away everything
but piercing ecstasy. With a shivering, broken cry,
she gave herself to the pleasure of being fully joined
with her dark warrior.

"Can you feel how much I want you now?"
Duncan asked through clenched teeth.

"I can feel you within me. All of you."

"Is there pain?"

"Nay. 'Tis a pleasure so intense it's frightening.
Your desire and mine together."

Smiling rather fiercely, Duncan slowly began to
withdraw from the silken depths he had taken with
such excruciating care.

"Nay," Amber said almost frantically. "I need
you!"

"No more than I need you."

Her breath broke as Duncan returned, sliding
deeply into her, filling her once more. He repeated
the movement with a restrained power that was all
the more exciting because Amber so clearly knew
the wildness of his desire.

A strange, fey shimmering spread out from their
joined bodies. Amber's eyes widened as she felt
herself being consumed by a fire both tender and
fierce. She began trembling helplessly.

"Duncan, I am coming undone. I cannot—"

Amber's voice splintered. Her body convulsed
delicately, repeatedly, and each motion served only
to draw him more tightly to her, increasing the ravishing fire.

Duncan drank the rippling cry from Amber's lips as her release washed over him, caressing him with each deep, hidden pulse of ecstasy. Every breath he took was infused with her passion.

For sweet, agonizing moments, Duncan held himself motionless above Amber as he savored the certainty of the pleasure he had given to her.

When he could bear no more, he began to move with increasing power. Every motion he made within her brought forth more silky pulses. Her face was taut, drawn with effort as she flew higher and higher, spurred by the potency of his body driving into her.

Suddenly Amber arched and shivered, transfixed by wild ecstasy. The rippling cry she gave was Duncan's name. She clung to him with all her strength, for he was both the storm and the shelter surrounding her.

The sleek, primal heat of Amber tugged at Duncan, caressing him, promising him a pleasure greater than he had ever known. He felt control slipping away and fought against it, for he wanted to hang suspended forever between the certainty of her ecstasy and the anticipation of his own.

"You are perfect," Duncan said hoarsely. "God help me, I want you more than I want anything, even my own memory."

Then he could endure no more. With a groan of surrender, he let go his savage restraint and poured himself into the amber witch whose passionate depths matched his so completely.

15

FULLY dressed for battle, Simon rode his huge war stallion up to Blackthorne Keep at a swift canter. On one side of him rode another knight in chain mail and battle helm. On Simon's other side he led a dark brown stallion that was fully as big as his own mount.

The brown stallion was riderless, his saddle empty of all but a sheathed broadsword and a long, teardrop-shaped shield. On the shield was a drawing of a black wolf's head, sign of Dominic le Sabre, the Glendruid Wolf.

All around horses and men swirled the cold, silent mists of autumn. The horses thundered over the lowered drawbridge that opened into Blackthorne Keep's inner bailey. Moments later cobblestones rang beneath the three stallions' steel-shod hooves.

A woman appeared at the forebuilding's stairs, looking anxiously toward the bailey. When she saw the riderless stallion, she picked up her rich green skirts and raced down the steps. Her cowl slipped off, revealing hair as red as flame, and like flame, her hair lifted on the wind as she ran across the bailey.

Heedless of the danger of being trampled, she went right up to the horses. With each rapid motion of her body, the tiny golden bells she wore shivered and sang.

"Simon!" she cried. "Where is Duncan? What has happened? Why do you have his war-horse?"

Simon's stallion half reared as his rider pulled hard on the reins.

"Stay back, Meg!" Simon commanded. "If one of the horses steps on you, Dominic will have my head."

"I'll have more than that," said a voice from the direction of the gatehouse. "I'll have your heart on a roasting spit."

Simon turned and saw his brother striding across the cobblestones.

Dominic's mantle was long, as black as his hair, and devoid of any decoration save the large silver pin that secured the heavy cloth. Nor was more decoration needed to proclaim Dominic's status. The pin was solid silver, shaped like a wolf's head, and had uncanny crystal eyes that looked out on the world with ancient knowledge.

Wolf of Glendruid, lost for a thousand years, then found and given to a warrior who was not of the Glendruid clan.

Dominic walked past the restive stallions until he could stand between them and his wife. Only when Meg was safe did Dominic turn and address Simon.

"Is Duncan alive?" Dominic asked bluntly.

"Yes."

Meg closed her eyes and said a prayer of thanks as Dominic's arm went around her. He pulled her close and murmured something against her hair. She moved closer still, accepting her husband's support.

"Is Duncan injured?" Dominic asked.

"Yes. And no."

Silver eyes narrowed as Dominic measured the suppressed emotion vibrating within Simon.

Eyes of Glendruid green also studied Simon, for Meg had sensed the hatred that seethed beneath his outward calm. She had not seen him like this since

he had accused her of poisoning Dominic shortly
after their marriage.

Dominic turned and looked at the second knight.
His helm concealed his fair hair, but not the winter
paleness of his eyes. A slight motion of Sven's head
confirmed what Dominic already suspected.

No more should be said about Duncan of Maxwell where all ears could overhear.

"Come into the solar," Dominic said.

A gesture from Dominic sent several grooms
hurrying across the bailey to take the horses. A
word to one of the squires who hovered in the
background sent the boy running to another
quarter of the bailey to have food brought from
the kitchen.

No one spoke again until the privacy of the lord's
solar was reached. After mist-drenched mantles
were removed and hung to dry, Dominic turned
to his brother.

"Tell me how it goes with Duncan."

"He has been bewitched," Simon said flatly.

The hatred in Simon was no longer disguised. It
crackled in his voice like lightning.

"Bewitched?" Meg said. "How so?"

"He remembers nothing of Blackthorne, nothing
of his vow of fealty to Dominic, nothing of his
betrothal to Ariane."

A single black eyebrow lifted, giving Dominic's
face a sardonic look.

"God's teeth," Dominic said. "That could be
inconvenient. King Henry was particularly pleased
to have found a Saxon match for the Norman
heiress."

"A safe match, you mean. As your vassal, Duncan
is indirectly beholden to Henry," Sven said. "I
understand that the lord of Deguerre Hold was
not pleased by the proposed alliance."

Dominic's smile was as savage as the savage
wolf's head pin he wore.

"Lord Charles," Dominic said softly, "dreamed of expanding his empire with his daughter's marriage. Instead, Ariane's wedding will solidify Henry's empire."

"And yours," Sven said with satisfaction.

"Yes. Did you see sign of Charles's men in the Disputed Lands?"

"Nay," Sven said.

"Simon?"

"All I saw sign of was witchery," his brother said grimly.

Dominic glanced sideways at his wife.

"Witchery is your realm, not mine," he said, smiling.

"So speaks the Glendruid Wolf," Sven muttered.

Dominic's smile widened, but he made no effort to further question Simon.

"What kind of spell or enchantment do you suspect?" Meg asked her brother-in-law.

"Ask the hell-witch who lives in the Disputed Lands."

"From the beginning, please," Meg said.

It was a command as much as a request.

Simon took no offense. He had both affection and respect for the Glendruid woman who had saved Dominic's life at great risk to her own.

"Sven and I parted ways at Sea Home," Simon said. "He wanted to chase rumors of a fully outfitted battle stallion roaming the forest like a wild animal, eluding all men who attempted to capture him. A great stallion of darkest brown . . ."

Meg looked at Sven.

"Duncan's stallion?" she asked.

"I suspected as much. I had heard Duncan whistling to him like a falcon. So I whistled through the forest until Shield came trotting up like a great hound, happy to be home again."

Meg turned back to Simon.

"While Sven was combing the forest," Simon said,

"I chased rumors of odd comings and goings to Sea Home."

Meg's breath was released swiftly.

"That was a dangerous thing to do," she said. "Sir Erik is reputed to be a sorcerer. Sea Home is ruled by him."

Simon's clear black eyes gleamed with concealed laughter. Being fussed and worried over by a woman was new to him. He discovered that he rather liked it.

Still smiling, Simon swept off his helm and set it on a trestle table next to Sven's well-used helm.

"Sir Erik's sorcery—if such existed—didn't extend to knowing my mind," Simon said. "He accepted my story of being on a private religious quest."

Meg made a sound that could have meant anything, including impatience with her beloved brother-in-law.

"I had been there only a few days when a man and a maid rode up to Sea Home," Simon said. "The maid was dressed in shades of gold and wore precious amber as though it were brass."

"Amber?" Meg said intently.

"Aye. It was her name, too."

Dominic sensed his wife's sudden tension. He looked down at her in concern, but all her attention was on Simon.

"Amber," Meg repeated. "Just that?"

"She was called the Untouched," Sven said softly, "because no one, man or woman, was permitted to touch her."

A stillness came over Meg.

"Continue," she said to Simon.

"I think rumor overstated the matter," Simon said sardonically. "Amber clung to her companion like ivy to a powerful oak."

"Truly?" Meg asked, startled. "Then it couldn't have been Amber the Untouched."

Simon and Sven looked at each other. It was

Simon who contradicted his lord's Glendruid wife.

"Perhaps not," Simon said carefully, "but the knights and squires of Sea Home thought it was Amber, and they had known her for many years."

"How curious."

"Erik the Undefeated also called her Amber," Simon added. "He used her to scry the truth of her companion's thoughts."

"Ah, that is why she was touching the man, to gain knowledge," Meg said. "She is one of the Learned."

"What are you talking about?" Dominic asked.

"Don't you remember?" Meg said. "When you were planning various ways to take Stone Ring Keep, I told you about the Learned."

Dominic frowned. "Aye, but frankly I didn't credit the foolishness about sorcerers and shape-changers and prophecies and the like."

Amusement danced in Meg's green eyes. Her husband wore the ancient likeness of the Glendruid Wolf, yet had little patience for things he couldn't touch, measure, fight, lay siege to.

Or make love to.

"In some cases, my lord," Meg murmured, "that which cannot be touched is more powerful than that which can be touched."

"A difficult truth for a warrior such as I," Dominic said.

Meg nodded.

"But I have a very fine teacher," he added, smiling. "I now know that the love of a Glendruid healer can take a warrior's frozen heart, turn it inside out, and make it warm again."

The smile Meg and Dominic exchanged reminded Simon of nothing so much as Amber and Duncan. The comparison made him both angry and uncomfortable.

"So," Meg said, turning to Simon once more, "Amber was scrying her companion. Go on."

Simon and Sven exchanged another glance.

"She may have been touching the man for the purpose of gaining knowledge," Simon said in a clipped voice, "but she looked more like a maid with her lover."

"What does it matter?" Dominic asked with growing impatience. "It is Duncan who concerns me, not some Celtic witch."

"That is just the problem," Simon retorted. "The witch's companion was Duncan of Maxwell."

Instantly Dominic's posture changed. He became like a falcon spotting prey from afar, poised for the sudden stoop.

And the kill.

"Was Duncan captive?" Dominic demanded.

"He wore no *visible* bonds, save Amber's fingers laid against his wrist."

"Hardly enough to restrain a warrior of Duncan's size," Dominic said dryly. "Unless this Amber is a new Boadicea come to slay men with her mighty sword."

"The sword she used to slay Duncan—"

"What?" Meg interrupted starkly. "You said Duncan was well!"

Simon looked into Meg's clear green eyes and wished himself anywhere else.

"I know you have tenderness for him," Simon said.

Dominic looked grim. Despite his certainty of Meg's love, Dominic found he had little liking of his wife's affection for her childhood friend, Duncan of Maxwell.

"But," Simon continued grimly, "I fear the hell-witch Amber has taken Duncan's soul."

"Is he dead?" Dominic demanded.

"No. Nor is he alive, not in the way we knew him."

"Explain."

The quality of Dominic's voice made Sven shift

and look at his lord's mantle uneasily. The eyes of the great pin glittered with reflected firelight as though intelligent, alive, and every bit as savage as the man who wore it.

"It is as I told you," Simon said distinctly. "Duncan remembers nothing of the time before he came to the Disputed Lands."

"Are you certain?" Dominic asked. "Could he not be like Sven, pretending to be someone he isn't in order to spy out the land?"

"I prayed that was the truth," Simon said.

Meg simply shook her head. Tears glittered in her eyes as she remembered Duncan's forthright nature.

"He is not like Sven," Meg said, "an actor capable of many roles."

"A man may learn to act when his life depends on it," Dominic pointed out.

Meg closed her eyes for a moment. When they opened again, they were those of an unflinching Glendruid healer. It was the same when she spoke, her voice devoid of all emotion.

"Continue, Simon," Meg said. "I would hear more of Duncan's transformation. I would hear *everything*."

Uneasily Simon looked at Dominic. There was nothing in Dominic's face to comfort Simon.

"I showed no sign I recognized Duncan," Simon said, turning back to Meg. "He kept staring at me as though trying to decide if he knew me."

"How was he introduced to you?" she asked.

"As a man whose memory was gone."

"What did they call him?"

"Duncan," Simon said.

"Why?"

"Because he is dark and a warrior. At least, that is what Erik said."

"Did they explain how Duncan lost his memory?"

"Nay," Simon said savagely. "Erik said he found Duncan in a storm, senseless and naked but for that amber talisman you had given him."

"Sven?" Meg asked.

"I heard naught but what Simon did."

"The talisman saved his life," Simon said.

"How so?" Dominic asked.

"Erik was expecting Duncan of Maxwell or his knights. A common stranger would have been killed as a spy or an outlaw. But a stranger wearing an amber talisman was different."

"They took Duncan to Amber the Untouched," Meg summarized.

Simon looked curiously at her, wondering how she had known.

"Yes," Sven said quietly. "It is said that all things amber belong to her."

"Yes," Meg said.

For the space of several slow breaths she looked into a distance only Glendruid eyes could see.

"Did you know, small falcon?" Dominic asked Meg softly. "Is that why you gave the talisman to Duncan?"

"I dreamed of amber," she said. "And I dreamed that Duncan was going into great danger."

Dominic smiled slightly. "I knew about the danger while wide awake. 'Tis why I sent Duncan to secure Stone Ring Keep. Only a powerful warrior could take an estate in the Disputed Lands."

"And only a wealthy knight could hire enough fighters to hold such an estate," Simon added.

"Aye," Dominic said. " 'Tis why King Henry arranged a wedding with the daughter of Charles, the Baron of Deguerre."

"Don't count on the marriage," Simon said bluntly.

"Why not?"

"The people of Sea Home were making wagers on how soon Amber would wed Duncan the

Nameless, the one man whom she could touch with pleasure."

"God's teeth." snarled Dominic. "Duncan must be mad. Lady Ariane arrived here three days ago!"

Simon looked surprised. "I saw no strange men or servants in the bailey."

"She came alone but for a lady's maid and three knights to guard her dowry," Meg said.

"The knights left as soon as they saw the dowry safely inside the keep," Dominic added.

"Hardly the way I would expect a great baron to treat his hounds," Simon muttered, "much less his only daughter."

"The baron was much put out by having to marry his daughter to a Saxon," Dominic said neutrally.

"Then the baron may be pleased to get his daughter back."

"If Duncan jilts Ariane, he will have no means of supporting the knights he must have to hold Stone Ring Keep," Dominic said flatly. "And I, along with my unruly vassal, would suffer the displeasure of both the King of England and the King of Normandy."

"All this," Meg said quietly, "at a time when the last of the warriors you sent with Duncan are only now straggling back to Blackthorne Keep on foot, muttering about lightning from a clear sky that drove their horses mad."

"Are you quite certain," Dominic asked Simon, "that Duncan hasn't forsworn himself and cast his lot with Erik?"

"Never!" Meg said before anyone could speak.

"That is what I feared at first," Simon said calmly. "It would have explained much."

"And?" Dominic asked.

"Rather quickly, I decided it wasn't a simple matter of betrayal. If it had been, Duncan would have given me away to Sir Erik."

Sven nodded, silently agreeing. "It would have meant Simon's death."

"So you decided he was bewitched," Meg said, "and truly didn't know you."

"Yes. What else could it be?"

"Sometimes," Meg said, "a man who is kicked in the head by a horse or hit with a battle hammer . . . if they survive, sometimes such men lose all knowledge of themselves for a time."

"How long?" Dominic asked sharply.

"Sometimes days. Sometimes months. Sometimes . . . forever."

Sven crossed himself and muttered, "You call it accident. I call it Satan, who knows more disguises than I do."

"Truly?" Simon asked innocently. "A bemusing thought."

Dominic ignored them and looked at Meg.

"What do you say, Glendruid healer?" he asked.

"I can't know whether it is accident or bewitchment until I see Duncan."

"While Duncan and I fought—," Simon began.

"You fought?" Meg asked, appalled. "Why?"

"Sir Erik wanted to know the temper of the two new warriors he had found," Simon said dryly. "So Duncan and I fought to display our skills with the sword."

Dominic's smile was as thin as the edge of a dagger.

"I would like to have seen that," he said. "Your quickness against his strength."

Simon's black eyes gleamed with laughter and a warrior's love of testing himself against another warrior's skill.

"It was like fighting you," Simon admitted, "but every bruise was rewarded by the certainty that Duncan hadn't betrayed his oath of fealty to you."

"How so?"

"When I said the words 'Blackthorne Keep,'

Duncan faltered as though at a blow. For an instant the darkness in his eyes lifted and he almost knew me."

"What happened next?" Meg asked intently.

"I put him on his back in the field. Then I asked him if what Erik had said about his memory was true."

"And?"

"Duncan said it was."

"You believed him," Meg said.

"Aye. He remembered nothing. The hell-witch has stolen his soul."

Meg flinched at the naked loathing in Simon's voice. She knew he hated necromancy as few men hated anything.

But she didn't know why.

"I now knew all that was required," Simon said. "I made my excuses to Erik, found Sven, and set off for Blackthorne Keep as fast as our horses could carry us."

Absently, Dominic ran his fingertips over the cool silver of the Glendruid Wolf. Then he turned and looked at Simon and Sven with eyes whose icy clarity precisely matched those of the huge pin.

"Rest for a time," Dominic said. "When you are ready, the three of us will ride for the Disputed Lands."

"What will you accomplish with just three men?" Meg asked. "Stone Ring Keep can hold out for months against such a small force."

"To take any more warriors would endanger Blackthorne Keep."

Dominic's expression softened as he smiled at his red-haired wife. He touched Meg's lower lip with his thumb in a brief, sensual caress.

"Besides," Dominic added, "don't you remember what I taught you about the best way to take a well-defended keep?"

"Treachery," Meg said huskily. "From within."

"Aye."

"What will you do?" she asked.

"Somehow they stole Duncan from us. We shall steal him back."

"How?" Simon asked.

"With a net," Dominic said succinctly.

"And then?"

"We will teach Duncan who he is," Dominic said. "Then we will send him back to Stone Ring Keep. When he is inside, he will open the gates for us."

Sven laughed softly.

Simon simply smiled. "How like you, brother. Bold, yet bloodless."

"There's little point to killing good men when better means are available," Dominic said, shrugging.

"We had best hurry to be about our treacherous business," Meg said. "The sooner we—"

"We?" Dominic interrupted.

"Aye, husband. We."

All amusement and sensual indulgence vanished from Dominic's expression.

"Nay," he said flatly. "You're carrying the future of Blackthorne Keep in your womb. You will stay here."

Meg's mouth tightened.

"I am many months from birthing your heir," she said. "I'm as fit as any of your knights to ride. I'm no frail lady unable to pick up a dropped shoe."

Her voice and expression were every bit as determined as her lord's.

"*Nay*," Dominic said.

Simon looked at his brother, cursed silently, and did what few men would have the courage to do when Dominic looked so fierce. Deliberately Simon cleared his throat, drawing his brother's attention.

And his ire.

"What is it?" Dominic snarled.

"If Duncan is injured, Meg can treat him. If he is

enthralled . . ." Simon shrugged. "What one witch has done, another witch might undo."

"We were going to move the household to Carlysle Manor for several fortnights in any case," Meg said calmly. "The Disputed Lands are but a few days' gentle ride from Carlysle."

Dominic remained as silent and forbidding as a drawn sword. Then he lifted his hand and set it beneath Meg's chin.

"If God willed it, I could bear losing the babe," Dominic said softly, "but not you. You are my heart."

Meg turned her head and kissed the scarred hand that held her so gently.

"I have dreamed no Glendruid dreams of death," she said, "and being parted from you is a kind of dying. Take me with you. Let me do what I was born to do."

"Heal?"

"Aye."

There was a long silence. Then Dominic released his wife with a gentle touch and turned to Sven.

"Inform the grooms to ready horses for dawn."

"How many horses, lord?"

Dominic paused, looked at Meg's unflinching Glendruid eyes, and knew what he must do whether it pleased him or not.

"Four."

❧❀ 16

T HE flicker of a dying candle
flame beyond the bed's luxurious draperies made
Duncan start from his uneasy sleep.

Danger!

He reached for his sword as he had so often in
the twelve days since his marriage. Belatedly he
realized he was only half awake and fully nude.

Even as Duncan told himself it was but a dream
that had disturbed him, he eased out of the bed
and lit candles around the room until there were no
shadows where enemies could hide. Only then did
he go back to bed as silently as he had arisen.

"Duncan?"

He started again, then turned on his side toward
the soft voice that was both familiar and oddly
alien. Thoughts like black lightning raged through
the shades of darkness that were his mind.

She is not part of my past.

Danger!

I am surrounded by enemies.

Danger!

Yet even as part of Duncan's mind cried of peril,
his recent memories scoffed, for nothing but kindness and incandescent passion had come to him at
Stone Ring Keep.

Am I going mad?

Will I be torn in two and die writhing while shades

of darkness and amber light battle for my soul?

The only answer that came to Duncan was an inner silence which seethed with contradictions.

The unremembered past was taking shape in his mind as random threads and fragmented patterns, names and no faces, places and no names, faces and no places. He was a tapestry rent and shredded, unraveled as much as woven, threads all snarled and frayed.

Sometimes, the worst times, he saw the shadows retreat, revealing his memory. And that was when he truly knew despair like black ice, freezing everything.

He feared his returning memory.

What is happening to me? God's wounds, why do I fear the very thing that I long for!

With a harsh sound Duncan grabbed his head in both hands. An instant later, fingers that were both gentle and insistent stroked his clenched fingers.

"Dark warrior," Amber whispered. "Be at peace."

If Duncan heard, he made no sound.

Tears slid hotly down Amber's cheeks as she shared Duncan's anguish.

And his fear.

Like Duncan, Amber sensed the slow healing of his memory. She saw faces where only shadows had been, heard names where only silence had been, sensed time's shuttle at work. The pattern which would weave all together was lacking, but it, too, would return. She was certain of it.

And then she would know the wrath of a proud warrior who had been defeated in secret rather than allowed to fight as he had been born to do.

It is too soon. Duncan has had so little time with me. A fortnight before we became lovers. Barely a fortnight since we wed. Not enough time to learn to love me.

Dear God, not nearly enough time.

Only love could forgive so great a deception. If he remembers too soon, he will never forgive me.

Never love me.

And great death will surely flow.

Amber never knew whether she called Duncan's name with her lips or with her heart. She knew only that suddenly they were holding each other so tightly she couldn't breathe.

"Precious Amber," Duncan said in a raw voice. "What would I do without you?"

Tears burned against her eyes and filled her throat.

"You would fare better than I would without you," she whispered. "You are the heart in my body."

Duncan felt the hot flow of Amber's tears. Slowly he eased his grip on her.

"Don't cry," he said. "It was but a dream I had, naught to disturb yourself over."

Amber knew with Learned precision just how little of what had gone on in Duncan's mind resembled a dream, and she knew that he knew it as well as she did.

Yet she said nothing about the gentle lie. She had no more desire than Duncan to search among the tangled, agonizing threads of his memory for the truth she feared more than she feared death itself.

"Duncan," she whispered.

The sound was more a caress than it was a word, for she spoke with her lips pressed against the pulse that beat in his neck.

Duncan's body stilled for an instant before he shuddered and tightened with a different kind of tension than that of a warring mind. He felt an answering ripple of sensation pass through Amber and knew how clearly she felt his desire.

Yet he knew now that it was also *her* desire. In the brief time of their marriage, she not only responded when he cast the sensual lure, she wanted him whether or not he was touching her.

She came to him when he stood brooding and

watching the rain through the keep's narrow windows.

If she awakened before he did, she curled against him, stroking her slender hands the length of his body and laughing softly when he rose to meet her touch.

Each day before dinner she rode with him, sharing her knowledge of the forest and fields and the people of the keep.

In the evenings she dismissed his attendant and bathed Duncan with great pleasure, teaching him the Learned way of purifying the flesh and then shivering with delight when he taught her how the Saracen sultans bathed.

And always her eyes brightened when he came to her after hearing the complaints of serf and villein in the morning. She smiled with happiness when she turned and saw him standing in a doorway, watching her decipher ancient manuscripts.

In a thousand ways she came to him, telling him how much she was pleased to be his mate.

"You are sunlight when all else is rain," Duncan said.

More tears seeped from Amber's eyes to glide hotly over Duncan's skin. He shifted onto his back, pulling her close against his side.

"Without you," he whispered, "I don't know how I could have survived the battleground that is my mind."

"Dark warrior . . ."

Pain twisted in Amber, squeezing her throat shut more surely than tears. The words of love she wanted to give Duncan were fire burning within her silence.

Blindly Amber moved to lie even more closely against her husband's body. His heat and power were a lure that grew greater every hour she spent with him. The thought of losing Duncan was a dagger turning in her soul.

"Duncan," she whispered.

Amber's ragged voice and the hot glide of her tears against Duncan's shoulder sent a wave of tenderness through him. Gently he stroked her hair. She shifted and a moist heat traced the length of Duncan's jaw.

For an instant he thought it was her tears. Then he understood that it was the tip of her tongue in a lover's caress.

"You tempt me," Duncan said huskily.

A ripple of pleasure went through Amber, a sweet echo of the sensual anticipation sweeping through Duncan. He no longer fought the wild surging of his desire when she touched him, for he no longer worried whose hunger rose first to the sensual lure and whose followed.

Duncan had learned that Amber's passion was a fire that burned brightly whether alone or entwined with his.

Small teeth delicately tested the pad of muscle on Duncan's shoulder. Hidden within the caress was a sensual tasting of his skin. Surrounding and enhancing the kiss was a shivering sigh.

"Do you want me, precious Amber?"

Another trembling sigh.

"Yes," she whispered.

Yet when Duncan moved to hold her, she pulled away.

"No," she whispered.

"It appears you are of two minds," Duncan said, smiling. "Is there anything I can do to—"

His teasing words broke over a groan of pleasure as Amber's leg moved to lie between his.

"The flower is already blooming," Duncan said thickly. "I can feel its heat."

"The flower knows that the sun will soon rise. It wants each petal already open to drink the first golden shaft of the sun."

"The sun is already risen," he said thickly.

"Is it?"

Beneath the bed covers, a small hand trailed down Duncan's bare torso.

The rest of him was equally naked.

Delicate fingertips brushed over Duncan, measuring and caressing his aroused flesh. A soft palm fitted itself around him. He made a sound that was laughter and passion at once.

"You know fair well it is risen," he said. "You are holding the proof in your palm."

"Only part of the proof. I fear the full proof would overrun both of my hands together."

"A waste."

"Aye," Amber murmured.

"There is a solution for that."

"I'm considering it."

"Lie on your back, precious Amber. You will consider things much more deeply from that perspective."

"I think . . . not."

The laughter and husky sensuality curling through Amber's voice made Duncan smile. Passion and anticipation coiled more tightly within him.

"What are you thinking of, then?" he asked.

"I fear it would shock you into swooning," she said.

"I'm lying down."

"Not all of you is supine."

"The greater part is."

Amber smiled and drew her fingertips up the part of Duncan which was not at rest.

"Such a sweet, witchy little smile," he said thickly. "What are you thinking of that makes you smile so?"

"Two hands . . . and a mouth. Will that suffice?"

For an instant Duncan didn't comprehend. Then Amber's hands circled him and the velvet heat of her tongue caressed him. His whole body tightened in a savage rush.

"Amber."

She looked up at him.

"Did I hurt you?" she asked.

As she spoke, she stroked the length of his rigid flesh. Blood beat visibly beneath her caress, hardening him even more.

"Nay," Duncan said.

"Shock you?"

"Yes. No."

He forced breath into a body that was clamoring for another intimate kiss, for the sleek glide of her tongue tasting him.

"Can't you decide?" Amber asked, knowing full well how deep Duncan's pleasure had been. "Perhaps this will help."

She repeated the wild caress, lingering over the part of him that was most intriguingly different.

And most sensitive.

"Have I told you," Amber murmured between caresses, "how much your body pleases me?"

"If you please me any more, I will come unraveled."

"Then I shall just have to knit you up again."

"The heart falters at the thought."

"The heart, perhaps, but not the flesh. It tugs like a stallion too closely tied."

Duncan laughed despite the heat flooding through him, driven by the wild rush of his blood and the feel of Amber caressing him with her words, her hands, her tongue.

Smiling, knowing how much she was exciting him, Amber shook her head until her hair fell like a veil over Duncan's loins. But not all of him could be easily veiled. Passion stood forth proudly, demanding to be eased.

Or teased.

"I particularly like this," Amber said. "Hard, yet so smooth to my fingertips, like polished silver warmed by the sun."

A deep shudder went through Duncan as he watched and felt the pink flame of her tongue licking over him, setting him utterly ablaze. Strong hands buried themselves in her hair.

"Come here," Duncan said hoarsely.

"Soon," she whispered. "But first . . ."

Amber's mouth circled him, tasted him, tested his hardness and resolve with loving caresses. The wildness that gathered in him also gathered in her. At any instant she expected Duncan to overturn her, draw up her knees, and bury himself within her.

Abruptly Duncan sat up and drew Amber's leg across his thighs until she was astride him, open to him. He found her drenched with the same passion that made his body gleam as though polished with oil.

His hand moved between her thighs, testing and savoring her in the same caress. His fingers came away glistening with her desire. Watching her, he lifted his hand and breathed in deeply, infusing himself with her fragrance.

"Next time," he said, "I shall know your taste as well. But not this time. This time I am already undone by your sweet mouth."

"You look quite whole," she whispered.

Her fingertip rested for an instant on him, just long enough to steal the single, hot drop that had eluded his control. When she brushed her fingertip over her lips, tasted, and smiled, Duncan made the sound of a man in torment. Another drop welled up, called by her pleasure in him.

"Come, witch. Ride the dragon you have summoned from mortal flesh."

"How does a maid ride a dragon?"

"Like this."

Duncan's hands closed on Amber's hips, pulling her closer even as he lifted her. A instant later his blunt, eager flesh parted her. With a cry of fulfillment, she slid down on him, claiming him as deeply as he was claiming her.

Amber tried to say Duncan's name, but could not. His pleasure in her had stolen her voice. The sudden clenching of his hands on her hips scattered her thoughts and focused her desire. She began moving, riding him more surely with each slow motion of her hips, feeling his passion and her own with unusual clarity.

When he would have speeded the pace of the ride, Amber lifted one of his hands, kissed it, and put it on her breast.

"You're enjoying tormenting me," Duncan said through his teeth.

"Aye."

His fingers closed on the taut peak of Amber's breast. A delicate convulsion shivered through her, forerunner of the ecstasy to come. When his hands caressed both nipples into hardness, her back arched and her breath tore. The sweet heat of her passion flowed between their joined bodies.

"Yes," Duncan whispered. "Let me feel your pleasure."

Without warning, ecstasy ravished Amber, setting her to shivering and crying. He thrust into her, fusing their bodies together with the searing pulses of his own release.

Feeling Duncan's ecstasy increased Amber's, driving her even higher. He rocked his hips against her until she called his name and came completely undone once more.

Then he held her against his chest until both of them could breathe evenly again. Only then did he move, reversing positions until he lay between her legs. He kissed her slowly, deeply.

"Each time you please me more," Duncan said.

"And you please me more. 'Tis almost frightening."

"Why?"

"If I enjoyed you any more," Amber whispered, "I would die."

"And I would bring you back to life."

" 'Tis impossible."

"Nay. 'Tis inevitable."

"We can't," she whispered, understanding what he intended. "Can we?"

"We must. We will. Watch me as I watched you. Learn how much I cherish you."

Slowly Duncan slid down Amber's body, turning his face from side to side, caressing her with his lips and his words.

"Take me to the place where there are no shadows, only fire," he said. "Give me the flower that blooms more beautifully each time."

Amber had no defenses against Duncan's aching need. Nor did he. It was a passion more complex than any he had ever felt. It was an emotion whose name he did not know, for he had never guessed such a feeling existed.

It was thirst in the midst of sweet water, need in the midst of plenty, hunger in the midst of a feast.

He could not get close enough to her.

Tears filled Amber's eyes and overflowed onto her cheeks. Never had she thought to be cherished so sweetly, tiny kisses and secret tastes, his breath warm against her breasts, her navel, her thighs.

Then Duncan's mouth discovered her, tasted her, circled the bud that was the burning center of her passion. The unexpected caress was like lightning transfixing her, startling a cry from the back of her throat.

"Precious Amber," Duncan said, shivering with a torrent of desire. "I swear I can feel your passion like lightning transfixing you."

Delicately he caught her tender bud between his teeth. She cried out his name with each slow move-

ment of his tongue. Then she could speak no more
for she had no breath, she was splintering, crying,
dying, consumed by an ecstasy that had no beginning and no end.

In the midst of fire he came to her, and they
burned together in a place where there were no
shades of darkness, only fire.

AMBER looked out upon the great
hall. There were still many serfs, freeholders, and
villeins standing about. Only a few of them had
expressions that suggested they were still waiting
for their seneschal's attention.

"Are you finished, my lord?" Amber asked.

She had left Duncan long enough to translate a
particularly difficult fragment of a manuscript so
that Cassandra would have it when she returned
from the north. But as soon as the translation was
done, she had sought out Duncan.

When Amber wasn't with him, she felt uneasy,
as though he would somehow be taken from her
without warning.

"Come sit beside me," Duncan said, holding out
his hand. "I'll be finished soon."

The instant Duncan touched Amber, she sensed
some of the tension leave both of them. At the
moment, his memories weren't stirring. He was
concentrating only on the present and his duties
as Erik's seneschal.

While Amber sat beside Duncan on the raised
dais in the great hall, he listened to complaints,
resolved them, and listened again. As he listened,
he caressed her hand, recalling for both of them the
pleasure and peace they had found in the hours
before dawn, when their interlocked bodies had
defeated the memories which stalked Duncan like
a pack of wolves.

"Has it been a tedious morning?" Amber murmured.

"I have come to believe that all pigs should be hamstrung," Duncan muttered as the next vassals stepped forward.

Amber saw who the petitioners were and hid her smile.

"Ethelrod must have let his pig root about in the Widow Mary's garden again," Amber said.

"Does it happen often?" Duncan asked.

"As often as Ethelrod and the widow lie with each other."

Duncan gave Amber a sideways glance.

"The pig is quite fond of Ethelrod, you see," Amber said in a voice that carried no farther than her husband.

"No, I don't see," Duncan muttered.

"The pig follows Ethelrod like a faithful hound."

Duncan's smile was a white flash beneath his mustache.

"I begin to comprehend," he said. "Does Ethelrod have an enclosure stout enough to hold a pig?"

"No. Nor can he afford one. He is but a serf."

"Do they wish to marry?"

"The widow is a freeholder. If they marry, any children they have would be serfs."

Frowning, Duncan watched the couple who stood so uneasily in front of their new seneschal.

"Does Erik lack for serfs?" Duncan asked very softly.

"Nay. He is a strict lord, but not harsh," Amber said. "No one flees his service."

"Has Ethelrod been a faithful vassal?"

"Aye. He has never shirked."

"How is he thought of by the people of the keep?" Duncan asked.

"They bring their problems to him sooner than they bring them to the priest or to the lord of the keep."

Duncan kept Amber's hand within his as he turned back to address the couple standing in front of him.

"Widow Mary," Duncan said. "Other than Ethelrod's status as serf, have you any objection to him as a husband?"

The woman was so startled by the question, it took her a moment to answer.

"Nay, lord. He be a hard worker and a kind man to those as is weaker. But . . ."

"But?" Duncan said encouragingly. "Speak, woman."

"That pig of his will nae see the inside of my cottage save it enter on a roasting spit!"

The vassals who had remained to watch their new seneschal at work laughed. The running battle between the widow and the pig was a source of much amusement at the keep.

Smiling, Duncan switched his hazel glance to the serf who stood uneasily in the great hall, his cap in his gnarled hands and his ill-shod feet flat as a cart bottom.

"Ethelrod, have you any objection to the widow as a wife?" Duncan asked.

Red crept up the man's bearded cheeks to his weathered forehead.

"Nay, s-sir," he stuttered. "She be a f-fine lass."

"Then the solution to the problem of the pig becomes clear," Duncan said. "The day you wed Widow Mary, you will no longer be a serf."

Ethelrod was too stunned to do more than open and close his mouth.

"Sir Erik's present to you on your wedding day," Duncan continued, "will be enough wood to build a stout swine pen."

A shout compounded of laughter, approval, and celebration went up in the great hall. In less than a fortnight, the vassals had come to fully approve the keep's seneschal.

Before the commotion had settled, Duncan stood up, drawing Amber with him.

"Come and ride with me," he said. "I find I enjoy your knowledge of the keep and its vassals as much as I need it."

"Where shall we ride this time?"

"Where we have ridden every day since we wed," Duncan said, nodding to the vassals as they cleared a way for him through their ranks.

"The southern trail through Wild Rose hamlet and the fields to the forest," Amber said, smiling. " 'Tis my favorite ride. Wild Rose creek sounds like laughter."

Only two horses waited out in the bailey. There were so few fighting men left at Stone Ring Keep that Duncan refused to put them to work as an unneeded escort when he and Amber rode out over the keep's land. No outlaws had been seen or heard within half a day's ride of the keep since one of their kind had been hanged by Erik.

Duncan lifted Amber onto her horse, then mounted his own. As always after settling into the saddle, he checked the position of his sword and that of the hammer. To Duncan, the gestures were as natural as breathing.

Side by side, the two horses clattered through the bailey and thumped over the stout wooden drawbridge. As they rode, Amber answered questions concerning the history of the various fields, who tilled them and how well, who was freeholder and who was serf, who was well and who was ill.

"I don't think you ride out along this path to hear the creek," Amber said finally as they rode into the forest.

"I ride out to have you teach me about the keep."

"And Hawk Hill, which lies close to our way, is a good viewpoint to look out upon the keep's land," she said.

Duncan nodded.

"You will make Erik a fine seneschal."

"I would make him a better warrior."

"He doesn't doubt your mettle," Amber said.

"Then why won't he use me at Winterlance, where Norsemen are rumored to be thick as summer grass in the fields?" Duncan asked angrily.

"You are more valuable to him here. Only Saturday last, one of his cousins was sniffing about the vassals, testing their will."

Duncan grunted.

"By now," Amber said, "Erik's cousins know that Stone Ring Keep has a new seneschal who is much respected by the vassals."

When Duncan didn't answer, Amber looked at him unhappily. He was glancing around with narrowed eyes, as though searching for something.

And his hand lay on his sword hilt.

"Duncan? Is something amiss?"

He started and looked toward Amber. Her heart stopped, then quickened fiercely.

For an instant he hadn't known her.

Duncan looked down at his partially drawn sword and then over his shoulder. Behind them, fanning out from the point where cart path and forest merged, the keep's fields lay darkly beneath a peaceful sky.

Beyond the fields, clouds lay against the fells like languid harem girls awaiting their lord's pleasure. Over all poured the sun, its rich golden light a healing benediction.

Turning in the saddle, Duncan looked ahead. The lord's forest still wore an autumnal blaze of yellow and red and orange. Frost-killed weeds clung in brittle disarray to rocks and fallen limbs. Leaves dried by three windy, rainless days swirled around the horses' fetlocks as they walked side by side along the cart road.

When Duncan showed no sign of answering her question, Amber braced herself in the stirrups and leaned toward him. Fingers that trembled slightly closed over the wrist of his sword hand.

Nothing came to Amber through the touch but the savage conflict within Duncan's mind.

"Do you know me?" Amber asked, her voice urgent.

Duncan's eyes focused on her and he laughed in surprise. He picked up her hand and kissed her palm.

"I know you as well as I know my own heart," he said.

"But a moment ago you looked at me as though I were a stranger!"

Amusement faded from Duncan's eyes, leaving only the shadows that haunted him relentlessly.

"A moment ago," he said, "I was lost in shades of darkness."

Amber made an unhappy sound.

"Part of me constantly cries danger," Duncan added grimly. "Part of me constantly scoffs. I feel like a haunch being gnawed by two wolves."

He laced Amber's fingers between his. For a time they rode slowly, side by side, talking little, letting the brilliant colors of autumn brighten all shadows.

Duncan and Amber were still holding hands when a weighted net sailed out of the forest and wrapped around the Scots Hammer.

❧ 17

INSTANTLY Duncan fought to free his sword hand, but only succeeded in tangling himself more tightly within the net's coils. Crying Duncan's name, Amber pulled out her dagger and leaned toward him.

Before she could slash at the net, a man appeared beside her and grabbed her wrist. The hatred that poured through the contact was more painful than anything she had ever felt. Amber gave a horrifying cry and fell senseless to the ground. Nor did she move again, even when Duncan called her name.

Duncan went mad.

He clawed at the net, ripping its tough fibers as though they were straw.

"Now!" cried the man who had grabbed Amber.

Two more men ran from the forest. One of them seized Duncan's left foot and heaved upward, sending him tumbling to the ground.

All three men jumped on their captive, trying to subdue him. Though one of the men was as big as Duncan, and the others hardly smaller, Duncan had a berserker's strength.

"Simon, grab his other arm!" Dominic said harshly.

"I'm trying!" Simon retorted through his teeth.

"God's blood," Sven said, "he's strong as an ox."

"Duncan!" Meg called. "*Duncan!* You're safe! Don't you remember us?"

For an instant Duncan hesitated, caught between past and present, held by a half-remembered voice.

An instant was all that Dominic required. His thumbs dug savagely on either side of Duncan's neck. The Scots Hammer kicked once, then fought no more.

When Dominic lifted his hands again, Duncan lay as senseless as Amber. Simon wasted no time in removing the net while Sven bound hands and feet as they became untangled.

"It is done," Sven said. "Even a white bear couldn't break free of these bonds."

"Take his feet," Dominic said to Simon. "And remember—we ask questions of him, but offer no answers of our own beyond our friendship and his bewitchment."

Simon bent and grabbed Duncan's feet.

"I still think," Simon muttered, "we should just tell him and be done with the mummery."

"Aye, but Meg said otherwise, and she is the healer."

"God's teeth," hissed Simon.

"And Hell's, too," Dominic agreed.

Together, Dominic and Simon heaved Duncan facedown over his horse's back. Walking on either side, they quickly vanished into the forest. Sven bent, scooped up Amber, and followed at a trot.

Meg caught the remaining horse's reins and led it to the rough, hidden camp Dominic had made while he waited for the best moment to grab Duncan. With each movement Meg made, the tiny golden bells she wore at her wrists and waist chimed sweetly.

While Sven tied the horses, Meg went to where Duncan was lying motionless on the ground. As she knelt, Dominic came to stand nearby.

Only Simon noted that Dominic's hand was on his sword.

Meg put her palm on Duncan's chest. His heart beat steadily. His skin was warm. His breathing was even. She let out a sigh of relief and removed her hand.

"That was a nasty Saracen trick, husband."

"Better than the butt of an axe handle," Dominic said bluntly. "Duncan is dazed, that's all."

"His neck will be bruised."

"He is fortunate to still have his precious neck," Dominic retorted.

Meg didn't argue. It was the simple truth.

"Dominic is the only lord I know," Simon said, "who wouldn't have hanged Duncan out of hand as a traitor."

With a muted chiming of bells, Meg stood and touched her husband's cheek.

"I know," she said proudly. "That is why you are the Glendruid Wolf. You are strong enough *not* to kill."

Dominic smiled and covered his wife's hand with his own.

"You had better see to the witch," Sven said as he threw a blanket over Amber. "She's pale and cold as frost."

Bells sang softly as Meg hurried to Amber, knelt, and touched her. Amber's skin was indeed cold. Her breathing was erratic, too shallow. Her heartbeat was too rapid.

Frowning, Meg turned to Simon.

"What did you do to her?" she asked.

"I grabbed her wrist."

"Harshly enough to break bones?" Meg asked.

"No, though I wouldn't weep if I had," Simon said. "The hell-witch deserves worse than a few broken bones for what she did to Duncan."

"I saw it, lady," Sven said to Meg. "He barely touched the girl, yet she screamed like a soul feeling the fires of hell for the first time."

Meg tilted her head in the manner of someone listening to a distant sound.

"It fits," she said finally.

Meg flicked a corner of the blanket back. Amber's wrists were tied neatly together in front of her.

" 'Tis said that anyone's touch is painful to her," Sven added.

"Aye," Meg said.

Her fingers stopped short of Amber's wrists. There were no obvious marks of bruising, no sign of swelling. Nor was there any other injury visible on her body.

Yet Amber lay senseless, her skin cold to the touch, her heartbeat too rapid, her breathing too light.

After pulling Amber's mantle and the blanket more closely around her, Meg stood and went to check on Duncan again. When she would have knelt beside him, Dominic's hand shot out. He pulled her aside, putting her behind his broad back.

Now Meg was well beyond Duncan's reach, even if he were free to seize her.

"Leave Duncan be," Dominic said. "He is like a stranger. He knows us not."

"He knew me," Meg said.

"Did he?" Simon muttered. "Or was he simply surprised to hear a woman's voice?"

"Ask him," Dominic said curtly. "He is only pretending to sleep now."

As Dominic spoke, he watched the knight who had sworn fealty to him . . . the knight who now watched Dominic with the eyes of a man half mad with hatred.

"What have you done to Amber?" Duncan snarled.

"Naught but pull her from her horse," Dominic said.

"You *touched* her?"

Dominic shrugged. "I? No. Simon did. Most gently, if you think on the circumstances."

"Let me see her!"

"No," Dominic said distinctly. "I think you have seen far too much of your leman."

"She is my wife!"

A stillness came over Dominic. "Is she? Since when?"

"Twelve days."

Muscles bunched and strained visibly as Duncan fought his bonds.

With outward calm Dominic waited until Duncan was panting, sweating, and convinced that he was well and truly bound.

"I must be with Amber," Duncan said urgently. "She is not like others. A stranger's touch can be a sword cutting her. Whether you meant to or not, you have sorely hurt her. Let me go to her."

Dominic sensed Meg's movement behind him. He countered it, keeping her from Duncan's view.

The half step Dominic took put him into full sunlight. He swept off his battle helm and looked down at Duncan. The clear, bright light heightened the contrast between Dominic's black hair and his crystalline gray eyes.

On the shoulder of Dominic's black mantle, the eyes of the Glendruid Wolf gleamed as though alive, infused with ancient wisdom.

"Do you know me?" Dominic asked.

Duncan's only answer was a feral snarl.

"You have been bewitched," Dominic said. "We are your friends, yet you have no memory of us."

A shudder coursed through Duncan.

"Nay, I was but ill," he said hoarsely.

"Do you remember the time before you came to the Disputed Lands?" Dominic asked.

"No."

"Do you know that man?" Dominic asked, pointing to Sven.

Duncan looked. A expression of strain came to his face as he tried to rip shadows aside to get at the truth beneath.

"I . . ." Duncan's voice faded to a hoarse whisper. "I have no memory."

"Do you know this woman?"

Dominic stepped aside, leaving Meg alone in a shaft of sunlight. Her loosely bound hair blazed like fire. Her matchless eyes were an intense, burning green given only to Glendruid women.

Duncan made an odd sound.

"Don't you know me, Duncan?" Meg asked gently. "Once, we chased butterflies together."

An agonized expression crossed Duncan's face. Memories glittered like moonlight on disturbed water.

"You taught me to ride," Meg continued, her voice soft, relentless, "to hunt, and to cast the lure for a falcon. We were betrothed when I was but nine."

Abruptly memory flowed together—a face, a name, a childhood stitched through with a girl's laughter.

"Meggie?" Duncan whispered.

A smile transformed Meg's face.

"Aye, Duncan. Meggie. Of all the people in Blackthorne Keep, only you call me that."

The mention of Blackthorne Keep made shadows within Duncan swirl and churn. He turned and looked at Simon.

"You talked of Blackthorne Keep when we fought."

"Aye. 'Tis how I defeated you," Simon said.

"Blackthorne . . ."

A shudder tore through Duncan's powerful body. More fragments of memory touched and wove together.

"Lord John," Duncan said, looking at Meg. "My . . . father?"

"Your father," she agreed. "Though he wasn't free to wed your mother."

Duncan made an odd sound. "Somehow I remembered that."

"John?"

"Nay. Being a bastard." Duncan closed his eyes. "Meggie, for the love of God, *let me go to Amber.*"

The naked plea in Duncan's voice made Meg's throat ache.

"Hold a dagger to Duncan's throat if you must," she said to Dominic, "but let me see into his eyes."

Without a word Dominic drew his battle dagger, knelt, and laid the blade across Duncan's throat.

"Be very still," Dominic said calmly. "I value you, but I value my wife above all else."

Duncan ignored the dagger, having attention only for the Glendruid woman who was kneeling close to him, attended by a muted murmuring of bells. Eyes the burning green of spring unleashed looked into Duncan's own eyes, *seeing* him in the uncanny way of Glendruid women.

For a long time there was silence but for the wind pulling bright autumn leaves from branches.

"Let Duncan go to her," Meg said finally.

"Nay!" Simon said, his voice as fierce as his eyes. "Duncan was my friend and that hell-witch stole his mind!"

With a graceful motion, Meg stood and went to her brother-in-law. His fair hair gleamed like gold in the sun, but his eyes were slices of moonless night.

"Duncan is not bewitched," Meg said.

Simon looked into the fathomless green of Glendruid eyes. Then he looked away to the girl who lay unmoving beneath a blanket.

"How can you say that? The hell-witch took his memory," Simon said savagely. " 'Tis as clear as day!"

"To practice the black arts thus would have left

a mark on Duncan's soul that nothing save God could erase," Meg said. "Duncan has no such mark."

Simon looked back at Meg.

"Do you think," she asked softly, "that I would knowingly set an enemy in our midst?"

"No."

"Do you think I would put Dominic's life at risk in any way?"

"Nay," Simon said. "Never."

The certainty in his voice was reflected in his eyes. He knew to the depths of his soul that Meg loved his brother in a way Simon had never thought to see a woman love any man.

Meg saw Simon's faith in her and touched his cheek in brief thanks.

"Then believe me," she whispered, "when I say that Duncan is not bewitched."

"If it were anyone but you speaking . . ." Simon said, raking his fingers through his fair hair.

Meg waited.

With a resigned gesture, Simon turned away. "I'll bring the hell-witch to him myself."

"Nay!" Duncan said violently. "Don't you understand? *Your hatred wounds her.*"

Simon looked at Meg.

"Duncan," Meg said, "if we untie you, will you vow not to attack us?"

"As long as you don't further wound Amber, yes."

Dominic put his hand on Meg's arm when she would have drawn her own dagger to cut Duncan free.

"Slowly, small falcon," Dominic said. "We have had Duncan's word in the past and found it without value."

When Duncan realized what Dominic was saying, he flushed with anger.

And then he turned pale.

"Am I forsworn?" Duncan asked starkly. "Do you know of any vow I have broken?"

Dominic saw the depth of Duncan's emotion and knew that whatever had happened since Duncan had come to the Disputed Lands, the Scots Hammer had not knowingly broken his word.

"Do you know me?" Dominic asked almost gently.

Duncan stared at the Glendruid Wolf as though sight alone could put together the elusive fragments of the past.

But it could not.

"I . . . should." Duncan's voice was hoarse with effort. "I sense it, but . . ."

"You don't know me," Dominic finished.

"No," Duncan whispered.

"Then you are not forsworn," Dominic said simply. "Cut his bonds, Meg. Duncan has given his word not to attack unless we harm the witch."

Dagger in hand, Meg bent over the cords. No sooner had she cut through them than Duncan sprang to his feet and went to where Amber lay.

The coolness of her skin shocked an oath from him.

Hurriedly Duncan lay down beside Amber, lifted her slack body against his, and wrapped the blanket around both of them, trying to warm her flesh with his own.

"Precious Amber," he whispered. "What has happened to you?"

There was no answer.

The Scots Hammer bent his head, hiding his face in the unbound gold of Amber's hair.

"I did but pull her from her horse," Simon said, baffled. "I swear it."

"It isn't your fault," Meg said. "Whether Learned or Glendruid, a gift is also a curse."

"I suspect that Amber's is more curse than gift," Dominic said in a low voice.

"Are you saying that my touch alone did that to her?" Simon asked, appalled.

"Your touch told her of your hatred," Meg said. "You have little trust in women, especially those with gifts."

Simon didn't deny it. "I make an exception for you, Meg."

"I know. I have *seen* it in you."

"Are you smiling lovingly at my brother?" Dominic asked Meg in an ambiguous tone.

Simon gave Dominic a sideways, wary glance.

Meg laughed softly.

"Of all men who walk the land," she said, "you have the least cause to be jealous."

"Aye. But Simon is a handsome devil."

"So is Duncan," Simon retorted.

Dominic grunted. "Seeing him with his witch, I no longer worry that he looks at Meg with more than friendship in his eyes."

Simon followed Dominic's glance to where Duncan lay cradling Amber against his body.

"Aye," Simon whispered. "What do we do now?"

"What we must," Dominic said quietly.

"And that is?"

"Question him before the witch awakens."

"Let me," Meg said.

After a brief hesitation, Dominic nodded.

"All right, small falcon. He remembers you with . . . affection." Dominic smiled thinly. "His memories of me might be somewhat different."

"Particularly if he remembers what happened in the church," Simon said sardonically.

Meg gave Dominic a sideways glance. She knew quite well how little her husband liked remembering Duncan and John's plan to wed her to the Scots Hammer—over Dominic's freshly killed body.

"Duncan," Meg said.

Though her voice was gentle, it wasn't timid. She was the lady of a great keep and a Glendruid healer, and she meant to have Duncan's attention.

He looked up, his eyes wild with shades of darkness.

"Is she better?" Meg asked.

"Her skin feels less cool," Duncan said.

Muted cries of bells marked Meg's progress toward the girl who lay unmoving in Duncan's arms. Meg bent closer but didn't touch Amber.

"How does her heart feel beneath your hand?" Meg asked.

"Strong. Steady."

"Excellent. She appears to be in a healing sleep rather than in a stupor. When she is ready, she will wake without lasting harm."

Meg stood and watched Duncan's large hand smooth hair back from Amber's face. Though asleep, Amber seemed almost to follow the caress the way a flower follows the sun across the sky.

"I take it your touch doesn't wound her," Meg murmured.

"Nay."

"Odd," Meg said.

"Aye. The people of Stone Ring Keep were much surprised."

Meg sensed Dominic's sudden, intense interest at Duncan's mention of the contested keep.

"Is Amber from Stone Ring Keep?" Meg asked.

"Yes."

"Vassal to Erik, called the Undefeated?"

Duncan smiled strangely. "Aye. They were childhood friends, much as you and I were. He and a Learned witch called Cassandra are Amber's closest friends."

A gust of wind blew through the camp, stirring Meg's robes and setting hidden golden bells to crying. The sound caught Duncan's attention.

"You never used to wear such jewelry," he said. "Did you?"

"No. They were my husband's gift. Golden jesses for his small falcon."

Duncan looked back down at Amber's face. He stroked her cheek tenderly. It was warm beneath his touch.

The icy fist that had squeezed Duncan's heart eased somewhat. With a silent prayer of thanks, he pulled Amber even closer to his own warmth.

"What do you remember of the time before you came to the Disputed Lands?" Meg asked.

"Very little. Not even my true name."

"Duncan is your true name."

"Nay. Duncan is the name Amber gave me when I awakened with no more memory than a babe has." He brushed his lips over Amber's eyelids. "She touched me, *knew* me, and named me dark warrior. Duncan."

A single black eyebrow rose, emphasizing Dominic's skepticism. But a quick warning look from Meg ensured his silence.

"How did you find Amber?" Meg asked.

"I didn't. Erik discovered me inside Stone Ring, at the foot of the sacred rowan."

Meg became very still.

"I was naked," Duncan said, "senseless, and had nothing of my possessions with me but an amber talisman."

His head snapped up suddenly.

"You gave it to me," he said to Meg.

"Yes."

"I remembered that as in a misty dream, the color of your hair and eyes, but not your name or where you were or why you would give something so valuable to me."

"Are you certain you were found *inside* the Stone Ring?" Meg asked, ignoring Duncan's implied question.

"Yes. That—and the talisman—was why Erik brought me to Amber. All things amber belong to her."

"Is she the one called Untouched?"

"Yes," Duncan said huskily. "Until I came to her."

"And then?"

"She burned at my touch, but there was no pain. I burned at her touch and found Paradise."

Duncan looked up at Meg, wanting her to understand what he himself was still discovering.

"There has never been another woman like Amber for me," he said slowly. "There never will be. It is as though God made her solely for me, and me solely for her."

Simon and Dominic exchanged a look, but neither man spoke. There was nothing they could say to parry the certainty in Duncan's voice.

"So Erik brought you to Amber," Meg said carefully, "because all things amber belong to her."

"Yes. I lay senseless in her cottage for two days."

"Dear God," Meg whispered.

"Somehow Amber called me from the fell darkness that had taken me. Without her I would have never wakened."

"So you married her out of gratitude," Dominic said in a low voice.

Duncan shook his head. "I vowed if I took her, I would marry her."

"So she seduced you," Dominic muttered.

"Nay. She was a virgin when we lay together beneath the sacred rowan in Stone Ring."

Delicate chills coursed down Meg's spine. She, too, had once lain as a virgin with a warrior in a sacred place. She, too, had arisen no longer a maid. She, too, had been a participant in a destiny whose choices were not always obvious.

And not always her own.

"What is your memory like now?" Meg asked.

"Leaves scattered by a dark wind," Duncan said bitterly.

"Has there been no improvement since you first awakened?"

Duncan let out a harsh breath he hadn't been aware of holding.

"Instants of understanding, no more," he said. "Just enough to tantalize me."

"Do these memories come at any special time or place?"

"When I first saw Simon at Sea Home," Duncan said, "I had a memory of candles burning, chants, and a knife blade cold between my thighs."

Duncan turned to look at Simon.

"Did that happen?" Duncan asked. "Did I stand in a church with a woman's silver shoe in my hand and a knife blade between my thighs?"

Simon looked swiftly at Meg. She nodded.

"Yes," Simon said. "It was my blade."

Memory shivered and bright fragments wove together, giving Duncan more of the past.

"It was your shoe," Duncan said to Meg.

"Yes."

"John was too ill to take part in the ritual, so I stood in his place," Duncan said slowly.

"Yes."

"And I . . . and I . . ."

Shades of darkness descended, baffling Duncan's efforts to recall his lost past.

"I am so close to remembering it all," he said harshly. "I know it! Yet something holds me back. *God, let me remember!*"

Amber stirred as though called by Duncan's anguish. Golden eyes opened. She had no need to ask what was wrong. She sensed the thinning shadows very clearly, the siren lure of memory glittering through the shades of darkness.

Just as clearly she sensed Duncan's fear of knowing. It was a fear she shared.

Yet there was no choice but to confront that fear. She could no longer leave Duncan torn between past and future, bleeding invisibly, edging relentlessly toward madness.

As I feared, it is destroying him.

And as I feared, it will destroy me.

It is too soon, my dark warrior, my love, heart of my heart . . . too soon.

And it is too late.

Slowly Amber looked past Duncan to the three warriors watching silently, held in check by no more than the upraised hand of a Glendruid witch.

When Amber saw the silver pin glittering on one man's mantle, she knew she had lost her gamble. The past had overtaken Duncan.

And the name of the past was Dominic le Sabre.

"Let go of me," Amber whispered.

It took Duncan a moment to realize that Amber had spoken to him. When he would have answered, her hand lifted, sealing his lips.

"If you would remember the past," Amber said shakily, "you must first let go of me."

Why?

The demand was silent, but as clear as a spoken word to Amber.

"Because you can't have both," she said simply.

Why?

Amber closed her eyes against the pain coiling more tightly through her with each breath. She had suspected the truth even before she had given herself to Duncan beneath the sacred rowan. Suspected, but not known.

She knew now.

Too late.

"Because you can't truly love me until the shadows are gone," Amber whispered, "and when the shadows are gone, *you won't love me at all.*"

Her hand dropped from his lips. Knowing she

shouldn't, unable to resist, she brushed her mouth over his.

"You make no sense," Duncan said, searching Amber's shadowed eyes. "Your fall addled you."

"Nay. It made me see clearly how I have wronged you in the name of protecting you."

"Wronged me? What nonsense. You called me from a terrible darkness."

Shaking her head slowly, ignoring the slow fall of her own tears, Amber forced herself to give Duncan what no longer could be denied.

"Let go of me, dark warrior. Your past is all around you."

"What do you mean?"

"Let go of me," she whispered.

Puzzled, Duncan opened his arms, releasing Amber. She sat up and would have stood, but knew her legs would refuse to take her weight.

Like Duncan, she was at war with herself, knowing what must be and rejecting it at one and the same moment.

"Now that we aren't touching, do you see?" Amber asked starkly.

"I see only your tears."

"Then hear my words. The Glendruid witch is your childhood friend."

"I know. Meggie."

"The fair-haired, black-eyed knight who hates me so—do you know him?"

Duncan glanced at Simon.

"Aye. He is Simon, called . . . the Loyal!" Duncan finished, triumph clear in his voice. "Aye! I know him!"

"And to whom is he loyal?" Amber asked softly.

"His brother."

"Who is the brother of Simon the Loyal?"

Abruptly Duncan came to his feet and faced the tall, powerful knight who was watching him with sword half drawn and eyes the color of winter rain.

"Dominic le Sabre," Duncan said.

The knight nodded.

"And who are you, dark warrior?" Amber whispered raggedly. *"What is your true name?"*

Duncan closed his eyes and tried to speak. Shadows writhed as they fought against the bright memories flowing together, weaving a tapestry of knowledge fragment by shimmering fragment, until even a thousand shades of darkness could no longer conceal the burning pattern of the truth.

When Duncan's eyes opened once more, Amber was grateful not to be touching him.

"I am Duncan of Maxwell, the Scots Hammer," he said savagely.

Again Dominic nodded.

"I am Duncan of Maxwell, steward to Erik the Sorcerer in the very keep that you, my rightful lord, gave me to hold in fief for you."

Dominic would have spoken, but there was no chance. Duncan's words were still falling like bitter rain. The pride, humiliation, and rage in him were strong enough to taste.

"I am Duncan of Maxwell, a man brought to ruin by a witch with golden eyes and a lying tongue.

"I am Duncan of Maxwell, the Forsworn."

❦ 18

WITHDRAWN, silent, Amber watched while the last of the rude camp was loaded onto horses.

"Can you mount unaided?" Meg asked.

"Yes."

"Good. We wouldn't want to hurt you again."

"And Duncan can no longer bear to touch me," Amber said with outward calm.

Reluctantly, Meg nodded. Her intent glance missed neither the pallor of Amber's face nor the dark brackets of pain on either side of her mouth.

"I have lived without touch before," Amber said. "I will do so again."

"Before, you didn't know . . ." Meg's voice died.

"Aye. Knowledge is my punishment."

The bleakness of Amber's voice made Meg flinch in silent sympathy.

"I'm sorry," Meg said.

"Don't be. Better that I live untouched than be touched by Duncan now."

"He would never lift a hand to you," Meg said quickly.

"He wouldn't have to. I can feel his fury like black wings beating against my soul."

Instinctively Meg held out her hand in a gesture of comfort, then remembered that pain rather than ease would flow from her touch. Her hand dropped to her side.

"Duncan will soften," Meg said. "I've never seen him so tender with anyone as he was with you before he knew that . . ."

"That I was less than I seemed and he was far more?" Amber's mouth turned down in a sad curve.

"His temper is like a summer storm," Meg said, "loud and even frightening, but it passes quickly."

"The rocky fells will melt and run like honey before the Scots Hammer forgives me for tarnishing his honor," Amber said. "Such forgiveness would require great love. Duncan loves me not."

The combination of anguish and acceptance in Amber's voice told Meg more than words could have.

"You knew this would happen, didn't you?" Meg whispered.

"I knew it might. I hoped it wouldn't." Amber closed her eyes. "I wagered . . . everything. I lost."

"Why did you do it?"

"Duncan came to me in shades of darkness . . . and touching him taught me that the darkness was mine, not his."

"I don't understand."

Amber smiled oddly. "I doubt that anyone could unless they were cursed with my 'gift.'"

Motionless, Meg waited, *seeing* Amber's truth and sorrow with Glendruid eyes.

"Mine was a lifetime of night," Amber said simply. "Duncan was my dawn. How could I let Erik hang him?"

"Hang Duncan?" Meg asked, appalled.

"Aye."

As though chilled, Amber wrapped her arms around herself and whispered, " '*Death will surely flow*.' "

Coolness coursed down Meg's spine. "What was that?"

"Cassandra's prophecy, the one I hoped to evade."

"What prophecy?"

Amber's laugh was a cry of throttled pain.

"More fool I," Amber said bleakly. "Rich life was the lure, death is the truth. Better that I had never been born."

"What prophecy?" Meg asked again, sharply.

The tone of her voice brought Dominic immediately to his wife's side.

"What is it, small falcon?"

"I don't know. I know only that something is wrong, black wings beating . . ."

The echo of her own words brought Amber's attention back to Meg. The compassion in the Glendruid healer's eyes was as clear as it was unexpected.

"A prophecy attended my birth," Amber said. " 'A man with no name may you claim, heart and body and soul. Then rich life might grow, but death will surely flow.' "

Dominic's eyes narrowed into slivers of beaten silver as he listened. He would have dismissed the words, but his own marriage had taught him that some prophecies were as real, and as deadly, as a drawn sword.

" 'In shades of darkness he will come to you. If you touch him, you will know life that might or death that will.

" 'Be therefore as sunlight, hidden in amber, untouched by man, not touching.

" 'Forbidden.' "

When Amber finished speaking, there was a silence unbroken by even the wind. She turned around and found what she had feared she would— Duncan standing behind her, watching her with wintry contempt in his eyes.

"You came to me in shades of darkness," Amber said, "a man with no name. And I touched you. You claimed my heart and my body. We had better pray that my soul is still unclaimed, or death will surely flow."

"Then we are lost, witch. Your soul was sold to the devil a long time ago."

"*Duncan!*" Meg said, appalled.

"Don't let your soft heart lead you astray, Meggie," Duncan said. "There is naught but hell's own calculations in that sweet-faced witch."

"You are wrong. I have *seen* her."

"So have I," he retorted sardonically. "I have seen her bend to me and whisper of love at the very instant she most deeply betrayed me."

Amber's head came up. She watched him with a falcon's proud eyes.

"I have never betrayed you," she said distinctly.

"You didn't tell me my own name. I call that a betrayal."

"I didn't know who you were until you fought the outlaws with such lethal skill."

Duncan said nothing.

"And even then I wasn't certain beyond all doubt," Amber said. "It made no sense. You had flashes of Learning, yet Duncan of Maxwell wasn't Learned."

Meg looked curiously at Duncan, as though seeing a side of him that she hadn't known existed before.

"There could have been other warriors," Amber said, her voice subtly pleading, "men whose names I didn't know, men who had a strong hand with the hammer, men who were Learned."

"Did you know who I was before we married?" Duncan asked bitterly.

Amber's spine straightened and her chin came up. "Yes."

"Did you know I was betrothed to another, a marriage arranged by my true lord, Dominic le Sabre?"

"Erik . . . told me."

"Before we were married?"

"Yes."

"And you say you never betrayed me. Such fine calculations they must teach the Learned, all the ways to split hairs until nothing remains but dishonor."

The contempt in Duncan's voice made Amber feel as though she were being flayed with a thin whip.

"I had to marry you," she said desperately. "It was either that or watch you hanged!"

"Better I had been hanged than live to know myself an ill-begotten bastard whose vows are worth less than sheep dung."

Dominic stepped up to Duncan and put both hands on his broad shoulders.

"I don't consider you a man without honor," Dominic said. "You, *and your oath,* are much valued by your lord."

Duncan became very still. Then a visible shudder went through him. He went down on one knee in silent reaffirmation of his oath of fealty to Dominic le Sabre.

"You are generous, lord," Duncan said in a strained voice.

"I hope Lord Erik thinks so," Dominic said ironically, "when he returns from Winterlance and discovers that I have taken Stone Ring Keep."

DUNCAN rode alone over the lowered drawbridge and into Stone Ring Keep's bailey. His shout brought the keep's men-at-arms running.

"Go to Amber's cottage," Duncan ordered them. "She has much to bring to the keep."

The men obeyed quickly, leaving the bailey at a trot. The remaining guardians of the keep were more boys than men, squires who dreamed of someday being knights.

"I will take the gatehouse watch," Duncan said to Egbert. "If either of you sees aught amiss, *don't cry out.* Come to me swiftly and silently. Do you understand?"

"Aye," the two boys said as one.

As the squires trotted off to their posts, Duncan went quickly to the armory. The weapons that remained there after Erik's departure were ill-assorted but quite sufficient for the keep's defense.

Duncan locked the armory door and kept the key. Then he went to the gatehouse to wait for the Glendruid Wolf.

And while he waited, he tried not to think of the amber witch who had set fire to him as no other woman ever had.

My body knows you. It responds to you as to none other.

How many times have we lain in darkness together, our bodies joined and slick with desire?

How many times have I undressed you, kissed your breasts, your belly, the creamy smoothness of your thighs?

How many times have I opened your legs and sheathed myself within your eager heat?

She had come to him so perfectly.

So falsely.

Come heaven, come hell, I will protect you with my life. We are . . . joined.

The echo of Amber's vow twisted through Duncan's memory, and with it came the pain of a betrayal so deep he would spend a lifetime measuring it.

I believed her. By all the saints, I am a fool!

Yet even as Duncan told himself he was a fool, he couldn't help but remember his own burning need, a hunger greater than any he had ever imagined.

You're a fire in my blood, in my flesh, in my soul. If I touch you again, I'll take you.

Then touch me.

Amber—
Take me.
And he had, despite all.
I am afraid for you, for me, for us.
Because I can't remember?
No. Because you might.
And he had done that, too.
Would to God I could forget her more thoroughly than I ever did the past!

But that Duncan could not do. The memory of Amber was a thousand torches afire in his mind, his body, his soul.

Touch me.
Take me.

With a throttled sound, Duncan fought his brightly burning memories as savagely as he had once fought a thousand shades of darkness.

Without success. He was a man torn by conflicting needs. The part of Duncan that was ruled by rage hoped that Amber would take the men-at-arms he had sent to her and run for Sea Home or Winterlance.

And part of Duncan feared she would do just that.

Then he would never again hear her laughter, never again turn and find her watching him with eyes of fire, never again feel the sultry yielding of her body as he sheathed himself in her.

"Sir?"

The whispered word came from behind Duncan. He spun with such fierce speed that Egbert backed up in alarm.

"What is it?" Duncan asked.

"Three knights and a lady are riding up to the keep. They have a small amount of baggage with them."

"Just one lady?"

Duncan's voice and eyes were a blunt warning of his temper. Egbert swallowed and backed up.

"Aye," the squire said nervously.

"Amber?"

"I recognize neither the lady nor the knights."

Rage and pain struggled for control of Duncan's voice. Neither won. He was unable to speak.

Duncan turned his back on Egbert and looked out through the open gate to the road. There were indeed horses coming up the road. One of them was Shield, his own battle-trained stallion. Shield's saddle was empty, but the broadsword was now at Duncan's side rather than in its riding sheath.

"Sir?" Egbert prompted.

"Go back to your post."

Egbert hesitated, then turned and sped away, wondering what had caused Duncan's expression to be as bleak as a stone carving of hell.

Motionless, Duncan watched Dominic le Sabre canter up to Stone Ring Keep, his Glendruid wife at his side.

"Was there any difficulty?" Dominic asked.

Duncan shook his head.

"For a man who has just secured his own keep without bloodletting, you look quite grim," Dominic said, dismounting.

"Not my keep, lord. Yours."

"No longer. As of this moment I give you Stone Ring Keep outright, without let or hindrance. You are lord here, Duncan, not my tenant-in-chief."

Smiling, Dominic watched understanding sink slowly into Duncan. Born a bastard with no name, no estate, no prospects other than his strong right arm and a burning need for land of his own ... and now Duncan had that land.

Dominic understood the complex emotions exploding in Duncan, for Dominic, too, had been born a bastard with no prospects other than his skill with a sword.

And he, too, had won wealth and land because of that skill.

"My own keep," Duncan said oddly.

He glanced around the keep as though it were new to him. In a sense, it was. He had never looked at it as his own before.

"It hardly seems real," Duncan said softly. "To go from a man with no name to this, all in a day . . ."

A lifetime's dream had come true. It was as solid as the cobbles beneath his feet, the weight of a sword by his side, and the smell of food from the kitchen in the bailey.

Stone Ring Keep was his and his alone, held in fief for no other man. The keep and all its lands and people were Duncan's as long as he could hold them with his sword and his wisdom. He was no longer Duncan of Maxwell.

He was Duncan, Lord of Stone Ring.

" 'Tis a great gift you have given me," Duncan said, turning back to Dominic.

" 'Tis a great gift you have given me," Dominic countered softly, dismounting.

"I? What have I given you save a long ride and doubts of my worthiness?"

"You have given me what I crave above all else. Peace for Blackthorne."

"Peace?"

"You returned alone to Stone Ring Keep. Had you wished it, you could have drawn up the bridge and told me to go forthwith to hell and take my knights with me."

"I would never—" Duncan began.

"I know," Dominic interrupted. "Beyond all doubt, beyond all temptation, you are a man of your word. And your word was given to me."

Duncan let out a long breath, feeling as though a huge weight had slipped from his shoulders.

"With you on my north," Dominic said, "I will never need to fear for the safety of my Carlysle estates."

"You have my oath on it."

"And you have mine, Duncan of Stone Ring. If you ever need help to defend what is yours, send word to Blackthorne. The Glendruid Wolf will come to fight by your side."

Clasping sword hand to sword hand, the two men sealed their vows as equals.

"I fear that I won't be long in claiming your aid," Duncan said. "As soon as Amber gets to Winterlance, Erik will be on his way with more knights than I have men-at-arms."

"Amber?"

"Aye," Duncan said bleakly. "The witch will waste no time crying the word of your coming and my true name throughout the countryside."

"Turn around, Duncan. Tell me what you see."

Puzzled, Duncan turned—and saw Amber riding up to Stone Ring Keep, surrounded by the keep's men-at-arms.

Relief and rage warred within Duncan. He waited until the small party was across the bridge and through the gate. Then his gauntleted hand clamped around Whitefoot's reins, bringing the mare to a stop.

"Go about your tasks," Duncan told the men curtly.

The men-at-arms left without a backward look. Their speedy departure said more clearly than words that they would be quite pleased not to be within sight or sound of Duncan when he looked so fierce.

Even Amber, braced for Duncan's rage, knew a chill when he looked up at her with eyes as hard as agates.

"Why did you come here?" he demanded.

"Where else would a wife be but with her husband?"

Duncan became utterly still.

"Or had you forgotten we are wed?" Amber asked with a bittersweet smile.

"I have forgotten nothing, *witch*."

The chill she had felt returned doubly, becoming fingernails of ice along her spine.

"Then, husband, release Whitefoot so that a groom may see to her comfort."

Duncan turned his head just enough to see Dominic without taking his eyes off Amber.

"Dominic," said Duncan distinctly, "I trust your months as Lord of Blackthorne Keep have not caused to you forget how to close gates and lift a drawbridge?"

The Glendruid Wolf laughed.

"Good," Duncan said. "If you would be so kind as to see to those small tasks for me . . ."

Before Duncan had finished speaking, Dominic was working the mechanism that lifted the drawbridge until it fit like a heavy barrier across the opening to the keep. Bolts thumped home one after another, mating the bridge to the thick stone walls. The inner gate soon followed, closing with thick sounds of timber on timber.

It seemed very dark in the bailey without sunlight slanting through the gate.

"You should have run while you could," Duncan said silkily to Amber.

"To what purpose?"

"To bring Erik, of course."

"Then death would surely come as well," Amber said. "As long as I am within the keep, Erik won't attack."

"Let him come!" Duncan snarled.

Amber looked past Duncan to the man who wore the Glendruid Wolf.

"Is that what you want, lord?" she asked. "War?"

"What I want is of little moment," Dominic said. "The keep and all that comes with it are Duncan's, not mine. The decisions that pass here will also be his."

Amber's breath caught swiftly.

"You gave it to Duncan?" she asked, stunned.

"Aye," Dominic said, walking forward to stand next to Duncan.

"And to his heirs, without let or hindrance?"

"Aye."

"You are a man as generous as you are shrewd, Dominic le Sabre," she said. " 'Tis no wonder Duncan's unremembered oath to you caused him such unease."

"If you knew going back on his oath was causing him so much distress," Dominic said coolly, "why didn't you help him to remember?"

Shadowed golden eyes looked from one man to the other. Both men looked very much alike at the moment. Tall. Powerful. Fierce.

Proud.

Drawing a hidden, shaking breath, Amber forced herself to meet the savage, disapproving eyes of the Glendruid Wolf. As she did, she remembered the way those eyes changed when Dominic looked at Meg.

It gave Amber hope. Not much, but a spark seems brightest when all else is dark.

"If you knew a time was coming when your wife would look at you with loathing," Amber said, "what would you do to delay that day?"

Dominic's eyes widened fractionally, then narrowed into opaque slices of silver.

"Meg said as much on the ride in," Dominic muttered, "but I find it hard to believe."

"What is that?" Amber asked.

"That a woman can love a man, yet not love his honor, too."

Amber's skin became even more pale, until even her lips were bloodless.

"Then you believe as Duncan does," she said, "that it would have been better to let him hang."

"It would have been better not to force the marriage in the first place," Dominic said bluntly.

"Yes," she tonelessly. "But Erik forestalled that possibility, too."

"What?" demanded Duncan and Dominic as one.

"I have had much time to think since you left me at the cottage," Amber said.

Duncan grunted.

"Men call Erik a sorcerer, but I think often that he is simply shrewd in the way the Glendruid Wolf is shrewd," Amber said.

"Meaning?" Dominic asked her softly.

"Meaning that he understands what moves people and what leaves them unmoved."

Stillness came over Dominic. "My brother said as much."

"Simon?"

Dominic nodded and asked, "What did Erik know that he used against Duncan?"

"He knew that Duncan didn't love me."

Duncan didn't deny it.

Amber hadn't expected him to, but his silence stung like salt in an oozing wound. She drew another hidden, shaking breath and was grateful Meg wasn't there to measure her distress with Glendruid eyes that saw too deeply, too clearly.

When Amber spoke again, it was to Duncan rather than to the Glendruid Wolf.

"Erik knew you wouldn't marry me if you remembered," Amber said with aching calm. "And he knew how much you desired me. He knew I wanted you . . . dawn after a lifetime of night . . ."

Her voice thinned into splinters of silence.

"So he left us utterly alone but for his most foolish squire," Duncan finished savagely, "and all the time you allowed me to believe you weren't a maiden."

"Nay," Amber said fiercely. "That was your own doing, Duncan. Erik and I both swore otherwise, but you didn't listen. You didn't want to know the truth, because if you believed me a virgin you wouldn't have allowed yourself to take me."

"Aye," he said in a cold tone.

" 'Aye,' " she mimicked. "Or maybe *nay*, Duncan of the broad shoulders and thick skull! Maybe you wouldn't have been able to stop yourself even if you knew. Then you would have hated yourself for breaking your vow!"

Memories arced like summer lightning between Amber and Duncan, the wild instant when he had taken her beneath the sacred rowan with a single, unexpected thrust of his body.

" 'Tis much easier to hate me than yourself, isn't it?" Amber asked.

She yanked on the reins, freeing them from Duncan's grasp before he could recover. Whitefoot backed up in a frantic clatter of metal shoes on cobblestones, taking her rider beyond Duncan's reach.

"The bridge is drawn up," Duncan said savagely. "It's too late to run."

"I know. I've known it since I first touched you. Now you know it, too."

❦ 19

WORD of Cassandra's appearance went through the keep almost as quickly as word of Duncan's true name had two days before. Amber heard rumors of the Learned woman whispered by the serving men who brought steaming bathwater to the room where Amber and Duncan had once slept together.

But no more.

Amber hadn't seen Duncan since he had requested that Simon escort her to the luxurious room. She had become a prisoner in all but name, her only company the servants who came and went without warning.

And without conversation. It was as though they were terrified of being caught speaking to the lady of the keep.

A shout from the bailey below drifted through the partially open shutters. Amber stood poised on the edge of entering the big wooden tub, where water gently steamed.

"She be here, I tell you! Saw her with me own two eyes. Blood-red robes and silver hair!"

Amber listened, but nothing more about Cassandra's presence could be heard from the high room. With a sigh, Amber slid into the water.

Will Duncan come to me now? Will he finally admit that he needs me as much as I need him?

Only silence answered Amber's half-fearful, half-yearning thoughts.

That same silence had once been her customary state, but she had never noticed it. She hadn't known then what it was like to wake up feeling herself surrounded by Duncan's arms. She hadn't known then what it was like to feel his warmth, his laughter, his hunger, his peace, his strength, all that was Duncan enfolding her in a richness of emotion she had never imagined.

Having known that sharing, Amber now knew what true loneliness was. She measured its extent in the echoing emptiness that was inside her.

No, Duncan won't come to me.

'Tis just as well. I dream of black wings beating at me, whispering unthinkable rage, unspeakable grief.

I fear what would happen if I touched him now.

For both of us.

I fear.

And yet I yearn . . .

The coolness of the bath told Amber that she had spent too long in useless regrets. Despite the hearth's cheerful fire close by, she felt chilled.

Amber reached for a pot of soap and began washing quickly, barely noticing the complex fragrance of evergreen and spices that rose from the soap. Soon the scent drifted through the room, as did the sound of soft splashes as she bathed.

"My lady," Egbert called from the hallway beyond the room.

"Again?" muttered Amber under her breath. Then, "What is it?"

"May I enter?"

Though the bath was shielded by wooden screens both for privacy and to hold the hearth's warmth close to the wooden tub, Amber had no desire for Egbert's company.

"As I told you a few minutes ago, I'm bathing," she said tartly.

There was an odd silence followed by the sound of feet shifting against the wooden floor.

"Lord Duncan requires your presence in the solar," Egbert said.

"I will be down presently."

Nothing in Amber's voice suggested that she was excited to have her time of forced seclusion end.

Or that she was longing to see her husband.

"The lord was most, um, urgent in his requirement."

"Ask him, then, if he would like to see me in the great hall, wearing only the liquid remains of my bath?"

The sound of rapidly retreating footsteps was Egbert's answer.

Moments later, candle flames dipped and trembled as a draft moved through the room. Amber didn't notice, for she was rinsing her face. But an instant later, she looked up and froze. A frisson of awareness shot through her.

Someone was in the room with her, standing just beyond the the wooden screens. Watching her.

Duncan.

She was certain of it.

"Yes, lord?" Amber asked.

Despite her best efforts at calm, her voice wasn't steady. Her heart was beating far too rapidly with the knowledge that Duncan was so close.

For the space of several breaths, no answer came. Rage and desire fought for control of Duncan. Every breath he took was infused with the scent of evergreen and spice. The silence shivered with the tiny sounds of water gliding over skin. Each instant announced in a new way that Amber was nearby, fragrant, warm.

Naked.

The hammer blow of desire that went through Duncan made him sway.

"Cassandra has asked after you," he said finally.

But Duncan's voice said much more, husky and
heavy, telling of blood racing hotly, flesh hardening, a body yearning to be completed. He could
not have told Amber of his desire more clearly if
he had touched her.

His mind might be closed like a fist against her,
but his body wasn't.

Amber made a soft sound as her own body softened in a heated rush. She prayed that Duncan
hadn't heard the telltale break and thickening of
her breath.

And she prayed that he had.

The same instinct that had told Amber about
Duncan in that first single touch had been
whispering relentlessly to her since he had looked
at her and seen his betrayer rather than his lover.

Instinct and gift combined told Amber that she
must somehow get past Duncan's rage before it
destroyed both of them, and the people of Stone
Ring Keep as well. If desire was the only way to
reach him . . .

Then let it burn.

"Tell Cassandra I am bathing," Amber said
huskily.

Deliberately she shifted in the tub so that her
profile rather than her back was to the screens.
Slowly, gracefully, she trickled fragrant water over
her shoulders and breasts. Crystal drops ran down
the shadow cleft between her breasts and gathered
in glittering crowns on nipples that had tightened
simply at the sound of Duncan's voice.

Amber heard Duncan draw in his breath. As
she had hoped, he was watching her through the
space where the screens didn't completely meet.
She wished she could see him as well as he was
seeing her.

And as naked.

"You don't usually bathe at this time of day,"
Duncan said.

Like Amber's voice, Duncan's said more than his words.

She shrugged, sending intriguing patterns of light, shadow, and moisture over her breasts.

"I'm not usually held prisoner," Amber said.

She lifted her arms and reached behind her head to tuck up stray strands of her hair. Her breasts swayed gently. The nipples gathered into even higher crowns. Silhouetted against the fire, she appeared to be licked by amorous flames.

With a throttled sound, Duncan forced himself to look away. The first thing he saw was the dinner that had been brought hours before to Amber's room. Little had been touched. Less had been eaten.

"Is something wrong with your food?" he asked roughly.

"No."

"You must eat more," he said.

"Why? It takes little strength to be a prisoner."

The calm question infuriated Duncan. He had no answer save that the thought of her fasting when there was no religious need disturbed him.

Abruptly Duncan turned and headed for the door. This time he made no attempt to be silent. The clink and rub of chain-mail hauberk and hood, chausses, gauntlets, and sword announced that the lord of the keep was prepared for battle.

But he hadn't been prepared to find his enemy naked.

"Finish your bath," Duncan said in a harsh voice. "Be quick about it. If you aren't in the great hall before I become impatient, I'll send a scullery wench in to dress you and drag you forth."

The door to the room shut with emphasis, announcing that Duncan had left.

Anger and disappointment swept through Amber, but she wasn't foolish enough to test her husband's temper by dragging her feet. Whether Duncan knew it or not, she would rather have been whipped than forced to endure being touched by all but three people in the world.

Cassandra was one of them. Erik was another. The third had just left in a fury.

It was a very short time before Amber appeared in the solar, wearing a gown the color of highland pines. Against the dark green of her gown, the ancient amber pendant glowed as though on fire. Her hair was a loose, flowing cloud held back from her face by a silver circlet set with amber gems the precise color of her eyes.

Duncan looked at Amber as though she were a stranger. A glance, no more, before he turned again to watch the Learned woman whose gray eyes had never looked more like a winter sky.

"As you see," Duncan said curtly, gesturing toward the doorway, "Amber is unharmed."

Cassandra turned and looked at the girl she had raised as her own daughter.

"How goes it with you?" Cassandra asked.

"It is as you foresaw."

Pain passed like a shadow over the Learned woman's face at Amber's soft words. Cassandra bowed her head for a moment. When she looked up again, there was no expression on her face at all. She turned toward Duncan.

"Thank you, lord," Cassandra said quietly. "I will trouble you no more."

"Hold," Duncan said when Cassandra would have turned away.

"Yes?" she asked calmly.

"What did you foresee for Amber?"

"Nothing that would affect your ability to rule Stone Ring Keep, its people, or its lands."

"Amber," Duncan said without looking away from Cassandra. "Touch the Learned woman while I question her."

Disbelief showed in Amber's face for an instant. Then anger came.

"There is no reason to doubt her word," Amber said stiffly.

Duncan's smile was as cold as Cassandra's eyes.

"No reason for you, perhaps," he said. "She has no affection for me."

"Daughter," Cassandra said, holding out her hand. "Your husband is uneasy. Reassure him."

Amber took the other woman's elegant fingers between her own. The emotions that poured into Amber were complex, powerful, darkly seething with all that had been risked.

And lost.

Closing her eyes, Amber fought against the tears that Cassandra would not shed.

"I have foreseen nothing that would affect your hold on Stone Ring Keep, its people, or its lands," Cassandra repeated.

"It is the truth," Amber said.

She put Cassandra's palm against her cheek in a brief caress and released her.

Unease rippled through Duncan. Though nothing more was said, he could feel the sadness flowing between the two women.

It was as though they were saying good-bye.

"What did you foresee for Amber?" he demanded again.

Neither woman spoke.

"What did you foresee?"

Cassandra looked at Amber. She shook her head.

"That is a matter between Amber and myself," Cassandra said, looking back at Duncan.

"I am lord of this keep. You will answer me!"

"Aye," the Learned woman said, "you are lord of this keep. My answer is that what passed between

Amber and myself has naught to do with the safety of this keep."

Duncan looked into Cassandra's calm gray eyes and knew that he would get no better answer from her.

"Amber," he said, "you will tell me what I seek."

"To use my gift merely to satisfy idle curiosity would be a sin. You are lord of the people's bodies, not of their minds."

Duncan came out of the riven oak chair as though shot from a bow. His hand clamped around Amber's arm. She barely had time to prepare herself for whatever pain might come along with the pleasure of his touch.

But there was no preparation possible for what poured into Amber with Duncan's touch. Rage and desire, contempt and yearning, restraint and grief, a torment that knew no bounds. There was no beginning to it, no end, no place to hide.

His pain and her own combined.

A keening sound of anguish was dragged from between Amber's clenched teeth.

"Amber?" he said roughly.

She didn't answer. She couldn't. It was all she could do simply to stand upright against the combined torrent of their emotions.

"It would be kinder to take a whip to her," Cassandra said bitterly. "But you feel no kindness toward her now, do you?"

"What in the name of God are you chattering about?" Duncan shot back. "I'm not holding her tightly enough to give pain."

"You could break her bones and she would feel no worse."

"Make sense, woman!" Duncan snarled.

"I am. Whether light or heavy, your touch is agony to her."

Duncan looked at Amber, seeing *her* rather than his own rage. She was as pale as salt. The centers of her eyes had dilated until there were only glittering rims of gold. A sheen of sweat stood on her cold skin. Strength visibly drained from her with every quick, shallow breath she took.

Shaken, Duncan released Amber as though she were a burning brand.

She sank to her knees, put her arms around her cold body, and fought to bring the pain under control. It was possible now that Duncan wasn't touching her.

Possible, but agonizing.

"I don't understand," Duncan said, baffled and angry at once. "My touch used to give you pleasure. Is it because my mind is whole now?"

Amber shook her head.

"Then what in the name of Mary and Jesus is happening!" Duncan demanded.

For a moment Amber struggled to speak. Then she simply shook her head again.

"Your rage," Cassandra said simply.

Duncan spun toward her. The look in his eyes would have made an armed knight flinch, but the Learned woman made no move away from the lord of Stone Ring Keep.

"Speak plainly," he ordered.

" 'Tis simple. You are consumed by rage. When you touch Amber, she feels your hatred of her as greatly as she once felt your pleasure. Beating her with a whip would cause less pain."

Stunned, Duncan looked at his own hands as though they belonged to a stranger. Never had he beaten a horse, a woman, or a child. The thought of causing such pain with no more than a touch sickened him.

"How could Erik have used her gift to discover truth?" Duncan asked in a low voice. "He is a monster!"

"Nay," Amber said raggedly. "Most people give me but a few instants of pain."

"What of Simon?" Duncan demanded. "You fainted."

"Simon had but one thought when he grabbed my wrist. Loathing for me. He is a man of intense passion. It overwhelmed me."

"What of Erik?" Duncan asked bluntly. "I doubt that his passions are timid."

"Nay. Nor do they wound me. He has tenderness for me, and I for him."

Duncan grimaced.

Cassandra looked from Duncan to Amber.

"Duncan is a man of great passion," Cassandra said softly to Amber. "Why didn't his hatred overwhelm you?"

"Because he feels other things for me as well. It is tearing him apart. It is tearing me as well."

With that, Amber came back to her feet. She took a step, stumbled, and would have fallen if Duncan hadn't caught her before he thought of the hurt his touch would cause. He released her as quickly as he had caught her.

"I didn't mean to . . ."

Duncan's voice faded and he made a baffled gesture with his hands. No matter how furious he was with the witch who had betrayed him, the thought of his simple touch causing such pain for her bothered him in ways he didn't want to name.

" 'Tis all right," Amber said in a low voice. "It wasn't nearly so hurtful the second time."

"Why?"

"The rage was still there, but it was overwhelmed by your horror at causing me such pain."

A shuttered look came over Duncan's face as he realized how clearly Amber saw him.

More clearly than he saw himself.

More clearly than he wanted to see.

"Then," Cassandra said, "there is hope."

"Duncan is a decent man," Amber said wearily.

"Weave your hopes upon that, rather than upon my future."

"Hope?" Duncan asked. "Of what?"

Neither woman spoke.

Duncan turned on his heel and sat again in the lord's chair.

"I see that you are quite restored," he challenged.

A chill gathered in Amber. Duncan's softening toward her had been only momentary.

"Yes," she said tonelessly.

"Then we will continue. Are the Learned plotting against me?" Duncan asked.

Cassandra's hand lifted to brush against Amber's cheek.

"No," Cassandra said.

"No," Amber echoed.

"Does Cassandra hope that they will?"

"No," Cassandra said.

"No," Amber echoed.

For a time there was silence but for the cry of wind around the keep and the whistling of a servant as he drew water from the well below the solar.

Then Amber sensed people coming into the room behind her. She didn't look to see who it was. She had attention only for the proud warrior who was gazing at her with far too much darkness in his eyes.

"As you requested," Simon said from the doorway. "Although what you will do with this lazy lout is beyond me."

Duncan looked beyond Amber and smiled slightly.

"Stay by the door, Simon, if you please."

Simon nodded.

"Egbert," Duncan said. "Step forward."

Amber heard the squire's footsteps begin, hesitate, and then set off at a different angle, giving her a wide berth.

"No," Duncan said. "Stand close to the witch."

"Which one, lord?"

Duncan shot the squire a cold glance. "Amber."

Egbert edged close enough that Amber could see his shock of reddish hair from the corner of her eye.

"Touch him," Duncan said distinctly, looking at Amber.

A chill gathered in Amber.

"A few moments of discomfort, I believe you said?" Duncan asked in a soft voice.

Amber turned to Egbert, who was watching her with fear in his eyes.

"This won't hurt you," she said quietly. "Hold out your hand."

"But Erik will hang me if I touch you!"

"Erik," Duncan said in a dangerous voice, "is no longer lord of this keep. I am. Your hand, squire."

Jerkily, Egbert held out his hand to Amber. She put a single fingertip against it, flinched subtly, and turned to Duncan.

The pallor of Amber's skin angered Duncan all over again.

"Why so pale, witch?" he asked. "Egbert is but a half-grown boy. Compared to a man's passion, it must be less than a candle flame against a roaring hearth fire."

"Is that a question?" Amber asked.

Duncan's mouth flattened. He switched his savage attention to the squire.

"If you remain at the keep, will you be loyal to me?" Duncan asked.

"I—I—"

"Amber?" Duncan demanded.

"No," she said tonelessly. "He would be forsworn. His oath has been given to Erik. Egbert may be lazy, but he values his honor."

Duncan grunted.

"You will leave for Winterlance at dawn,"

Duncan said to Egbert. "If you are seen outside your quarters before then, you will be presumed to be an enemy bent on treachery, and you will be treated as such. Go."

Egbert all but ran from the solar.

"Bring the next one, Simon."

Cassandra made an involuntary motion of her hand as though to intervene.

"Be still or begone," Duncan said coldly. "The witch was Erik's weapon once. Now she is mine."

THE hearth fire was freshened three times before Duncan sorted through the keep's squires, men-at-arms, and servants. The squires were all loyal to their oaths and to Erik. The men-at-arms were locally born. They were loyal to the keep rather than to any one lord. It was the same for the servants, who were drawn from the keep's families.

When the last scrying was done, Amber slumped in a chair near the fire, too weary even to hold her cold hands out to the flames. Pale and tightly drawn, her face was a silent rebuke to the man who had used her too hard.

"May I offer my daughter refreshment?" Cassandra asked.

Though the Learned woman's voice was neutral, Duncan felt as though he had been slapped.

"It is within her reach," he said curtly. "If she wishes to eat or drink, she has but to stretch out her hand."

"She is too spent."

"Why?" Duncan's voice was angry. "She said it was but a few moments of discomfort."

"There is a candle next to you," Cassandra said. "Hold your hand on the tip of the flame.

He looked at her as though she had lost her mind.

"Do you think I'm mad?" he asked.

"I think you wouldn't ask your knights to do anything that you wouldn't do yourself. Am I correct?"

"Aye."

"Excellent," Cassandra hissed. "Then hold your hand over the candle flame, lord. The space of two breaths, no more than three."

"No," Amber said dully. "He didn't know."

"Then he will learn. Won't you, proud lord?"

Duncan narrowed his eyes at the naked challenge in Cassandra's voice. Without a word he stripped off one gauntlet and held his hand over the candle flame for the space of one breath.

Two breaths.

Three.

"And now?" he challenged Cassandra, drawing back from the flame.

"Do it again. Same hand. Same skin."

"No!" Amber said, reaching for the wine. "I'm well, mentor. See? I drink and eat."

Duncan put his hand in the flame again. Same hand. Same place on his palm.

One breath, two, three.

Then he withdrew and looked at Cassandra.

She smiled savagely. "Again."

"Are you—" Duncan began.

"Then again," Cassandra continued. "And then again. Thirty-two times—"

Comprehension came to Duncan in a wave of coldness. That was the exact number of people whose truth Amber had questioned by touch.

"—until your flesh smokes and burns and you want to cry out, but don't, for it would change nothing, especially the pain."

"*Enough.*"

"Why so shocked, proud lord?" Cassandra mocked softly. "As you said, the candle is only a shadow of the hearth fire. But the flame . . . the flame burns just as deeply in time."

"I didn't know," Duncan said through his teeth.

"Then you had better learn the nature of the weapon you wield, lest you break it in your ignorance and arrogance!"

"I had to know what the people of the keep were thinking."

"Yes," Cassandra acknowledged. "But it could have been more gently done."

"You could have spoken," Duncan said, turning to Amber.

"Weapons don't speak," Amber said. "They are simply used. Are you through wielding me for now?"

Slowly Duncan's hands closed into fists. Just as slowly they opened once more.

"Return to your room," he said.

Amber set aside the wine goblet and left the solar without a look or a word.

Nor did Duncan call her back.

But when Cassandra would have followed, he gestured to another chair.

"Be seated," Duncan said. "You have no loyalty to me, but you will do what you can to help the amber witch, won't you?"

Cassandra's lips thinned. "Amber is Learned, not a witch."

"Answer my question."

"Aye. Whatever I can do to help Amber, I will do."

"Then stay nearby and speak for the weapon that is too stubborn to speak for herself."

"Ah, then you value her."

"More than my dagger and less than my sword," Duncan retorted.

"Erik should see you now."

"Why?"

"He thought your feeling for Amber would be stronger than your pride. I would like to show him how wrong he was," Cassandra said bitingly. " 'Tis a pity that he isn't the one to bear the pain of his misjudgment."

Before Duncan could speak, Simon and Dominic came into the solar. They looked from Cassandra to Duncan to the untouched supper arrayed on a table near the hearth.

"I have news that should whet your appetite," Dominic said.

"What is it?" Duncan asked, turning away from Cassandra.

"Sven assures me that the people of the keep are quite willing to accept you as their lord."

Duncan smiled and turned to Cassandra.

"Disappointed?" he taunted.

"Only in your treatment of your wife."

"Then you need not worry for long," Simon said. "The marriage will be set aside."

Duncan and Cassandra turned as one to face Simon.

" 'Tis a true marriage," Cassandra said. "Ask Duncan if he hasn't had carnal knowledge of his wife!"

"Whether she is maiden or madam," Dominic said, "it matters not. The marriage was conducted under false pretenses. No bishop would uphold it."

"Especially if a church or a monastery were offered as a gesture of respect," Simon said sardonically.

"You exchanged sacred vows," Cassandra said to Duncan. "Will you go back on your word?"

"Vows." Duncan's mouth flattened in pain or contempt or both together. "Nay, I won't go back on my true word."

Cassandra closed her eyes in a relief she couldn't hide.

"I will keep the *true* vow I made when my mind was whole," Duncan said. "I will marry Lady Ariane of Deguerre."

"What of Amber?" Cassandra asked.

Duncan turned to Dominic without answering.

"Send for my betrothed," Duncan said flatly. "The wedding will take place as soon as the Church agrees."

"What of Amber?" Cassandra demanded.

Duncan rose and walked out of the solar, looking at no one.

"What of Amber!" Cassandra shouted.

Cassandra's cry echoed through the great hall, following Duncan. Even when the last echo had faded, he heard the words crying within the bleak silence of his mind.

What of Amber?

What of your sacred vow?

Amber.

Sacred.

Amber. Amber. Amber . . .

There was no peace for Duncan in any part of the keep. The cry was a part of him, as deeply embedded as the pain of his old memory and his new betrayal.

The past turning, returning, tormenting him first with Amber's voice and then with his own.

Truly I am safe with you.

Always, my golden witch. I would sooner cut off my own sword hand than harm you.

The memory was too sad, too savage. Duncan pushed it away, buried it among the thousand shades of darkness where he could no longer hide.

Cassandra's voice pursued him, the Learned woman's words raining down like drops of fire.

To deny the truth of the past or the present will destroy you as surely as cleaving your head in two with a sword.

Remember what I have said when the past returns and seems to make a lie of the present.

Remember it.

Long after others slept, Duncan paced the halls

and winding stairways of his own keep. Voices spoke within his silence, words echoing through his seething mind, Amber's voice describing passion, pride, and honor being used as tools of war.

Erik knew that you didn't love me. He knew that you wouldn't marry me if you remembered.

And he knew how much you desired me.

Duncan desired her still. False or true, witch or woman, leman or wife, she made his body burn for her with all the fires of hell. The violence of his need overwhelmed everything.

Even betrayal.

Gradually Duncan realized he was standing in front of Amber's door, his fists clenched at his sides. He didn't know how long he had been standing there. He knew only that he must be inside with her.

The door to the bedchamber made no sound when Duncan pushed it open. The candles had burned low. The hearth held little more than embers. Draperies around the bed gleamed darkly as he drew them aside.

Amber lay in uneasy sleep, the covers twisted and her hair a tumbled golden cloud spread across the pillows. For an instant Duncan saw her as she had been in the bath, her breasts gilded with water and reflected fire. He had wanted then to be like the fire licking over her.

He still wanted it.

Duncan released the draperies and began stripping off the heavy battle clothes he had worn throughout the day. When he was as naked as a candle flame, he drew back the draperies again and lowered himself into Amber's bed.

Slowly he reached out to touch her. Just before his fingertips brushed her lips, he remembered what had happened in the solar—Amber white with pain, hardly able to stand, and Cassandra's cool words describing what had happened.

She feels your rage. Beating her with a whip would cause less pain.

Yet Amber hadn't flinched the second time Duncan had touched her, when his concern for her pain had been greater than his anger at her betrayal.

For a long time Duncan lay motionless, torn between desire and anger. Instinctively he divided his mind as though Learned, yet without Learned understanding of the danger to himself of what he did. A divided mind would soon curl back upon itself like a leaf shriveled by fire. And like a leaf, the mind would wither and die.

Duncan forced himself to concentrate not on his bleak rage at being betrayed, but rather on his desire. Then he focused on Amber's passion for him, a passion she had never been able to conceal.

Erik knew I wanted you . . . dawn after a lifetime of night.

The thought of being wanted like that again swept through Duncan. All that held him in check was his fear of hurting rather than arousing Amber with his touch. He wanted her hungry, not beaten, as wild for the joining of their bodies as he was.

A wave of heat burst through Duncan as he remembered what if was like to thrust into Amber, feeling her body close around him, holding him with tight, sultry perfection.

Breathing a word that was prayer and curse at once, Duncan speared his hand into Amber's hair until her scalp lay warm against his palm. The burning focus of his mind was desire. The corrosive shadows he held at bay served only to make the fire even hotter by contrast.

Amber awoke into a torrent of passion. She needed no candlelight to tell her who was lying next to her, his body hot and hard, his need too great to be described in words.

"Duncan. My God, your hunger . . ."

She tried to breathe, to talk, but all she could do was shiver as her own body changed to meet his with the speed of a falcon leaping into the sky.

"You tremble," Duncan said roughly. "Pain or desire?"

She couldn't speak for the waves of his desire breaking over her. Then his hand swept down her body, seeking answers in another, surer way.

The sultry riches that greeted him nearly drove him over the edge.

He moved over her with catlike swiftness, opening her legs and thrusting into her even as she arched up to him. The hot perfection of the joining undid him. With a raw cry of completion, he poured himself into her.

But it wasn't enough.

He wanted to fuse their bodies together, wanted the fire to burn forever, wanted . . .

Amber.

Duncan lowered his mouth to hers and began to move again, driving into her, joining with her in the only way he would permit himself, burning with her in the heart of his fire.

And when neither could burn any longer, they slept in the ashes of their shared passion.

Their nightmares were also shared, a thousand cold shades of darkness and betrayal, vows that could not be kept without forswearing other vows, rage at what could not be undone, a primal hunger for all that could not be . . .

Slowly Amber withdrew until she no longer touched her sleeping husband. Eyes open, staring at the darkness, Amber drank to the last bitter drop the knowledge of what she had done to him and to herself.

The Glendruid Wolf had truly seen into Duncan's soul. Beyond all doubt, beyond all temptation, Duncan was a man of his word.

And his word had been given to Dominic le Sabre.

Amber knew it now.

Too late.

If Duncan lets himself love me, he cannot permit our marriage to be set aside. He must turn his back on honor and on Dominic le Sabre.

Duncan of Maxwell, the Forsworn.

If he turns his back on honor, he will hate himself.

And me.

20

TWELVE days later, Cassandra entered the luxurious room that served as Amber's prison.

Amber looked up from the manuscript she had been trying to decipher. Trying, and failing. Her mind was on one thing and one thing only.

Duncan.

"Ariane is here," Cassandra said bluntly. "Duncan requires your presence in the solar."

For a moment Amber became as still as death. Then she let out a long, soundless breath and looked around the luxurious bedchamber with eyes that saw only a thousand shades of darkness.

"Simon brought a Norman priest along with the Norman heiress," Cassandra continued. "There is no doubt that your marriage will be set aside."

Amber said nothing.

"What will you do?" Cassandra asked.

"What I must."

"Do you still hope that Duncan will allow himself to love you?"

"No."

But the flare of emotion in Amber's eyes said *yes*.

"Does he still come to you in the darkest part of the night, when he can bear his own hunger no longer?" Cassandra asked.

"Yes."

327

"And when the hunger is spent?"

"Then comes anger at himself and at me and at the lies and vows that have trapped both of us. Then he doesn't touch me again. It hurts too much."

"At least he has that much tenderness for you."

Amber's smile was worse than any cry of pain would have been.

"Yes," she whispered. "Though he doesn't know it, my pain hurts him, too."

"You still hope he will someday come to love you?"

Long lashes swept down, concealing Amber's eyes.

"Each time we touch," she whispered, "there is more torment beneath the passion, more darkness. Surely where so much emotion is, there is also a chance . . ."

"You will stay as long as you have hope," Cassandra said.

Amber nodded.

"And then?" Cassandra asked. "What will you do when hope is gone and only a thousand shades of darkness remain?"

There was no answer.

"May I see your pendant?" the Learned woman asked.

Amber looked startled. After a moment of hesitation, she reached inside her robe to pull out the ancient pendant.

Transparent, precious, golden, it hung from the glittering chain. Yet for all its beauty, the amber had changed in ways so subtle that only a Learned person would see . . . darkness drawing a veil over light.

Cassandra touched the pendant with a fingertip that displayed a very fine trembling despite her best efforts at concealing the grief that raged beneath her Learned calm.

"You know that Duncan is destroying you," the older woman said.

Silence was Amber's only answer.

"Drop by drop, bleeding in secret," Cassandra whispered, "until there will be nothing left of light and life in you, only darkness."

Again Amber said nothing.

"It is destroying Duncan as well," Cassandra said flatly.

Only then did Amber cry out, denial and pain and the same rage that Duncan knew. For she was trapped with him, and each day was another shade of darkness wrapped around them. Day after day, until there would be nothing left of light and life.

Only darkness.

"He must not set you aside," Cassandra said fiercely. "I have never wished death on anyone, but I wish death to the Norman bitch who—"

"Nay!" Amber said sharply. "Don't drag your soul into darkness over something I have done. You taught me to make choices and to live with those choices."

"Or die."

"Or die," Amber agreed. "In any case, if it were not this heiress, then it would be another. We can't be slaughtering hapless maids, can we?"

Cassandra's laugh was as sad as her eyes.

"No," agreed the Learned woman. "There aren't enough rich maids in the world to slay before your thick-skulled lord will awaken to the riches that lie within his grasp."

Not touching, yet close in every other way, the Learned woman and her chosen daughter went down to the lord's solar. The sight that greeted them was illuminated by hearth, torches, and the misty light pouring through the solar's high window.

Duncan sat in the chair of riven oak. Simon was carving a cold joint of meat with his dagger and deftly piling the thin slices on a silver plate.

At first Amber thought no one else was in the room. Only when Duncan spoke did she realize that Simon was slicing up food not for himself, but for another.

"Lady Ariane," Duncan said, rising from the lord's chair, "I would like you to meet my weapon, a witch called Amber."

A woman dressed in a gown of black wool turned around. In her hands was a small harp.

At first Amber thought Ariane was wearing a cowl of darkly shining black cloth embroidered with silver and violet threads. Then Amber realized that the cowl was Ariane's hair, thickly plaited and coiled. Silver ornaments gleamed in the midnight blackness, and amethysts glittered almost secretly with Ariane's smallest movement.

"Go to her, Amber," Duncan said.

For a moment Amber couldn't force herself to move. Then her feet obeyed the commands of her mind rather than her heart. She walked up to the Norman heiress.

"Lady Ariane," she said, nodding.

For an instant, curiosity animated eyes that were as richly violet as the gems woven into Ariane's hair. Then the woman's thick black eyelashes swept down.

When her eyes opened again it was as though a door had closed. Nothing of curiosity or any other emotion remained. The heiress's eyes were as cold and remote as the amethysts she wore.

"A pleasure," Ariane said.

Her voice was cool, her words accented by her birth in Normandy. She made no offer to touch Amber in any way, even the most trivial brush of fingers in greeting.

Amber suspected it was Ariane's nature, rather than any special warning on Duncan's part about touching Amber, that kept the Norman aloof.

"You have had a long journey," Amber said.

"A chattel goes where it is bidden." Ariane shrugged gracefully and set the harp aside.

Chill fingers caressed Amber's spine. It was obvious that Ariane no more wanted the forthcoming marriage to Duncan than Amber did.

"Now you see why I require you," Duncan said sardonically. "My betrothed's enthusiasm for the match reminds me that her father considers Saxons his enemy. God—or more likely the Devil—knows what Baron Deguerre thinks of Scots."

Ariane neither moved nor spoke in response to Duncan. Within the pale perfection of her face, her eyes were the only thing alive; and they were alive only as a gem is alive, reflecting light rather than having light of their own.

"It reminded me of Dominic's marriage," Duncan added.

Simon sliced through another bit of roast with a single swift stroke.

"Aye," Simon said. "John gave his daughter as an act of vengeance rather than as a true joining of clans."

"Exactly," Duncan retorted. "I have no wish to wake up and find myself wed to a maid who can't give me heirs."

Amber sensed the involuntary shrinking that went through the heiress who sat so still amid her splendor of rich black clothes and extraordinary jewelry.

Cassandra also sensed the Norman woman's inner flinching. She looked at Ariane with true interest for the first time.

Simon put a plate of meats, cheeses, and spiced fruits in front of Ariane. When his hand brushed her sleeve, she started and looked at him with the wildness of a trapped animal in her amethyst eyes.

"Ale?" he asked calmly.

"No. Thank you."

Ignoring Ariane's refusal, Simon put a mug of gently seething ale in front of her.

"You're too frail," he said bluntly. "Eat."

Simon stepped back, no longer leaning over Ariane. She let out a ragged breath. When she reached for a sliver of meat, her hand trembled.

Impassively, Simon watched until Ariane chewed, swallowed, and reached for a bit of cheese. When she began eating that as well, he looked at Duncan.

"Lady Ariane needs rest," Simon said. "We rode without pausing during the day. Nights were little better. After Carlysle, there was no shelter from the storms."

"I won't keep her long," Duncan said. He looked at Amber. "Take her hand, witch."

Amber had known this was coming since she had heard Duncan's fears about heirs. Knowing, she had prepared herself. Her hand was steady when she held it out to Ariane.

The Norman girl's expression said quite clearly that she disliked being touched by anyone. She glanced at Duncan, saw no comfort, and took Amber's hand.

Despite Amber's preparation, the chaos of terror, humiliation, and betrayal that lay at Ariane's core nearly brought Amber to her knees.

Ariane was a woman of great passion, and all of it was dark.

"Lady Ariane," Duncan said, "are you sterile?"

"No."

"Will you accept your duty as my wife?"

"Yes."

Amber swayed, fighting the savage emotions that lay beneath the Norman girl's rigid control.

"Amber?" Duncan said.

She didn't hear. All she could hear was the vast scream of betrayal that filled Ariane's core.

"Amber." Duncan's voice was sharp.

"She is—telling the truth," Amber said raggedly.

Then she let go of Ariane's hand, for she could no longer bear the grief and fury that filled Ariane's soul.

It was too like Duncan's.

"Daughter, are you all right?" asked Cassandra.

"What she feels is—bearable."

Ariane looked at Amber with dawning outrage.

"You know," Ariane said tightly. "*You know.* Cursed witch, who gives you the right to harrow my soul?"

"Silence," Cassandra said savagely.

She walked swiftly to the two women, her scarlet robes burning vividly against the black of Ariane's clothes and the gold of Amber's.

"All that has been harrowed is Amber," Cassandra said. "Look at her and know that whatever black fires burn you in secret have also burned her."

Ariane went white.

"Know also that whatever your secret is," the Learned woman continued, "it is secret still. Amber touches emotions, not facts."

Silence stretched while Ariane gazed at Amber, seeing the pallor of her face and the strained line of her mouth.

"Emotions only?" Ariane whispered.

Amber nodded.

"Tell me," the Norman woman said. "What do I feel?"

"You can't be serious."

"Nay. I thought I no longer had feelings. What do I feel?"

It was the tone of simple curiosity that jarred Amber into replying.

"Fury," Amber whispered. "A scream never voiced. A betrayal so deep it all but killed your soul."

Silence stretched and stretched.

Then Ariane turned to Duncan with contempt flashing in her narrowed eyes.

"You have forced me to share what I have hidden even from myself," she said. "You have forced her to endure what she never earned."

"I have a right to know the truth of our betrothal," Duncan said.

Ariane made a cutting gesture with one hand.

"You have diminished my honor and the honor of the one you call your 'weapon,' " she said tersely.

Duncan's open hand slammed down on the arm of the chair.

"I have been betrayed by those I trusted," he said in a clipped voice. "This is my way of being certain it doesn't happen again."

"Betrayed," Ariane repeated tonelessly.

"Aye."

"We have that in common." She shrugged. "But is it enough for marriage?"

"We have no choice but to marry."

Duncan leaned forward, his eyes hard as stones.

"Will you be a faithful wife," he asked coldly, "loyal to your husband rather than to your Norman father?"

Ariane studied Duncan's fierce expression for a long moment before she turned to Amber.

And held out her hand.

"Yes," Ariane said.

"Yes," Amber echoed.

"Will that change if I take Amber as my leman, living in my keep and sharing my bed whenever I wish it?"

Amber's Learned discipline shattered. Even as Ariane's relief and hope soared, Amber's emotions all but overwhelmed the truth of what she was learning by touch.

"Not at all," Ariane said clearly. "I would welcome it."

Duncan looked surprised.

"I will do my duty," Ariane said in her cool

voice, "but I am repelled by the prospect of the marriage bed."

"Does your heart belong to another?" Duncan asked.

"I have no heart."

Dark brown eyebrows lifted, but Duncan said only, "Amber?"

Silence was Amber's answer. She was too busy trying to control her own seething emotions to speak.

Leman.

Whore.

Day after day, darkness condensing, destroying . . . Everything.

"Well, witch?" Duncan asked.

Amber forced air into her rigid body.

"She tells the truth," Amber said hoarsely. "All of it."

Duncan settled back with a curt nod and an expression that was as bleak as winter itself.

"Then it is done," he said. "We will be married on the morrow."

As though in answer, a wolf's savage howl echoed from just beyond the keep's wall.

Amber and Cassandra spun toward the sound.

Even as they turned, another cry came, the scream of an outraged peregrine. Before the cry had faded, Erik walked into the great hall. He was alone but for the sword sheathed at his side. Beneath his long crimson cape he wore chain mail. A battle helm hid all but his dark gold beard.

Duncan came to his feet in a fierce movement. With one hand he swept up his battle helm from the back of the chair. The hammer that was never far from his reach appeared in his other hand. Smoothly he put the helm on.

Like Erik, Duncan now was dressed from head to feet in links of steel.

"Greetings, Duncan of Maxwell," Erik said gently. "How is your wife?"

"I have no true wife."

"Does the Church agree?"

"Aye," Dominic said from the doorway behind Erik.

Erik didn't turn around. He watched Duncan with the unflinching stare of a falcon.

"Is it done, then?" Erik asked.

The gentleness of his voice made Amber long to scream a warning to everyone within the room.

"I have only to fix my seal to the document," Dominic said.

Again Erik didn't look away from Duncan.

"And you, Duncan," Erik said. "Do you agree to this?"

"Yes."

The wolf called again, and was answered by the peregrine's high scream. Erik smiled savagely.

"I demand blood right," he said. "Single combat."

"You have no kin here," Duncan said.

"You are wrong, *bastard*. Amber is my sister."

A shocked silence spread in the wake of Erik's words. Amber was the most stunned of all.

Erik looked at her for the first time since he had walked into the great hall. Smiling almost sadly, he held out his hand.

"Touch me, sister. Know the truth. Finally."

In a daze, Amber walked to Erik and placed her fingers on his hand.

"You are the daughter of Lord Robert of the North and Emma the Barren," Erik said distinctly. "You were born minutes after I was. We are twins, Amber."

The truth of what Erik was saying went through Amber like thunder through a narrow glen, shaking everything.

"But why . . . ?" whispered Amber.

Then she could say no more.

"Why were you denied your birthright?" Erik asked.

She nodded.

"I don't know," Erik said. "But I suspect that it was the price of my conception."

"That I be denied?" Amber asked.

"That you be given to the Learned woman who would suffer no man long enough to quicken with her own babe."

Cassandra made a stifled sound.

Erik looked at her for a moment only. Then he looked back at the girl whose true paternity he had discovered when he first had regarded the problem with Learned eyes.

"Is that true?" Amber asked, turning to Cassandra.

"When you were born . . ." Cassandra's voice thinned into silence.

"The prophecy," Amber said.

Death will surely flow.

"Aye. The amber prophecy," Cassandra said, sighing. "Emma feared it, and you. She refused to nurse you."

Amber closed her eyes. Tears glittered among the lashes that rested against her pale cheeks.

"But I loved you from your first breath," Cassandra said fiercely. "You were so tiny, so perfect. I believed if I could teach you enough Learning, rich life might flow."

Amber's laugh was sadder than her tears.

Better you had left me for the wolves.

Yet the words were never spoken aloud, for Amber had no wish to wound the woman who had taken an unwanted babe and raised her as her own.

"In the end, my lack of talent for Learning doomed your hopes," Amber said.

"The fault was in my lack of teaching," Cassandra said.

Amber simply shook her head.

After a moment she opened her eyes, looked at Erik . . . and saw her brother for the first time. Tears came again, but differently. She touched his cheek, his hair, his lips, letting the truth of him sink into her.

"The river always runs down to the sea," Amber said, "no matter how you try to stay its true course. Let it go, my brother. Let it go."

Before Erik's answer came, the peregrine flew at the partially opened shutters that kept her from her master. The falcon's shriek was as shrill as Erik's voice was gentle.

"Never," Erik said.

"I don't want you to do this!"

"I know. But it must be done."

"Nay!" Amber cried, gripping Erik's arm with one hand.

"A gentle, sheltered girl called Duncan's soul from darkness," Erik said.

Abruptly links of metal chain began to chant of death, sliding one over another as the hammer moved restlessly in Duncan's grasp.

"And then," Erik said gently, implacably, "the girl gave Duncan her own soul to fill the emptiness in his. For this priceless gift, he would make her a whore."

Steel links clicked and writhed as though alive with the rage that was pouring through Duncan.

Erik lifted the cold fingers that gripped his arm, kissed them, and stepped back from Amber. For the first time he turned around and confronted Dominic le Sabre. The pin that held Dominic's mantle in place glittered fiercely.

"As you see, Wolf of Glendruid," Erik said, "the blood relationship is clear."

"Yes."

"Then you will grant leave for your vassal to meet me in single combat."

"Duncan is my equal, not my vassal."

"Ah, so that, too, is true. I wondered." Erik smiled sardonically. "You are indeed a formidable tactician, Dominic le Sabre."

"As are you. No one less could have held three large estates in the Disputed Lands with a handful of knights and the reputation of being a sorcerer," Dominic said.

Erik began to turn toward Duncan, only to be stopped by Dominic's dry words.

"Your penchant for entering keeps through bolt-holes unknown to others is no doubt useful to your reputation," Dominic said.

"No doubt," Erik said gently.

"But there will be no problem in the future."

"Oh? Why?"

"Your shrewdness didn't extend to letting Duncan challenge *you* to single combat. You are a dead man, Erik, son of Robert."

Dominic looked past Erik to the Scots Hammer.

"Insomuch as you once were my vassal," Dominic said, "I entreat you to choose the hammer for your coming battle."

Cassandra's body jerked as though she had been whipped.

Absently, Duncan glanced down at the weapon that was quivering and twisting at the end of its steel leash, eager for the combat to come. Until that moment, he hadn't really been aware of holding the hammer.

"Erik is undefeated with the sword," Dominic said, "but he isn't known for any extraordinary skill with the hammer. *And I need you alive.*"

Surprised, Duncan looked at Dominic.

"Without you holding Stone Ring Keep," Dominic said simply, "there is little chance for Blackthorne's survival in the coming years. Grant this favor to one who was once your lord."

Duncan looked at the hammer that waited within

his grasp, as much a part of him as his own arms.

Then he looked at Amber.

Her eyes were wide, wild, and her hands were pressed against her mouth as though to hold back a scream. No matter who won the coming battle, she lost.

Duncan knew it as well as she.

"While you are considering the matter," Dominic added, "remember that Erik is the highborn lord who thought a man born a bastard had so little honor he wouldn't notice being forsworn."

Metal links snapped and snarled as Duncan played with the hammer. The people in the great hall were so still that each movement of the chain carried throughout.

"So be it," Duncan said. "I will fight with the hammer."

Amber closed her eyes.

Erik nodded, unsurprised.

"Have a hammer brought for me from the armory," Erik said.

"If you wish," Duncan said carelessly. "But if you choose to fight with sword and dagger instead, then you may do so."

A howl lifted beyond the walls, a wolf's throat crying Erik's pleasure.

"Sword and dagger," Erik said succinctly.

Duncan smiled with feral anticipation.

"Simon," Duncan said, "bring shields from the armory."

Without a word, Simon left. He returned quickly carrying two long, teardrop-shaped shields. One of them was emblazoned with the black outline of the Glendruid Wolf on a silver field. The other had on it the silver head of a wolf on a black field.

Two wolves circling, testing.

Cassandra went to Amber while the keep's chaplain shrived both men.

"I would take your place if I could," Cassandra

said in a low tone, "live in your skin, feel your emotions, weep your tears, voice your screams, endure your pain . . ."

"Whatever passes, the blame isn't yours," Amber said. "Nor is the death that is gathering like a black river. And like a river, it will flow."

The sound of Amber's voice made even the Learned woman flinch. Cassandra laced her fingers together inside her long sleeves and gathered what comfort she could from her Learning.

When the chaplain was finished and both men were shriven, Dominic went to Duncan and Erik.

"You have made the challenge, Erik, son of Robert," Dominic said. "Do you wish to give quarter?"

"Nay."

"So be it. No quarter given. No quarter received."

Dominic stepped back with a swiftness that made the black folds of his mantle swirl.

"Let it begin!" cried the Glendruid Wolf.

Erik leaped forward with a quickness that drew a gasp from the people in the hall. His sword swung in an arc so swift it was scarcely visible.

Duncan barely brought up his shield in time. Metal crashed on metal with a force that echoed through the hall.

A weaker man would have been flattened by the sudden attack. As it was, the force of the blow sent Duncan reeling. He went to one knee before he caught himself.

Erik's sword whistled and descended with hellish speed. It was clear he meant to end the battle with the next blow.

Again Duncan raised the shield without an instant to spare. But this time he was braced for the blow. Even as he absorbed it, his other arm moved in a powerful sweeping motion.

The hammer began to sing.

The eerie steel moan quivered in the hall, making

the hairs rise on Amber's neck. Though her eyes were closed, the hammer's death song told her Duncan had survived the first, incredibly quick moments of Erik's attack.

Amber's eyes remained closed when metal sounded on metal once more. Just as she hadn't wanted to see Erik's attack, the inhuman swiftness that killed with the speed of a peregrine, she didn't want to see Duncan now, the hammer circling with vicious speed, driven by the unusual power of his arm.

Amber wouldn't need to see either man's death in order to *know* he had died.

The hammer's song ended with a crash of steel on steel that drew cries and groans from the people in the hall. So great was the impact of the blow that it dented Erik's shield and knocked him off his feet. He rolled aside and leaped up with a quickness that drew a surprised oath from Simon.

The hammer descended again. Erik spun with the shield, giving way even as the blow struck, taking the force from it. As he spun, he slashed with the sword.

Duncan jerked his shield into place, but not quite as quickly as before. It was as though his arm had been deadened by the punishment it had already received.

Erik grinned like hell unleashed. The sword whistled and slashed blow after blow onto Duncan's shield, driving him backward toward a wall. Once within reach of the wall, Duncan's weapon would be as harmless as a handful of stones. There would be no room to swing the hammer if his back was to a wall.

Another sword slash sent Duncan to his knees. The hammer faltered in its song. Erik surged forward, sending the sword in a vicious arc meant to cleave Duncan in two.

Abruptly, the hammer whipped with renewed

force—and it came from the opposite direction, less
than a handspan off the floor.

Chain wrapped around steel chausses. Duncan
yanked, jerking Erik's feet from beneath him. He
hit the floor with a force so great his helm flew off
and his breath was knocked from him.

With a hoarse cry, Duncan pulled his battle dagger and knelt astride Erik before he could recover.
Unable to breathe, much less to fight, Erik looked
into the eyes of the dark warrior who would soon
kill him.

A mailed fist raised, a dagger gleamed, and
steel flashed downward while a woman's scream
wrenched the silence.

At the last instant, Duncan turned the blade aside.

The dagger struck the wooden floor with such
power that the blade slammed all the way through
the heavy plank and broke from the haft.

"I can't kill one who looks at me with Amber's
eyes!" Duncan raged. "I give him to you, Dominic.
Do to him what you will!"

With that, Duncan stood and threw the dagger's
heavy haft across the hall. It smashed into a far wall
with enough strength to chip stone. A vicious snap
of Duncan's wrist called the chain back from Erik's
ankles, freeing him.

Amber started toward both men, only to be
restrained by Cassandra's hand.

"It isn't done yet," Cassandra said tautly. "Now
we will see if Dominic le Sabre is truly fit to wear
the Glendruid Wolf on his mantle."

The harp Ariane held sounded an odd chord as
her fingers abruptly relaxed. It was the only outward sign that she had been in the least moved by
what she had seen.

Dominic drew his sword and slid the tip between
the chain-mail hood and Erik's chin.

For a long time the two men measured each
other.

"I would prefer an alliance to a funeral," Dominic said finally.

"Nay," Erik said, his voice hoarse.

"If you die, your father will be stirred from his clan rivalries. There will be war between the Glendruid Wolf and the clans of the north."

"And the Learned will be first to fight," Cassandra vowed. "I will lead them myself!"

No one who heard the Learned woman's voice doubted her.

"You will lose," Dominic said. "King Henry won't let his northern borders go to Saxons and Scots."

"Perhaps he won't have a choice," Erik said.

"Perhaps. But Henry has held every bit of land he has fought for."

Erik said nothing.

"If Ariane is jilted," Dominic continued, "there will be war as well. Baron Deguerre is a proud noble. King Henry is most pleased with the match."

Ariane stiffened subtly but said not one word.

"Aye," Erik said fiercely. "But if you have allies in the north, you might win that war against Henry and Deguerre."

Dominic nodded slightly and waited, not easing the pressure of the sword point at Erik's throat.

"If you have no allies, you will lose," Erik pointed out, "for you will be caught between two enemies— me on the northern border and Baron Deguerre's allies on the south."

"Do you relish the thought of war?" Dominic asked curiously.

"No. Neither do I relish seeing my sister turned into Duncan's whore."

Dominic's eyes narrowed. "The witch was not without a part in Duncan's betrayal."

"Losing Duncan is a greater punishment for Amber than you can imagine," Erik said.

"And you? How will you be punished for arranging things so that Duncan would be forsworn?"

"Watching what comes to Amber will be my punishment. It will be suitable in ways only the Learned can comprehend."

Dominic flicked at glance at Cassandra. She nodded once, but it was the pain bracketing her mouth that told Dominic what he needed to know. He turned back to Erik.

"And Duncan's punishment?" Dominic asked softly. "For you wish to punish him, too, I suspect."

A falcon called wildly from beyond the walls, triumph and fury at once.

Erik's smile was as cruel as the falcon's cry.

"Erik!" Amber cried. "No! Duncan doesn't understand! You can't scourge him for that!"

"Duncan will be the first to know his punishment," Erik said gently, never looking away from the Glendruid Wolf. "And he will know it too late to do anything but rage at himself for the fool that he was."

Silence filled the hall while Dominic measured Erik with eyes like quicksilver.

"Will Duncan survive this 'punishment'?" Dominic asked.

"I don't know."

"*Can* he survive?"

"I don't know."

Delicately Dominic allowed a bit more of the broadsword's weight to rest on Erik's flesh.

"What *do* you know, proud lord?" Dominic asked softly.

"That Duncan and Amber are joined in ways that defy measure. In denying her, he denies himself. In humiliating her, he humiliates himself. In hurting her—"

"He hurts himself," Dominic interrupted curtly. "A man can survive hurt. A man can't survive in the Disputed Lands with no money to buy knights."

"Amber is in Duncan's very blood," Erik said flatly. "Tell me, Glendruid Wolf, how long can a man live without blood? *How long would he want to live?*"

Dominic looked at Duncan. The Scots Hammer's back was turned. Quite plainly he had no further interest in what passed between Dominic and Erik.

The Glendruid Wolf looked at Amber. The paleness of her face and the stark fear in her eyes told him more than he wanted to know. Dominic sheathed the sword with a smooth, powerful stroke.

"You owe me your life," Dominic said. "Use it to help Duncan. I must have him alive and in power at Stone Ring Keep. It is the only way war can be avoided."

Erik said nothing.

"I am merciful only once with the same man," Dominic said coolly. "If war comes, you will die. You have my word on it."

Motionless on the floor, sword still in his hand, Erik took the measure of the Glendruid Wolf. Erik knew he could attack Dominic, possibly kill him—and surely die himself—or he could accept the terms as offered.

"If Learning can help Duncan," Erik said, "he will be helped."

Cassandra's soft laughter shocked everyone.

"Indeed, lord, you are fit to wear the Glendruid Wolf," she said coolly.

Dominic lifted a black eyebrow and said only, "You have seven days to find a solution to Duncan's problem. Then I will put my seal on the annulment and let the devil take what he will."

"Just seven days?"

"Yes."

"Done." Erik came to his feet in a lithe surge, sword in hand.

Simon leaped forward with a quickness that was

as surprising as Erik's had been. Smiling slightly, Erik sheathed his sword and turned to Dominic.

"You have my oath," Erik said. "Amber will verify it."

"It isn't necessary," Dominic said.

"It will assure the Learned that my oath is freely given, and as such, should be honored by *all* Learned."

Dominic lifted a black eyebrow. Silently he decided that the next time Meg chose to lecture him on the subject of the Learned, he would listen more attentively.

"Sister," Erik said, holding out his hand.

"Go," Cassandra said softly to Amber. "Take the gift the Glendruid Wolf saw fit to give."

Amber walked forward on unsteady legs. Instead of taking Erik's hand, she threw her arms around him and held him as though he were an anchor in a storm. Erik held her in return, feeling her tears hot against his neck.

"I love you, brother," Amber said.

"As I love you, sister, I will be good to my oath."

"Yes," Amber said, shaken by what she felt pouring into her from Erik. "I feel it raging in you. You want this very badly."

Slowly she released him. Even when they were no longer touching, she stood very close to her newly discovered brother.

Yet it was Duncan whose every move Amber's eyes followed. She wanted to go to him, to hold him, to assure herself in an elemental way that he truly was alive.

But Duncan hadn't looked at her since he had spared Erik's life.

Simon sheathed the sword he had drawn the instant Dominic had sheathed his own. Duncan slung the hammer over his shoulder in rest position. Dominic went to Meg and smiled down at her reassuringly.

Cassandra watched it all with a ruthless smile.

"Odd, isn't it, Glendruid Wolf?" she asked.

"That Erik's life was spared?" Dominic asked.

"Nay. That all of you accept the word of a girl who is being deeply wronged."

Dominic shrugged. "I have only to look at Amber to know that she wouldn't betray Duncan."

"Aye," Cassandra said in a low voice. "You know what the proud warrior refuses to acknowledge. Amber loves Duncan."

"She helped to betray him."

"Without that 'betrayal,' Duncan would be hanged and we would be at war. Bleak death rather than rich life."

"Yes."

"Then tell me," Cassandra said, "in what way did Amber truly betray her dark warrior?"

"Ask Duncan," Dominic said quietly. "He is the one whose back is turned to her. He is the one who wishes for both wife and leman."

"Duncan," Cassandra said.

There was that in her voice which could not be denied.

Abruptly Duncan turned to face the Learned woman.

"Let Amber go," Cassandra said simply.

"Never. She is *mine*."

Cassandra's breath came out in an aching sigh. When she spoke again, her voice was soft. And it carried through the hall like the sound of a sword being drawn from a steel sheath.

"Amber said exactly the same thing to me," Cassandra murmured, "and in exactly the same way, when I suggested taking you back to Stone Ring before you recovered your senses."

A tremor ripped through Duncan. It was so small that only someone looking for it would have seen it.

Cassandra was looking for it with a falcon's predatory eyes.

"Tell me," Cassandra said distinctly. "Will dishonoring Amber salve your honor . . . or only wound it more?"

Duncan said nothing.

"Let her go," Cassandra said.

"I will not."

Cassandra smiled with a savagery that made Dominic's hand itch to hold a sword once more.

"Will not?" she repeated mockingly. "Nay. You *cannot* let Amber go."

Duncan neither moved nor spoke.

"Once I thought I would destroy you when you finished flaying Amber's soul from her body," Cassandra said. "Now I know I will not."

"Mercy from the Learned witch?" Duncan asked, his voice as mocking as hers.

"Mercy?"

Cassandra laughed. It was worse than her smile.

"Nay, dark warrior. I would rather you survive and learn too late what you have done."

Duncan became still.

"Then," Cassandra said, "I will watch your soul die in the same way you are killing Amber's . . . one cruel breath at a time."

∂ 21

AMBER lay awake in the luxurious bed that had been hers since she had married Duncan. Each time the wind shifted or sleet rattled against stone or a voice drifted up from the floors below, her heartbeat doubled.

Then she would hold her breath, listening with every fiber of her being for the sound of footsteps approaching her door.

Duncan will come to me tonight.

He must.

Come to me, dark warrior. Let me touch you in the only way you allow yourself to be touched.

Let me be one with you once more.

Just once.

I can touch your soul if you will let me.

Just once . . .

But none of the sounds Amber heard were those made by Duncan climbing the spiral stone stairway to her bedchamber.

As the night lengthened and the autumn sleet beat against stone, Amber understood that she would remain alone in the storm. Duncan would not come to her on this night of all nights, when nearly dying at Erik's hand had renewed his appreciation of life, of living, of simply being alive.

Tonight Duncan would be vulnerable to his amber witch in ways he didn't want to be.

She knew it.

And so did he.

Abruptly Amber sat up and threw the rich bed coverings aside. The fine, fragile linen of her nightdress glowed with ghostly light, reflection of the dying hearth fire. The amber pendant she wore had the shuttered gleam of banked coals.

Her eyes gleamed in the same way, veiled by a darkness that had nothing to do with night.

Amber whirled her mantle around her shoulders, pulled the cowl into place, and set off for the bedchamber of the lord of the keep. She needed neither candle nor lamp to light her way. Duncan's presence was a fire burning against the night, as certain a guide to him as dawn is to the day that follows.

The path to Duncan could have been through a strange forest or a tangled glen, and it would have been the same to Amber. Clear. Certain.

No one was about in the hall. The voices of the sentries from the battlements above were the only noises not made by the storm. Amber's feet moved soundlessly over the wood of the floor. Her mantle lifted and fell around her ankles with every swift step.

No squire slept outside Duncan's door, for he hadn't had time to choose among the young, wellborn boys who were eager to be trained in the ways of war by the legendary Scots Hammer. Indeed, the door to the lord's bedchamber was half open, announcing the confidence of the warrior who slept within.

A glance around the room told Amber that Duncan must have gone late to bed. Flames still leaped within the hearth. Candles still burned in their sconces. On a chest near the bed, an oil lamp burned at low ebb, sending the scent of rosemary through the room. Next to the lamp, a battle hammer lay in readiness, gleaming coldly with reflected fire.

The golden light of the candles wavered when Amber walked in and shut the door quietly behind. Duncan didn't stir. Nor did she expect him to do so. Though untrained, Duncan had a Learned warrior's appreciation of when danger was nearby.

And when it was not.

Amber's mantle slid to the floor with a hushed sound. Her nightdress followed, settling like a cloud over her mantle. Her golden hair shimmered with firelight. Golden amber gleamed between her breasts. Making no more noise than a candle flame, she eased into bed beside Duncan.

The subtle smell of spices on Duncan's skin told Amber that he had sought whatever peace could be found in a warm bath before going to bed alone. The same scent was on her own skin, for she, too, had sought water's soothing embrace.

But what she truly wanted was an embrace less soothing, more fiery, Duncan locked within her body.

Deftly Amber drew the bed covers aside. Duncan's bare back gleamed in the muted light. He was lying on his side, facing away from her. The naked power of his shoulders was both a lure and a warning.

Dark warrior, who could make the hammer sing as no other.

With the delicacy of a butterfly sipping nectar, Amber's fingertips stroked from the nape of Duncan's neck down the length of his spine. Though she had hungered to touch him, it was painful to her. Even while he slept, the savage conflict within his soul raged on, truth set against truth.

And you say you never betrayed me. Such fine calculations they must teach the Learned, all the ways to split hairs until nothing remains but dishonor.

My body knows you. It responds to you as to none other.

We are lost, witch. Your soul was sold to the devil a long time ago.

You're a fire in my blood, in my flesh, in my soul.

Yet when all truths were weighed and measured, one remained against which there was no measure, the Glendruid Wolf's words ringing like thunder through every silence.

Beyond all doubt, beyond all temptation, you are a man of your word. And your word was given to me.

For Duncan to go back on that word would be to destroy himself. To keep his word meant destroying Amber. Neither was bearable.

One was inevitable.

If I loved her, I could not do what must be done.

Pain that was both Duncan's and her own lanced through Amber, cutting her, scoring her soul.

"As I feared," she whispered, "it will destroy you."

Were it not for the equally great need in Duncan to touch Amber, to lie with her, to lose himself within her until he was too spent to battle himself for a time . . . were it not for that, touching Duncan would have been as agonizing to Amber as putting her hand within the hearth fire.

As it was, touching Duncan was a bittersweet torment that cut her until she bled.

And not touching him also cut her until she bled.

Drop by drop, bleeding into darkness.

And as I feared, it is destroying me.

Yet Amber didn't lift her hand. Duncan's skin was smooth, supple, warm. The layers of muscle on either side of his spine lured her. She stroked the resilient flesh with gentle sweeps of her hand, savoring the sheer power of him, ignoring the pain.

"You are strong in so many ways, dark warrior," Amber whispered. "Why can't you be strong enough to accept what can't be changed?"

You're a fire in my blood, in my flesh, in my soul.

Muscles shifted and coiled as Duncan rolled onto

his back. His head turned toward Amber. She held her breath, but he didn't awaken.

"If you could accept," she whispered, "then you could love me despite all the truths known too soon and told too late."

Duncan's deep, even breathing remained unchanged. The amber pendant he wore shifted and gleamed with each breath.

Sighing, Amber gave in to the temptation to smooth her hand over the hair that curled so intriguingly across Duncan's chest. The crisp mat tickled and aroused and pleased, making her hand tingle with heightened sensitivity.

Amber lowered her head, kissed Duncan's shoulder, and laid her cheek on the muscular pad of flesh over his heart. The sound of his life beating so close beneath her cheek swept through her.

"If only I could touch you. *Just once.*"

Somewhere in his mind, Duncan was aware of Amber's presence. She could tell by the change rippling through him, savage arguments fading, muffled by the sleek, sensual tide that was rising in him, called by her touch.

Though Duncan had allowed nothing but the most basic physical connection between himself and Amber since he had learned his true name, he had once enjoyed being stroked and petted by her. He had held his own arousal in check simply to savor a less urgent exchange of caresses with his lover.

In sleep, Duncan was enjoying being stroked again, absorbing Amber's pleasure in touching him as avidly as dry ground absorbed a gentle rain.

"You, too, missed this," Amber whispered. "You, too, hungered to share tenderness as well as wildfire."

Relief shivered through Amber. She had feared that the darkness growing at Duncan's core had eaten away all softness in him. She bent down to brush her lips over his skin once more.

An instant later his hand gripped her hair with painful force. Duncan was fully awake.

And fully furious.

"I don't want you," he said through his clenched teeth. "I don't even want to touch you."

Though the currents of desire swirling between their bodies made a mockery of his words, his rejection still stung.

"Is that a promise?" Amber asked silkily.

"What?"

"That you won't touch me tonight."

"Aye, witch. I won't touch you!"

Amber's triumphant smile was as primitive as the light in Duncan's eyes. Had he been less angry he would have been wary. The feminine ruthlessness in Amber was almost tangible.

"Then take your hand off me," she said distinctly, "or find yourself forsworn before you've drawn another breath."

Duncan let go of Amber as though she were the burning end of a candle.

"Get out," he said flatly.

Amber simply looked at Duncan for a time. Then her hand moved with a speed that rivaled Simon's. The last of the bed coverings were raked aside, revealing that Duncan was like her, naked but for an amber pendant.

Equally naked was his desire. Rigid, erect, his flesh stirred with each quickening beat of his heart.

Amber made a sound of pleasure that was almost feline.

"Get. Out." Duncan's voice was icy.

Smiling slightly, Amber trailed her fingertips down his chest to his navel, slowly approaching the center of his need.

Duncan started to grab Amber's hand, then realized that he could not.

Not without being forsworn.

"Witch."

Furious and savagely aroused at once, Duncan watched Amber's elegant, teasing fingers prowl closer and closer to his straining flesh. At the last moment she turned aside, tracing a half circle in the thick nest of hair.

"You could call for Simon," Amber suggested.

Her smile said just how much she enjoyed Duncan's dilemma. Her fingertip traced the creases where muscular torso and legs joined.

Duncan hissed through clenched teeth.

"Simon has little trust in me," Amber pointed out, "and less liking."

Her nails bit delicately into the taut skin of Duncan's thighs. She felt the hot explosion of his desire.

His finger's dug into the soft mattress. He willed himself to feel nothing.

Amber laughed softly, knowing everything he felt. No matter what his mind said, his body knew what it must have.

Soon.

"Simon would be pleased to drag me from your bed," Amber murmured.

She fitted her palm over Duncan's thigh, openly savoring the strength of him. The contrast between her graceful fingers and the blunt, clenched power of his body aroused Duncan until he could barely stifle a groan.

"But I wouldn't be pleased to be dragged from you," Amber whispered, bending over Duncan.

Her hair spilled across his thighs in a cool cascade. He groaned despite his determination not to respond.

Amber smiled even as her teeth bit sweetly into the long muscle of his thigh. The center of the bite was a hot touch of her tongue.

The shudder that went through Duncan went through Amber as well.

"Tonight you are like winter wine to me," she said in a low voice. "Dark, potent."

Duncan made a thick sound.

"I would like to taste you from your forehead to your heels," Amber murmured.

The tip of her tongue traced a line of fire from Duncan's knees to his navel.

"I would like to do . . . everything."

With a throttled sound, Duncan clenched the muscles of his legs and covered himself with his hands, trying to prevent further intimacy.

"Wouldn't you rather my hands were holding you?" Amber asked.

"Nay," he said through gritted teeth.

"Truly? Is that why you grow more formidable with each breath? You hope to frighten me away?"

Duncan had no answer save the one he was trying to conceal or ignore.

Amber knew it as well as he did. Better. His desire and her own combined.

"It won't work, dark warrior. No matter how formidable you become, I can sheathe you. You know it as surely as I do."

Then Amber laughed softly. "Nay, you know my sheath better than I, for you have measured it full well."

Duncan's answer was a low sound that had no meaning but frustration. She was bringing him to bay with her words alone. His body knew what it wanted. It clamored for it.

And his body knew where to find what it must have.

"Move your hands," Amber said huskily. "Give me the freedom we both desire."

"Nay! I don't want you!"

Amber couldn't help laughing despite the slice of pain that came with his repeated denial of her.

"Not so, coy knight," she said. "You can scarce conceal your desire with both hands."

There was also no way Duncan could hide from Amber the fire burning within him. Each time their skin met, his hunger poured through him into her, truth known through touch.

And Amber made certain their skin was always touching.

Laughing, she began to seduce Duncan's hands away from his body. Her teeth nipped boldly. Her lips brushed tantalizingly. Her breath was a sultry warmth bathing him. The tip of her tongue traced each line between his tightly held fingers.

In time, Amber's hand sought the shadow line between Duncan's tightly held thighs, stroking in the same rhythms as her tongue probing between his thumb and forefinger. Then she caught his smallest finger between her teeth and pulled it into her mouth. The movements of her tongue silently offered him another, even more intimate caress.

A groan was dragged from deep in Duncan's chest. Desire shook him until his hands jerked. Instantly Amber's hand slid beneath one of his. Slender fingers curled possessively around him. His body jerked again, as though he had been struck by a whip rather than by a tender caress.

"Amber," Duncan said between his teeth. "No!"

"Yes," she whispered raggedly. "Dear God, yes!"

Her hand moved beneath his, and then her breath, and then her tongue.

"Amber."

"Aye, dark warrior. 'Tis Amber. And this . . ."

Her tongue swirled, tasting and caressing in the same motion.

" . . . this is magnificent. Warm as a cat. Hard as a fist. Surging like a storm."

When Amber's tongue circled Duncan teasingly, he made a last effort at escaping her by turning away from her onto his side.

She was too quick. She turned with Duncan, flowing over him like a hot rain.

Then Duncan found he could retreat no farther. He was caught between Amber's mouth and her hand sliding up between his thighs. She cupped him in her palm, weighed him, and laughed with pleasure at his readiness.

"Every part of you is hard," Amber said. "You burn very hotly, dark warrior, but I would have you hotter still."

She bent to Duncan again, caught him against her tongue with loving care, and stroked him until sweat glistened on his skin like rain.

"Stop," he said hoarsely.

"Stop?" Amber's laugh was low, delighted, a bit savage. "Nay, my stubborn warrior. You have barely begun to burn."

"I cannot—hold—much longer."

"I know." A delicious shivering went over Amber. "I like that knowledge."

"Witch," he said thickly.

But there was more pleasure than anger in his voice.

Amber's teeth closed delicately. Duncan said something dark as he fought the desire consuming him with every breath, every heartbeat, every hot caress.

Yet just when ecstasy was on the brink of overcoming his restraint, Amber stopped. Torn between relief and disappointment, Duncan breathed deeply, trying to calm the wildness of his need.

Tenderly, soothingly, Amber stroked hair back from Duncan's heated face and kissed his cheek as though he were a child who needed calming. Finally passion's claws eased in Duncan, allowing him to breathe evenly once more. With a groan, he rolled over onto his back.

Amber smiled at him, kissed his shoulder, and slid like fire back down his body.

And like fire, she burned him.

Soon Duncan was hotter than before, harder,

shaking with what it cost not to give in to Amber.
When he was no more than a breath from ecstasy,
she stopped and calmed him again.

And in time she set him to burning all over
again.

"Finish it," Duncan said through his teeth. "You
will drive me mad!"

"Soon," Amber murmured.

"Soon I will be mad!"

Laughing, she drew her nails over his clenched
thighs and between his legs, goading him ever
higher, yet always knowing when to draw him
back from the sensual brink.

Sweat gathered and ran on Duncan's loins.
Amber tasted it, found it good, and tasted again,
elsewhere. She found that good as well.

Fire poured over Duncan, burning him to the
marrow of his bones. Never had he known Amber
to be like this, waging a sultry, determined seduc-
tion over every bit of his body. She wanted him,
and she meant to have him.

All of him, in every way there was.

"Release me from my promise," Duncan said
thickly.

The warmth of Amber's laughter washed over
him.

"Not yet."

" 'Tis beyond reason. I must touch you!"

"How?"

The word was as much a purr as a question.
Low, husky, breathless with desire, the sound
of Amber's voice sent a shudder of anticipation
through Duncan.

Suddenly she moved astride his thighs and he
sensed her opening to him. She radiated heat and
wept with desire. The scent of her made him wild.

Yet Amber stayed where she was, poised just
above him, brushing against the very flesh she had
tormented so thoroughly.

"Finish it," he said hoarsely. "You want me as much as I want you. I can feel it."

"That will never change as long as I draw breath."

"Then let me take you and end this torment!"

"That can't be your hand upon my thigh, pushing me down, can it?" Amber asked.

With a dark curse Duncan snatched back his hand.

"I didn't mean to," he said.

"I know. I felt your surprise."

"Have I no secrets from you?" Duncan asked angrily.

"Many. But only one that matters."

"What?"

"Your soul, dark warrior. It is shut away from me."

"So is yours from me."

"Nay," Amber whispered. "Tonight I am giving it to you one breath at a time."

Whatever Duncan might have said in answer was lost in the husky cry he gave as Amber slid down over him, taking all of him in a slow, caressing glide.

Before the taking was half complete, Amber came undone. Her shivering flesh and rippling cries undid Duncan. Even as she took him fully, he gave himself to her in a succession of deep pulses that left him shaking.

And then it began all over again.

The tempting and the teasing, the intimate caresses and the sweet torment. Whispered words and touches that made Duncan jerk with pleasure. Unexpected kisses, love bites that stung and pleasured at once.

While candles guttered and flames winked out, Amber burned on undimmed, pouring herself into Duncan as surely as he poured himself into her, burning with her because he could do no less, consuming her as certainly as he was himself being consumed.

A whispered plea, a vow given back, and
Duncan's hands were at last free to touch, his
mouth to kiss, his body to sink deeply into the
wildness that was Amber burning. She drank his
passion and gave it back to him redoubled, driving
both of them higher and higher, speaking to him in
wild silence, describing a love that could not be put
into words, expressing an unspeakable need.

*Let me reach into you as you have reached into me.
Then rich life might grow.*

When finally nothing was left undone, when both
were so spent they slid from shattering ecstasy into
sleep in the space of a breath, still Amber clung to
Duncan, wanting to share her dreams as deeply as
she had shared the rest of herself.

Let me touch your soul.

Just once.

But it was Duncan's dreams that were shared,
bleak turmoil redoubled rather than relieved by
Amber's wild giving and taking of self.

Soon Amber awakened, dragged into awareness
by the conflict raging through Duncan's soul. When
she realized what had been gambled and what had
been lost, cold seeped through her.

The last part of the prophecy had been fulfilled.

Yet Duncan was farther from her than ever,
locked in battle with himself. His word had been
given.

It had not been given to her.

Yet he was part of her.

Darkness gathering, drop by drop, breath by
breath, one soul given, one soul locked away.
Untouched.

*Cassandra is wrong. His soul won't wither, for he
does not love me.*

Slowly Amber drew away from Duncan and slid
from the bed, unable to bear the agony of touching him any longer. With hands that trembled, she
removed her amber pendant and placed it across

the coiled metal of the war hammer that had given
Duncan his name. She reached out to him one last
time, but did not touch him.

"God be with you, dark warrior," Amber whispered, "for I cannot be."

MEG looked across the table at her
husband. Their cold breakfast of bread, meat, and
ale lay largely ignored on the trestle table in the
great hall. Dominic was leaning back in his chair,
eyes narrowed. The fingers of his right hand
drummed softly on his thigh in time to the haunting tune Ariane was playing on a lap harp.

Simon carved another slice of venison, poured
some ale into a dainty goblet, and set both in front
of Ariane.

"Leave off making the harp weep and eat," he
said tersely.

"Again? I feel like a goose being fattened for a
feast," she muttered.

But Ariane set aside the harp and began to eat.
It was easier than arguing with Simon when he had
that determined look in his eyes.

"Have you dreamed, Meg?" Dominic asked
abruptly.

"Yes."

"Glendruid dreams?' he asked.

"Yes."

The fact that Meg said no more told Dominic that
the dreams had been unhappy . . . and that they
had offered no solutions. The backs of his fingers
stroked her cheek.

"Small falcon," he said in a low voice, "I must
find a way to give Blackthorne peace. I want our
child to be born into a time and a place not torn
apart by war."

Meg kissed Dominic's palm and watched him
with eyes made luminous by love.

"Come what will, Glendruid Wolf," she whispered, "I will never regret bearing your child."

Ignoring the others in the room, Dominic lifted Meg into his lap. Golden bells braided into her hair shivered and chimed. He held her close, whispering his love.

After a time, the haunting cry of the harp resumed, beautiful music describing all the shades of sadness.

"What a cheerful gathering," Erik mocked as he entered the great hall, his peregrine on his wrist. "Do you play often for funerals, Lady Ariane?"

"That is one of her lighthearted tunes," Simon said.

"God save us," Erik muttered. "Leave off, lady. You will have my peregrine in tears."

The peregrine in question flared her wings briefly before she settled to watching the gathered humans with inhuman curiosity.

"I would have expected you to be with Duncan," Dominic said, "driving Learning into his thick skull."

"My sister tried a more certain method," Erik said, smiling slightly. "She went to Duncan last night."

Dominic's smile was an exact reflection of Erik's. "That explains their absence at morning chapel."

"Aye."

"Did it help my quest for peace?"

Erik hesitated. Then he shrugged. The peregrine shifted restlessly on his wrist, making silver bells on her jesses ring.

"Something has changed," Erik said. "I can sense it. But I don't know what."

"Permit me to educate you," Cassandra said from behind Erik.

The quality of the Learned woman's voice brought a hush to the room.

Erik stepped aside, allowing Cassandra room to pass. He saw that her normally braided and concealed hair was loose, a seething silver glory rippling freely over her scarlet cloak. Ancient silver rune stones glittered in her hands.

The peregrine flared her wings again and gave a keening cry.

"You have just come from casting silver runes," Erik said, his voice toneless.

There was no answer. None was needed. The hammered silver markers in the Learned woman's hands spoke for themselves.

"What did you learn?" Erik asked.

"More than I wished. Less than I hoped."

Cassandra walked until she stood in front of Dominic and Meg.

"Witch of Glendruid," Cassandra said formally, "do you dream?"

A single glance at Cassandra's silver eyes brought Meg to her feet.

"Yes," Meg said. "I dream."

"Will you share your dreams?"

"A scream the color of amber. A darkness being torn apart like tough cloth, one fiber at a time."

Cassandra bowed her head for a moment. "Thank you."

"For what? There is neither comfort nor answer in my dream."

"It was confirmation I sought, not comfort."

Meg gave the older woman a curious look.

"When my emotions are involved," Cassandra said calmly, "I have to be wary of casting the silver stones. Sometimes I see what I wish rather than what is."

"What did you see?" Meg asked. "Will you share it?"

"The amber prophecy is complete. She has given her heart and her body and her soul to Duncan."

"You didn't need to cast the silver stones to see that was coming," Erik said.

Cassandra nodded agreement.

"Then why did you cast them?" Erik asked. "They are not to be used lightly."

"Aye."

Silently Cassandra looked from Erik to Dominic. Then she looked at no one at all.

"Erik, son of Robert," she said. "Dominic, Wolf of Glendruid. If you go to war now, it is because you wish to. Amber is no longer your excuse. She has—"

"What are you saying?" Erik interrupted roughly.

"—removed herself from your masculine equations of pride and power and death."

"*What has she done?*" Erik demanded.

"She gave her amber pendant to Duncan."

The peregrine shrieked as though its blood had turned to fire.

But even the falcon's scream couldn't drown the chilling scream of masculine rage that came echoing down the keep's great hall from above.

Cassandra tilted her head as though savoring the sound. Her smile was as cruel as winter.

"Duncan's suffering has begun," she said softly. "Amber's soon will end."

Dominic looked from the Learned woman to Erik.

"What is she talking about?" Dominic demanded.

Erik simply shook his head, unable either to speak or to calm his falcon's wild cries. He looked as though he had been struck by a mailed fist.

Another scream of anger echoed. Before it ended there were horrible sounds of smashing and clashing and rending, as though a battle were being fought in the lord's bedchamber.

"Simon," Dominic said, coming swiftly to his feet.

"Aye!"

Side by side, the two brothers raced up the stone stairway to Duncan's bedchamber. What they saw there made them pull up short in the doorway.

Duncan was a man possessed. Naked but for two amber talismans, he stood with the battle hammer in one hand. His lips were drawn back from his teeth in a grimace of pain or rage or both in unholy communion.

With a lunge, he ripped covers from the bed and flung them into the hearth. Smoke bloomed sullenly, then burst into savage flames, burning even higher than before.

The hammer whistled and hummed in a deadly blur, driven by the mad power of Duncan's arm. The hammer descended, a wooden table exploded, and he kicked the pieces into the fire. Then the hammer sang again, cutting circles around Duncan's head, its moan in ghastly duet with his scream of fury. The bed frame was smashed to kindling and fed to the ravening fire.

Dominic had seen men like this before, in the heat of battle, when the leash was slipped on all that was human and only rage remained.

"There will be no reasoning with him," Dominic said softly to Simon.

"Aye."

"We have to take him before he turns on the people of the keep."

"I'll get some rope from the armory."

Dominic drew his sword. "Don't be long, brother."

He was talking to himself. Simon already was sprinting toward the staircase.

Very quickly Simon reappeared with a coil of rope in his hand. Dominic was waiting in the doorway, his heavy black mantle in one hand and his sword in the other. As soon as he saw Simon, he sheathed the sword.

"When I tangle the hammer in my mantle," Dominic said, "get enough rope on Duncan to hold a bear."

Just as Dominic started forward, he sensed Meg coming up behind him. His arm shot out, barring her from the room.

"Stay back," Dominic said in a low voice. "Duncan is in a berserker's rage. He doesn't know anyone right now, least of all himself."

The hammer moaned and whipped through the air. Wood shattered like pottery. The chest was destroyed in a single blow and kicked into the fire. All that remained was a smaller chest and a wardrobe.

As soon as the hammer began to circle again, Dominic struck. His mantle fouled the hammer. Before Duncan could jerk it free, Dominic dove at him low and hard, sweeping Duncan off his feet. He landed with a crash that drove the breath from his body.

Even that wasn't enough to subdue Duncan. If it hadn't been for Simon's quickness, Duncan would have shaken off the attack with the strength of the madness that had claimed him.

But in the end, the two brothers finally managed to truss Duncan like a fowl for the spit.

Duncan gave a last, terrible cry and strained against his bonds until his face was dark. Even his great strength wasn't enough to throw off Dominic, Simon, and the ropes that bound him. Slowly the violent tension began to leave Duncan's body.

Breathing heavily, Simon and Dominic wiped sweat from their faces and came warily to their feet. Duncan lay unmoving, his eyes open, staring at nothing. Dominic retrieved his mantle and spread it over Duncan's nakedness.

"Now, Meg," Dominic said. "He knows you best."

"Duncan," Meg said softly. "*Duncan.*"

Slowly Duncan's head turned until he could look at her.

"Meggie?" he asked.

"Aye, Duncan. What is wrong?"

The last light of madness left Duncan's eyes, leaving no light at all.

"Gone," Duncan said simply.

"What?"

There was no answer.

Meg came forward and knelt by Duncan's shoulder. Gently she stroked the hair back from his sweat-drenched forehead.

"Amber?" asked Meg. "Is she gone?"

"The light . . ." A shudder went through Duncan's big body. "She took the light with her, Meggie."

22

"THE drawbridge is up," Simon said to Dominic. "The gate is sealed. Amber can't be gone."

"Every keep has at least one bolt-hole."

"Then she can't have gone far," Simon said. "She left at night in a storm."

Cool laughter came from the hallway beyond the bedchamber. When Simon and Dominic turned, they saw Erik. He was watching Duncan with a combination of anger and pity in his eyes.

"Amber is Learned," Erik said. "If you blink, she will be out of your sight. If you blink twice, she will be beyond your reach."

"Set your hounds after her," Dominic said.

Erik shrugged. "As you wish."

"You don't sound enthusiastic about finding your sister," Simon said.

"She will head for sacred ground. The dogs won't follow once she reaches a stone circle."

Simon muttered something under his breath about witches, but didn't argue the matter. He had learned in trailing Meg that the ancient stone rings had secrets they yielded to no outsider.

"We have to try," Dominic said.

"Why?" Erik asked bluntly.

"I don't want war with you."

"You won't get it."

"In six days," Dominic said, "I will put my seal to the decree setting aside Duncan's marriage to Amber."

"In six days it won't matter."

"Why?"

"Why do you care, Wolf? War has been avoided."

Erik turned on his heel and stalked down the hall. Cassandra was waiting for him at the head of the stairway.

Dominic watched as Erik took the Learned woman's hands between his own. Though neither wept, their mourning was almost tangible. Uneasily Dominic looked back at Duncan.

Duncan's suffering has begun. Amber's soon will end. The light . . . She took the light with her, Meggie.

Abruptly Dominic was afraid that he knew what Cassandra had meant, and what Duncan's suffering would be.

It must not be allowed to happen.

"Simon," Dominic said sharply.

"Aye. The war-horses?"

"Yes. One of us should stay here."

"Is Meg riding?"

Dominic looked over his shoulder. Meg was still kneeling next to Duncan, stroking his forehead. Tears were falling slowly down her cheeks. Duncan's eyes were open, but he was seeing nothing except what he had lost.

"Meg," Dominic said gently.

She looked up.

"We're going to put the hounds on Amber's trail," Dominic said. "If it ends in one of the ancient places, would you be able to pick the trail up again?"

"If Old Gwyn were here, perhaps she could." Meg looked down at Duncan. "I don't know if I can. I do know that Duncan needs . . . something. And I am a Glendruid healer."

"Stay here and guard your wife," Simon said

quickly to his brother. "She's worth more than all of the Disputed Lands put together."

"What of your safety? Sven is still out in the countryside measuring the temper of the people."

"I'll take Erik with me."

"He might attack you."

Simon's smile was swift and savage. "That would be a pity, wouldn't it?"

Dominic gave a crack of laughter and said no more.

Shouted orders went out. Soon three horses were thundering over the lowered drawbridge. Two were battle stallions ridden by knights in chain mail. Against all custom, one of those knights carried a peregrine on his wrist. The third horse was a white stallion ridden by a Learned woman whose long silver hair blew in the breeze without restraint.

A single, large wolfhound waited on the far side of the bridge. There was no hound master in sight.

"Just one hound?" Simon asked.

"If there is a scent," Erik said, "Stagkiller will find it. If the scent can be followed, he will follow it."

At an unseen signal from his master, Stagkiller began casting about for Amber's scent. He found it in a thicket of willows fifty yards from the keep's wall.

"Exit from the bolt-hole?" Simon asked blandly.

If Erik answered, it was lost in the deep baying of Stagkiller as he took to the scent trail. The rough-coated hound ran with the long, tireless strides of a wolf. The horses followed.

Serfs and villeins looked up as the trio of horses galloped by. When the men saw Cassandra's unbound hair, they crossed themselves and wondered who had been foolish enough to call down the wrath of the Learned.

The horses galloped down the cart road until the trail cut to a lane that zigzagged between fields and cottages. Mud leaped from beneath the horses' big hooves and stuck to the drystone fences that rose from the ground on both sides of the lane.

Soon the last of the keep's farmland lay behind. The forest began abruptly, looming up from the misty land in shades of pale bark and rich brown, lingering oranges and yellows and reds, and the startling evergreen fire of holly and ivy.

Stagkiller coursed the scent with lean intensity, never easing the pace no matter what the terrain or vegetation. After a time, mist-wreathed hills rose all around and a brook glinted darkly as it snaked between hills.

A long, low ridge of land lifted slowly beneath the horses' feet. When they crested it, a circle of stones lay beyond. Nose to the ground, Stagkiller loped up to the ancient place.

And then the hound stopped as though he had run into a wall.

With a howl of disappointment, Stagkiller looked to his master. Erik sent the peregrine into the air with a swift movement of his arm.

"Search," he ordered the hound curtly.

Stagkiller began casting for scent around the edges of the circle. It quickly became obvious that there was no scent to be found.

"God's teeth," Simon snarled. " 'Tis just like Blackthorne."

Cassandra gave him a curious look.

"I tracked Meg once to an ancient place," Simon said without looking away from Stagkiller. "The dogs lost her scent."

"Did they pick it up again?" Erik asked.

"No."

"Did you search the place?"

"No."

"Why not?" asked Cassandra.

"I was backtracking. I already knew where Meg was."

Cassandra and Erik looked at each other.

"Search Stone Ring," Erik invited.

Simon reined his horse over to the stones. The stallion refused to walk between. Circling the ring, Simon tried several more times, finally using his spurs. No matter where he pointed the stallion, or what prodding he gave the horse, it refused the trail.

Dismounting, Simon walked warily up to the circle. When he looked inside, he saw nothing remarkable. Rocks. Random weeds. Stones canted and covered with moss. A low mound. Mist writhing and lifting in a thousand silver veils.

With an impatient oath, Simon set off between the stones on foot. Every instinct he had was on edge, quivering with alertness. Yet he saw nothing. He heard nothing.

No tracks but his own showed in the mist-drenched grass. A quick turn around the base of the mound and over its top told him that the mound had neither an entrance nor any rock large enough to hide behind.

Relieved, Simon turned his back on the mound and headed for the standing stones where his battle stallion nervously waited. Just as Simon reached for the reins, he stopped, remembering something he had been told when he had first come to Stone Ring Keep as a knight on a quest.

"Is this where you found Duncan?" Simon called to Erik.

"Aye. On top of the mound, at the foot of the rowan tree, inside the second ring of stones."

Simon spun back toward the mound. He narrowed his eyes against the watery sunlight that was somehow so brilliant it forced him to squint. For a moment he thought he saw the elegant line of a rowan, but it was only a curl of mist rising.

Uneasily Simon looked around once more. As he had thought, there was only one ring of stones.

Even so, he kept glimpsing a second, ghostly ring from the corner of his eye.

Yet when he looked straight on, there was nothing but mist.

With an impatient curse, Simon mounted and rode back to where Cassandra and Erik waited with a thoroughly downcast Stagkiller.

"That can't be where you found Duncan," Simon said. "There is no rowan here, and only one ring of stones."

"If you say so, then it must be so," Cassandra said.

"What do you say?" Simon demanded of Erik.

"Sometimes Learned eyes see differently."

"Then in the name of God, *go and look.*"

Without a word, Erik and Cassandra rode to the ring of stones. Their horses switched their tails and minced warily between the large standing stones, but otherwise made no protest. A few yards farther into the ring, the animals visibly calmed. When their riders dismounted, both horses set to grazing as though in a familiar meadow.

Simon watched the two figures climb the mound. Silhouetted against the brilliant, misty sky, they were almost impossible to see. Using his hand, Simon shaded his eyes against the light that was both soft and yet so intense it made his eyes water to stare directly. Finally he managed to clear his vision.

Erik and Cassandra were gone.

A chill went over Simon in the instant before he realized that they must have walked down the far side of the mound and out of his sight. With a savage word, he blinked rapidly, then narrowed his eyes against the light.

There was no one on the mound.

His horse snorted and yanked on the rein. Simon looked at the stallion, saw that it wanted only to graze, and looked back at the mound.

Cassandra and Erik were silhouetted against the sky once more. Their outlines wavered for a moment, as though they were reflections on the surface of a slightly disturbed pond.

Simon blinked.

When he looked again at the mound, Erik and Cassandra were walking toward him, talking in low voices. A peregrine arrowed down from the brilliant gray sky to land on Erik's wrist.

"What did you find?" Simon asked impatiently.

"Amber was here," Cassandra said.

"And?"

"Now she is gone," Erik said.

"But your hound found no trail," Simon objected.

"Did your hounds do better at Blackthorne Keep?"

Simon grunted. "Where is Amber?"

Erik looked at Cassandra. The Learned woman was braiding her hair with fingers that shook.

"Where is Amber?" Simon asked Cassandra harshly.

"I don't know."

"What does your Learning tell you?" he demanded.

"Something I can scarce believe."

"God's teeth," Simon hissed. "What is it?"

"She took the Druid way," Cassandra said simply.

"Then follow!"

"We can't."

"Why not?"

Cassandra turned and looked at Simon with glittering silver eyes.

"You haven't the Learning to understand," she said. "Nor do you wish it. You have contempt for anything less tangible than a sword."

With a snarled word, Simon vaulted onto his war stallion. Soon the three riders were headed back for

Stone Ring Keep at an even faster pace than they had left it.

"HOW is Duncan?" Dominic and Simon asked Meg simultaneously.

Meg looked from the great hall where she was sitting to the lord's solar just beyond. Duncan was there at a table, listening to Ariane's mournful tunes while staring into the costly, ancient pendant that Amber had once worn.

At least Meg assumed that was what had captured Duncan's attention. He had his hands cupped around the pendant, protecting and concealing it as though it were a fragile flame in the wind.

"Duncan is the same as he was yesterday," Meg said. "If I speak loudly enough, he will answer. Otherwise, he ignores everyone but Dominic, to whom he feels indebted."

Simon grimaced. "God's blood. 'Tis like he has no . . ."

"Soul?" Meg offered.

"No emotions, certainly," Dominic said.

" 'Tis the cost of locking away much of yourself in order to survive," she said. "You should understand that, husband. You once did the same."

"Aye. But I hadn't met you then. Duncan has already met his witch. If he cuts off so much of himself in order to live . . ." Dominic shrugged. "I fear it will be like a poisoned wound, with no healing short of death."

Simon muttered something about the foolishness of giving that much of yourself to a woman and stalked into the lord's solar. Meg and Dominic followed. Even when all three stood in front of Duncan, he didn't look up from his study of the amber pendant.

"He is bewitched," Simon said bluntly.

"He is no more bewitched than Dominic is,"

Meg said. "Duncan's heart and body and soul have chosen a mate despite his vow. That mate is not Ariane."

"Yes," Dominic said simply. "I fear you are right."
Duncan's suffering has just begun.

Simon looked over at the violet-eyed heiress who drew such mourning from the harp's taut strings.

"Don't you know any joyful airs?" Simon asked. " 'Tis enough to make a stone snivel."

Ariane glanced at him and set aside the harp without a word.

"Duncan," Dominic said.

Though quiet, Dominic's voice commanded Duncan's attention. He looked away from the pendant concealed by his hands.

"I cannot watch you die. I release you from all obligation to me," Dominic said clearly. "Your marriage to Amber is intact. It will remain so."

Duncan's fingers tightened on the pendant's chain, making the concealed amber jerk against the tabletop. He looked at the gemstone again. It was dulled, as though from too much handling.

Yet he had touched it only once. The grief he had felt then had brought him to his knees.

He had been careful not to touch the amber again.

"I am released from no obligation," Duncan said.

His voice, like his eyes, lacked animation. Neither lacked conviction, however. He meant what he said.

"Don't be—" Dominic began.

"Without Stone Ring Keep as your ally," Duncan said, ignoring Dominic's attempt to speak, "Blackthorne will soon be at war with the Disputed Lands."

Dominic wanted to deny it. He couldn't. He badly needed allies, for he couldn't afford to hire more knights until he brought Blackthorne back from the ruin its previous lord had made of it.

"Without Ariane's dowry, I can't hold Stone Ring Keep," Duncan said. "Nor can you give me money without stripping Blackthorne to the bone."

A low curse was Dominic's only answer.

"In five days I will wed Ariane," Duncan concluded.

"Nay! I'll not see you live like a man half alive," Dominic said grimly. "Or worse."

"You have no control over the matter. You are no longer my lord."

"I'll refuse to put my seal on the annulment."

" 'Tis but a formality," Duncan said indifferently. "The Church won't care. The keep's chaplain will marry us. I am lord of this keep, not you."

Dominic opened his mouth to argue further, but Meg's hand on his wrist restrained him.

Duncan didn't notice. He was looking at the amber again, lost in its cloudy depths. Sometimes he almost believed he could see Amber there.

Sometimes . . .

A peregrine called softly. The trill was too sweet to have come from a falcon's throat. It hung in the air like light made into music.

Duncan looked up.

Erik stood nearby, his uncanny peregrine on his wrist.

"I will match Ariane's dowry," Erik said.

For a moment life flared in Duncan's eyes. Then it died, leaving him darker than before.

" 'Tis generous of you," Duncan said tonelessly, "but Baron Deguerre would go to war if his daughter were jilted by a Scots bastard. In the end it would be the same—Blackthorne lost because of a broken vow."

Erik looked to Dominic.

The Glendruid Wolf nodded reluctantly.

"Deguerre was furious at having to wed his daughter to a nameless bastard knight," Dominic said slowly. "If Duncan refuses Ariane, Deguerre will go to war against both of us. And he will have King Henry's blessing."

"Ariane and I will be wed in five days," Duncan said. "It matters not. *Amber is gone.*"

For a time there was no sound but the crackling of the fire and the distant moan of wind. Then Ariane took up the harp again. The tune she played caught the mood of the room with eerie accuracy: frustration and grief, a cold trap irrevocably closing, grinding life and hope between its cruel teeth.

Simon looked from his brother to the aloof Norman heiress. His mouth flattened into a grim line. Then he turned to Dominic once more.

"I'll marry the Norman wench," Simon said curtly.

Though Duncan didn't look up, the harp music stopped in a jangle of startled notes.

"What did you say?" Dominic asked.

"We will present it to the world as a love match," Simon continued, giving the last two words a sardonic emphasis. "A drawing together of hearts that resulted in elopement. We defied English king and Norman father equally. For *love*, of course."

The irony resonating in Simon's voice made Meg wince, but she raised no argument.

"What do you think?" Erik asked Dominic.

"King Henry won't object, for he will get what he wanted," Dominic said slowly.

"Which is?" Erik asked.

"Deguerre's daughter wed to a noble who is loyal to King Henry," Simon said bluntly.

"And Deguerre? Will he object?" Erik asked.

"No," Dominic said. "Simon is my brother and my strong right arm. As such, he is a more advantageous mate than Duncan of Maxwell would be."

"Lady Ariane," Erik said. "What say you?"

"I understand now why Simon is called the Loyal," Ariane answered. "What a treasure such fealty must be, more precious than rubies . . ."

Ariane plucked two strings. The purity of their harmony vibrated in the room for a moment, then died to a haunting whisper.

"I would prefer a nunnery to the marriage bed," Ariane said, "but neither my father nor God has seen fit to offer such to me."

"Nor can we," Dominic said bluntly.

" 'A drawing together of hearts . . . ' " Ariane repeated.

Her hand flashed, her fingers raked, and clashing cords filled the silence.

"Duncan. Simon." Ariane shrugged. "One man is much the same as another. Proud and cruel in equal parts. I will do my duty."

"You deserve a better wife than this cold Norman heiress," Dominic said to Simon.

"Blackthorne deserves better than war, brother. And so do you." Simon smiled thinly. "Surely marriage can be no worse than the sultan's hell you endured to ransom me."

Silently Dominic clasped his brother's shoulder.

"I will do what I can to sweeten your life," Dominic said simply. "I had hoped for a better match for you."

"You'll find none richer nor more useful than Ariane, daughter of Baron Deguerre," Simon said.

"I meant that I had hoped to find a woman who would love you as well as bring you wealth."

"Love? God's teeth." Simon looked sideways at his brother. "When I can hold love in my hand, see it, touch it, and weigh it, I'll worry about its lack. Until then, I'll take a good dowry and count myself lucky."

Shaking his head and smiling at the same time, Dominic turned to the one man who had yet to agree.

"Duncan?" Dominic asked.

Duncan didn't look up from the gemstone that lay on the table beneath his cupped hands, shielded from all other eyes but his own.

"Duncan," Dominic said in a clear voice. "Do you agree to the marriage of Simon and Ariane?"

"Do as you will," Duncan said indifferently. "Either way, *Amber is gone.* Not even the Learned can find her."

"Aye," Erik said. "But you might be able to reach her, Duncan."

Slowly Duncan's head came up. Hope struggled against despair in his eyes.

"You are her dark warrior and she is your golden light," Erik said. "The rowan gave you to Amber and Amber to you."

The words ran through Duncan like lightning. He stood in a rush, dragging the pendant with him. When the cool amber brushed his hand, he made a sound as though he had been raked by steel talons.

For the first time, Erik saw the dull pendant. Color drained from his face. The cry the peregrine gave was a naked lament.

Moments later Cassandra appeared in the doorway to the great hall, her scarlet robes flying. A single look at the pendant told her why the falcon had screamed.

Instinctively Meg came to her feet and stood next to the Glendruid Wolf.

"What is it?" Meg asked. "What has happened?"

"Amber," Cassandra said. "Taking the Druid way all but cost her life."

Duncan yanked Erik around to face him.

"Tell me how to get to Amber," Duncan said curtly.

"God's blood," Erik said. "Look at the pendant! 'Tis too late. She is dying."

"Tell me what I must know," Duncan commanded. "Quickly!"

"You aren't Learned," Cassandra said. "The only way is the Druid way, and even I—"

"Bring the pendant over to the fire," Erik interrupted.

Cassandra started to object, but a glance at Erik's savage yellow eyes stopped her words in her throat. She laced her hands together and let her long scarlet sleeves hide her fingers.

Swiftly Duncan followed Erik to the fire.

"Cup the pendant in your hands," Erik ordered.

Duncan's breath hissed between his teeth as he did what Erik asked. The amber was cool, but it burned viciously.

" 'Tis like holding a live coal," Duncan said in a strained voice.

"Now you know why she left," Erik said.

"What?"

" 'Tis Amber's pain you are feeling."

But Erik's voice wasn't without sympathy, for he knew the pain had become Duncan's also.

It gave Erik hope.

"Breathe over the pendant gently," Erik said. "Don't blow. Just open your mouth and let air flow out until the amber fogs with the breath of your own life."

Duncan closed his eyes, grappled with the pain as though it were a living enemy, and then exhaled gently into his cupped hands.

"Again," Erik said.

In taut silence everyone watched. Cassandra watched the most keenly, for what Erik was doing had never been tried with someone who wasn't Learned.

"Is the amber hazed?" Erik asked.

"Aye," Duncan said.

"Hold it just above the tips of the flames. Think of Amber as the haze clears. Then tell me what you see."

Frowning, trying to see past the vicious pain that

still burned in his palms, Duncan dangled the pendant just above the flames. As the fog cleared, he saw . . .

"Nothing," Duncan said.

"Again," Erik said.

Grimacing against the agony of holding the pendant against his skin once more, Duncan cupped the amber in his hands.

"Ignore the pain," Erik said curtly. "She did. Think of the woman who gave you her heart and her body and her soul."

The amber in Duncan's hands burned so fiercely he expected it to burst into fire.

"Did you give her nothing in return but your body?" Erik continued relentlessly. "Did nothing of you leave with her? Let go of your tightly held spirit. Let it seek her and make both of you whole."

Erik's words echoed in Duncan's head, drowning out the cries of his body. Raggedly he exhaled, giving the breath of his life to the amber he held cupped in his hands.

"Again," Erik commanded. "Think of Amber. You must want her beyond all else. Do you understand? *You must want her more than you want life itself.*"

Again Duncan breathed tenderly over the amber, infusing its coldly burning surface with his own warmth.

"To the fire," Erik said. "Quickly! As the haze clears you will see Amber."

Duncan let the gem slip on its chain until it was just within reach of the flames. He stared deeply into the pendant, to the place where shadows shifted and turned. He searched each shade of darkness for Amber, staring at the pendant until nothing was real but the darkness and the elusive fragments of gold . . .

The keening, questioning cry of an eagle piercing the air.

Mist clearing and re-forming, a dizzying view of hills and ridges, cliff-clinging trees and a glen falling away to an invisible sea.

Over all, enfolding all, the thousand whisperings of wind through an autumn marsh.

She is there, in the heart of silence, surrounded by whisperings she cannot hear.

" . . . hear me?" Erik demanded, shaking him harshly. "Duncan!"

Slowly Duncan lifted his head, breaking the amber enchantment. Sweat stood on his face. His hands were shaking.

"God's blood," Erik said roughly. "I thought we had lost you."

Duncan drew a deep breath. "Amber."

"Did you see her?"

"Nay."

Disappointment flattened Erik's mouth. "Rest. We'll try again later."

"I know where she is," Duncan said as though Erik hadn't spoken.

"Where?" Erik and Cassandra demanded simultaneously.

"Ghost Glen."

Erik looked at Cassandra. The Learned woman shrugged.

"We can but try," she said.

"What do you mean?" Duncan demanded.

"The sacred places accept or reject us," Cassandra said. "Ghost Glen has accepted no one but Amber within my lifetime."

"But I went there!" Duncan said.

"Aye," Erik said. "With Amber."

Duncan's hand closed around the pendant. Pain radiated through his hand, his arm, his body. He welcomed the pain.

It told him that Amber was still alive.

"I will be there again," Duncan vowed. "With Amber."

"Cassandra and I will come with you," Erik said.

"So will Simon," Dominic said. "He went to ready the horses. He is bringing Whitefoot, too. Amber will need a mount."

No one said what each feared, that Amber was lost to them.

"It will be a grueling ride," Erik said. "Ghost Glen may not reveal itself to him. Or to us."

"No matter how bewitched the rest of you become, Simon will see only what is real. That is his gift."

"It sounds more like a curse," Erik muttered.

A hound howled like a wolf just beyond the keep. A peregrine keened, calling for the hunt to begin.

"Do what you can for Duncan," Dominic said to Erik. "I value him as much as you value your sister."

"You have my vow on that, Wolf."

"I will hold the keep for whoever returns," Dominic said. "You have my vow."

"THE pendant," Erik said. "How is it affecting you?"

"It tells me Amber is still alive."

Erik asked no more. The pale line of Duncan's lips beneath his dark mustache said all that was needed. He had been haunted by what Amber had once said to him, in the golden time before his memory returned.

Precious Amber. What would I do without you?

You would fare better than I would without you. You are the heart in my body.

The memory was even more painful than the searing pendant.

"Take it away from your skin," Erik said.

"Nay. Pain is all we have between us now. If I deny it, I deny her. I'll not do that again. Ever."

Simon looked from Duncan to Erik, and from

there to Cassandra. No one spoke for many miles,
until Cassandra reined in sharply.

"There is something odd ahead of us," she said.

Erik gazed at the land ahead and nodded slowly. "Aye."

Without a pause, Duncan urged his horse forward. His eyes were fixed on the ridge that looked
rocky and impassable from this vantage point, but
had proved to be much easier when Amber had
chosen the way.

Just below the crest of the ridge, Duncan's horse
balked. He urged his battle stallion forward, but
still the horse refused.

Without a word, Duncan leaped off, vaulted into
Whitefoot's empty saddle, and went forward again.
Whitefoot minced and flattened her ears, but didn't
refuse the trail. Within moments she was over the
ridge and out of sight.

An eagle's majestic cry came through the mist
like a shaft of light. Duncan answered as he had
before, the hunting call taught to him long ago.

The eagle did not cry out again.

"I knew Duncan could find the way!" Erik said
exultantly. "Learned or not, I knew it! The rowan
wouldn't give Amber an inferior mate."

"Thick-skulled, stubborn, proud," Cassandra
muttered.

"Courageous, strong, honorable," Erik amended
dryly, remembering what Amber had once told
him. "In short, a good man."

Cassandra crossed herself, breathed a silent
prayer, and urged her own mount forward.

The white stallion refused the trail.

So did Erik's mount.

So did Simon's.

Of the three, Simon was the only one who was
surprised. What surprised him more was that even
when he dismounted, he couldn't find the trail
Duncan had followed. Mist swirled, lifted, teased,

confused, concealed . . . and Simon found himself back where he had started.

Neither Erik nor Cassandra fared any better. Ghost Glen was as it had always been to them.

Closed.

Duncan didn't notice that no one had followed him down the ridge into Ghost Glen. He knew only that the way became clearer with each step forward.

Without a thought to safety, Duncan urged Whitefoot to greater and greater speeds. Soon the mare was galloping swiftly down the glen, leaping brooks and fallen branches, skirting sacred circles, devouring the ground as though she had been born to run through the glen's ancient stillness.

Gradually, almost secretly, the rhythmic pounding of hooves was consumed by the myriad cries of geese. Calls lifted and tumbled, soared and turned, stirred by a restless wind. Answers stitched over other calls, other answers, countless wild voices weaving a tapestry of sound over marsh and sea.

A standing stone loomed out of the mist ahead. Duncan knew what the stone would look like when it was only a handspan away, knew what the thick cushion of growing things felt like at the stone's feet, knew that there of all places in the world Amber would be waiting for him, remembering as he remembered what it had been like to burn together in a golden fire that knew no pain, only passion.

Duncan kicked out of the stirrups and dismounted with a knight's skill, landing on his feet, running. But it wasn't a sword he held in his hand, nor was it a war hammer. It was a pendant as venerable as the land itself.

And it burned as only hope could.

"Amber!" Duncan called.

Nothing answered but thousands upon thousands of geese rising into the mist, black wings beating fiercely.

"Amber, don't hide! 'Tis Duncan!"

Heart hammering, Duncan stood at the foot of the ancient stone, listening for an answer.

It never came, though he called until his throat was raw.

Stunned, Duncan stood without moving, holding the pendant that had unlocked so much. But not enough. He had been so certain that Amber would be there, waiting for him.

So certain.

And so wrong.

Then he saw her from the corner of his eye, standing in front of the ancient stone. Her image wavered as though seen through water.

"*Amber,*" Duncan cried, reaching out to draw her close.

But his fingers touched only mist-drenched stone.

The ragged cry that came from Duncan's throat sent more clouds of geese hurtling from the marsh, wings beating blackly, voices calling back in their thousands, telling Duncan that he had learned Amber's truth too late.

She was beyond his reach.

Duncan cupped the pendant in his hands, trying to find her once more. He found nothing but the tears that blinded him.

He buried his face in his hands, knowing his own truth too late. He wanted the very thing he had driven away from himself, and he wanted it more than he wanted life itself.

"*Amber! Come back to me!*"

No geese lifted in response to Duncan's raw cry. No wings beat against air. No wind stirred dried marsh grasses. There was no sound at all.

Whispering Fen's uncanny silence touched

Duncan as no cry could have. He came to his feet and looked around wildly.

What he saw was a fen such as he had never known.

Where there had been myriad birds there was nothing. Where there had been wind there was stillness. Where there had been misty silver light there was now clear gold.

And there was silence, complete and perfect.

It was as though the fen had been cut adrift from time and life, caught like a bubble in sacred amber, neither touching nor being touched by anything of the world.

Duncan closed his eyes and wondered if this was what death felt like.

"Dark warrior . . ."

The soft whisper pulled the ground from beneath Duncan's feet. He spun around.

She was there, within reach, wrapped in her golden robes, watching him with eyes that were too dark in a face that was far too pale. She looked ethereal, more fragile than flame.

"Amber," Duncan said, reaching for her.

In the moment before he would have touched her, she flinched away.

"No more," she whispered. "Please. No more. I can't bear it."

"I won't hurt you."

"You won't mean to. But you will."

"*Amber.*"

She stepped back as Duncan stepped forward.

"You must go from this place," Amber said urgently. "It is too dangerous for you. Erik and Cassandra never should have guided you here."

"They didn't."

"They must have. There is no other way."

Duncan opened his hand. Amber's pendant lay on his palm.

"You guided me," he said simply.

"That cannot be. We aren't joined in that deep and final way!"

"But we are. I am here. If you will not come away with me, I will stay with you in this amber silence."

Amber closed her eyes and fought against the grief and hope that were destroying her equally.

"I'm sorry, dark warrior. I meant for you to be free."

"Without you there is no freedom except death."

She sensed his movement and would have retreated again, but the ancient stone was against her back. With the last of her strength, she gathered herself not to cry out at the touch that would come.

What Amber felt was a pendant being gently placed against her fingers. The instant she felt the weight, her eyes flew open. It was not only her own pendant that had been given to her.

It was Duncan's as well.

"Take them back!" she cried. "You will die here!"

"Breath of my breath," Duncan whispered. "Heart of my heart. Soul of my soul. *Touch me.*"

Slowly Amber lifted her hand. When her fingers brushed against Duncan's palm, she cried out.

Pleasure not pain.

A pleasure more exquisite than any she had ever known before.

Crying, laughing, she threw her arms around her dark warrior and held him, simply held him, drowning in the radiant truth revealed by his touch.

Around them the air shimmered and changed, sound pouring in as though a bubble had burst, life returning in a rush, geese calling, wind stirring long grasses until the fen overflowed with whispers and sighs, the same words endlessly repeated, weaving a spell that knew no boundaries of time or place . . .

I love you.

IN a distant, sacred circle, a rowan bloomed for the first time in a thousand years.

❧ Epilogue

STONE Ring Keep thrived with the blessings of the sacred rowan. Crops stood thick in the fields, fish and fowl swirled through water and sky, and children's laughter wove through green meadows as they played tag with the golden sun.

Duncan and Amber went often to Stone Ring and the sacred rowan. They stayed at the rowan's foot, sharing the enduring wonder of a tree that bloomed through all seasons, through all times, against all understanding, keeping a promise so old that only the rowan remembered to whom it had been given, and why.

The legend of the lord and lady of Stone Ring Keep spread through the Disputed Lands, a tale of an amber witch who loved too well and a dark warrior who would not be forsworn no matter how great the temptation.

It was a story of loss and daring, of an unLearned warrior braving the Druid way between time and place, life and death. It told of a knight vanishing into the mist on a dangerous quest and riding out once more with his lady in his arms. It was a story of love that bloomed as the sacred rowan bloomed, unexpectedly, bringing life to everything it touched.

*   *   *

THE rowan still grows inside the ring of sacred stones, for the promise was made for as long as rivers run down to the sea.

In time, other honorable men will come in shades of darkness to other brave women who will risk heart and body and soul . . .

And they, too, will find the place where there are no shades of darkness, only fire, and the rowan blooms forever.